STAR MARQUE RISING

SHAMI STOVALL

CAPITAL
• STATION BOOKS •

Published by
CS BOOKS, LLC

Star Marque Rising
Copyright © 2018 Shami Stovall
All rights reserved.
https://sastovallauthor.com/

Cover Design: Darko Paganus
Editor: Erin Grey, Abigail Stefaniak

**IF YOU WANT TO BE NOTIFIED WHEN SHAMI STOVALL'S NEXT BOOK
RELEASES, PLEASE CONTACT HER DIRECTLY AT
s.adelle.s@gmail.com**

ISBN: 978-0-9980452-0-7

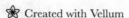 Created with Vellum

Star Marque Rising

by Shami Stovall

To John, for being the first to see.
To Beka, for making this possible.
To Gail and Big John, for all the support.
To Robert A. Heinlein, for all the books.
To Erin Grey and Abigail Stefaniak, for being amazing editors.
To all my writing buddies, this couldn't happen without you.
And finally, to everyone unnamed, thank you for everything.

ONE

Ambition

The dregs of Capital Station gathered for their blood sport, and I was more than happy to give them a show.

Section Six, the armpit of our massive space station, was the only section to condone violence, so long as it was kept to competitions. Thousands squeezed themselves into makeshift stands built atop gas lines and water pipes. The foul odor of sweat and vomit lingered like fog, but that didn't deter the crowds. I doubted anyone would miss a battle royale.

"We have ten participants, ladies and gentlemen," the game announcer said through a voice amplifier strapped over his mouth. Damn thing looked like a black surgical mask, but it sent his statement over all the speakers, blanketing the massive maintenance room with the declaration.

"Place your wagers while you still have a chance," he continued. "Perhaps you, too, can be lucky enough to win big!"

I stood among the competitors, but I kept my gaze fixed on the audience. The oil-stained jumpsuits of the crowd blended together in a sea of gray and blue. The physically deformed sat in the far back, right alongside the sick. I recognized no one, which was for the best. I didn't want my old "friends" from Section Two interfering. I refused to be their gunrunning hatchet man. I was done with that life.

"We have plenty of ambitious fighters this year. It's bound to be quite a show!"

I smiled after the comment. Ambition killed fools who overestimated their own pathetic abilities. But I wasn't one of them. My aspirations wouldn't be snuffed out by the likes of mouth-breathers and petty convicts. I had talent to back up my ambitions.

All I wanted was to step foot on a planet—*any planet*—at least once in my life. And I'd get there, even if I had to carve up all of Capital Station in the process.

The other combatants sized each other up. A few glowered in my direction, and one offered a lopsided smirk.

"You're too clean for this fight," the guy said. He tapped a piece of cyborg machinery protruding from the flesh of his shoulder, and out between poorly-fitted pieces of body armor. He flexed to show off his artificial strength.

I crossed my arms and ignored him. I was the only competitor without cyborg implants, and that gave all the fools a false sense of security. Worked for me. I loved capitalizing on stupidity.

The announcer, a gaunt man dressed in heavy boots, a blue jumpsuit, and gloves, was less shabby than the audience, but not by much. He walked along the outside of a metal stage, waving his hands to encourage the crowd. The cheering grew so intense, I swear it could be heard from the anchor planet our station circled.

The electric energy of a death fight got my blood going. Excitement spread through the crowd. Each competitor stepped onto the stage—a square loading platform devoid of siding—and I took my place at the corner.

"Remember, today's fights are brought to you by the Maccarus Felseven Grain Corporation! Eat like you live planetside with MF Grain!"

The announcer jumped onto the platform, and the lights dimmed over the crowd, putting the ring in the spotlight. The other fighters shifted their weight from one foot to another, sweat pouring from them like leaky pipes. Only schmoes entered a death fight without hardening themselves to the reality of dying. They must have been more desperate than I originally thought.

I shouldn't judge. I didn't have a credit to my name, and I had burned all my bridges before I arrived. I needed the money to pay for a carrier off this insufferable island in space. I couldn't go another sleepless night thinking every little creak might be one of my old associates come to put a plasma bolt through my head.

The prize awarded to the last man standing was half a million—twenty-five years of work for a typical sad sack of Capital Station.

One of the other competitors walked up to me, his body armor two sizes too big, and his shoulders slumped. The stiff vest, cracked helmet, and gloves wouldn't save him. I gave him a sideways glance and he flinched backward, but not far.

"This is really happening," he said. A normal man might not have heard his weak voice over the audience's commotion, but I picked up the words with little trouble.

He stared at the other fighters, a picture of uncertainty. "Pull it together, Darryl," he muttered to himself. "Pull it together. This is the only way…"

I had a feeling that if Darryl were at one end of a "remarkable persons" list, it wouldn't be the top. He was the type of man ambition killed on a regular basis.

"Forfeit," I told him, my voice strong enough to pierce the cheers.

Darryl shook his head. "I… I have a family. They need the money."

"Yet, here you are, saddling them with a funeral bill."

"Oh? What's this?" the announcer asked. "Here comes the man we've all been waiting for!"

Lights swiveled and shone onto the beast stepping up to the platform. I recognized him straightaway. He was hard to miss.

"The bookies favor him to win, and I can see why!"

Vorgo Dilucca—part-machine, part-flesh—towered over the other combatants the moment he stepped into the ring. Metal jutted from all parts of his body, the shoddy craftsmanship a signature of the Capital Station "doctors." The machines enhanced his strength beyond human capacity, sure, but those low-quality parts must have cut his life expectancy in half.

Vorgo probably thought he only needed a few minutes to win this fight, but he had picked the wrong battle royale.

"I've seen Vorgo throw a punch," the game announcer said, prancing across the ring. "He's got a mean left hook, like my ex!"

Laughter mixed with the cheering. Vorgo held up his massive, steel-girder arms and garbled something indecipherable. Those piece-of-shit cyborg implants messed with a person's insides—with each breath he sounded like he was swallowing his own tongue, and his head was shaped like a cinderblock. Too bad those surgeons couldn't give the man some common sense while they were tinkering with his noggin.

The whooping and hollering reached new levels. I bet people put a lot of money on a certain someone to win.

"Uh-oh! Looks like a few competitors are getting cold feet!"

Boos washed down from the crowd as six men stepped off the platform, forfeiting their participation. They ducked away with their heads hung and their hands shaking.

Ringside bouncers hit the fleeing men with electric prods, much to the delight of the audience. Those damn prods had enough amperage to burn skin on contact, and that would be coupled with a bruise left from the strike.

The announcer stared at me with a cocked eyebrow. "What do we have here? A brave fighter without any enhancements? He's got moxie, ladies and gentlemen!" He walked over and patted my bare shoulder. "No armor?" He examined my black tank top and Federation-standard cargo pants. "Maybe I misspoke. An *idiotic* fighter without any enhancements!"

More laughter. More cheering.

I had grown bored with the charade.

"Start the fight," I said.

"Heh. You're so… succinct. But first, what's your name, pal?"

"Clevon Demarco."

I shouldn't have used my real name, but would it really matter? I doubted anyone was going to verify my off-the-cuff statement. They wanted blood, not fact-checking.

"Demarco? I like your style." The announcer held up his hands, calling for silence. "And now, it's time! Will our plucky underdog, Demarco, last more than thirty seconds? I sure hope so! Let's find out!"

He leapt from the platform, and a metallic ring heralded the start of the competition. There were four of us. It was me versus a man-turned-metal-abomination, versus Darryl, of all people, versus a barely-enhanced schlub. The entertainment wouldn't last long.

Before things got interesting, the ringside bouncers tossed us a handful of melee weapons—a duralumin pipe, three seven-inch, military-grade knives, and one of those damn electric prods.

Darryl dove for the prod, and the schlub scrambled for the pipe. I leaned down and picked up a knife.

Vorgo charged forward.

With superhuman strength, Vorgo swung his heavy fist into the side of the pipe-wielder's small head, smashing teeth and cascading blood across the spectators sitting in the front row. People snatched up molars for souvenirs, and hundreds took pictures and vids.

"Oh!" the announcer said. "Brutal!"

The crowd roared as Vorgo continued his assault on the unmoving man, pummeling his opponent without a hint of remorse. He bashed him until his skull caved in and his eyes ruptured.

Darryl stood, frozen, his gaze glued to the gore and his grip loose on his electric prod. My pulse quickened with the exuberant cheering, and I probably should've killed Darryl while he was rattled, but my attention snapped to a pair of off-station enforcers, watching from the edge of the ring.

I hated off-station enforcers.

They were basically bounty hunters and starfighters hired by the Capital Station overseer to keep the peace by suppressing anything that looked like trouble. They wore high-quality, black enviro-suits—skin-tight armor mesh from their necks down to their toes—and they stood out like blood on white linen compared to the denizens of Section Six.

They couldn't possibly be here for me. I had taken precautions to avoid any trouble with the authorities.

The game announcer lifted his hands in the air, conducting the audience like an orchestra of clapping and shouting.

"There's no kill like *overkill!*"

Vorgo stood straight, gulping down air, a twisted smile on his misshapen face. The guy gave Frankenstein's monster a run for his money, and the blood-stained pants and ripped knuckles added an air of psychopath to his overall look.

Darryl turned to me. I stood motionless as he ran, full-tilt, in my direction, his weapon at the ready. At the moment of his swing, I shifted to the side, precision in my movement as I avoided the strike. I met his gaze with an unblinking focus, living the second as though in slow motion. I could've ended it with minimal effort, but I waited. There was little thrill in beating someone so far beneath me, and a part of me still hoped Darryl would throw in the towel.

Darryl caught his breath when I leapt around him, his eyes struggling to follow my movements. The shock didn't surprise me. Only a rare educated few knew the secret to my speed.

Vorgo lumbered over and entered the brawl, yelling. He swung, striking Darryl with bone-shattering intensity, breaking the prod—and Darryl's face—in a single blow. The patchwork body armor didn't protect Darryl from Vorgo's next two punches to the gut.

I doubted Darryl could see, not with his eye sockets bashed in—the name "Meatloaf Face" would have been more accurate at that point.

But that wasn't as interesting as Vorgo's fighting style. His stubby legs, strained from the additional weight of machinery, didn't move as fast as they should have for a brawl. He planted himself in a stance and only changed when necessary.

It would be his downfall.

Meatloaf Face attempted to jump off the platform to surrender, but bouncers prodded him back on, encouraging him to finish what he'd started. What bullshit. They'd let the others tap out, why not him? Their jeers and laughter betrayed their sadism, and that didn't surprise me either. Section Six was filled with fucked-up individuals.

Vorgo stomped over to Darryl, winded, and pity got the better of me. I whistled, harsh enough to pierce the cheers, until I got Vorgo's attention.

"Deal with him after," I said. "I'm the only thing standing in your way to victory."

"And Demarco has the balls to taunt his competitor," the announcer shouted with a laugh. "I knew there was a reason I liked this guy!"

Although Vorgo gulped down air with ragged breaths, he faced me with a glower.

The announcer continued, "It's the eleventh hour! Demarco versus Vorgo! Who will end up a bloodstain across the floor?"

Best to wait for Vorgo to come to me—the more energy he wasted, the better.

I gripped my knife tight.

Sure enough, Vorgo charged, his heavy fist balled for a glorious Hail Mary. His punch whistled through the air past me as I side-stepped away, and it only stopped once it collided with the solid platform. The clang of metal-on-metal echoed throughout Section Six.

I stepped away when Vorgo swung with his other arm, dancing around the dangerous blows. Vorgo inhaled deep, sucking in pink, blood-laced sweat that misted from his overclocked machinery. He grunted, but I was in no hurry. All I needed was an opening.

The bouncers pushed Darryl until he fell over, chanting for his death. Vorgo must have needed a confidence booster, because he faced the half-beaten man and lumbered toward him.

Good enough for me.

In that instant, I went in low and slashed. I sliced Vorgo's femoral artery, right where the leg meets the body, and then darted away, avoiding a slow, third swing. Vorgo's death wouldn't come all at once, but now, it was set.

While Vorgo grabbed at the stream of blood gushing from his body, I jogged over to Darryl and kicked him off the edge. The bouncers booed, but I ignored them.

"Looks like another fighter is officially out of the running!"

As I turned back around, the machines deep within Vorgo strained and twitched into movement. He swung wide. Trapped between Vorgo and the edge of the ring, I didn't have space to escape. He clipped me with a second powerful strike. The glancing blow to my left shoulder sent me tumbling back across the hot, unforgiving platform, dislocating my arm and cracking my collarbone.

Goddammit. That was what I got for sticking my neck out for someone. I should've learned my lesson years ago—the Darryls of the world would never be worth it.

I got back to my feet before the announcer could make a quip, hiding the grimace of agony as I faced Vorgo. Fighting, in part, was psychological. Every stab—either to the opponent's body or confidence—brought me one step closer to victory. My olive skin hid bruising well, and I returned to my combat stance, my knife still in hand.

Bits of food and boos rained down from the stands.

"What's this? Demarco's still in the fight? Unreal, ladies and gentlemen! Unreal!"

Vorgo grabbed at his injury, his fat lips quavering, sweat rolling off the grooves of his face.

"Vorgo's struggling! What a fight!"

With undeniable desperation, Vorgo lunged forward, overheating his cyborg implants for a slight increase in speed and power.

As graceful as any matador, I stepped aside.

In the split-second that Vorgo passed by, I slammed my blade deep into his neck, cutting both wires and veins. Choking on his own blood, Vorgo half-stumbled and half-ran off the edge of the platform, heedless of the bouncers and their prods. He crashed onto the walkway, twitching and convulsing as the machines ran through their power reserves.

"Demarco's the winner! What an upset!"

Cheers and violence erupted from the audience. The announcer tried to calm them, but it was to no avail. Instead, he grabbed my good arm and held it high. The bouncers kept the rabble away—

thanks to their unpleasant weaponry—but my attention was once again drawn to the off-station enforcers.

The enforcers pointed and talked before disappearing into the agitated crowd, their gaze set on me until they were gone.

I pulled my hand from the announcer's and turned to leave the platform. My arm and shoulder pulsed with pain, but I knew the fight wasn't over. I couldn't show weakness. No one won half a million credits on Capital Station without attracting unwanted attention. The eyes of scavengers followed me all the way to the winner's terminal.

The screen on the computer station displayed the vice-overseer of Section Six—some old, bald guy with surgery scars from a botched facelift.

"Congratulations on your victory," the vice-overseer said. "Please, hold your arm up to the terminal to receive your prize winnings."

I pocketed my souvenir knife, and then held up my right arm. Buried deep between the ulna and radius sat a small identification chip that contained personal information, such as bank accounts and criminal records. I held my breath as I ran my arm over the scanner.

The chip wasn't my own. I had purchased a stolen one from my old gangbanger associates. Felons weren't allowed to hold decent jobs or receive prize money, after all. A stolen chip was my only option. How else would I get off the godforsaken space station?

The terminal buzzed with acceptance, and I exhaled.

"Section Six thanks you for your participation. Join us again next year!"

I bit back a laugh. The generic recording, probably made as simple as possible to accommodate all sorts of "festivities," sounded rather morbid, since it was essentially asking someone to return next year for another death match.

Without waiting for a formal dismissal, I turned away from the computer terminal and headed straight for the small lift out of Section Six. I pressed the button for the business district, eager to escape the maintenance level as fast as possible. I wasn't going to miss the dim lighting, poor upkeep, occasional gas leaks, or rampant muggings, that was for sure.

I had earned my freedom. I could start a new life away from all this squalor, and finally see places other than Capital Station. I would've given my left testicle to stand planetside and take a breath of fresh air.

I entered the lift, rode up, and exited into the business district a few seconds later with single-minded focus.

I needed to get to the main lift and take it to Section Four—the docks—to secure a ride. Unlike the smaller, elevator-like lifts around each section, the main lift was a massive loading room, meant to carry tons of resources from one section of Capital Station to another—and it was the only way out of each section.

Not twelve meters into my trek, the lift door opened behind me. I glanced back and spotted a group of four off-station enforcers. They had followed me. I knew they would.

I picked up my pace, cursing my limited options. Every level in each section of the space station was essentially one long corridor. Sure, there were doors to shops and restaurants on either side of me, and there was a stream of people flowing like water, but I was a few centimeters taller than the average man and muscular to boot— I would be easy enough to spot.

As my adrenaline waned, my pain intensified. I gritted my teeth and slowed halfway through the district. Passersby knocked my injured shoulder, but I soldiered through, unwilling to get caught by wannabe cops. I glanced back every few meters, losing sight of the enforcers in the waves of people rushing to buy the latest shipment of MF Grain products.

The moment I arrived at the main lift, I slid my right arm over the scanner, smiling once the light flashed green.

This was it. I was going to make it.

The main lift was a warehouse. Empty, two-ton, steel cargo crates sat stacked against the walls, ready to be filled with merchandise. I could hide out until the warehouse elevator shifted over to the docks.

Before I did anything, however, I forced my left arm back into the socket. It wasn't as painful as everyone assumed, but a dull ache remained. The collar bone bothered me more, and it would prevent me from using my entire shoulder. Nothing I couldn't handle. I had gone through far worse.

"There ya are, Clevon," a man drawled.

I turned my attention to a handful of men leaning against two of the crates. They carried plasma rifles and wore white enviro-suits. The suits could sustain a man in space, but the cheap white ones weren't as armored as the enforcer suits. Their helmets hung like hoods between their shoulder blades, flimsy until secured over the head, where they snapped into a hardened shell, becoming legitimate protection.

"I told you I was done, Reggie," I said, counting five men in total. Two atop crates, three in front of me. They had cut a few zigzags into the shoulders of their suits, but I knew them even without the gang markings. My old "friends."

"You don't look happy to see us," Reggie said, stroking his oily chin. The man had all the charm of a used wares dealer.

"I paid my debts," I said. "Our agreement was that you wouldn't come after me."

"You didn't say nothin' about takin' credits with you."

"How'd you think I was going to leave Section Six? It's either this or prostitution, and I'd make a terrible prostitute."

Reggie scowled. "I never found you funny, Clevon."

"That's why I'm leaving," I quipped.

He hefted his plasma rifle and rested it on his shoulder, enough for me to get a good look at it. It was one of the better rifles on the market, not one of the low-power, homebrew laser guns I saw kids packing on the station.

"It's our chip," Reggie said. "Therefore, our credits. You ain't goin' nowhere."

"*Your* chip?" Damn. "You took the credits out of the account already, didn't you?"

"What didja expect? Did ya honestly think it would end well for you?"

"You should've asked yourself the same damn question while you were sitting here, waiting for me."

"You might be good, but I saw your fight over the telecast. That was a nasty spill you had. Besides, boss doesn't want ya trying anything stupid. You're a loose end. Come back and meet him or else things are gonna get worse for ya."

"I feel sorry for you, Reggie," I said, tensing my sore body for a second run, "which is why I'm going to give you a chance to return my credits."

"We ain't gonna do that." Reggie stepped away from the crate and motioned to the others. "We're gonna—"

I lunged forward, pulled my knife, and stabbed it straight into one of Reggie's bloodshot eyes. Bastard should've kept his helmet up.

The world slowed as I took in every bit of information—I lived each quarter of a second as though in full. I dropped my knife, ripped Reggie's rifle from his dead hands, and cursed my useless arm, all before those thugs could even comprehend what was going on.

I shot twice, hitting both men next to me, the plasma bolts leaving seared holes through their faces. The remaining two men snapped their helmets into place and opened fire. I rolled to the side and took cover behind a crate, cursing the pain that flared from my cracked collarbone.

The rapid-fire exchange triggered the automatic alarms. Red lights flooded the area, and sirens screeched in short bursts. Much to my displeasure, the lift doors opened within seconds to reveal my stalkers.

Four off-station enforcers took defensive positions on the other side of the warehouse door. I scooted around the side of the crate, keeping an object between myself and everyone else.

"You have violated Capital Station's plasma rifle protocol," an enforcer called out, her voice feminine even through the speaker of her enviro-suit. "Stand down or we'll be forced to return fire!"

Those thugs wouldn't know a good decision from a piece of

toast. They fired on the enforcers, missing their targets like only shaken men could.

I slid out of cover and shot at the distracted gunrunners. I struck one in the gut, blowing a hole in his suit and stomach. He fell off his crate and hit the floor, writhing.

Served him right. If they wanted to send me to hell, they would have to drag me there.

I ducked behind the crate as the enforcers blanketed the area with a series of organized shots. Thankfully they weren't using plasma bolts, but I recognized the crackle of high-powered shock rounds. One hit could stun a small whale.

One enforcer tossed out a paralysis grenade, and I knew things wouldn't end well for my old associates. Raw, electrical energy burst from the grenade, incapacitating the last goon and killing the guy I'd shot in the stomach, but the burst didn't reach me.

With bated breath, I listened.

The enforcers hustled into the warehouse.

"Lysander, report."

"One active, four dead, one neutralized," a man, Lysander, replied.

"Scour the area. Incapacitate, if possible."

Fuck.

I exhaled and stared at the duralumin wall in front of me. With off-station enforcers involved, I was sure to land myself a life sentence, or worse. And in my condition, it wasn't like I could kill them all.

Dread crept into my thoughts.

A small part of me wanted to surrender, but I couldn't stomach the idea. I would get off Capital Station or I would die trying.

I slung Reggie's rifle over my shoulder and stood.

The enforcers moved around the room with purpose—well, all of them but one. I could distinguish the soft and hesitant steps of an enforcer trailing behind. They walked along the wall, pausing at odd moments.

Piecing a plan together as I went, I crouched and ran behind the crates, keeping the positions of the other enforcers clear in my mind, thanks to their heavy footfalls. The moment I heard the cautious foot-steps of someone on the other side of a crate, I rushed out of cover. The others enforcers had their rifles up and ready, and one speedy bastard managed to fire a single shock round before I reached my target.

I evaded the shot and tackled the hesitant enforcer to the ground, careful to use my good shoulder.

"He's fast!" an enforcer yelled. "Watch yourself!"

With superior agility and strength, I forced the barrel of the enforcer's rifle up under his chin and fired. The black enviro-suit—worn properly with the helmet up—absorbed most of the discharged electricity, but the shock and awe of the attack left the enforcer shaken. He was small, and I assumed young, and new to combat. He froze up the moment I grabbed his arm and torqued it to the side.

I jumped to my feet, hauling the kid with me.

Maybe I could escape to the slums with this newbie as my hostage. Maybe I could still make this work.

Twisting the enforcer's arm behind his back, I positioned him as a meat shield, always keeping him between myself and the others who rushed toward us. They shot several shock rounds, but each hit the kid, discharging with little harm off the side of his suit.

"There's no escape!" the female enforcer shouted. "Surrender now!"

Even with an aching shoulder—and the kid wearing an expen-sive enviro-suit—I effortlessly overpowered him and kept him in front of me. As they approached, the other three enforcers hesitated more than professionals should.

I shuffled closer to the door. "I'll let him live, but first, you let me go."

"This isn't a negotiation. You will release the enforcer and stand down!"

To my surprise, the door opened. I stepped away, dragging the enforcer with me, and cursed under my breath when I spotted a squad of ten black-suited enforcers stepping into the warehouse.

The first three enforcers parted and surrendered authority to the one decorated commander who walked forward. She was taller than most, and wore her star insignia on the shoulder of her enviro-suit.

"Endellion," Lysander said, saluting the commander. "The situation, it's—"

"Stand down," she replied. "I will handle it from here."

"But—he's the one from the death game! He's the superhuman!"

"Is he?" The commander turned towards me, but I couldn't see her face beneath the tinted mesh glass of her enviro-suit helmet. "Just the one I've been looking for."

With speed on par with my own, the commander pulled her sidearm—a four-round plasma pistol—and fired. Her aim was so precise, it missed my meat shield by millimeters and clipped my shin, burning a straight line through my pants and searing a chunk of flesh from my calf.

I twisted in pain and stumbled to the side, catching myself on the young enforcer and nearly toppling over, but I corrected my footing and stayed standing.

During the two seconds I spent staggering, the commander closed the distance between us. Fifteen meters. She sprinted fifteen goddamn meters. And then she brought a shock gun to bear directly on my body.

I had lost.

In the fraction of a second it took the gun to fire the cartridge, I glimpsed through the tint of the visor and met the commander's gaze straight on.

Her eyes...

Within them teemed passion and ambition, the likes of which I had never known.

But then the cartridge left the barrel of the gun, pumping my already-injured body with 50,000 volts of electricity, and a single tranquilizer.

TWO

The Star Marque

I awoke submerged in liquid.

It took me a panicked moment to realize I wasn't drowning. I was immersed in the fluid of a healing vat—a thick, jelly-like substance composed of DNA-linked "mother cells," cells with the potential to become any type of cell within the body. The vat identified problem areas, and the mother cells filled in the wounds while speeding up metabolism to ensure a quick recovery.

A single air tube ran from the top of the vat down through my mouth and lungs. Then I realized I had nothing.

No clothes.

No weapons.

Tiny LED lights barely illuminated the inside of the vat. I looked around. The fluid, contaminated with my dead skin cells and bubbles of blood, sat stagnant. Healing vats only did that when they were close to finished, or so the educational videos said. How long had I been in the damn thing?

The vat itself had steel alloy sides and a sealed top, preventing any sort of escape and blocking my view of the outside world. I didn't have much of a choice at that point. I could wait for the vat to open or I could remove the air tube and breathe deep. Otherwise, I was stuck.

And where the fuck was I, exactly?

Not Section Six. The doctors there were butchers in disguise, and if they could withhold lifesaving procedures until they were paid more than twice the worth, they would. It would take a miracle to walk away from the infirmary without deep scars and shoddy cybernetics. A healing vat would reduce the clientele, so none had been installed.

Stuck in the gel, my mind wandered.

If I wasn't on Capital Station, where else could I be?

I supposed, on the opposite end of the spectrum, far from Capital Station, there were planetside hospitals with superhuman doctors and pharmacists. I had seen them on the news, and everyone was aware of their miraculous new procedures and medications.

Was I planetside? Or was I dreaming? I supposed the latter was more likely.

A loud clink heralded the draining of the mother-cell fluid. A small hole at the bottom of the vat opened, and everything spun down the drain. I braced myself as one side of the vat slid down, creating an opening.

I unceremoniously pulled the air tube from my trachea and coughed.

"*Rejuvenation complete*," a machine-like voice said, chipper and feminine in tone, but artificial. "*Fractures in the left clavicle and humerus have been mended. The anterior and posterior tibial muscles have been reconstructed. Please, speak to a physician if any pain persists.*"

I wheezed and hacked as I stepped out of the vat. The slimy fluid filled my nose and ears, and it took me a moment to snort them clear.

The bright lighting of the room hurt my eyes, but I adjusted in a matter of moments. I got a quick look around and froze up.

Everything was so well ventilated and clean...

I wasn't in Section Six.

It was a medium-sized room with a single metal door. My

healing vat sat in the back corner, extending from the floor to the ceiling. There was a computer terminal and two large, steel crates with the words *Medical Supplies* stamped across the side. But those things paled in comparison to the viewing window on the far wall.

I walked over, eyes wide, and stared out into the depths of space.

Capital Station hung in orbit around Galvis-4, a brown-and-turquoise planet that acted as the station's anchor. The space station —white and pristine from the outside—didn't look half bad from a distance. It was a hexagonal torus, forever spinning to maintain gravity, powering itself from the rays of the system's star. From the outside, one would never know of the filth that dwelled inside. From space, it was impossible to see the overcrowding and meaningless death that had made the station so infamous.

We had left the dock, but the starship I was on hadn't left for its destination. Why? My thoughts didn't linger on it for long.

Man, my new skin felt great.

I rubbed my arms and shins, impressed by how supple everything had become. I wiped away as much excess mother-cell fluid as possible, but the stuff was everywhere. Just… *everywhere*.

The door to the room slid open. I tensed and whirled around on my heel.

A short girl walked in, her attention fixed to the Personal Assistant Device on her arm—or PAD, as the rich pricks called it—a paper-thin device that wrapped around the user's forearm and maintained power through their body heat. The girl poked at the touchscreen, scrolling through text.

I rushed over, grabbed her by the jumpsuit collar, and slammed her against the wall. The girl, lithe and slender, raised her hands and stared at me in wide-eyed shock.

"Whoa, whoa," she said. "W-Wait a minute! I'm not—"

"Where am I?" I growled, gripping her collar with ever-increasing intensity.

"*The Star Marque*. An enforcer starship."

I hesitated for a moment, but kept the girl pinned to the wall. It wasn't hard. She didn't look like she had any cyborg implants, and her physique screamed "computer worker with a bird's appetite."

Her olive-green jumpsuit was typical for engineers. How old was she? I didn't know—I would guess in her early twenties.

"Where're we headed?" I asked.

"We're about to set course for Ucova."

Ucova. The only place worse than Capital Station.

It was a prison that orbited a frozen desert planet—the perfect place to have inmates mine themselves to death. I'd heard the intense gravity caused most to die from heart failure within five years.

I could put one and two together. That was where they intended to take me. I supposed I would at least get to set foot on *one* planet before I died, if I didn't manage to find a way off this rig before then.

"You forgot to sedate me, didn't you?" I asked.

"No," the girl said. "I never forget such details."

"Then this was part of your plan?"

I lifted the girl a few millimeters off the floor and gave her the once-over. She had to be 30 centimeters shorter than I was, and a third of my weight. Her dark-red hair fell midway down her neck and angled forward rather messily. The hue contrasted nicely with her freckled skin.

"Our c-commander said we weren't to sedate or restrain you," she said, holding my arm for support.

I set her down, but kept my grip on her jumpsuit and mulled over the bizarre piece of information. "Your commander?"

"Endellion Voight."

Endellion.

That was the name of the woman who'd caught me, the commander who'd shot my shin.

"It's Federation standard to sedate prisoners," I said.

"I made that exact argument," the girl replied, sardonic irritation replacing all fear. "Perhaps you can talk some sense into her. Maybe attack *her* the moment she enters a room, and then try the 'I'm unstable' argument." She motioned to the grip on her clothing.

I smirked. She was a cheeky little shit.

Before I let her go, I slid my hands into her pockets. No

weapons, just a pouch full of microtools used for fixing computer hardware. She grew red in the face and avoided making eye contact with me, staring up at the ceiling as much as possible.

"I'm not going to do anything," I stated.

She cracked half a smile. "This is starting to remind me of a few disappointing dates."

I snorted, taken aback by her blasé attitude.

Her PAD beeped, and a blue light flashed near her wrist. The screen displayed caller information, but the view window never opened. Audio communication rang from the edges.

"Sawyer," a masculine voice from her PAD said. "What does the vat say? How much longer until our new guest wakes up?" His displeasure carried through the speakers. He sounded familiar. He'd been on Capital Station when I was captured.

Lysander. That was his name.

Sawyer met my gaze, her face still flushed. "Don't make this situation any worse than it already is. Calm down. We'll get you some clothes and pretend this never happened."

Her PAD blinked blue, waiting for a reply.

Taking a hostage hadn't worked for me last time.

I released Sawyer and took a step back. I was half-tempted to fight the enforcers, but I knew that was a younger, stupider version of me talking. They had the advantage. Armor. Weapons. Security codes. Like my fight with Vorgo, it was best to wait for an opening, rather than start with aggression.

Sawyer tapped her PAD and said, "Our guest awoke, Lysander." She examined me from head to toe, holding up a hand to block her view of my junk. "And the vat helped. He's up and kicking, if you catch my drift."

"Why didn't you say so earlier?" Lysander replied. "I'll be there in a moment to escort him to Endellion. And don't engage with him! He's unpredictable and dangerous."

"Oh, I'll certainly try."

For reasons I couldn't articulate, her attitude amused me. I swore she snuck a look or two right before returning her gaze to the ceiling. She couldn't have been that afraid of me, or else I doubted she would've cracked so many jokes. Then again, people got weird in life-or-death situations. I had seen everything from anger, to tears, to that one time a guy was so uncomfortable he couldn't stop himself from whistling.

Sawyer stole one last glance at me before returning her attention to her PAD.

"Like what you see?" I asked.

Of course she did. I was a paragon of fitness, and unlike most, I had potent pheromones. What wasn't to like?

To my surprise, Sawyer rolled her eyes and kept her hand up to block her view. "Yeah, yeah. I'm sure you're amazing. Endellion does her research before taking people aboard, after all."

Hm?

"What was that?" I asked.

The door slid open, and I tensed. A man walked through, dressed in his black enviro-suit, his helmet hanging like a hood on his back. He tossed a white jumpsuit to the floor and pulled his sidearm—a four-round plasma pistol—and though he didn't point it at me, he did keep it at the ready.

"Put on the jumpsuit," he commanded.

I recognized his voice straight away. Lysander.

He glanced over at Sawyer and motioned for her to come closer. "Don't worry. He won't try anything with me around."

The statement almost made me *want* to start something. Then again, the longer I looked at him, the more I realized Lysander wasn't just some chump. He had military training—I could see it in the way he held himself straight at all times.

Sawyer walked to his side and glued her eyes to her PAD. She poked at the screen, never bothering to look up while I dressed.

"What's your name?" Lysander asked.

"Kasey Dimes," I replied.

"Don't try to pull any tricks. We know your chip is stolen."

"Then I assume you already know my real name. Why bother asking?"

"To see if you would be upfront." He narrowed his dark eyes and sneered. "But I guess I should've known better."

The guy even had a military crewcut. No wonder he disapproved. I was sure assholes like him thought they were above people like me.

"Lysander?" Sawyer asked. "The readouts from—"

"Later," he snapped. "I have to take this thug to Endellion first."

Sawyer let out a strained exhale and returned her full attention to the PAD.

I pulled the jumpsuit up and slipped one arm into a long sleeve. As I went to do the same with the other, Lysander lifted his sidearm and planted it into my solar plexus, pressing the barrel against my torso.

"C'mon," he said. "You can finish on the way."

I grabbed his wrist and jerked it to the side. He attempted to break free, but I ripped the pistol from his grasp, and he tensed, panicked.

"If you're going to pull a gun on me," I said through clenched teeth, "you'd better be fuckin' ready to use it."

Lysander attempted to wrench his arm free, but my strength was greater. It must have grated at his pride, because all hints of fear were replaced by hot shame. He reached up to his chest and tapped along a seam.

His enviro-suit pulsed with electricity powerful enough to knock Vorgo on his ass. I hit the steel floor, my muscles tensed and unresponsive, my heart convulsing like it was beating out of rhythm. Searing pain filled me for a few moments before fading into a dull ache.

Goddammit. I didn't know their enviro-suits had anti-grappling shock defenses. Why didn't the kid use it on Capital Station? He could have downed me in an instant the moment I took him hostage.

"I told you he was dangerous," Lysander said as he snatched his pistol off the floor.

Sawyer shrugged. "I didn't have nearly as much trouble. This might be a self-fulfilling prophecy."

"He deserves it for what he did to Noah."

I rolled to my side, still hurting, but that didn't stop Lysander.

He stepped over me and torqued my arms behind my back. I didn't resist as he secured my wrists with some sort of corded metal ties. Once finished, he dragged me to my feet.

"Sawyer, stand back."

"Uh-huh," she muttered, poking at her PAD.

With a stiff push, Lysander directed me out of the infirmary. We stepped into a wide corridor, perfect for accommodating movement of heavy crates and cargo. Lysander held my elbow, his grip tight as he shoved me along.

What a bitch. He should hope we both didn't end up in a dark alley somewhere.

"If you so much as stumble out of line," Lysander said, terse, "I'll shock you again."

"Do all your suits have that capacity?"

"Of course. *Star Marque* standard."

Hm. It was still a mystery why the kid didn't use it.

The halls of the *Star Marque* hinted at its long history. Military ships hadn't been built since the United-Earth War. The weapon mounts by each door, along with the prevalence of escape hatches, told me the *Star Marque* was a vanguard-class starship. The type of ship that took on all the dangerous missions. A ship for the ambitious and foolhardy.

This ship had been modified, of course. Instead of escape pods, there seemed to be starfighter ships—small, highly-maneuverable crafts carrying hyperweapons, perfect for deep-space combat. However, should the *Star Marque* fail, the lack of escape pods could leave half the crew dead in the water.

That kind of choice spoke volumes about the captain. Either he didn't give a fuck about his crew, or he was just confident he'd never fail.

Enforcers walked the halls in their enviro-suits, though most kept their helmets down. The easily-collapsible nature of the enviro-suit helmet allowed for a quick transition from casual to combat without the hassle of changing, but I would've been too worried to ever wear it down.

I stopped in the middle of the hall to twist in my jumpsuit. It was half-on, and with my hands cuffed behind my back, it was awkward and falling out of place.

Lysander pressed his pistol into my spine.

I glanced over my shoulder and glared at the man. I was already heading for Ucova… what was one more body?

Lysander must have picked up on my animosity, because he took a moment and examined my jumpsuit. He straightened the sleeve over my shoulder.

"I should've let you finish dressing," he said, strained. "My apologies."

But that was the end of that. He shoved me forward, and we continued on our way. I returned my gaze to the surroundings, taking in as much information as possible.

The *Star Marque* wasn't meant for human comfort, that was for sure. With each room we passed, I got a better picture of the guts of the starship. The spaces were designed for military personnel and squads of starfighters. Capsule bunk beds. Small lockers for storage. Shared bathing areas.

The decks were few but long, and I was willing to bet this ship could hold a company of 250 soldiers with few problems.

"This is it," Lysander said. He stepped up to a door on the far end of the craft, right at the end of a massive corridor. "This is the conference room. Endellion wants to speak with you before we place you in the brig."

Lysander opened the sliding door and ushered me in. A gigantic viewing window made up the entire wall on the far end of the room, from floor to ceiling. The sight took my breath away. The black void of space, dotted with the stars of a billion galaxies. I didn't consider myself poetic, but even Capital Station was beautiful among the black tides that surrounded us. It reminded me I was a small fleck of matter in an otherwise cold and empty universe. It was humbling.

It took me a moment to register everything else. A long conference table, a few chairs, a computer terminal, and a hydration station. Endellion stood by the window, her back to the room. She was the sole occupant.

Lysander straightened his posture more than before, if that was even possible.

"I brought the criminal," he said.

"I told you not to restrain him," Endellion replied, her gaze fixed on the outside. I wasn't even entirely sure how she knew I was restrained, considering she wasn't looking in my direction.

"He's dangerous. He attacked me and could have attacked Sawyer, and—"

"That's quite enough," she stated. "Undo his restraints. He's no danger while I'm around."

Everyone on this ship underestimated me, it seemed. It reminded me of Section Six all over again. When people thought I was a failure, they ignored everything I had to offer. I got so angry to prove myself, I did whatever they wanted—ten times better than they could have hoped—but that was a losing game when I worked with losers themselves.

But still… I wouldn't be talked down to ever again.

Lysander didn't speak as he undid my restraints. Once free, I rubbed my wrists and waited. Lysander stared at Endellion for a moment before muttering some sort of apology and stepping out the door.

I rotated my shoulder and pulled on the last half of my jumpsuit, irritated by the sticky, clingy feeling left over by the vat fluid.

I opened my mouth to say something, but Endellion beat me to it.

"Clevon Demarco."

Her statement caught me off-guard. I zipped up and waited, knowing she had more to say. Why bring me here? If I was her bounty and prisoner, what was there to gain by speaking with me? I should have been in the brig, floating up to my eyes in tranquilizers.

Endellion turned around, and I was struck by her silhouette, backlit by the system's star. The reflective properties of the viewing window prevented the glare from burning my eyes, but it still hurt enough to squint. She walked toward me, casual yet confident. I found myself straightening my own posture as she drew near.

"You have a long criminal record," she said, stopping a meter away, the light still highlighting her from behind. "Vandalism. Petty theft. Grand theft. Extortion. Money laundering. Obstruction of justice. Assault. Battery. Murder."

"Are you sure that's *my* rap sheet?" I quipped. "That could describe any random schlub from Capital Station."

"Why are you wasting your gifts, Clevon?" Endellion asked, ignoring my levity.

I snorted. "Are you trying to lecture me? Is that why you called me here?"

Her silence made me uneasy.

Actually, *everything* about her made me uneasy.

Like the rest of the crew, Endellion wore a black enviro-suit with the helmet back. Her long, auburn hair was tied in a braid and hung over her shoulder, not a strand out of place. She was tall— damn near my height—and her gaze pierced my core. It was the same gaze she'd had on Capital Station. Calculating and severe. Not a hint of hesitation.

When the silence persisted, I chanced a glance at the rest of her. I could see the skin of her face, blemish-free and smooth. Her curves were prominent, her stance powerful.

But her eyes... I kept returning my attention to her eyes. Without the tinted visor of the helmet, I could see they were a deep, emerald green. Unnaturally so.

Endellion smiled. "My subcommander is disappointed. He thought you were one of the genetic elite. He thought you were a superhuman."

"Not quite," I said.

"I know. You're a genetically-modified human."

"That's right." That was the secret to all my power and advantage. Genetic modifications could turn even the simplest of fuck-ups into a talented specimen of mankind. Increased strength. Increased speed. I would outlive the standard schmoe any day.

"From the records I found," Endellion said, "your mother was one of the lucky few Homo sapiens who got to live on Vectin-14. She worked planetside as a housekeeper for one of the Homo superior, did she not?"

I held my tongue, both amazed that she knew so much and angry that my information had been that easy to find.

Homo superior…

That was the fancy scientific term for superhumans. They were genetically separate from humans—the two couldn't interbreed— and there was a reason some pompous asshole gave them the species name of "superior." They were better. Stronger, faster, smarter. More so than genetically-modified humans, like myself. Wild stories of their accomplishments could be heard in every back alley on Capital Station. They were a thing of legend, but real.

Endellion continued, "Your mother had fetal modifications on her unborn child right before being removed from Vectin-14. The geneticist improved your reflexes, strength, and mental capacity, but from what I can tell, you've done nothing worthwhile with your talents."

"What do you know?" I said. "My mother was deported to Capital Station. *No one* makes it on Capital Station. No one."

"You're not on Capital Station anymore."

"Yeah. Now I'm on an enforcer ship, heading straight for my prolonged death."

Endellion tossed her long braid over her shoulder. "Your record was a fascinating read. You always managed to worm yourself out of any given situation. If you really think you're being sent to Ucova for the rest of your days, how do you plan to worm your way out of this?"

"I'll think of something."

She smiled. "Did you know that the *Star Marque* is registered with the Vectin Quadrant Naval Fleet? I hold the title of commodore."

What kind of tangent was this? I crossed my arms and narrowed my eyes. "Prissy titles handed out to the superhumans' dogs don't impress me."

"It means," she said, amusement in her unwavering stare, "I can pardon crimes within my jurisdiction and recruit whomever I deem fit to serve as a member of my enforcers."

I opened my mouth to make another quip but stopped myself before I took a breath.

She meant to recruit me? Was that what this was all about? Why? She knew of my criminal background. Felons didn't make for good law enforcement, or so I'd heard. I knew I was talented, but surely someone with some formal training would be better than a guy with raw capabilities.

"What do you want from me?" I asked.

"Genetically-modified humans make the best starfighters. Outside of superhuman starfighters, that is. And I'm in need of a few good pilots."

"I don't know jack shit about piloting a starfighter."

"You can learn. I prefer high-quality individuals who need training, rather than men who have hit the boundaries of their limits and will never improve."

I glanced around the conference room, taking note of how spacious and empty the place felt. Or maybe the view from the window distorted my perception.

"You're *that* hard-up for pilots?" I asked. "So much so that you'll take on a criminal?"

Endellion turned her back to me and returned to the viewing window. Her long legs captured my attention. Those enviro-suits hugged the skin tight.

"I deal with the worst of the worst," she said. "Corsairs, smugglers, *Capital Station*… but bigger problems are on the horizon. Problems that will require skilled individuals at my beck and call. I'm willing to take anyone on if they'll give me an advantage."

"So, let me get this straight. It's either *join you* or *get shipped off to Ucova*. Is that right?"

"Very astute," Endellion replied, a hint of mocking in her tone. "Truly, you live up to the high intellectual standards set by genetically-modified humans."

"What if I don't like either option?"

"I suppose I could execute you, if you'd rather."

Her casual threat got under my skin. I was half-tempted to play out our fight right there in the conference room. I had been injured on Capital Station and taken off-guard by her abilities. It wouldn't be that way this time.

Then again, her suit would incapacitate me in a heartbeat. I gritted my teeth and took a deep breath, suppressing my anger.

"The way I see it," she said as she glanced over her shoulder, "you can take your chances with the *Star Marque* and become an enforcer, or you can drown in a cesspool of your fellow lowly criminals."

"I'm not a lowly criminal," I stated.

"Then prove it."

My blood ran cold. She thought she could manipulate me? But still, she had a point. I never would have been given the option to become an enforcer before. They didn't recruit from places like Capital Station, after all. And going to Ucova was as good as signing my own death warrant.

But off-station enforcers traveled between stars and handled all sorts of dirty problems the superhumans didn't want to deal with themselves. It was the peak of occupational hazards. They died all the time.

"Fighting the filth of the outer colonies is an enforcer's job," I said. "I might live longer on Ucova."

Endellion turned around and walked back toward me, her gait powerful. This time, she got closer, less than 30 centimeters away.

"If you've given up, you've given up," she said. "Nothing I can do about that. But I should let you know, I don't lose to gangsters and lowlifes. I don't lose to smugglers or ex-soldiers or terrorists or even circumstance. If superhumans came to stop me, I'd fight them, too." She paused for a long moment, and I waited.

"Join me," she finally said, "and I'll take you to greatness. Nothing will stand in my way."

She held out her hand, like this was a crossroads of destiny—epic and shit—but as much as I wanted to mock her, I could feel the weight of the decision bearing down on me. She meant what she said.

I took her hand and shook it.

Her grip surprised me. Stronger than I imagined, and I questioned the source of her speed and strength. Was *she* genetically-

29

modified? I had never met another like me. It required special doctors and thousands of credits.

"Let's do this," I said.

"Excellent." Endellion tapped her left forearm. "Sawyer, did you get that?"

"Yes, Endellion," Sawyer's voice said through the communicators on the enviro-suit.

"Good. Then pull the ship back into port. We have things to complete in Capital Station."

"You're the captain?" I asked. "And a ground commander? And a commodore?"

Endellion nodded. "Welcome to the *Star Marque*, Clevon."

THREE

The Capital Station Docks

I pulled at the enviro-suit clinging to my body, hoping to let my skin breathe, but no matter what I did, it stuck as though suctioned in place. My movement wasn't restricted, and I rotated my arms to help alleviate the faux feeling of strangulation. I had never worn such a high-quality enviro-suit before.

"Endellion wants you as part of the dock security," Lysander said.

"What?" I asked. "She's just going to throw me in? No training? No nothing?"

"Endellion does things in a peculiar manner. She has her reasons. Unless you think you can't handle yourself."

I gave my enviro-suit one final adjustment around the crotch. "Oh, I can handle myself."

Lysander sneered as he motioned to our surroundings. "Then we'll be in charge of Dock Seven."

Ah, the glorious stench of Dock Seven. It was just as fragrant as the legends foretold—rotting sewage waste with a hint of decay.

"We?" I asked.

"You, me, and Lee."

Three of us? For all of Dock Seven?

I snorted and forced out a single laugh. Each dock was massive. Twenty to thirty starships clogged the docking hatches, and each starship required twenty station workers to handle it at the bare minimum. Not to mention the starship crews, which could be upwards of 2,000 personnel. And then each docking station had its own food stands, hookers, and other businessmen all looking to get a few credits from the weary travelers.

Three enforcers were not enough to wade through the masses.

"We're here to maintain order," Lysander said. "But we're also investigating a larger smuggling operation. A group of chem dealers are transporting their wares right through this dock."

"No shit," I said. "Standard fare."

"The chems we're looking for are different. Powerful neuro stimulants. They fry people's brains, killing them."

"And three chumps in high-tech enviro-suits are supposed to handle this?"

"No," Lysander snapped. "Two *professionals* are going to handle this, and one *chump* is going to sit back and watch how we operate."

I cocked an eyebrow, but he remained silent.

Lysander and I—we weren't going to get along. I hadn't decided that. He had.

"Endellion wants to evaluate you as an enforcer," he said. "Your actions today will be under the harshest scrutiny. If you don't mesh well, there's always Ucova."

"And I just happened to get assigned to you?"

"Endellion herself said you were to assist me on these docks. Consider it an honor."

The hiss of powerful hydraulics dragged my attention away from Lysander. One of the *Star Marque*'s loading doors lowered, revealing two dozen enforcers, suited up and ready to go. They exited in pairs, precise as ants, and headed straight for the section lifts. All except one.

The last man walked over to me and Lysander and gave us a nod.

He was short, and he had to stare up at me to make eye contact, but he held himself with confidence. Unlike most of the denizens in

Capital Station, he had a healthy bulk to him, and clean-cut, black hair. He offered half a smile, and I relaxed a bit.

"Lee?" I asked.

"Yeah," he said. Then he tapped my arm like we belonged to the same little brotherhood. "I haven't seen you before. What's your name?"

"Clevon Demarco."

"Gentlemen," Lysander said as he snapped his fingers. Like we were dogs. "We have work to do."

Lee pulled his helmet over his head and it clicked into its hardened state. Lysander stared, waiting for me to do the same. I hesitated for a moment, and when I finally pulled the thing over my head, it suctioned to my face like a second layer of skin.

I had never considered myself to be claustrophobic, but the new experience left me on edge. I took deep breaths, wondering if I was getting enough air, and I stared out of the flexi-glass visor, attempting to gauge how much of my vision had been limited.

The visor pulsed to life, revealing a screen of technical information. Once powered, the screen cleared, displaying minimal data at the periphery of my vision. The air had 78% nitrogen and 21% oxygen.

Lee motioned to the side of his helmet, tapping at the "ear," and then pointing to mine. I tapped my helmet, and the screen displayed that the comms had switched to a squad setting.

"Have you never used these before?" Lee asked, his voice crisp over the enviro-suit's comms system.

"He's Endellion's newest recruit," Lysander replied, his raucous voice right in my ear, grating away the last of my patience.

"He's the one we picked up the other day? The guy from the fights?"

"The criminal, yes."

"Oh. Endellion has... eccentric recruitment methods."

Lee and Lysander both tapped their helmets a second time. A strained silence fell over my comms. The visors for the enviro-suits were one-way mirrors unless you were up close, but I didn't need to see Lee and Lysander's faces to know they were discussing my dubious background. They had the subtlety of an out-of-control crane careening through a busy section corridor.

And then Lee stepped away from me and gave me the once-over. No doubt Lysander had filled him in about my past. Made me wonder if I should even be there, but I thought back to Endellion. She was something else. Something more than Lysander's pettiness. But was she enough to keep me there?

The comms clicked back to squad, and Lysander pointed to the section doors. Lee and I followed him into the docking station, a corridor that led to the central hub of Dock Seven. Before we were more than a couple meters in, we were bombarded by the shouting and megaphones that dominated the area. Rickety stands and mobile kitchens were set up all along the dull, gray walls, each manned by aggressive salesmen, all trying to outdo each other in the hopes of gaining attention.

Their ragged jumpsuits and thin frames told me business hadn't been good. Then again, it never was, not unless you were MF Grain.

I could mute the sound outside my enviro-suit—at least, according to the display screen—but I didn't. There were too many advantages to hearing my surroundings that I wouldn't want to forsake.

Lysander walked up to the first mobile kitchen. He slung his plasma rifle off his back, and the old bag manning the hot plate cringed away, her leathery skin coated in sweat.

"You, uh, hungry?" she asked as she tapped her spatula against the heated metal surface of her grimy cooking area.

My helmet indicated that the hot plate was 250 degrees Celsius and that the "food" was primarily made of cellulose and glucose—cardboard and sugar.

Lysander double-tapped the side of his helmet. "We need to inspect your equipment," he said aloud, his comms set to vocalize.

Really? *This* was how we were going to go about finding the smugglers? A systematic search of each rinky-dink stand?

I tapped my comms and cycled through until I had Lee in a

private little communication. He gave me a sideways glance, and I snorted.

"Is this how it usually goes?" I asked.

Lee nodded. "Well, there's typically a lot more of us. We comb the docking station, and then inspect the area using the suit's scanners. If there's anything suspicious, we report to Sawyer."

"Suspicious?"

"The usual. Known criminals. Illegal substances. Off-the-book cybernetics. Right now we're supposed to be tracking down some sort of smuggler who trades in faulty chems."

"Where are all the other fucking enforcers? This place is huge."

"Endellion won the bid for enforcement of the area. She insisted we were all that was needed for Section Four security."

I mulled over the information while Lysander continued harassing the crone at the hot plate.

Off-station enforcers got hired through a bid system. Whoever offered the lowest estimate for their services got picked up by the cheapskate overseer of Capital Station. Normally, a few teams were hired to police the lowlifes that infested the corridors, but I guessed Endellion had faith in her crew. That, or the pressure of being a captain, commodore, and ground commander had impaired her judgment.

"The food you're serving is below regulation standard," Lysander said.

"It's edible," the woman said, her voice rising. "And biodegradable!"

"Let me see a list of your suppliers."

"I don't got any, and you don't need to see them! It's edible, I tell you! It is!"

Lysander snapped his fingers again, and I turned to him, glaring.

I switched my comms back to squad. "You got a problem?"

"It looks like we'll be needing restraints. You two go and fetch some."

"Two of us?"

"Lee will get what I need. You watch him work."

There was no point in addressing the flaws in Lysander's tactics. Instead, I walked with Lee back toward the *Star Marque*. The moment Lysander returned his attention to the old, screaming woman, I grabbed Lee by the arm and returned to our private chat. "You get the restraints. I'm gonna talk to some people."

"Lysander wants us to stay together."

"You and I both know that's a waste of time. Besides, I'm familiar with Capital Station. Someone comfortable with the ins and outs is better suited for gathering information than doing simple fetch-quests."

Lee shifted his weight from one foot to the other, biding his time in silence. If we hadn't been wearing our enviro-suits, I knew the man would have eventually seen things my way. The pheromones that wafted from my body often got people to trust me when they were on the fence. Without them, I'd have to rely on logic.

Lee took in a ragged breath, probably ready to deny my request, but I cut him off and said, "Endellion recruited me. Don't you trust her judgment?"

I asked partly to sway him and partly to see what he would say about his commander.

To my surprise, he said, "She's never let us down. I guess... talking to the denizens won't hurt. Just don't take long. I'll get Lysander the equipment he needs."

"Good."

Smiling, I headed deeper into the dock.

Lee stood stiff, and I glanced back to catch him watching me walk through the crowd of sweat-coated workers. The longer he stared, the more I thought he regretted his decision, but his faith in Endellion got me thinking. If she'd recruited me from the dregs of humanity, where had the rest of her crew come from?

I shook my head and approached a group of loitering thugs. They hustled away, pushing past anyone in their path. I shouldn't have been surprised—I was an idiot for thinking this could even work. One whiff of off-station enforcers would cause anxiety for anyone on Capital Station. Enforcers didn't play by the rules. They were rough and never had to answer for their lack of due process.

That kind of authority created a chasm between me and every fool in this corridor. No one was going to trust me for shit.

With a heavy sigh, I pulled back my helmet. I took a couple quick breaths, and already I regretted my decision. The stench. I choked on it.

My usual tactics weren't going to work. When I was *Demarco the Gunrunner*, I was one of them—scum from the same urinal—but now there was no reason to talk to me, and a hundred reasons to keep their mouth shut. Snitches get stitches and all that.

I strode forward, half-smiling as the crowd parted, their heads down, and their eyes glued to the muck-covered floor. Children ran to their parents, and a few halfwit teens fingered their knives, but no one approached. Even the whores zipped up their jumpsuits and shimmied on to the next guy looking to burn some credits.

I would have to think of a different tactic.

If I were smuggling chems through Dock Seven, where would I do it? Through the food service workers, just as Lysander suspected. Those mobile kitchens were designed to be driven all over Capital Station. They flitted from dock to dock, chasing the starships and offering whatever they had for a meager amount of credits. That kind of mobility was the key to getting chems into the hands of potential buyers.

But Lysander's methods would tip off the smugglers. We needed to be clever—or at least, subtle—with our investigation. Perhaps we should have even ditched our enviro-suits. The smugglers were thugs, but thugs sure got clever when it came to avoiding the authorities. No doubt word had spread that enforcers were shaking down anyone and everyone, which would scare away our targets.

I stopped walking and glanced around.

Reality hit me.

I was wearing an expensive enviro-suit and carrying a plasma rifle. With Lee and Lysander busy, I could walk to the nearest departing starship and sell my equipment for a few thousand credits. I would be off this station and halfway to a planetside destination in a matter of minutes. There would be little chance I would ever see any of them again. Sure, I would probably see dirt and sky while working as an enforcer, but how long would that take?

This would be so much easier.

And it was their fault for giving me all the tools for my escape. Why would Endellion send me here untrained? Maybe she wanted to use me as a meat shield—making me a pilot was just a pretense. Maybe *I was* the fool for trusting her in the first place, and if I didn't run now, I would be squandering a golden opportunity. They should have—

"Oh, it's you!"

A flailing woman cut off my train of thought. She hustled over to me and stared, wide-eyed, while I regarded her with a cocked eyebrow.

"You're the one," she said through puffs of breath, her bony frame clearly unaccustomed to quick movement. "The one from the death fights."

"Yeah," I drawled.

"You won."

"Obviously."

"I didn't know you were an enforcer."

I went to correct her, but she cut me off with a bow, sweat from her forehead dripping onto the boot of my enviro-suit. "Never mind. Please, come with me."

I glanced around, wondering if this was a trap. Didn't matter. My old associates had rivets for brains. If they didn't take Reggie's death as a warning sign, they deserved what was coming to them.

The woman guided me through the flea-infested crowd and over to a mobile kitchen, no fancier than any other and half as busy. Two women, just as thin and wan as her, operated the hot plate. They scraped together "omelets" made of *factory mold*—an organic substance grown on the station in a mossy lump. Supposedly it was healthy, but I hated looking at the shit. When heated, it congealed into a slime-like substance. The omelets were garnished with pureed roaches.

Fancy.

"This is him, Lissa," my guide said. "The one who won the fights in Section Six!"

Lissa, a short woman with puffed cheeks that betrayed a glandular problem, turned her attention to me. She stopped her cooking and exited the kitchen, wiping her hands on her oil-stained apron.

With tears at the edges of her red eyes, she grabbed my forearm and bowed her head. "Thank you, thank you," she muttered.

I ripped my arm away. "What is this?"

She flinched back. "I'm sorry, uh, but—"

"Do I know you?"

Maybe I had slept with her. I had been with a lot of people on Capital Station—men and women—there was no way I could remember them all. She didn't look like my type. Too sickly and withdrawn. And she stood with slumped shoulders and a slight hunch.

I wouldn't have said no if she'd offered, of course.

"My husband," Lissa said as she wiped her face dry. "He entered the death fights after I begged him not to. Thank you so much for saving him. I don't know what I'd do without my Darryl."

Ah. She was Mrs. Meatloaf Face.

Well, more like Meat*ball* Face, what with the puffy cheeks, but still.

"He lived?" I asked as I scratched my chin. "After that beating? He's got tenacity."

"He owes it all to you. We all saw what you did to save him."

"Don't mention it."

I had contemplated killing the man. I didn't deserve a pat on the back for tossing him out of the arena.

"You can have a free meal whenever you come by," Lissa said, motioning to the sludge she mistook for food. "My family and I will accommodate you. Anything you want. It's the least we could do."

"Anything, huh?"

Wait, wasn't I on my way out of there? There was no need to get involved if I was not really an enforcer. Of course, showing up Lysander would be worth the effort. And if the crew of the *Star*

Marque trusted me alone now, they would trust me later. I could always leave if things started to look questionable.

"Do you know what's going on?" I asked. "About a new batch of chems that've been killing people?"

Lissa caught her breath. She turned and gave the other two women hesitant glances. They regarded her with furrowed brows and stiff head-shakes. When Lissa turned back to me, I could almost see the fear pouring off her. She balled her hands and held them close against her chest.

"We know nothing," she said, her voice half-drowned by the commotion of the busy market corridor.

She was as good a liar as Darryl was a fighter.

"I could have killed your husband," I said. "And I could arrest you for lying to an enforcer. But I didn't, and I won't. If you really want to thank me for kicking Darryl off that arena, you'll point me in the right direction."

Lissa walked back to the other women, and they argued amongst themselves in hushed voices—something about business and needing money—but I tried not to listen. I didn't actually want to cause the lady grief. Her husband had gotten thrown through a blender, and she didn't look much better. They might have both been genetic defects, given all the sickness in their appearance. Harassing her with threat of enforcer involvement would be the last bit of stress needed to complete her suicide sundae.

Lissa scrounged around the kitchen and withdrew an aluminum bag from one of the crates. She walked it over to me and presented it with her arms outstretched.

"Here," she said.

I took the bag and ripped it open.

The shine of a quick injection needle startled me. I closed the bag, my mind grinding to a halt. It was full of chems. Needles. The reusable kind. Buyers got a quick shot, and then the dealer took it back to fill it with some more chems before the next guy came to get a hit. Disgusting practice, but it cut down on costs.

"*You're* the smuggler?" I asked under my breath.

She shook her head. "I was… just dealing chems on the side."

"These kill people."

"Only if you take too much. I told 'em not to take more than one hit every twelve hours. It isn't fatal then. It just gives 'em vivid dreams."

The whole Meatloaf family apparently made idiotic decisions. Then again, who could blame them? Capital Station was a ruthless bitch that didn't take kindly to the meek and timid. People got desperate, and good judgment went out the window.

"So, the smugglers gave you a supply to sell, and you take a cut afterward?"

"Th-That's right." She stepped forward. "You said you wouldn't arrest us."

"Who's the guy? The one who gave you the bag?"

"His name is Slaight. He runs—"

"I know Slaight," I said, cutting her off. "He's a dockhand."

"That's right."

He was a notorious gambler, too. I had met him several times across a dice table. The guy didn't understand strategy or game theory—he just liked the rush when large numbers were involved.

Slaight always dabbled in this line of work whenever he got down on his luck. It was either *run chems* or *have his vital organs sold*. Not much of a choice.

A hand came down on my shoulder. I glanced over to find Lee standing next to me. I wrapped up the aluminum bag, handed it to Lissa, and gave her one final nod. "Make sure your husband stays out of the arena next year, yeah?"

"I will," she said.

"And no more of this." I didn't want to see her arrested.

"O-Okay."

I moved Lee away from the kitchen. Lee peeled back his helmet and let it fall between his shoulder blades.

"Did they have any chems?" he asked.

"No," I said. "They're clean. But I did get a tip." I motioned to the maintenance office built into the side of the station. "That's where our smuggler is."

"You think so?"

"Yeah."

"We've been on these docks for weeks. We've searched the maintenance office hundreds of times. We never found anything."

"You weren't looking in the right places or asking the right people."

I slid my helmet back on and slung my plasma rifle into the ready position. Lee followed my lead.

"We should tell Lysander," Lee said over the personal comms. "He's already pissed you went off without us. And you weren't answering his summons."

"We'll tell him as we head over there."

FOUR

Cyborg

S laight had the wits of a tire, and a spine as limp as the cardboard paste sizzling on the hot plates. I was never impressed with the man when he ran errands for the syndicate. His deliveries were late, and his goods questionable. If he was the weasel handing out faulty chems, this bust was as good as done.

"Lysander," I said once I'd switched the comms. "We're heading into the maintenance office."

He huffed. "What? You are to retur——"

I cut communication, switched to vocalize, and strode up to the heavy doors of the office without hesitation. Lysander could dick around all he wanted, but I knew what needed to be done.

"This is going far beyond questioning the locals," Lee said.

I tapped on the communicator next to the maintenance office door. A screen built into the wall flickered to life, revealing the secretary with a pixelated quality that made him look like he was being censored for obscenity. I didn't even need to say anything—the guy got one look at my enforcer enviro-suit and automatically unlocked the door. A second later and the screen shut off, almost like he wanted to escape the situation as fast as possible.

Lee grabbed my arm the moment I stepped inside. "Look,

you're breaking all sorts of protocols. I know you're new, and I know Endellion must have recruited you for a reason, but we don't operate like loose cannons around here. We have a chain of command and—"

"How can we help you off-station enforcers?" a dockhand asked, cutting Lee off.

I gave the dockhand my full attention. Three workers crowded around, blocking my view of the data-entry sad sacks poking away at their computer stations. I wouldn't have described the maintenance office as "large." Five computer terminals cluttered up the space, and the dockhands themselves were bulky with muscle. The three guys surrounding us made for claustrophobic conditions.

And the grime of the area made everything worse. Dried fluid was crusted over the touchscreens, filth was piled in the corner, and my enviro-suit detected an uptick in carbon monoxide, probably from unmitigated flatulence. I was already itching to leave, even though I was protected in my suit.

"Where's Slaight?" I asked, not bothering with pretentious formalities.

Lee turned his head but remained silent. He murmured something about seniority into the comms, but he didn't articulate his disapproval.

The dockhands—all of them men with twenty years' worth of hard work blistered onto their hands—regarded each other with quick glances.

"Slaight's busy," the first guy said. "We'll answer your questions."

"I don't need questions answered," I replied. "I need to arrest a guy for distributing chems. Any of you want to take Slaight's place for that?"

"You need to wait a moment. We got procedures."

"That's where you're wrong. I don't need to wait for jack shit."

Again, the meatheads exchanged glances.

I placed my hand on my plasma rifle, and everyone tensed. Before I said another word, the men stepped apart and motioned to the heavy door that led into the maintenance halls of Dock Seven. They offered nothing else as I stepped past them.

Lee jumped to my side. We walked to the door, tapped on the controls, and the door shot upward in a jarring split-second. The door was solid duralumin—it must have weighed a good two tons. After we stepped through, it slammed shut behind us with the same force, sending a shiver down my spine. I swore Capital Station would be the death of me. One wrong step under that door and I would have been severed in half.

"Jeez," Lee said with a sigh. "Lysander's going to break the comms. This isn't how he likes to do things."

I replied with a dismissive wave of my hand. "You can wait here for him, if that's what you want."

I strode forward. Lee hung back for a moment before jogging to catch up.

"We're not questioning the men back there?" he asked.

"They were trying to stall us."

"Is that right?"

"Slaight's up to no good back here."

"This is either going to be epic, or we're going straight to the brig."

The maintenance halls acted as the guts of Capital Station. Wires, pipes, and corded cables hung exposed on all sides, each marked with yellow-and-black signs for easy identification. Years of half-assed repairs had left most of the identifying marks too worn to read, and some pipes were covered completely in emergency sealant foam. The foam was meant for temporary patchwork, but I guessed some boob didn't understand the word "temporary."

I walked past several heavy-duty doors—the same as the one up front—but I didn't stop. I knew where Slaight would be.

Some maintenance halls had electromagnetic power generators. They were exposed and just as shitty as the rest of the hall, resulting in ambient fields of disruptive electrical power. It didn't physically hurt the workers, but it messed with nearby electronics and comms signals. It was the perfect place to conduct shady business. No one recording. No one listening.

"You're moving kind of fast," Lee said as I rounded a corner. He kept my pace, which was good because we couldn't slow down.

I snorted. "They're going to run."

"You've got a lot of theories."

The dockhands couldn't get a message to the goons near the electromagnetic generators, but they *would* get a message to someone nearby, and that someone would run ahead and alert everyone of enforcer presence. I'd worked with the Capital Station gangs for years. I knew their tricks.

"Trust me," I said. "We're almost there."

Before Lee responded, I dashed forward and ducked under wires strung around the pipes.

I rounded one more corner, and I spotted two guys rushing down the hall. When they spotted me, they picked up their pace.

"Hey!" one of them yelled. "They're here! They're here!"

"Freeze," I said, hefting my plasma rifle.

Lee readied his weapon as well. "We're station authority, hired by the overseer! Stand down!"

The men whipped around and opened fire with their hand cannons. Their laser rounds impacted my torso, the black mesh absorbing the heat. If I hadn't been wearing an enviro-suit, I would have been a dead man.

I chortled. Nothing beat having all the advantages.

Faster than the punks could comprehend their situation, I lifted my rifle, aimed, and fired. The plasma bolt ripped a chunk from one man's arm and sent him tumbling to the steel grating of the maintenance hall floors. The other guy—smarter than I took him for—turned and smashed his fist on an emergency rupture button.

The familiar red lights of the warning system blanketed the hall, and a siren rang with such piercing intensity, even the deaf could have heard it.

Maintenance workers from all directions started hustling through the area, following evacuation protocols. Before the button-pushing lunatic could disappear into the crowds, I took aim and fired. My plasma bolt ripped a hole in his neck, and the guy hit the floor, twitching.

Through the commotion, I spotted Slaight. He had a shaved head and tattoos along the back of his neck and ears. He ran for the generator room, so uncoordinated that I suspected he might have been soaked in chems himself.

I fired and clipped Slaight in the calf. He tumbled face-first into a pipe, blood exploding from his nose and coating his green jumpsuit.

Eh. He would be fine. The *Star Marque* had a healing vat. And now he wasn't going anywhere anytime soon.

Then valves opened all around us, and it took me a moment to realize the station was going through emergency procedures. I jumped out of the way before a geyser of cement foam gushed out of a nearby pipe. The opaque substance, thick and lumpy, coated the corridor. It was meant to protect against breaches, to seal cracks and holes that would lead to the vacuum of space, or to stave off radiation. The damn stuff dried within a fraction of a second, so I could stand on the new, lumpy section of corridor, but there was less room now, and everything had become uneven.

A few maintenance workers got hit with the initial jet stream of sealant. The foam got into their mouth, hardening before they could scratch it out, choking them while they staggered away. One unlucky bastard fell into a hardening pile, trapping himself in a cage of suffocation.

Although I'd dodged the foam, Lee wasn't as quick. He stumbled and got his leg stuck in a mound by the wall, trapping him in place. No matter how hard or frantically he yanked his leg, the cement foam wouldn't release him.

Maintenance workers ran around in droves, the hall filled with their presence. I headed for the generator room, pushing people out of my way as I walked.

"Hey, wait!" Lee said through the comms.

I glanced over my shoulder. Was Lee really in any danger? Lasers wouldn't damage his enviro-suit, the thugs weren't using plasma bolts, and the foam had stopped gushing into our section of the maintenance hall.

With a sigh, I hung back.

As I dwelled on the situation, a passing maintenance worker pulled a plasma knife, clicked it on, and swung. I leapt aside faster than he'd anticipated, and I slammed the butt of my rifle across his pockmarked face. Unlike lasers that did no harm to a high-quality enviro-suit, active plasma would slice clean through just about anything.

Three other workers—likely thugs in disguise—headed for Lee. One pulled a four-shooter plasma pistol from his jumpsuit pocket.

I leaned away as my attacker swung a second time, despite the swelling around his right eye. The glowing edge of his plasma blade, made of whitish-blue ionized gas, seared the air. The information on my visor highlighted the weapon in red and warned that the temperature at the edge of the blade was 2,700 degrees Celsius and dropping at a slow rate. That scorching ionized gas wouldn't last more than a few hours, but that was long enough to gut me.

And my attacker aimed to do just that. I could see it in his frantic mannerisms, his wide swing, and the tight grip he had on his blade.

We must've stumbled into the right nest. That was the only explanation for this level of desperation.

When I went to shoot, the man stabbed the barrel of my rifle, melting the steel and warping the weapon beyond use. I grabbed the madman and shoved him into the pipes, busting his forehead open.

The pistol gunman took his opportunity to fire at me, but his four rounds missed everything, almost like he was afraid he would hit one of his buddies instead. And four shots meant he would need to reload.

I wheeled around and found Lee struggling to stave off two attackers. He fired his rifle, but because of his predicament, he couldn't aim properly, and his bolts pierced through pipe after pipe, spilling heated water into the area. It hindered his two attackers, who slipped on the slick, bumpy surface.

Much to my frustration, I needed to concentrate as I ran to Lee's side. The floor no longer gave me adequate footing. A man with a knife, a guy with a pistol, some random brawler, and their backup punk wouldn't be a problem under normal conditions, but here I was struggling.

When I reached Lee, I ripped the brawler off him and punched the guy across the face. The impact hurt me more than him thanks to the metal skull beneath the brawler's skin.

He was a cyborg.

He swung once, and I leaned out of the way, but I slipped. When he swung again, he struck me across the helmet, his iron-hard knuckles undeniable, and the blow crumpled the flexi-glass of my visor. I stumbled, the display screen on the fritz. Information flickered in front of my eyes, blocking a good portion of my view.

Stabby the Knife Guy came up behind me, his plasma blade at the ready, but I pushed his scrawny ass back with a quick jab to the throat. He staggered and tripped on the hardened foam, allowing me enough time to return to Lee.

The last punk wrapped an arm around Lee's neck and pulled a Federation-standard steel alloy knife. He got it close to Lee's throat, but Lee held him off—he was strong for such a short guy. I reached the pair with enough time to wrench the weapon from the thug's grasp. I was stronger, despite the obvious mechanical finger alterations the guy had.

However, he punched me square in the face, messing with my display screen even further. I couldn't see, and the follow-up strike to my gut made me nauseous. I ripped off my helmet, knowing I would be in trouble if more laser weapons got added to the mix, but it was better than fighting blind.

I caught my breath.

Endellion leapt over a pile of cement foam, kicked off a pipe, and fired her plasma rifle mid-jump. She struck the four-shooter gunman, killing him while he was in the midst of reloading.

Endellion hit the floor, whipped around, and fired another round, leaving the brawler with a gory hole through his chest. When the knife guy stood, she shot him through the back of his head, her aim on a level I had never seen before.

The last punk attempted to attack her from behind, but Endellion—not even looking in his direction—stepped aside, evaded his strike, and kicked him. The force of her boot to his gut caused the man to vomit as he sailed back and hit a nearby doorframe. He couldn't stand. Instead, he curled in on himself, his jumpsuit bloody from the kick, like Endellion had ruptured his skin with her unnatural strength.

He attempted to crawl away, whimpering something that not even I could hear over the emergency sirens. While he writhed and sobbed, Endellion walked over to the door and hit her palm on the control screen. The heavy, metal door slammed down before the guy got through, severing his legs from his body in one quick blow.

The detached limbs, filled with electronics, blood, and synthetic muscle, squirmed across the hall as they twitched. Left without direction, the cybernetics went haywire, until their power reserves drained. The two stumpy legs were at either end of the hall before they were done flailing.

Slaight, like the idiot he was, rolled to his feet and attempted to limp away.

Endellion lifted her rifle, but I got my hand in the air before she could fire.

"He knows things," I said. "We want to question that one."

She put her rifle down and ran Slaight down like a dog. Within seconds, she had her rifle so far up his ass, he was choking on it. Slaight didn't resist as she restrained him with steel-cord cuffs.

The sirens stopped, and although water still gushed into the area, quietness settled over the corridors. The other maintenance workers had booked it out of there, and the chem-toting thugs were nothing more than corpses. The red emergency lights added a satisfying tint to the gore.

"What happened to the others?" Slaight asked.

"Don't worry," I said. "They died doing what they loved most— being stupid fuckin' gangsters."

Slaight shook his head. "Don't kill me. I got credits. I got—"

"You're under arrest," Endellion said. "The overseer and his justiciars will see to your hearing and sentence."

Slaight blubbered something else, but nothing worth noting.

I glanced over at Endellion, stunned by how quickly she had

dispatched those fools. She didn't mess around. One shot, dead. Second shot, dead. Another shot, dead. Door-to-legs, dead—or at least, bleeding out. It made me a little nervous—I was usually the one with all the tricks, all the advantages.

She was like me. She had to be. So why was she so much better? What did she have that I didn't? I had never met anyone with her capabilities before.

But I would deal with that later.

I stepped past Slaight and Endellion and headed to the electromagnetic generator room. The door was locked, but I grabbed the key card hanging from one of the corpses. He wasn't going to need it anymore.

Once the door opened, I strode in. The hum of the generator could be heard from half a kilometer away, and I gritted my teeth, wishing my helmet wasn't busted. I walked into the massive room and found the machine whirling at high speeds, the moving parts exposed to the world without guardrails or shielding. A shield would have stifled the electric effect, but Capital Station wasn't known for its safety protocols.

It wasn't hard to see why everyone had run. Five mobile kitchens sat parked around the generator, but they didn't cook food anymore —they cooked chems. The powerful chemical stench could kill roaches, and I was sure I lost a handful of brain cells from a single whiff. Those piece-of-shit labs made all sorts of toxic concoctions.

I returned to the hall and inspected the carnage. Most thugs had machinery and wires embedded in their system. Their mechanical parts were hidden underneath their jumpsuits, but now that they were sprawled out on the floor, it was easy to see the lumps.

Cyborgs disgusted me. They disgusted everyone on Capital Station, really. Most of their implants were taken from corpses, and it was a stereotype that only the desperate submitted themselves to the hack-job doctors. It was like a payday advance loan. One cyborg implant led to medical problems, which led to more implants, which led to more problems, and so on. Anyone stupid enough to take the quick enhancements was destined to die in a maintenance hall, forgotten.

"Pathetic," I said as I scratched my chin. "Cyborg scum crop up more and more these days."

Endellion turned to me, her visor a black mirror that reflected my image.

"Cyborg scum?" she asked, a hint of amusement in her tone.

"I've never known a cyborg that wasn't a complete dumpster fire. They get those machine bits to rise up to mediocrity because they couldn't do it any other way."

"Such disdain. You disappoint me, Clevon. I figured you, of all people, would see the vast potential of cybernetic enhancements."

"Whatever. Put your money where your mouth is. If you think it's so wonderful, why aren't you shoving machines into your body left and right?"

Endellion peeled back her helmet and allowed her dark, braided hair to spill over her shoulder. She smiled, her face and teeth perfect and proportionate in every way, but her eyes—I swore they said more than the rest of her. They said she was amused, like a parent entertained by a child.

"Clevon, I'm more machine than flesh. I've had over a hundred procedures."

I examined her a second time.

No. She wasn't a cyborg. She was perfect in every way. Sleek. Powerful. Her skin unmarred by surgery scars. Over one hundred procedures?

"Bullshit," I said.

Endellion laughed, but it sounded forced.

Other black-suited *Star Marque* enforcers entered the hall. A couple climbed over the piles of cement foam and sprayed it with dissolving liquid. Lee thanked them as two pried him from his prison. I heard Lysander barking orders, but I didn't have any fucks to give him.

"You're genetically modified, right?" I asked Endellion. "Like me. You started at a higher base. Those machines don't do that much for you."

"It's rare to find someone like you, Clevon. I wasn't so lucky." She hauled Slaight to his feet. "There's more to the universe than

52

Capital Station. The superhumans have perfected cybernetic enhancement. Their doctors produce cyborgs with unparalleled talents."

"You had superhuman doctors perform your enhancements?"

I couldn't hold back the shock in my voice. How? They almost never enhanced Homo sapiens. And getting into one of their hospitals was unheard of.

"Uncomfortable with superhumans?" she asked.

"I've never met one before."

"Then steel yourself. We're reporting to one in a few hours."

"YOU REALLY SAVED my ass back there," Lee whispered to me.

"I got you into that mess," I said in a hushed tone. "Let's call it a wash. Besides, Endellion came in and finished things up, anyway."

"Still. I'm impressed. You move like her. I've never seen anyone else do things like that."

Lysander peered over his shoulder, giving me and Lee a prolonged glower. He said to keep quiet, but what the fuck was the point? We were the only ones waiting in the conference room.

And this place wasn't something I was used to. Luxury accommodations weren't found in the slums of Section Six. I was almost in disbelief that this place existed inside Capital Station, but the more I glanced around, the more I came to terms with it. The floors sparkled, the table had clear water pitchers and actual food—even the air smelled sweet. The overseer and vice-overseer had decent quarters, but this outclassed everything else.

I leaned over in my seat—a soft, fine-weave chair that swiveled, super-fancy shit—and I got closer to Lee. "How did Endellion know where we were?"

Lee replied, "Sawyer monitors our comms at all times. She must have reported our actions to Endellion."

"But I switched my comms to personal. And I walked around without my helmet on for a bit."

"It doesn't matter. Sawyer hears everything, even with the helmet down. I, uh, discovered that the hard way."

Lee grew red and silent.

"She didn't report our activities to Lysander?" I asked. "It would've saved him a heart attack."

"She doesn't like communicating with anyone other than Endellion."

I stared at Sawyer. She sat in her posh chair, her feet on the seat, her legs up and pressed against the edge of the conference room table. With undivided concentration, she stared at the PAD on her arm, poking away at the touchscreen and typing with one hand. With her disheveled, red hair falling in front of her face, she didn't look too professional, but I guessed it didn't matter. Endellion didn't reprimand her.

Me, Lysander, Lee, Endellion, and Sawyer... and there was another woman I didn't recognize who'd joined us. She sat next to Endellion, her black hair spun into tiny braids and held back in a collective ponytail. Her enviro-suit marked her as some sort of subcommander.

Lee elbowed my arm. "I see you checkin' out Quinn."

I gave Lee a sidelong glance. "Who is she?"

"She's the starfighter subcommander for the *Star Marque*."

A starfighter. So, she was a combat pilot.

Lee leaned in closer. "How would you rate her? A ten, right?"

I didn't realize we were buddy-buddy, but ever since we'd exited the maintenance halls, Lee had been chatting it up like he would die if he didn't get enough conversation in his life.

I returned my gaze to Quinn. She was athletic, but feminine. Small earrings adorned the edge of her ear, her skin had a clean smoothness, and her eyes had an inner light of intelligence. The enviro-suit hugged the curve of her muscles—not too bulky, but capable.

"A nine," I said.

Endellion, though... it was a shame Quinn was sitting next to her. Even without the accessories, Endellion demanded attention.

"So, you agree Quinn's smokin' hot?" Lee asked.

"Yeah. Of course."

Lee ran a hand over his face, attempting to hide his smile but failing miserably.

"You gonna hit on her or something?" I asked.

"She's my wife."

I snorted and held back a laugh. What a dog. And he looked so pleased with himself, too.

My mirth irritated Lysander. He shot me another glare, but I ignored him. We were still waiting on the damn superhuman—the one who owned all of Capital Station and MF Grain—Maccarus Felseven. Everyone else, right down to the station's overseer, was just his underpaid minion.

"Anyone here ever met this superhuman?" I asked the group.

Sawyer, Lysander, and Quinn flinched at the sound of my gruff voice, betraying their high-strung nerves. They shook their heads, but Endellion didn't react. Her gaze remained locked on the far door.

"I've heard Maccarus Felseven over the comms systems on the ship," Sawyer said. "But I've never met him in person. He made it quite clear he doesn't like wasting time with hired guns."

"He doesn't like enforcers? Or he doesn't want to mingle with lessers?"

"Lessers?" Endellion intoned.

She swiveled her chair around and faced me. A cold silence settled over the room, like the others had caught and held their breath.

I chuckled and shrugged. "Everyone here knows superhumans are in a league of their own. Don't pretend otherwise. They're off governing quadrants of space while we're here playing cops and robbers with the filth of Capital Station."

"Have you met one?" Sawyer asked.

"No. But that's common knowledge."

Only members of Homo superior governed. Period.

They governed quadrants, planets, asteroid fields. Homo sapiens lost that privilege when they lost the war. Even major military positions within the Federation were now exclusively held by superhumans. And why would it be different? Everyone knew of their outrageous talents. There was a hierarchy of genetics—Homo superior at the top, Homo sapiens mucking around the middle, and the mutants and deformed got shafted.

I didn't write the rules. I just reported them.

No one else said anything. They gave Endellion fleeting glances as she swiveled her chair back around and resumed her staring. I couldn't help but feel I was missing something crucial.

"Has anyone here met a superhuman?" I asked. "Besides Endellion?"

Sawyer raised her hand. Again, no one else said anything.

"And they look different?"

Sawyer nodded with a smirk. "If you've never seen one, you're in for a treat."

I knew that. *Everyone* knew that. Superhumans were different. Perfect, or so people said. Imposing without effort, intelligence on par with a station mainframe, sleek and fit. Humans had five senses. They had six.

What did that even look like?

As if on cue, the door to the conference room opened. Endellion stood, her jaw tight, and her shoulders squared. Everyone else followed suit, and I did the same.

For the first time in a long time, nerves got the better of me, and I found myself tense.

FIVE

Governor

A fat slob masquerading as a person walked into the conference room.

That was no superhuman. It was Overseer Tobin Grank.

I had seen his giant mug all over Capital Station's monitors. He delivered speeches, announced the appointment of new justicars, and his recordings sounded every six hours, reminding people to report crimes.

Not that he gave a shit.

His apathy washed through the room in waves as he waddled over to the nearest chair, his brow set low in a scowl. His attendant —a thin man a third his size—kept the PAD on his left forearm close. He must have been the overseer's personal accountant. That or he was the PR guy. Overseer Grank wasn't known for his even temper.

"Where is Maccarus Felseven?" Endellion asked, not even bothering to greet the overseer.

"He's busy," Overseer Grank croaked.

His fussy little assistant typed away on his PAD. Definitely a PR guy. This whole meeting was being recorded—it was this guy's job to spin everything to shine a good light on Overseer Grank.

Endellion turned. "Then we'll return when he's available."

"Hmpf," the overseer grunted. "Don't bother. Felseven's busy every day you're free."

Everyone at the table gave each other subtle glances. I was surprised Lysander hadn't interjected himself into the conversation, but he sat stiller than the rest.

"I completed Felseven's assignments," Endellion said. "All of them. And all within half the allotted time."

"You found the individuals involved in smuggling on Dock Seven?" the overseer asked.

"I have."

"Impossible." Overseer Grank almost sounded irritated. It wouldn't have surprised me to find he was fueling half the crime on Capital Station. I knew my old boss had gotten "permission" to run drugs through certain sections. And the overseer looked like the type of guy who needed extra credits for his frequent trips to the buffet.

"We got a lucky break," Endellion said, her calm façade never wavering. "We found a few maintenance workers wrapped up in the cooking of illegal chems. Fortunately for us, they're the type to squeal the moment we applied pressure. My enforcers have already rounded up over a hundred criminals. Dock Seven has been secured —long before any other team of enforcers said they could do it."

Lucky break, my ass. That was all me. I was the one with the contacts. I was the one who knew the movers and shakers. I was the one who'd lived on Capital Station for—

My thoughts ground to a halt.

Son of a bitch.

Endellion had placed me on Dock Seven just so I would find those smugglers for her. No training? A tiny team? Had she wanted me to wander off and handle things myself? Or had it all been a coincidence? No. Endellion had my rap sheet. She'd banked on my insubordination.

"Felseven thanks you for your services," Overseer Grank said with a sneer. "You've done remarkably well. Your payment has already been transferred."

"And what further assignments can I complete for Felseven?"

"There are none."

Overseer Grank's lips twitched upward into a slimy smile. He took way too much pleasure in his response, like he wouldn't mind slipping a hand into his pants while he said it. It was the attitude of a man accustomed to ruling an empire of trash. If everything else was shitty, his filth didn't look half-bad by comparison.

"We've never failed to complete a task within the given time-frame," Endellion said. "Felseven said he would meet with me once these were completed. He said we had more important arrangements to discuss."

"Felseven doesn't want to associate with an overreaching cyborg."

Endellion didn't reply.

"He's gotten wind of your governorship petition, and he's already voiced his disapproval. Felseven doesn't see the point to this charade. You can stop your begging and sniveling."

I didn't know what Endellion was petitioning for, but the situation was now clear. This was a snub. A petty, political snub. Endellion must have agreed to take care of a few things under budget, and faster than expected, in exchange for Felseven's favor. And then he decided he wasn't going to give it to her. He should have at least had the balls to reject Endellion himself, rather than sending a human trash bag in his stead.

Lysander crossed his arms and his fingers dug into the black mesh of his enviro-suit. The others stood with stiff postures, each quiet, but I could sense them seething. The PR guy stopped poking at his PAD as the silence thickened.

Endellion gave the overseer a nod. "Then our business is concluded. Have a nice day, Overseer."

She turned on her heel and motioned to us with a jut of her chin. I followed, but Lysander jumped to her side before I could say anything. Once out of the conference room and back into the grimy halls of Capital Station, he huffed.

"We can submit a formal complaint," he said. "The Vectin High Governor can—"

"There's no point," Endellion interjected.

"You're on good terms with the high governor. He might intervene."

"I won't be calling in any favors over this. Felseven will regret crossing me, but now isn't the time."

"We did all this work for next-to-nothing. He took advantage of us!"

Endellion gave him a sidelong glance. "Patience is a virtue. And I have other matters to deal with."

Her tone carried a finality that killed the conversation.

I stepped up to her other side, my curiosity burning all other thoughts. "You sent me to Dock Seven hoping I'd finish your assignment, didn't you?"

"It was a calculated risk," Endellion replied. "And you didn't disappoint."

"I could've ditched the team. It would've been easy."

"You gave it serious thought, I see."

"Of course he did," Lysander said through clenched teeth.

"I could still do it," I said, half-wanting to see her reaction.

Lysander shook his head. "I told you he'd be like this."

Endellion silenced Lysander with a wave of her hand. When we reached the lift, she glanced to me, a half-smile on her face. "Look around, Clevon. Day one and you're dealing with the highest levels of Capital Station. Imagine day two. *Imagine day four hundred.*"

The lift doors opened. Lysander and Endellion stepped through. I stood in the doorframe as Sawyer, Quinn, and Lee took their time catching up. They entered without a word, no doubt lost in their own thoughts.

Imagine day four hundred, huh?

I WAS SURPRISED by how much access I had been granted on the *Star Marque*. If I were in charge, I wouldn't have been nearly as trusting with new recruits, especially not men like me. Not that I *wanted* to do anything to the *Star Marque*, but I was more than capable.

The cold duralumin and steel alloy of the ship gave it a dark color. Even with the full force of the lights, walking through the halls was like walking through space itself. There was light, but there was always darkness. Always.

I walked by the mess hall as cheering permeated that entire section of the ship. I glanced in, taken aback by the merriment. Groups of enforcers crowded tables that had been pushed together to form a circle. Whisky, beer, rum, and brandy pouches of all flavors were being liberally passed around the group. Half the enforcers were still in their enviro-suits while the other half were dressed down in nothing but pants and a tank top.

One table sat in the middle, like a stage. Lee stood next to it, one foot on a bench and a brandy pouch in hand. He was a showboat who shouted at the top of his lungs, gesturing to the crowd like a damn ringside entertainer.

"—and then the emergency foam *gushed* out of the valves!" Lee said with a slur. But then he spotted me. "There he is! That's the guy!"

I tensed, waiting for the inevitable. Lysander had probably gotten to the crew before me. They would be chanting "criminal" any second, which was exactly why I'd separated myself from the other enforcers the moment we loaded up to leave Capital Station.

"He saved my life," Lee said, removing his foot from the bench. "And he's the one who tracked down the smugglers."

One by one, the enforcers held up their shiny aluminum pouches, toasting me as I stood in the doorway of the mess hall.

"Join us," someone shouted from the crowd. There must have been over 60 people in the room.

"Yeah," another person chimed in. "Lee's been telling us all about you."

The jovial atmosphere enticed me. Back on Capital Station, getting drunk meant fucking or fighting—sometimes both—and it never ended pretty. PADs went missing. People wound up dead. It seemed different here on the *Star Marque*, almost like everyone was enjoying themselves, even if they were tipsy.

I entered the room, but I kept my wits about me.

Lee motioned me close, and I sauntered up to his impromptu stage. Some lady tossed me a pouch. I caught it, turned it over, and examined the date. There was always a good chance shit was expired on Capital Station.

The *Star Marque* must have had quality suppliers, though. My pouch didn't expire for another two years. I cracked open the straw nozzle and took a drink. Fresh and crisp. That was a new experience. The pouches were meant to keep liquid contained in case of a gravity failure, but I had always found the damn things made it too difficult to get a good mouthful of anything. Not that it mattered. My enhanced metabolism made it difficult to get buzzed regardless.

Lee staggered to me and threw an arm over my shoulder. "This guy. *This guy.* He had my back. Six—no, *ten*—guys came to rough us up. Cyborg thugs. You should've seen this guy move. He fights like Endellion. Super-fast. Duckin' and weavin'.."

In a pathetic attempt to mimic my fighting style, Lee pushed away from me and spun around. If I didn't know he was drunk, I would've said he was having a seizure. The enforcers got a kick out of it, laughing and cheering him on, and I couldn't help but chuckle.

"Guys, come meet, uh," Lee thought for a moment. "What's your name again?"

"Clevon Demarco."

"Right. Yeah. Meet my usual crew. Quinn, Mara, Advik, Yuan! Get over here!"

Quinn emerged from the crowd of enforcers, still adorned in her enviro-suit. "Okay, babe. It's time to take a seat. Let someone else tell a story." She handled her husband with gentle gestures until he was leaning his weight on her shoulder. "You were starting to sound like a lunatic."

Quinn motioned with a jerk of her head, and I followed her into the group, away from the "stage." Enforcers patted me on the shoulder, either offering quick nods of approval or outright stating I did a good job for my first day. I half-smiled, rubbing my face to conceal it from the others. I wasn't used to camaraderie. Capital Station thugs would shoot up and get high to celebrate, but there was a good chance everything they owned would be looted the second they lost consciousness. Not the best environment for teamwork.

"I got a story," some large woman said as she stepped up to the center table. "I chased after three smugglers that defeated themselves, basically. After two minutes of running, they all had to vomit up that cardboard paste they ate for lunch. Then they keeled over!"

The laughter got to me. I joined in, amused by the stupid kids who thought they could run around after ingesting sludge.

Quinn grabbed the front of my enviro-suit and pulled me to the only table left in the corner of the mess hall. I wanted to rip my suit out of her grip, but I stopped once I spotted the mirth in her smile. She wasn't attacking me. This was some sort of playful gesture.

She allowed Lee to slide onto a bench. The four others at the table—who I assumed were Lee's usual crew—toasted his arrival.

"Thank you," Quinn said.

I cocked an eyebrow. "For?"

"For keeping Lee off the deceased list." She pushed me toward the bench. "And thank you for getting Endellion those smugglers. You made us look like titans."

I took a seat and downed another mouthful of my brandy pouch. Good shit.

Quinn motioned to the four around the table. "Clevon, meet Mara, Advik, Yuan, and Noah. Everyone, this is Clevon."

"Call me Demarco," I said.

"I thought only thugs went by their last names?" Lee asked. He gulped down the last of his drink and tossed the empty pouch onto the table.

I chuckled. "Yeah, well, I have a rap sheet from here to Galvis-4 and back. I think that classifies me as a 'thug.'"

Quinn hit me on the shoulder with more oomph than I thought possible from a girl her size. "You're not a thug anymore. You're an enforcer on the *Star Marque*. That makes you one of the crew."

The others at the table nodded, each uttering, "Hear, hear." All except for Noah, who kept his mouth shut and his eyes glued to the table.

But was that it? Was it over? They didn't care about my history?

"I mean it," I said. "I've done some messed-up shit in my life."

Quinn took a swig from her pouch and shrugged. "I used to hustle the defects on Midway Station. A real racketeering gig to make them pay all sorts of credits. I'm not proud of it, but Endellion knew talent when she saw it. Same with you." She motioned to the others. "Same with most of us."

Another round of, "Hear, hear."

"You must have a lot of faith in Endellion," I said.

"She's the greatest captain in the quadrant." Quinn smiled, and her volume increased. "And the best commodore. And soon-to-be the best—and first—human governor!"

The mere mention of Endellion's successes got the whole room cheering. Silver pouches were thrust into the air, people chanted her name, and another round was passed between the enforcers.

"Humans can't be governors," I said, my voice reaching Quinn but dying shortly after in the cacophony of cheers.

Quinn hit my shoulder again. "That's the thing. Endellion's petitioned the Vectin superhumans to grant her special permission. She's going to govern a planet. And we're all going to retire to a small piece of planetside property."

"She's going to govern a planet?"

"That's right. She's going be the first human to do it all."

"Why?" I asked.

Why would anyone want that kind of responsibility? It was hard work and effort, and she was going to get rejected.

Lee shook his head. "Endellion said that's what she wanted. And she's got the drive to make it happen."

Endellion could petition the superhumans from here to Earth and back, and it wouldn't make a difference. They would never let a human govern. Never.

I was no master of history, but every child got told the same damn thing in their earliest years of schooling. Colonists from Earth took the long trip to four sectors of space, each sector a close collection of 12-15 stars, ruled over by the antiquated United-Earth Governance.

But that didn't last long.

Human defects sprouted up at an all-time high. Mismanagement of planetside resources led to stalled construction and loss of countless lives. And once superhumans came into the picture, people saw them as a threat. Superhumans didn't develop genetic defects, and each one was three times as capable as any human. For every seat in the government a superhuman took, and for every company a superhuman controlled or created, more and more infighting occurred amongst the old rulers of the United-Earth Governance.

At first, superhumans took districts and turned them around. Then superhumans became governors and reformed their designated systems. When they called for a federation conference—a formal meeting to redesign the Cygnus Sector's constitution and change it into a federation of governors and planets, rather than one failing government—war broke out between the old United-Earth Homo sapiens and the supporters of the new Federation.

Needless to say, the Federation—those under the guidance of Grand Admiral Lone, a superhuman strategist with no equal—won the day.

Since then, superhumans had been at the top of all power structures, and they made rules to make sure it stayed that way. Most asshole instructors cited the failings of the United-Earth Governance as the reason the Cygnus Sector almost collapsed. The "old ways" were disastrous, and the Homo superior saved us from destruction—a justification for why humans didn't have much in the way of influence. That was what they said, day in and day out.

Restrictions were made after the United-Earth War.

Humans didn't even have the option to purchase planetside property—not unless they had a special invitation from a planetary governor.

If Endellion planned on using her influence to grant her crew property, that was an extraordinary reward. No wonder everyone was content with her dealings.

Fuck, I would have been satisfied living in one of those rent-a-box apartment complexes meant for menial workers. Anything to set foot on a planet. Endellion wanted to *rule* over one? She didn't shoot for mediocrity, did she? She had her sights set for heights most people couldn't fathom.

Quinn sat down on Lee's lap and locked her mouth with his. He ran his hands down her back and got a handful of her ass with no shame.

I liked Lee more and more. He was my kind of guy.

Lee detached his lips and gave me a half-smile. "Are you lookin' at my wife? It's okay to admit you're jealous."

Quinn ran her fingers through Lee's shiny, black hair. "*Everyone's* jealous, babe. No one knows passion like ours."

"Yeah, we're filled with passion."

Again, they mashed their faces together, like they wanted to choke one another with their tongues. I didn't mind watching if they were willing to put on a show, but the others at the table weren't as open-minded. One girl threw an empty pouch and hit Lee in the back of the head.

"You have your own quarters," the girl said as she motioned to the back door. "Besides, one more drink and you're gonna pass out."

Lee tore himself away from his wife and snorted. "Nah. I'm good."

"I think they're right," Quinn said. "We should go."

Before Lee could offer any more protests, she dragged him from his seat and headed for the door. Quinn knew what she wanted, and she wasn't going to get it from a limp noodle that passed out in the middle of the mess hall, that was for sure.

I took another long drink. I could get used to this. The atmosphere. The crew. This couldn't have been an elaborate trick—the camaraderie must have been real. Their faith in their captain was genuine.

Everything I'd heard about Endellion made me question my own capabilities. I had a ton of natural advantages, thanks to my genetic modification. Those advantages helped me in all sorts of situations, but I never thought outside of my limited personal goals.

400 days was a long time. How long had Endellion been reaching for her goals?

I turned to Mara, a cute little woman with short black hair and a button nose. "Hey. Endellion was born into some high-class family, right? One of the old human lines from the first mass transports?"

Mara shook her head. "No. Endellion was born on Ucova."

I caught my breath. Ucova? The prison planet?

Mara continued, "She lived there until her parents died in the mines."

"They were criminals?"

"No. Just blue-collar workers brought aboard to do mining and shipping."

The others at the table nodded, as though the story were common knowledge.

"She came from nothing?" I asked. No secret fortune? No family connections?

"That's right. She got her first job on Midway Station. Then she became an enforcer, and she's basically been the best ever since. Everyone knows it. We get extra consideration when we put in bids because of Endellion's reputation. She always delivers."

I turned away and finished the last of my brandy.

Endellion.

I couldn't stand being such a schmoe compared to her. It made me want to try that much harder. To show the others I was just as talented. Or maybe I only wanted her recognition. To impress her.

Maybe that was what I'd do.

SIX

Evaluation

T ime passed differently on the *Star Marque*.

Lights in the barracks dimmed and shone, depending on the schedule of the occupants. I stared at the fluorescent lighting as it transformed from black to full brightness over the course of 30 minutes. I think it was meant to simulate a planetside sunrise, but I didn't know. I had never seen one.

Capital Station wasn't so kind. Each section had its own "night-time" and "daytime." The transition was a harsh switch between 40% lighting to 100% lighting. Nothing in between.

I kicked open the door to my capsule and slid out.

Everyone got their own little room on the *Star Marque*. It was two-and-a-half meters deep, one-and-a-half meters wide, and two meters tall. Not enough room for me to stand and almost not enough room for me to stretch out. It didn't matter, since the capsules were solely for sleeping, but it was not something I was used to. Fortunately, every capsule came with its own monitor and entertainment, and the doors sealed to keep the snores of the others from penetrating my dreams.

It was like living in my own personal soup can.

I rotated my arms. Everyone said it would take six months

before we reached our destination—Vectin-14, capital planet for the whole quadrant. Six months was a long time to dick around on a starship. I was supposed to report to Sawyer, but first I wanted to bathe.

The others dressed in casual jumpsuits and headed out of the barracks in groups of four to six. I didn't have a crew of my own, and although the other enforcers were friendly, they didn't go out of their way to strike up a conversation or show me around.

That was fine. I could find my own way around the damn ship. I left without consulting anyone. I had seen enough of the interior to make it to the showers with little difficulty. I walked there in a few short minutes, realizing the starship paled in comparison to the size of Capital Station.

I stopped once I crossed the threshold of the shower room and was hit with a wall of steam and the smell of shampoo.

The first thing I noticed—probably because I'm a dog—was that the showers were co-ed. There hadn't been many women signing up to be gunrunners, so it wasn't like I'd worked with many on Capital Station. Men, on the other hand, were easy to come by. Tell a guy he was about to get laid, and he would be undressed before the end of the sentence, which made women more of a rarity for me.

But that was in the past. Although I wouldn't have minded getting to know my new enforcers in an intimate way, I kept to myself and locked my gaze on the floor—and my mind on dead orphans. If I was going to live in a polite society, I needed to at least attempt to be polite myself.

I undressed, left my jumpsuit in a locker, and headed into the open room of showerheads, some mounted to the bulkhead, and some mounted to floor-to-ceiling pipes scattered throughout the area. I walked past a few individuals and took up showering in the corner.

The showers—like those on Capital Station—had been set up to recycle water in the most efficient manner. The floor had drains that poured into a filtering system, which rerouted everything back to the showerheads. Every few minutes, I was hit with the same water from earlier—though unlike Capital Station, the filters actually worked. Nothing beat crisp water, free of particles and piss.

Damn. I already loved being on the *Star Marque*, and I had been there for less than a week.

"Hey," someone said. "Aren't you the guy from last night? Demarco?"

I glanced over and spotted Mara, rinsing herself off with the showerhead next to mine. She was three decimeters shorter, and probably half my weight, but that didn't mean she wasn't cut. I returned my attention to the much-less-interesting bulkhead in front of me, counting the droplets of water to keep myself from thinking of anything else.

"Yeah," I replied. "What do you want?"

"Quinn said you're the newest starfighter."

"So?"

"We'll be working together." She waited a moment before adding, "Have you ever flown a fighter before?"

"Listen," I said. "If we're going to talk, I'm going to stare. Otherwise, let me take my damn shower."

Mara's giggle was made of cuteness. "You're a lot different than I thought you would be."

I turned and stared down, not bothering to avert my gaze. I'd warned her. She had made her decision. To my surprise, she didn't seem embarrassed or disturbed by our nakedness. On the contrary, she continued as though nothing out of the ordinary were happening. Washing her hair. Smiling. She had an unusual happiness about her I found as alluring as her flesh.

"Lysander said you have an extensive criminal record," Mara said as she reached up to adjust the showerhead. "And Quinn says you've been genetically modified. I figured someone like that would be extra aggressive or a giant or something."

"Why would you think that?"

"I thought superhumans only modified humans for specific purposes. Maybe you were made to be a brute."

I hadn't been made for anybody.

Then again, genetic modification to humans had become rarer

and rarer, so I didn't blame her for assuming. Maybe a few centuries back, it had been more common, but that was when everyone was attempting to "break the ceiling" of human potential, back when superhumans didn't exist, and everyone wanted to create the first.

Once superhumans could reproduce with viable offspring—children who couldn't breed with humans because they were a different species altogether—fewer and fewer humans were in charge of medical research. They lost those roles to their superior creations.

And superhumans valued improving superhumans. Not the obsolete.

"Are you okay?" Mara asked.

She shut off her water and wrung out her short hair, giving me an odd look with a tilt of her head.

"Yeah," I said. "But I don't know of any other genetically-modified people, so it's hard to compare myself to them."

I'd thought Endellion was the first. I still couldn't believe she was a cyborg.

"There's only one other on the ship," Mara said. "You guys are pretty rare."

There was another on the ship?

A loud cough broke our conversation. I glanced over my shoulder, and then turned around, unable to restrain a smile.

"Sawyer," I said. "You're… fully dressed."

She stood outside the water, her gaze forever glued to the PAD on her arm. The other enforcers regarded her with chortles, a few nudging their buddies and pointing her out.

"It's time for your evaluation," Sawyer said, not looking at me. "I tried to reach you from your suit, but you weren't wearing it."

"Hello, Sawyer," Mara said.

"Hm."

"I never see you outside the control room. Your hair is adorable." Mara stroked Sawyer's red locks. "Why don't you wander around the ship more often? I'd love to talk to you in person from time to time."

Sawyer rolled her eyes. "I'm good." Then she motioned for me to follow. "Let's go. Your evaluation should've started already."

I turned off my showerhead and gave Mara a quick nod. She waved—seemed childish, but I wasn't going to complain—and then joined a group of enforcers chatting near the back of the room.

Sawyer thrust a towel into my gut, and I took it.

"I'm starting to think you *want* to see me naked," I said.

She got red in the face, but I admired her willpower. She *still* didn't look up from her PAD.

I patted myself dry. "Admit it. You didn't have to come get me in person. I'm sure this ship has comms."

"I don't like using the ship's shower comms."

With a few quick motions, I slipped into my jumpsuit and zipped it into place. "Mara's spunky. I think we'll get along."

"Hurray."

"I've got good credits she wants in my pants."

Sawyer snorted. "Yeah. I bet that's what she'll tell her girlfriend after her shift today."

Oh, goddammit. Just my luck.

Sawyer ignored the world around her as she ambled for the door. I followed, irritated for unreasonable reasons. "Is *everyone* on this rig in a quaint little monogamous pairing?"

"Not everyone."

"Endellion isn't worried about suspect loyalties?"

"People get removed from the *Star Marque* if they can't perform their duties."

Sawyer yawned as she rounded a corner. Passing enforcers greeted her, but she only returned the gesture one out of every five times. She was slow compared to my normal walking speed, but when I glanced down, I saw she was typing at a furious rate. Looked like code for a starship, the kind of complex code they used for the ship's main operating system. I had seen it dozens of times at the docks. A lot of ships went through updates while they resupplied, making sure they were up to Federation standards.

I was impressed. I didn't know anything about shit like that. It required a formal education and training. There hadn't been an abundance of schooling on Capital Station.

"You don't have any family, Demarco?" Sawyer asked, somehow

still typing her code while maintaining a conversation. "Or maybe you're leaving friends behind on Capital Station?"

"I had my mother. My mother died. I knew this one guy who had my back. He died, too. That's about it."

"Hm. A man with your amazing charisma, I'm surprised you don't have a bucket of friends, mourning your departure."

"I had a few friends. I'd say they were 'special,' but that could have a positive interpretation, so I'm going to describe them as 'fucked-up.' They aren't going to mourn my loss, and I'm not going to mourn theirs."

"Do you have a problem forming meaningful relationships?"

"What is this? A psych test?" I snapped. "From the sound of things, you're a space hermit. I don't think you can give me shit for this."

"Oh, I'm no psychologist," Sawyer said. "I'm just curious."

We reached a large, rectangular room, and I wished the place had a few port windows. I missed seeing the vastness of space. Well, the part with stars, anyway. Instead, the room was some sort of training facility, but it was the one guy milling around in the corner I took note of first.

"Thank you, Noah," Sawyer said. "I'm glad I didn't have to track you down as well."

Noah nodded, his shoulders and posture slumped, like a man cowed. I ignored him—he was no threat—and I examined my surroundings. Ten person-sized pods lined the back wall, and four stalls meant for holographic simulation sat in the center of the room. Sawyer grabbed a few wire headsets, then handed one to me and one to Noah.

"Put this on behind your ears," she commanded. "They monitor brain function. It'll help me evaluate your capabilities."

I did as she said, wrapping the thin wires around the back of my neck and hooking them to the shell of my ear. Noah watched me the entire time, and I shot him a glare. "Do I know you?"

"We met last night," he said.

Ah. Right. He'd been sitting at Lee's table.

"We also met on Capital Station," Noah continued. "I was… well, you took me hostage. When you were attempting to escape."

I laughed, amused by his sheepish tone. "Oh, you're *that* guy."

"Yeah. That guy."

"Which reminds me—why didn't you shock me with your enviro-suit's anti-grappling measures?"

"I…" Noah took a breath, and then exhaled. "I forgot it was an option."

"Heh. That's what they'll carve onto your tombstone, kid."

Noah looked away. From the side, he had the same hard edges to his features that Lysander had, but Noah had longer hair, not a military crewcut.

"You're Lysander's brother," I said, more accusatory than I'd intended.

"Yeah," Noah replied. "But we're nothing alike."

Sure, they weren't.

Sawyer motioned to a steel cabinet filled with training rifles. They were lasers—low power, non-lethal, but enough to register an impact—and I picked one up, surprised by how light it was. Noah took another, and I saw the way he hefted it. No enthusiasm. His lack of energy made me think he was sick.

"This is a competition," Sawyer said. "You both stand in those stalls and shoot all target prompts. The one with the highest score wins."

Noah narrowed his eyes. "Why is it a competition? Can't we be evaluated separately?"

"What's the matter?" I asked. "Afraid you're going to lose to me again?"

"There's that charisma I was talking about," Sawyer muttered.

She walked over to the holographic stalls and typed a few commands into the terminal. I stepped into one stall—it was open, no walls, just a ring of metal above and below me, held up by two posts—and Noah got into the next. The rings produced holograms. To someone standing in the stall, it appeared lifelike, but I had been outside them before. Everything from the outside looked flat. It was a trick of perspective.

I guessed the *Star Marque* used them for shooting practice. Guys on Capital Station used them for faux lap dances.

Noah regarded me with a quick glance. We were in competition with each other? This would be simple.

"Shoot the targets," Sawyer commanded.

Semi-transparent holograms appeared in 360 directions, and our laser fire got canceled by the refraction veil that accompanied the stall. No need to worry about shooting all around the room.

I fired.

Easy pickings.

The holographic images appeared to be far-off—making for small hit boxes—but they were the silhouettes of people, my most common target on Capital Station. And laser rifles had no kick. Hell, they didn't have any bullets or gas cartridges, so I could fire as fast as I could pull the trigger without losing any accuracy.

Only a schlub would have problems shooting with this weaponry.

"Time," Sawyer said, once 60 seconds had elapsed.

The holograms faded, and I lowered my weapon. On the post, written in bright-red LED letters, was my score. Shots fired: 67. Targets hit: 67.

I glanced over at Noah's. Shots fired: 52. Targets hit: 25.

He caught me staring at his score and glared.

"What?" he asked.

"Looks about right," I said. "For a guy of your caliber."

Noah tightened his grip on his rifle, and there was a part of me that wondered if he would turn it against me. I wouldn't have minded. It might have spiced things up. But the kid would have regretted it.

"Let's do it again," Noah said.

Sawyer, her hand over the computer terminal, gave us both a half-lidded, irritated stare. "We have other tests to run."

"I want to try this one again. I wasn't focused."

She sighed. "All right. One more time."

Kid thought he could beat me? Clearly he hadn't been paying attention.

The holograms shimmered into existence, and I whipped my rifle around to point it in Noah's direction. He flinched back, almost stumbling out of his stall.

I returned to my shooting, half-smiling. Noah was easily rattled. That was why he'd fucked up on Capital Station. That was why he'd forgotten his own suit's capabilities. Some men crumpled under pressure, broken by the weight of disastrous hypotheticals.

And that was why I was always going to win this challenge. Noah could practice 'til he was blue in the face, and while his aim might improve, it wouldn't toughen up his spine.

The kid wasn't suited for competition. He didn't have the ambition for it.

After 60 seconds, Sawyer called time.

I glanced at my score. Shots fired: 60. Targets hit: 60. Fucking with Noah had cost me my overall total, but my accuracy had remained at 100%.

Noah never recovered from my feint. His score got me chuckling. Shots fired: 54. Targets hit: 19. More shots. Fewer hits. And this time he didn't even bother making eye contact with me. He stared at the ground, a blank expression across his face.

"Put your rifles away and get into the pods," Sawyer said, motioning to the back of the room. "I'm going to run you through some basic starfighter-training runs."

"Finally," I said as I sauntered out of the holographic stall and tossed my rifle back onto the rack. "Let's get this started. I'm going to be the best damn starfighter on this ship."

"The best?"

"You heard me."

Noah placed his rifle among the others. "Endellion is the best," he muttered.

I gave him a sidelong glance before catching sight of Sawyer. She had the quirk of a smile on her face, like she'd enjoyed that comment.

"Endellion's also a starfighter?" I asked. What *didn't* she do?

"She has to be," Sawyer replied. "We're woefully lacking in

pilots. Counting you and Noah, we have eight. And you and Noah aren't trained."

"Are you serious?" I asked.

"Learning to pilot a starfighter is hard work. And most individuals can't handle the G-force. You'll be lucky if you don't pass out the first time you fly one."

Noah's shoulders bunched around his neck. I got a little uneasy myself, but I recovered the moment I imagined the look on Endellion's face if she had to rescue me from fainting in a starfighter. That wouldn't happen. I would master the starfighter.

"Again, I want you both to treat this like a competition," Sawyer said.

She walked over to the pods in the back—slightly smaller than my sleeping capsule—and opened two hatches. The insides were pitch black with a single reclined seat. No doubt they were some sort of simulation pods.

"I think I need a better opponent," I said.

Noah didn't offer an objection. He walked over to a pod and stepped in. Once he took his seat, the hatch closed, sealing him inside with a whoosh akin to a long sigh.

I had already won. Whatever we were doing, he had given up. I'd broken that spirit pretty quick. Probably not the right move. This wasn't Capital Station—this was a working enforcer unit. I wasn't about to be killed by my own gang brothers. And I might have to rely on Noah in the future.

Once I was certain he wouldn't hear me, I turned to Sawyer.

"Why the competition?" I asked as I walked over to my pod. "The kid isn't up for it."

"I need to monitor his hormone levels under stress," she said, disinterested. "Lysander believes he has a chemical imbalance. He wants to control the situation through injections and cybernetics."

"So, you had him compete with me?"

"He expressed anxiety about training with you."

"Me?" I blurt out. "Why? We hung out last night. I didn't fuck with him."

Sawyer stopped poking at her PAD and motioned to the pod. "Get in. We don't have all day."

I stepped inside, but my question still stood. Sawyer forced a quick sigh.

"I'm sure Lysander used colorful words to describe you," she said. "Just play along and allow me to monitor Noah's stress and hormone levels."

Feh. Lysander.

I figured Noah would be just like him, which was why I'd opted for total destruction in our competition, rather than playing nice, but perhaps I should've been easier on the kid.

"Don't be frustrated if you fail the first time," Sawyer said as I took a seat in the pod. "It's difficult."

"I got it," I snapped. "Worry more about the kid."

The hatch closed, leaving me to drown in darkness.

SEVEN

Training

I didn't like to admit it, but the bleakness of space unnerved me. Not the part twinkling with stars, but the dead blackness that filled the void between them. The port windows on Capital Station occasionally faced a patch of open space, lacking all light. It had given me nightmares as a child.

The darkness of my pod reminded me of those nightmares.

When a bead of sweat trickled down my forehead, I smiled. Was this what would break me? No. Definitely not. I had dealt with worse on Capital Station. I was ready for whatever bullshit this training required.

The pod condensed. It squeezed my lower legs, trapping them in place, and the chair fitted around my bulky frame, molding to hug every curve. I had never been claustrophobic—but I had never been in whatever this was, either.

"What the fuck is going on?" I yelled.

I attempted to jerk my legs out of the restraints, but there was no room left for me to move. The pod had a complete grip from my knees to my feet, applying pressure without causing me harm.

"Calm down," Sawyer said through the pod's comms. "This is standard undocking procedure for starfighters."

"Why?" was all I could ask.

"To regulate your blood flow. Extreme G-force causes your blood to pool in your extremities. The starfighter cockpit will prevent that from happening."

"This... is normal?"

Sawyer chuckled. "And here I thought someone with your bravado couldn't be shaken."

"I'm fine," I snapped.

"What the fuck is going on?" said a recording of my voice over the comms.

I gritted my teeth. "Get your quips out now. We have training to do."

"Hm. Suddenly all business."

Lights filled the inside of the pod—bright, sharp red-and-blue— and my heartrate kicked into high gear. There was a sophistication to the layout that drew my attention to the two side-stick control handles in front of me. I rested my hands on them before going any further.

"What is all this?" I asked as I tilted my head back and stared at the lit screens.

"Your fighter's hull integrity, your position within the Vectin star map, the number of torpedoes loaded, the number of hyperweapon bolts, a comms channel reader, a—"

"I'm supposed to keep track of all this during a dogfight?"

"You should keep your attention on the center screen. It indicates particles and objects you'll need to avoid. Other than that, I'll be monitoring your other systems."

I took a deep breath and relaxed. Starfighters were known for their high-tech ingenuity. Sure, they were tiny, one-person vessels, but they were quick and could change directions with precision befitting a master surgeon.

The center screen showed me the outside of the cockpit. It was a vision of space, with information overlaid like a transparency. Before me sat an asteroid field, and I admired the porous rocks, spinning together in groups. I knew it was a simulation, but sometimes I was reminded of just how small I was compared to the vastness of reality.

"Twist the right side-stick to accelerate and press the trigger on the left side-stick to fire your hyperweapons and torpedoes," Sawyer said.

"What are hyperweapons, exactly?"

"A super-heated plasma bolt. It's hot enough to vaporize most metals into gas, but that level of heat can only be maintained for a short period of time. You have to be close to your target—closer than any normal starship could get to another—for it to be effective."

Melt metal into gas, huh? Shit. That would annihilate human flesh in an instant.

I wondered if that had ever been tested.

Heh. Of course it had. Humanity was fucked up.

"Avoid the obstacles and shoot the targets," Sawyer said. "You may begin."

Even though I knew it was a simulation, the viewscreen had a lifelike quality that got me nervous all over again. With a hesitant grip, I accelerated. To my surprise, the starfighter darted forward with speed unlike anything I could have anticipated. The screen beeped twice—highlighting a chunk of asteroid in red—and then I collided with it.

My chair shook.

The screen went black. The lights powered down.

Then nothing.

"Sawyer?"

"You died," Sawyer replied with a sigh. "Try again."

"Wait, what? I *died?* How?"

"A fragment of asteroid pierced your hull, destroyed the integrity of your starfighter, and ignited one of the bolts in your ammunition stores. Don't worry, you died instantly. No pain."

Her snarky disregard for the severity of failure got my blood running hot.

"It's that easy to die in one of these things?" I gripped the chair, my fingers practically piercing the mesh fabric. "You didn't mention that!"

"I said, you should pay attention to the screen. Avoid the obstacles. Shoot the targets. Simple instructions, really."

"One fucking obstacle, and I'm dead? That's a thin goddamn margin of error!"

"That's why you're in a practice simulation," Sawyer drawled.

The lights and screens flickered back to life, and the asteroid field once again lay in front of me. Ice replaced all anger in my system. I had lived on Capital Station my entire life, never once taking a jaunt through space. It was hazardous. Every tiny mistake could lead to catastrophe.

The cold void of space wanted to rip the life out of everything it touched. Eyes boiled in their sockets from the heat, skin cracked open from the chill, and lungs swelled like a marshmallow in a microwave—I had seen the damn educational videos. Space wanted us dead. It wanted *everything* dead.

I stared into the distance. I could see the fleck of asteroid that had resulted in my failure—it was the size of a human head, maybe smaller.

"Your heartrate has accelerated," Sawyer said. "And you're not even moving."

And there I was, berating Noah for getting rattled. I should have stoned up and taken my own advice. I needed to focus. It was a simulation. Nothing would happen. The better I became, the less likely I would fall to a tiny mistake when it counted.

Noah's starfighter, shaped like a U and black to the point of fading into the darkness, flew into my field of view. The monitors of my starfighter had him tracked and mapped—even when he wasn't in front of me—but I ignored those in favor of watching him spin and head in my direction.

Could we fight each other in this simulation? Surely we could. Was that what he wanted to do? Get his revenge for my earlier feint?

"How is he flying around like that already?" I muttered.

"He's been training for a week or so," Sawyer said. "He already got his obligatory *deaths on the starter rock* out of the way."

I braced myself as he got close, ready to receive another death.

"Move," Sawyer commanded.

But I didn't. Part me of didn't want to run and give Noah the satisfaction.

Noah fired.

His torpedo streaked across space, almost too fast to track, but I had the reflexes. It smashed into the starter rock, destroying the obstacle and clearing my path. And then he spun and flew off, heading toward the targets on the other end of the asteroid field.

The gesture sunk into my thoughts like scrap metal in water.

"You really have no excuse to sit idle now," Sawyer said.

"Do these pods have comms to each other?" I asked, ignoring her derision.

"Yeah. We use them for team simulations."

I reached up and switched my comms signal to "team," but I said nothing as I placed my hands back on the side-sticks and accelerated. The starter rock wouldn't have given me the same trouble twice, but knowing it was gone did make me feel better. Like I had been avenged. Thinking about its dust particles gave me more satisfaction than it should have. It was a rock. It was not even a *real* rock, just a virtual one, but that was what it got for fucking with me.

The starfighter reacted with a near-instant response when I turned the side-stick. As the ship spun, I took in all the information, like I would in a fight. I could see the obstacles, I could anticipate my speed, and everything operated at a fourth its rate in my mind's eye, allowing me to calculate my path with time to spare. I wove through the rocks without a scratch.

"I did it," I said.

"Yeah," Sawyer said. "Pretty good. For your second try."

"Did you see the grace of my movements? I think congratulations are in order."

"Congratulations. You've learned to avoid obstacles at the speed of a sleepy snail. Truly, you are the best starfighter."

Noah chuckled.

I forced a long exhale. She wanted me to go faster? Fine. I was ready to impress. I had come to terms with the simulation.

I punched the speed, curious to see how fast this piece-of-shit could go.

Within seconds, the inside of the pod tripled in pressure. It created artificial G-forces, and the effect left me short on breath. The crushing force hadn't yet become painful, but it wasn't pleasant, either. I was pressed against my seat, like some invisible hand was out to crush me.

"You're at 3Gs," Sawyer said. "You need to be on the lookout for loss of light in your vision. The hypoxia can cause you to lose consciousness. Oh, and remember to breathe deep."

I continued accelerating. When an obstacle appeared on the screen, I tilted and avoided it by millimeters, but it was intentional. Why move a lot when a little would do?

"4Gs," Sawyer said. "5Gs. Hey. Breathe. You need to breathe."

I took in deep breaths, still dedicated to my forward momentum. The asteroids were spaced far enough apart that zipping through them was possible, but more and more, I needed to tilt the starfighter. It became a game. Go faster. Don't get hit. That realization relaxed me a bit.

Sawyer let out a quick exhale. "6Gs is the highest the pod can simulate."

When a larger asteroid blocked my path, I tilted the side-stick harder than expected. The jerk of the starfighter put even more stress on me, but I soldiered through. Unlike most humans, my body was designed to withstand high pressures. My muscles were corded, my blood highly oxygenated, and my mind processed a multitude of information with ease. Before I knew it, I'd gotten around the largest asteroid, still accelerating as fast as the simulation would allow.

"You've passed the targets," Sawyer said with a chuckle. "You realize that, right?"

"Yeah, yeah," I choked out. It was harder to speak than I'd imagined it would be.

And difficult to breathe.

But I ignored that and turned the starfighter around, trying to push the limits of the craft, as well as my own. The obstacles were hard to anticipate when turning—harder than flying straight—but my focus didn't break. I returned to the target area and saw Noah's fighter on my screen readout. And then I saw his fighter blink out of existence.

He had crashed.

I pulled back the speed and returned to a crawl. Once the G-force waned, and my lungs weren't being squeezed by death itself, I watched Noah's blip on my star map as he rushed back over to the targets. The asteroids around that area moved faster than the rest.

When Noah attempted to fly through the rocks a second time, he fired at the targets, hitting one but falling victim to another stray asteroid. He crashed, and his starfighter got returned to the starting position.

"Damn," Noah muttered, his voice faint over the comms.

With a forced exhale, I sped toward the targets. Noah reached them almost at the same time, but I flew around him. A twist of my left wrist brought up the torpedo options, and I targeted one of the asteroids. When I fired, it destroyed the rock, leaving the targeted area a little clearer than it had been before.

Noah aimed for the targets, but I didn't even bother. I fired at a few more asteroids, a feeling of power washing over me when I saw the massive chunks of rock fall to the might of my starfighter.

"What're you doing?" Noah asked, indignant.

"Clearing the area," I said.

"This is a competition. You should be focused on the targets."

"Fuck the competition. Nobody cares about that. It's a ruse, some bunk task given to manipulate us."

Noah scoffed. "Is that true, Sawyer?"

She said nothing. At least, nothing I could hear.

"Listen to me, kid," I said. "There's a time and a place for fretting. The middle of a fight isn't one of them. That's your problem. You let things get to you, and then you overthink them."

"How would you know?"

"I've seen a lot of guys get killed because they couldn't focus on the task at hand."

Noah's starfighter slowed down near the targets. "B-But there are so many things to keep track of, and—"

"Forget all that. Focus on getting good at *one skill,* and then move on to the next. When you're good at something, it builds confidence, trust me. And confidence buys you more skills in the future."

He didn't reply, and his silence grated on me.

"I'll destroy the obstacles," I said. "You focus on the targets. Get good at shooting, got it? Shooting."

In reality, we would *both* get good at shooting—I was just shooting different objects. Sure, mine were larger, but he had been doing this for a few weeks, apparently. It all worked out in the end.

Although he hadn't given me an answer, I hit the throttle and sped through the asteroid belt, my attention homing in on the rocks. I loved destroying them. It had now become a tiny obsession. No rock was going to kill me. Ever.

Noah flew toward the targets—gold circles that glinted with inner light—and shot them one by one, while I cleared out the obstacles.

"You ruined my testing," Sawyer said, her voice low.

She wasn't speaking through the group comms, but through an individual channel.

Sawyer continued, "His stress levels are already evening out."

That was good. For him, at least. I knew some guys who exceled under stress, but Noah wasn't one of them. Even as I destroyed asteroids, I could see him increasing his speed and hitting more targets faster than before. Neither of us crashed again, and by the time the last target was destroyed, I realized I was enjoying myself.

The pod powered down, and the pressure returned to normal. I exhaled as the hatch opened. When I stood, I caught my breath, surprised to see Endellion in the room, her arms folded, her piercing gaze locked on me. I got out and stood in place, waiting for her assessment. Her mere presence made everything tense.

"How're you feeling?" Sawyer asked. Unlike before, she wasn't on her PAD—she just stared, her brow furrowed.

"I'm fine," I replied. "Why wouldn't I be?"

"Most individuals vomit after experiencing G-forces for the first time. That or controlling a starfighter in a 360 environment leaves them with vertigo."

Noah stumbled out of his pod and gave Endellion a quick salute. "Commodore Voight. I didn't know you would be here."

Endellion offered him a quick smile, forced but not unpleasant. "Sawyer says you've improved. I'm glad to hear it. But you should give us a moment. I need to speak to Clevon about his evaluation."

"Yes, of course."

Noah gave me a glance before leaving, like he wanted to say something but didn't have the time to do so.

Once he exited the training room, Endellion dropped her arms and gave me the once-over. "Your evaluation says everything I thought it would."

"Oh?" I asked. "And what's that?"

"You're capable of handling a starfighter with ease."

"I handle *everything* with ease."

Sawyer cocked an eyebrow as she gave me a half-lidded, sardonic stare. Was she going to ride my ass for dying in the beginning? That was nothing. I'd gotten over it. I could handle myself.

"Sawyer has constructed your daily schedule for the next six months," Endellion said, drawing my attention back to her. "But I'm adding physical training to your schedule as well."

"Physical training? I'm stronger than any schlub on this starship."

"You're not stronger than me."

Her casual statement got under my skin. I had never handled taunts well—they got me ready to prove them wrong. But she *could* have been stronger than me. It was a real possibility.

"That's because you cheated," I said with a smirk. "Ditch your fancy machines and let's see how well you do, then."

Endellion flipped her beautiful, braided hair to the side. "I'm sorry, are we aiming for mediocrity, or are we aiming for greatness?"

"What does that—"

"I *could* stoop to your level," she said, cutting me off, "and we could wallow in your subpar test of strength, or you can join me in the top tier of humanity, where real power is measured."

Why did she enjoy challenging me? She was always ready with

some retort, pulling my strings and getting me to react the way she desired.

"You want me to get stronger," I said, realizing it was her goal.

"Of course," Endellion replied. "My enemies won't throw away their advantages because I childishly whine about the unfairness of it all. I'm not prone to excuses. I'm prone to succeeding. And success requires hard work. I expect that from you, Clevon. I expect you to meet me at my level."

It hit me then. I wanted to impress her, but that was no easy feat. She wasn't impressed that I was better than the others. That was what she already knew. And she wasn't impressed that I was climbing toward her. That was what she wanted. She was patiently waiting for me to catch up, no doubt because she wanted something from me. I may have even been disappointing her because I wasn't climbing fast enough.

"All this so you can have a starfighter pilot?" I asked. Was that really what Endellion wanted from me?

"You could be something more, if you have the ambition."

The way she said that rang in my ears, embedding itself in my thoughts. I took a step closer, her height on par with mine. When she smiled at me, it was more genuine than the smile she'd given Noah, but it was reserved as well. Her gaze measured me, like she judged my every move.

"Is it true?" I asked in a hushed tone. "You're going to give everyone on this starship planetside property when you become governor?"

"That's right."

"It's an outrageous reward for being a simple enforcer."

"Some would consider my goals outrageous." Endellion tilted her head. "Are you going to help me? And then claim your reward?"

There was no turning back, if that was my goal. No running away. No leaving. If I was going to take her offer—not just an offer to work for her, but an offer to claim my prize at the end of a long haul—I was in it for life. I would have to give her everything.

"I'm going to be the best starfighter here." I couldn't help myself. I knew it in my core. I would master piloting, or I would die on the first rock out. "And then I'm going to move up the ranks. All the way until I reach yours."

My statement got her smiling wider. She stepped closer to me until we were centimeters apart, her breath practically on my chin.

"I look forward to it," Endellion said. And then she turned away, leaving me with her sweet scent. "Sawyer will be updating me on your progress."

EIGHT

167 Days

It would take 167 days until we reached our destination—Vectin-14.

I thrust both arms forward, straining the weight machine until I touched both palms in front of me. Then I relaxed at a slow pace, allowing the cords to pull my arms open.

One more time.

After a deep breath, I did it again. The machine beeped and the screen displayed a readout of my physiology, highlighting the muscles I'd used, listing the calories I'd burned, and flashing a warning across the top—indicating I should stop.

One more time.

Quinn stopped her workout routine to watch. Lee, Noah, and Mara had already stopped a few minutes ago, all three of them glancing between me and the screen, some even counting my reps.

Shooting practice dominated the physical training room, with squad tactics, obstacle courses, and reflex machines coming in a close second. Only a small corner had been set aside for improving strength. It wasn't as important when each enforcer carried less than 20 kilograms of equipment—including their plasma rifle—but I wanted to be on par with a cyborg, and cyborgs always had high strength capabilities.

One more time.

Lee whistled. "220 kilograms. Crazy."

"I've never seen anyone get past 110," Mara said, both eyebrows up, a smile on her face. She sat on the edge of a cardio machine, one hand on her chin as she watched me with undivided attention. "And it's not like they did that consistently. It was for hilarious dares. When everyone got to drinking."

"I thought the machines wouldn't allow you to lift weights if there was alcohol in our system?"

"They don't. The drunk guys would challenge the sober guys. We had a lot of fun."

The screen on my machine said permanent damage might occur if I continued, but the machine didn't understand my advanced nature. It treated me like a normal human—one who couldn't handle my physical routine—and it made inappropriate suggestions.

Which was why I ignored it.

"I need more weight," I said as I stopped pulling and let go of the cords. The machine dropped the tension, and the warnings stopped.

I poked at the screen a little more ham-handed than I'd wanted, but that was what happened after a few hours of training. The machine buzzed and beeped. When I tried to set the weight higher than 220 kilograms, it asked for an authorization passcode.

"More weight?" Noah asked, eyes wide. "Seriously? Aren't you worn out after that?"

"I can handle more."

Nothing would stop me from getting better. Maybe I could slack off with the gangsters and chumps on Capital Station, but not on the *Star Marque*.

Fuck it. If I couldn't increase the weight, I would just go longer. Maybe faster, if the damn machine would cooperate.

Quinn let her braids fall loose to her shoulders as she threw back a water pouch. Once finished, she tossed me one, too. I took a long swig as she examined me.

"Don't hurt yourself," she said. "I'm your direct superior. It'll make me look bad."

"My superior, huh? Who all is in our unit?"

"It's me, you, Lee, Noah, Mara, Yuan, and Advik."

"And Endellion," I said. "She's a starfighter, too, right?"

Quinn shook her head. "She's not in our unit." She stood, sweat dappling her skin, highlighting her raw, athletic appearance. "We're heading out, Demarco. Stay safe."

She motioned with a tilt of her head, and Lee sprang to her side, all smiles. Mara followed suit, just as enthusiastic. Noah lingered, watching as I grabbed the weight cords for a second run. I gave him a sidelong glance, wondering what he wanted.

He focused his gaze on the floor. "Um…"

So, he wanted to talk to me. But he floundered like a chem-addict reaching for another hit.

"Out with it," I said. "I've got stuff to do."

After a silent moment, he said, "I want to keep a training schedule like you do."

I pulled the cords forward, enjoying the burn in my arms. "I don't know if you can handle it, kid."

He stood. "I'm a lot more confident now." He held his head high and squared his shoulders. "There's nothing I can't handle."

I had seen better acting in pornos.

But still, he had grit, which was admirable. Training could only help him—unless he overdid himself, but the weight and cardio machines had a way of nagging people into quitting if they reached their limits. Or they'd passive-aggressively shut off.

I relaxed, but I kept tension in the cords as they pulled my arms back.

"Fine," I said. "But I'm training twice as hard as the others."

"I know. I've seen."

"And confident men don't go around saying they're confident. They just are. Got it?"

Noah hung his head and nodded. He was tall—nearly my

height, which was already taller than most—but Noah's slumped posture didn't do him any favors.

"Pride isn't always a bad thing," I said as I went through another pull on the machine. I took in even breaths and continued, "It's your own source of approval. You don't need everyone else's recognition if you can learn to recognize yourself."

"Is that the kind of stuff you learn in the dark corridors of Capital Station?"

Nope. I was making this shit up as I went. It sounded good—maybe a little too schmaltzy, but it got the point across.

"Shut up and do your training," I said, unable to admit I was faking my way through the conversation.

Noah jumped to a machine and clicked through the settings, preparing his station for a workload he could handle. I liked that he didn't give me a hard time about everything I did. We would get along just fine.

WE STILL HAD 142 days until we reached our destination.

The thought got me antsy as I flew my simulation starfighter around one of the larger asteroids—50 kilometers in diameter. I shook my head and returned my focus to the squad maneuver. It was a three-way pincer attack, starfighters coming in from different directions, meant to disorient a single enemy pilot. The plan involved flitting about and diving at the target at the same moment.

"Starboard Leader, are you ready?" Quinn asked over the comms.

"Ready," I replied.

"Port Leader?"

"Always ready," Yuan said.

I switched off my comms, punched the speed, and whipped around the asteroid, my attention glued to my screen. I blinked half as often when I was in the damn starfighters. My nerves got to me, and I couldn't stand the idea of dying because my eyes needed a little more moisture.

The point of practice was to sync up our movements. The target didn't even defend or react—it just sat there, like a boob on a corpse.

The other technical information, like my location in relation to the other fighters or the three-dimensional intercepts, displayed along the side of my screen, helping me calculate maneuvers and distances, but I ignored them in favor of my instincts. All I needed was a few numbers, and I grasped the distances with an intuitive understanding, even within split-second reaction windows.

Almost like I was built for this type of piloting.

My screen beeped, letting me know I had hit 6Gs.

It had taken me some time to read up on it, but apparently, starfighters and starships were powered by plasma engines. Gas was kept in a magnetic containment field, and then ionized, similar to the gas in stars. The resulting intense heat powered everything. Starfighters used it for a burst of speed—which resulted in the G-force pressure—while the starships used a form of constant acculturation that allowed the passengers to acclimate to the force, resulting in a high top-end speed but slower acceleration.

Which was fancy talk for, "little ships reached speeds instantaneously, while big ships took their time."

And G-forces were just a measurement of the acceleration converted to pressure in comparison to Earth's gravity—1G was the equivalent pressure of gravity planetside on Earth, and 2Gs was double that. So on and so on. At least, that was what Sawyer said.

I reached our target first and fired. Yuan and Quinn reached it a second later, but the target had already been destroyed.

"I'm just too good," I said to myself. "You guys better keep up."

A hushed chuckle came through the speakers. I glanced around, confused, and I checked my settings. No one should have been able to hear me.

"Sawyer?" I asked in a quiet tone.

Nothing.

"I know it's you."

"Do you always compliment yourself?" she asked, not even

bothering to admit she was spying on me like an ex-lover-turned-stalker.

"Someone's got to do it," I said, cracking a smile. "Skills like mine *deserve* compliments."

"And what about your fuck-ups?"

"Those can be forgotten. No one talks about great figures in history to discuss the couple times the person died in a training simulation. Everyone talks about all their epic achievements."

"You're a little ahead of yourself. If I ever wanted to commit suicide, I could climb to the top of your ego and jump down to your number of epic achievements."

"Always busting my balls, Sawyer," I muttered as I flew my starfighter back into formation with the others.

The formation drills—while important—had all the excitement of a rotting carcass. I'd understood them the first time through, and now I completed them with muscle memory, my mind focused on a million other details. Even Noah had the formations ingrained into his reflexes. I wasn't going to complain. The low mental impact gave me time to mess with Sawyer.

"You ever talk dirty to any of the pilots over your private little communication channel?" I asked.

"No," Sawyer said. "I've never talked dirty to anyone while they're piloting a starfighter."

"That's a waste. You've got a nice voice. And it's right in my ear."

"Remember that thin margin of error you have while piloting? Do you really want to be distracted while you're maneuvering through a debris field?"

"This is a simulation," I said. "I can handle it."

And I had been. The formations were smooth, and I was capable of multitasking.

"Endellion would be upset if I disrupted your training, even a slight amount," Sawyer said.

"Okay, how about this? If I'm ever about to die, you whisper sweet nothings into my ear so my last few moments are pleasant."

"Deal."

"Yeah?" I asked, trying to hide the shock in my voice. "I was half-joking. I thought you'd never agree."

"Well, you're just *so good*," she said, thick with sarcasm, "that it'll never happen, right? You're *the best starfighter around*. Guys like you don't get close to death."

Touché.

"Demarco," Quinn said, disrupting my thoughts. "Are you ready for another squad maneuver?"

I switched my comms back to the group. "Yeah. Let's get this done."

"And try to keep in sync with Yuan. It's not a race to the target. It's a coordinated attack."

"Yes, ma'am."

Yuan connected to me in a private comms channel. I switched to hers and said, "What is it?"

"I was going slow because you're new."

"Don't bother."

She laughed. "I got that. But don't go thinking you need to slow down for me. Quinn wants us to be in sync, but I've been flying for years. If you want to go fast, I can go fast."

I had barely interacted with Yuan, but already I liked her.

"Good," I said. "I'm ready for round two."

ONLY 101 DAYS left until we reached our destination.

I entered the physical training area in the middle of our artificial night. Every deck had its own sleep schedule, so there was always someone up and ready to cover the duties of the 24/7 starship in flight, but Deck Three—my deck—was the only deck with a physical training room. Even now it was in use by enforcers from other decks getting their practice in.

Vanguard-class starships had little in terms of entertainment. The gray metal walls, grate flooring, and dim lighting made the rig a jail-like environment. The best areas were the mess hall and the recreational lounge because at least there people drank and played games, but routine killed all excitement.

Without a word to the others, I walked over to the weight machine and poked the screen. Damn thing still wouldn't let me go above 220 kilograms. I needed to find someone who could give me authorization.

"Here you are, Demarco."

I glanced over my shoulder and spotted Lysander.

"Hey," I said. "You're a subcommander, right? Can you override this weight machine to allow for a heavy pull? I've got goals to meet."

Lysander frowned. "I'm not going to do that."

"Of course you won't."

I turned away and set the machine to the maximum. He got up close to me, and I suspected he wanted to have a conversation, but he didn't want to be polite about it. I figured he wanted me to treat him like a military commander—maybe even salute him or some other pretentious shit—but he would have to wait a while before that happened.

His hovering grated on my nerves.

"You waiting for Noah?" I asked.

"Noah won't be joining you anymore."

"Because you told him no?"

"That's right."

I stopped with the machine and glared at the man. "You think I'm that bad an influence?"

"I've worked as an enforcer for years. I know lowlifes when I see them."

His statement didn't deserve a reply. I focused on my machine, hoping to jury-rig a solution. Maybe I could trick it into allowing more weight.

Lysander took a deep breath, and then exhaled. "I'm not worried about you influencing Noah's character, but he has already been to the infirmary twice to deal with injuries from your training. Noah doesn't need that."

What?

I had never seen the kid do anything super-strenuous. We went for a long time, sure, but never anything he couldn't handle. How had he hurt himself?

"He never complained to me," I said.

"That's because he doesn't want anyone to know."

I narrowed my gaze. That didn't sound right. I figured Noah would have told me he was injured if it came from the machine or working too long.

"What's wrong with him?" I asked. "You treat your brother like a child. Something else is going on here."

"I do *not* treat Noah like a child," Lysander said, strained.

"One grown-ass man doesn't tell another they can't do weightlifting. That's what a parent tells their kid. You're treating him like a child. Why?"

Lysander glanced over his shoulder and looked around. Not many people walked our way, but he got closer to me nonetheless and said, "Noah has a genetic defect."

"He doesn't look like the sick pukes I met on Capital Station."

"We have medicine for him."

I scratched my chin as I mulled over the new information. "So why can't he handle the physical training?"

"Membranes in his body degrade when put through stress. It causes... problems."

"Is he suffering?" I asked.

Lysander shook his head. "Noah won't talk about it, but he's been taking more painkillers than ever."

His gaze fell to the floor, and for a moment the man wasn't a complete overload of insufferable.

People with genetic defects had it bad. On Capital Station it was a crime to reproduce, and Midway Station had a forced-sterilization program. Every defect carried teratogens—agents that caused deformities in their children. The resulting freaks were the lowest of the low, often restricted from everything, including joining the Federation military or holding well-paying jobs. Some defects didn't have it bad in terms of physical deformities, but some were so misshapen, they might as well have been a lump of solidifying jelly.

I knew a guy with a tumor on his back so large a person could fit inside. He smuggled chems in an open sore because no one with a functioning stomach would touch it.

"Listen," I said, ending my own mental tangents. "Just let Noah train. Obviously, he thinks he can handle it."

Lysander glowered, his jaw clenched. "Easy for you to say. You don't give a damn about anyone. This training could have permanent repercussions for Noah."

"Can't he get into the healing vat and be done with it?"

"The mother cells aren't compatible with genetically-defective cells," Lysander said, heated. "When the mother cells try to replicate, they form malignant tumors instead of fresh tissue. Defects die in the healing vats."

I hadn't known that. But it didn't change my mind.

"If you keep telling Noah he's fragile, that's all he's ever going to be," I said.

"A guy like you wouldn't understand. You've never had to survive with an illness."

Realization struck me. Noah and Lysander were brothers.

Lysander was a defect, too.

He was also an asshole, so I guess it all balanced out, but I was still surprised.

However, his statement didn't ring true. I had lived a weird life. Lysander didn't know me, and he was jaded from his own experiences. I wanted to argue with the man—to tell him he was wrong— but there was no point. He'd convinced himself he was weak. I wasn't going to blow smoke up his ass, or throw him a pity party, or treat him like a pet that needed protecting.

He was a man, like any other man. Everyone had their own problems, and everyone dealt with them in their own way. If he allowed his disadvantages to shape his interactions and decisions, then he had chosen to be ruled by his weaknesses.

"You've heard my opinion," I said. "You and Noah do whatever you want."

"Don't try to convince Noah to go against my orders."

"I don't give a damn about anyone, remember?" I said. "I'm not going to talk to your brother. Now get out of my face. I have training to do."

I WAS on the verge of going stir-crazy.

We still had 86 days left until we reached our destination.

Capital Station was a hundred—maybe a thousand—times larger than the *Star Marque*. Being trapped on the starship had gotten me riled, like a caged child with a sugar tap straight to the arm. Drinking had become my only solace. I tried flirting, I really had—a fuckbuddy would have been nice—but I figured Sawyer lied when she said not everyone had paired off.

Lee and Quinn clung to each other with a honeymoon passion. Mara and Yuan remained a couple. Lysander and Noah had effectively become ghosts the moment Noah had stopped training with me. And I had interacted with Advik a grand total of two times outside of training and knew next to nothing about her, besides her skill as a pilot. Whenever I did try to find her, she disappeared. I swore she avoided me on purpose.

Maybe I should have taken a week off and mingled with other groups. *Someone* on our rig had to be as hard-up as I was. Anyone would do. I wasn't picky.

And there should've been another genetically-modified human somewhere on the *Star Marque*. I wanted to meet them, and if I was lucky, we would strike it up.

I rolled over in my capsule and turned on the screen built into the wall. The movies came in all flavors, including "entertainment for the single and lonely," which wasn't a label I ever wanted to give myself, but life had an unfortunate sense of humor. Luckily, the capsules had thick, steel-alloy doors and sound-dampening walls. I could watch whatever I wanted, and I wasn't going to disturb my neighbors.

After scrolling through a list of lackluster options, I went with *Bar Whores: Return of One-Eye*. Hadn't seen that one before.

I stretched out on my back and tossed off my sheets, ready to get the party started, but I stopped when my thoughts considered odd possibilities. I muted the screen and listened.

"Sawyer?" I whispered, wondering if she could hear me, even there.

For a second, all was quiet. But then I heard her soft chuckle.

"Yes?" she said over the capsule's comms.

I gritted my teeth, half-amused she'd answered and half-stunned that I'd never thought of it before.

"You've been listening in?" I asked, painfully aware of my nudity and prepared activity. "Can you see me, too?"

"The starship has comms and monitoring devices for every millimeter of its insides."

"How long?"

Her lack of response told me everything I needed to know.

I smiled. "You've been watching me since I boarded the *Star Marque*."

"Just about."

Exhaling, I relaxed back and stared up at the ceiling of my capsule. I wouldn't have taken that kind of behavior from someone I disliked, but Sawyer was a different story. Her creepy omnipresence fueled my imagination, and she was a good flirt when she wanted to be. I liked Sawyer.

"You don't need to watch," I said. "You could come join me."

"I'm busy," Sawyer said with a yawn.

I laughed. "Fuck you."

"It's the truth."

"You were about to watch me get it on with my hand. You're not busy."

She sighed. "Trust me, because I know, you yanking your wank isn't *that* entertaining. I just like to keep an eye on you while I code."

"If I had known you're a voyeur, I would've upped the show-manship."

Sawyer's laugh got me smiling wider.

"You've got no shame," she said.

"And you're awfully talkative for someone who's busy. I say you should take a break."

"I don't think you understand the complexities of a starship's operating system, Demarco. The main code keeps all systems working in tandem, and it allows for the ship to communicate with other ships and docking ports within the Vectin Quadrant. The latest mandated update really messed with some of the *Star Marque*'s core security and self-control systems, and—"

"Hey, hey," I said, holding up a hand, even though I was talking to the ceiling. "I get it. You're busy writing computer code for the ship we live in, and it's important. No need for the details."

"Endellion expects me to finish before we arrive at our destination. It's not a reasonable request, but it's one I intend to fulfill."

The insistence in her voice betrayed her loyalty to Endellion. It was important to Sawyer, either because she was afraid of failing or because she wanted recognition, I couldn't tell. And I was impressed she'd dedicated so much of herself to the project. Although I basically never saw her, anytime I did catch a glance, she was working.

Then it hit me—I hadn't seen Endellion in months.

"What is Endellion doing?" I asked.

"She's adjusting one of her cybernetic enhancements to work with our starfighter interface."

"So, she can be a better pilot?" I asked.

"That's right."

"Cyborg parts can do that?"

"They can do a great many things, so long as you have the right equipment."

The knowledge seeped into my thoughts, coloring old memories with confusion. I'd thought cybernetic enhancements only improved a person's strength and agility. Maybe mental speed as well, but creating an interface to deal with computers or ships wasn't something I'd thought possible. Endellion's improvements helped her in every way, not just physical.

"So, you're tweaking the ship's code, and Endellion is improving her skills as a pilot?" I asked.

And I was sitting around in my capsule, stewing in blue balls.

"Is something wrong?" Sawyer asked.

I sat up, grabbed my jumpsuit from the built-in drawer under the screen, and shoved both legs into the pants. If they were going to work every second of every day, then I supposed I knew what I needed to do to keep up.

Once I was somewhat decent, I kicked open the capsule's door and hopped into the walkway.

"Go back to work, Sawyer," I said. "I've got training to do."

ALMOST THERE–75 days left until we reached our destination.

That fact energized me as I aimed my laser pistol in the holographic targeting stall. Everyone else had finished their drills an hour ago, but I'd stayed to work on my spotting.

I had 100% accuracy in most situations, but when the computer included targets I *shouldn't* shoot—like innocents, or teammates not in uniform—I found I was a little trigger-happy. To curb my enthusiasm to kill, I had taken it upon myself to practice selective shooting.

While I plugged away at my targets, someone entered the room and programmed the stall next to mine. Once the simulation ended, and the holograms faded, I realized the newcomer was Noah. He'd set up his stall to join me for a run before stepping into it.

There was a brief moment when we were both standing and waiting for the next simulation to begin. He shouldn't have been here. That wasn't what Lysander wanted. But I didn't say anything.

Right before the simulation started, Noah tapped both our screens and paused the simulation.

"I'm going to continue with the extra training," he said, staring a hole in the floor.

Again, I opted for silence.

"I told Lysander I could handle it," he continued. "And I can. So, I will."

"I take it your brother isn't happy about this," I said.

Noah shook his head.

The kid didn't look great. Not like he was sick, but like he was hurting. I wasn't that great when it came to dealing with other people's emotional bullshit, and I tended to cut relationships off before anything substantial could develop. Despite that, I could tell this feud of theirs was taking a toll on both of them.

I sighed, removed his hand from my stall's screen, and gave him a sidelong glance. "Just tell him I pressured you back into training."

Noah cocked an eyebrow.

"Trust me," I said.

Lysander could be angry with me all he wanted—I didn't give a shit.

"I really can handle the training," Noah said.

"Sure, kid. I believe you."

Noah replied with a curt nod.

I got a little nervous because ambition could wreck a man before he was ready to face a challenge, but I figured Noah would be prepared. He already stood taller than he had before, and he had me backing him, after all.

I just hoped I wasn't misjudging him.

---

61 DAYS—TWO MONTHS—AND we would finally arrive.

When I was training or relaxing, the time didn't get to me, but when I tracked the days, it grated on my patience. I knew the solution. Don't fucking stare at the clock. But my self-control failed me now and again, and I found myself calculating the trek down to the minute.

"Are you paying attention?" Quinn asked me.

I took a long swig from my rum pouch and smiled. "Yeah. We're playing a game. You're explaining the rules. Poorly."

"Would *you* rather explain the rules?"

"I've never played Pirate's Gambit before."

Noah, Mara, Yuan, Advik, and Lee crowded around the table, each with an old key drive in their hand. Those key drives used to be the rage a generation ago. Everyone locked their doors and computer terminals with the KeyMAX locking systems. The thumb-sized key drive acted as a physical plug-in. Once inserted, the computer and door functioned properly. Without the key drive, everything remained locked. Hackers and knock-off models made the system obsolete, which was why people used them as betting chips or game tokens now.

I glanced down at mine. One side had the word *trust* etched into the metal. On the other side, the word *betray* was inked in red.

"It's a simple game," Quinn said, holding up her key drive. "We're in pairs, and each person has to decide whether they're going to trust or betray the other."

Lee nodded along with the words. "I've played this a few times." He threw back the last of his pouch. "Great game."

Mara smiled wide. "I've never done it before. How do you get points? Why trust or betray someone?"

Quinn held up a hand. "Without speaking or communication, you need to decide whether to trust or betray your partner. If you both trust each other, you each lose a point."

I raised an eyebrow. Lose a point, huh?

Quinn continued, "If you both betray each other, you each lose two points. But if one person trusts, and another person betrays, the person who trusted loses *three* points, and the person who betrayed doesn't lose anything."

"So, the highest score is zero?" I asked.

Yuan gave me a quick nod. "Yeah, but no one ends the game at zero."

"Is that right?"

"We switch pairs every round," Quinn said, ignoring our side conversation. "Until everyone has paired with each other. Since we have seven players, someone will have to sit out this round."

Advik scooted to the edge of the bench. "I'll watch," she whispered.

No one protested. No one even looked like they were surprised. Advik stared down at her key drive, examining the device as though it were infinitely more interesting than the conversation. Maybe she had a mental defect.

"Everyone, partner up," Quinn said.

I turned to Lee, and he gave me a smile.

Quinn slammed her hand down on the table. "No talking. Choose trust or betray and keep your token under your hand until the reveal."

I stared at Lee, and he narrowed his eyes. We fidgeted with our key drive, one hand held up to cover our decision. Everyone at the table did the same until the movement died down. Then Quinn motioned with her hand.

Everyone revealed their choice.

Lee moved his hand away. He chose to trust.

Figures. I chose betray.

Lee threw his hands in the air. "Seriously? First move? Damn."

"That's zero points for me," I said. "A big negative three for you."

"Yeah, but now you've got a reputation. You'd better watch your back."

The others at the table gave sideways glowers. I didn't care. I knew how this worked. Everyone was out for themselves, they just didn't want to admit it. My time on Capital Station had taught me nothing less.

We switched partners. Mara sat across from me and giggled, her cute button-nose red from drinking. I stared into her eyes. She gave me a playful scowl.

"Reveal your choices," Quinn said.

Mara chose to trust.

I chose to betray.

"Aw," she said. "Really? I thought you liked me more than that." But she never dropped her smile, not even once, not even after losing three points.

Zero points for me, so what did it matter? Lee shook his head and motioned to my key drive with wild arm gestures. "Can't you see what's happening? Demarco doesn't get the long-term game, you guys."

"New partners, babe," Quinn said.

Again, we switched. Noah slid into position across from me. Unlike Lee and Mara, when we locked eyes, I could have sworn he had an entire conversation prepared. He knit his eyebrows together, but I kept my face still, betraying nothing. Noah let out a quick sigh before fidgeting with his key drive. When he looked at me again, he frowned.

Did he think he would get pity points from me? He had another think coming.

We flipped over our key drives.

He chose to betray. Ah. So, he felt guilty.

I chose to betray. That made us even.

"Damn," Noah said. "You really are going to betray everyone around the table, aren't you?"

Yuan snorted. "Not the best strategy, but at least you know what you're getting into."

"Wait, wait," Mara shouted. "We need new drinks! I'll go get some." She bounded away from the table, and Yuan watched her every step with a slight smile.

"I'm going to hit the latrine," I said as I stood. My enviro-suit could technically collect human waste, but I wasn't so sloppy drunk that I would opt for that. I walked out of the mess hall, but my mind returned to Sawyer.

I pulled my helmet over my head and activated the comms.

"You've been watching, I assume?" I asked.

"That's right," she replied.

"If we were playing a round, what would you pick?"

"Betray, of course."

"*Of course?* What's that supposed to mean? Is it because I've betrayed each time? Or you just want to betray me specifically?"

"No," Sawyer said, a hint of boredom to her. "Because it's rational to betray. Game theory really boils down to how you can make yourself the winner. The worst possible outcome is to trust while your opponent betrays. However, if you always betray, you safeguard yourself from the least-desirable outcome."

"Uh-huh," I say. "So, you're saying the numbers add up in my favor, right? I'm playing the game better than they are?"

"Sure. Whatever helps you sleep at night."

"C'mon. Tell me the statistics or something. I know I'm right."

"Very well. In a game with a defined number of turns, it's best to betray on the last turn, no matter what you did in all previous rounds—that's true for everybody. So, why wouldn't you betray the round before that, and the round before that? All it takes is for one person to trust to net you the best outcome, and even if they betray, you both get the same negative score, resulting in a stalemate."

I mulled over the information and half-laughed. In theory, trusting all around would result in everyone having a similarly low score, but what did that matter? You wouldn't win.

I finished pissing, zipped my enviro-suit back up, and exited the latrine. When I returned to the table, I found Mara had supplied us all with two extra pouches of liquor. I was down with that.

Mara and Yuan whispered to each other, Mara giggling nonstop. Yuan smiled. I didn't think she did it often, because her face contorted a little for the effort.

"Here's the asshole now," Lee said with a smile, motioning me back to my seat. "Everybody ready?"

I could see it on Quinn and Yuan's faces—they knew I was going to betray, and that was what they were going to do, too. We were in a deadlock, knowing each other's strategies. But the path was set, so-to-speak. No pulling out now.

I felt a slight bit of guilt for being hasty with my decisions. Neither Lee nor Noah had appreciated the gesture, and now I felt like they didn't even want to sit that close to me at the table anymore. No one on Capital Station would've taken this personally. No one on Capital Station would've trusted, though.

Maybe I should've thought about the long-term.

I wondered what Endellion would do if she played a few rounds.

NINE

Unexpected Arrival

5 6 days to go.

I sat in my training pod and waited for the simulation to begin. Quinn said she needed to speak to Endellion before we started, but that had been several minutes ago. Left to my own devices, I switched through the comms channels until I had the others together.

"Any of you hate the smell of these pods?" I asked.

I got a chorus of stifled laughs and muttered agreements.

"Beats the starfighters we had back on the *Orbit Cruiser*," Mara said with a giggle in her voice.

"Yeah it does," Yuan said, her voice as hard and unfeeling as steel when compared to Mara's.

I smiled. "They reek or something?"

"They were constructed from scavenged starfighter parts," Mara said. "The parts that survived after they were wrecked by enemy fighters."

"So, you rode in the stitched-together corpses of old starfighters?"

"Yup! Not only were all the pilots certain it was bad luck, they all had a bizarre odor to them. Like death itself was trying to remind us that someone already died in our seat. It's pretty hilarious, thinking back on it."

Hilarious, huh? Mara was an odd one.

"Yeah, the *Orbit Cruiser* was terrible," Lee said with a sigh. "I thought I was going to die every time I got deployed. And it wasn't even because of the enemy—I just figured my ship would give out at any moment."

"Right?" Advik said, her quiet voice barely registering over everyone else's comments.

"Did you all serve on the *Orbit Cruiser?*" I asked.

Lee coughed a few times before replying, "Most of us. Me, Mara, Yuan, and Advik, at least. We served with the *Orbit Cruiser* enforcers, until the captain got himself killed on Midway Station. He got into a bar fight."

"A madman brawl, more like," Yuan said.

"Yeah. The guy got drunk, killed several people, destroyed a small section of the station, and then got gunned down by the station enforcers."

"Sounds like a stable dude," I quipped.

Lee said, "The station overseer seized the *Orbit Cruiser* to pay for the damage. We all thought we'd be stuck without a job, but there Endellion was. She said she'd heard about our piloting skills, and how well we flew—even with junkers—and we all got a new lease on life when she took us on."

"I like it better here," Mara interjected. "Lots of interesting people, and we find more every time we stop at a station. Great times!"

"Enough of that," Quinn said, joining us in the comms. "I'm back, and it's time to get to training. Endellion has some specific maneuvers she wants us to practice."

"Roger," everyone replied in semi-unison.

THE CLOSER WE got to our destination, the slower time ticked by.

We had 33 days remaining. I imagined this was how a convict on

Ucova felt. Spending each day waiting for the next. Waiting for the punchline—freedom.

"I think you'll like this lounge," Noah said as we walked the second deck corridor together. "It's for the ground enforcer units. You'll have a good time with them. It's a shame we don't inter-mingle more often."

When I thought back to everyone I had met on this rig, I realized I had never interacted with any of Endellion's ground enforcers. Even the people who'd grabbed me on Capital Station were Quinn, Noah, Lysander, Yuan, Advik, and Endellion. All members of the starfighter unit or officers. And when I'd accompa-nied Lysander at the docks, Lee was our only companion. Another starfighter.

The sounds of training echoed down the corridor. Although Noah wanted to make a turn away from the racket, I headed for it, curious to see the other enforcers. Noah picked up on my deviation and jogged to my side. I stopped once I reached an open door.

Forty, maybe fifty enforcers in enviro-suits stood in groups oppo-site each other. They hefted weapons in unison, practicing their formations. The large doors—meant for accommodating cargo—gave me enough room to see everything. Lysander stood at the back, observing everyone and calling out commands.

"What're we doing?" Noah whispered.

"There are a lot more ground enforcers than starfighters," I said.

"Yeah. That's how it is with most enforcer teams. We need boots on the ground when we take station-security jobs or mining-regula-tion runs."

"Your brother trains them?"

Noah perked up at the comment. "Of course. He was an officer and instructor in the Federation Navy HSN Corps, Ground Divi-sion. He knows what he's doing."

"Oh? Why'd he leave?"

"He was discharged when they found out."

Found out? Ah. They hadn't known Lysander was a defect. Although, that was rather unusual. They never overlooked bullshit like that. The HSN Corps—Homo sapiens corps—took only fit human beings and encouraged them to consort with "their own kind" for better breeding. They were some of the most anti-defect people in the whole Vectin Quadrant.

"Everyone is tested before they're accepted into the Federation's military," I said. "How did Lysander even get in?"

"Our father has a few doctor friends. Lysander served for eight years without trouble, but out of nowhere, his secret was leaked to his CO, and he was dishonorably discharged."

"Hm."

"It's messed-up," Noah said, his gaze on the floor. "Lysander was one of their best. They said it all the time. And he liked it there. He would have served until he died, if they had let him."

Although I said nothing, I agreed with Noah. Lysander seemed like the type to take to that kind of environment. As I watched him, I could see he craved order and discipline. He barked at anyone out of position and shouted about the need to focus. A real hard-ass.

Endellion's ground forces must have been plotting to kill him. I knew I would have been.

But his methods seemed to work. The enforcers held their rifles with confidence. They stood in groups, each understanding their role. Some knelt, others stood behind them, and another had a bandoleer of grenades—no doubt the group's heavy-weapons expert. A good little fighting unit. I bet Lysander had taken those kinds of tactics straight from the HSN Corps.

The knowledge made me pensive.

Knowing Endellion's long history of manipulating the circumstances to her favor, I wondered why she'd only ever sent less-than-ideal enforcers to deal with me. Or maybe purposefully sent them.

If I assumed Lysander was exceptional, like Noah had implied, perhaps the ground enforcers would have shot me in the Capital Station lifts without a second's hesitation. Maybe a trained soldier—loyal to Lysander—never would have let me wander off on my own when we'd patrolled Dock Seven.

But there was no way Endellion thought of circumstances in such detail. No way she'd thought out every little thing to maximize the odds of success. That level of plotting wasn't common fare, and I refused to believe Endellion considered hundreds of hypothetical scenarios.

Still, Endellion had picked me and Lee to accompany Lysander to search the dock. What a bizarre order, if not for a specific reason.

Or maybe I was overthinking it, like a drug addict overthinks the shape of his hands.

"You okay?" Noah asked.

"Yeah," I muttered. "I just need to relieve some pent-up frustrations." That was what was wrong with me. I wouldn't be considering lunacy as an explanation if I'd had someone to unwind with.

I gave Noah the once-over and exhaled. "What do you do when you're not with me?"

"I'm in the infirmary," Noah said, cracking half a smile. "Making sure I'm not going to fall apart anytime soon."

Good. He'd made a joke about it. Thank the stars, because I hadn't mentioned anything on the off-chance he would devolve into a weepy mess of existential dread. His levity made the situation less painful.

"So, you're busy?" I asked, sarcastic.

"Yeah. 'Busy' is one way to put it. I'm heading there right after I introduce you to this lounge."

I walked away from the training room and motioned to the hall. "Then lead the way. I need a good distraction."

———

"ALL RIGHT, that does it for today," Quinn said as she stepped out of her pod.

We were down to the crunch. By my count, we had 18 days left before we reached our destination. That was 18 days until I stepped foot on something that was *not* Capital Station. A measly 18 days, and I would have explored more of the universe than I ever had in my 25 years of life. It was an odd fact I couldn't get out of my head.

I exited my training pod and stretched. Exhaustion swept through my veins, and I wasn't used to the feeling. Probably a positive thing—after a good night's rest, I could take on ten Vorgos in a death match and walk away unscathed. Well, I could have done that regardless, but now I felt like I could do it in style. Enforcer fighting techniques and weaponry went a long way.

Yuan ambled over to me. She had a fit look about her—much like Quinn—but there was a harder edge to her appearance. She had short, black hair and dark eyes, and she walked with a stiff leg, like her knee gave her trouble, but only after a long day of training.

"The starfighters are faster than the simulation," she said. "You know that, right?"

I nodded. "That's what Sawyer said."

"You ready for the real deal?"

"How often do we fight punks in starfighters, anyway?" I wasn't looking forward to the day I had to fly around the void of space, but I wanted to be prepared.

"Not often, but Endellion's been pushing for it. I think she has some things in mind."

"Is that right?"

Mara leapt from her pod and jogged over. She had a laugh and vivaciousness that couldn't be understated, even as she embraced Yuan for a motionless two seconds. Once she broke away, she took off with a smirk, probably heading to the mess hall for drinks. Everyone met there after training, almost without fail.

"She's a little cheery to be an enforcer," I said.

Yuan's gaze was locked on the door Mara had exited through. "I like her better this way," she murmured.

"You mean, she wasn't always a precious little helium molecule?"

"No. Quite the opposite, actually."

The opposite, huh? I couldn't even imagine. She had been hyper and unabashed in all ways since I'd gotten on that rig. Everyone else had a visible toll taken on them from the long ride. Everyone but Mara.

Yuan never took her gaze off the door. After a silent moment, she said, "I'll see you around."

She limped off without a glance back.

Noah stuck close to me as the others filtered toward the door. He regarded them with nods, and they acknowledged him in kind, but I had noticed a shift in their attitude, ever since Lysander had gotten upset. Perhaps they were worried, but they thought it wasn't their place to comment. Or perhaps not. I wasn't sure.

"Demarco!"

I turned my attention to the door, tense in every regard. People yelling my name wasn't a good sign.

"Sawyer wants to see you," Quinn said. She untangled her many long braids as she approached. I saw why Lee found her so attractive. "Well? Get a move on."

"Where is she?" I asked.

"On the first deck, with all the other officers."

"Sawyer is an officer?"

Noah chuckled, and I shot him a glare.

Quinn shook her head. "Sawyer is the Chief Cyber Operations Officer."

I hadn't known that. It explained why she was always on the comms. She might have even been listening to our conversation, laughing to herself about my ignorance. But then why hadn't she summoned me herself? She hadn't hesitated to talk to me in the past, and we were surrounded on all sides by cameras, microphones, and speakers. This whole rig was a technological marvel.

An odd thought struck me. "Why is everyone so casual? No one uses titles. I would've known she was an officer if someone had called her 'Chief Cyber Operations Officer.'"

"I use titles," Noah interjected.

I gave him yet another glare, and Noah took a step back.

"It's habit," Quinn said. "A lot of us started with Endellion right when she broke away from the *Black Riser*—her last enforcer group. She wasn't a captain, then. She doesn't demand the formality—unless we're in official meetings—so, other officers followed suit."

"Seems lackadaisical," I said. "Most military units always use titles."

"We're a lot smaller than most military units. We barely have two hundred people."

"Isn't she a commodore?"

I was surprised she wasn't commanding a vast fleet. A single ship hardly seemed befitting for someone with such a title, but maybe I wasn't as familiar with the chain of command as I thought I was.

"She's had a meteoric rise through the ranks," Quinn said with a shrug, almost like she didn't know the answer. "Endellion always says she likes having her mobility and personalized crew. But maybe the people handing out titles and the people handing out ships aren't the same group."

"Whatever the reason." I hit Noah on the shoulder. "I'll see you around."

If I were being honest, Sawyer was my second-favorite person on this rig. I was eager to see her, and I walked around Quinn, and then exited the training room into the poorly-lit corridor without wasting any time.

The *Star Marque* had become home over the last five months. I could have navigated the place blind. Plus, I didn't get many questioning glances anymore. I felt like a cog in the machine—a working part all the other cogs relied on. It made it easy to find a comfortable rhythm.

The *Star Marque*'s lift was smaller than anything on Capital Station, but it ran faster. I hit the button, the door closed, and a few seconds later I was at my destination. I stepped off onto Deck One and found the layout similar to the other levels, but the halls deserted.

The same metallic color palette and cold atmosphere permeated the deck. I walked forward, glancing at each heavy door and reading the plates for directions. Most of the personal rooms were open and empty. I suspected the *Star Marque* was supposed to have more in terms of an officer crew, but there appeared to be only four —Quinn, Lysander, Endellion, and Sawyer. No engineering officer? No weapons officer? Surprising. Almost all enforcer ships had those positions filled.

My attention focused on the closed door labeled *Officer Lounge*. I was certain I would find Lysander within, but I doubted Sawyer would be anywhere near this area. She didn't have a single lazy bone in her body, and socialization had gone the way of her baby teeth.

I stopped when I read a plate labeled *Central Communications and IT Logistics*. That was it. Sawyer would be there. I pressed the door controls, waited for it to slide open, and stepped inside.

I caught my breath as I glanced around, taking in the unusual sight.

Multiple screens of information lined the back wall. A cluttered counter wrapped around the room, covered in a sloppy assortment of microtools and computer bits, like it was a bloody crime scene of electronics. Old chunks of machinery—person-sized, with the inner workings exposed—filled the rest of the area. Power cables and gas tubes hung from the ceiling and connected to the machines at odd angles. With the only light emanating from the wall of screens, the place had a thriller vibe that got under my skin.

Sawyer sat on top of a mutilated machine, her eyes glued to the PAD around her left forearm.

Before I said anything, a fish—*a fucking koi fish*, of all things—floated through the air in front of me. I jumped back and hit the closed door, seconds away from grabbing the thing and killing it with my bare hands.

"The fuck is that freak-fish-thing?" I said, word-vomiting as I stared down the demon fish.

Sawyer chortled. "I'm going to get a lot of good sound bites from you, aren't I?"

"What's that supposed to mean?"

She tapped on her PAD, and the comms replayed me saying, *"The fuck is that freak-fish-thing?"*

"Answer the damn question."

"The fish is named Blub. He's my only family in the universe."

"Blub?"

The fish swirled around the air, its mouth opening and closing in rhythm, like a heartbeat. The black eyes of the creature matched the black spots of its scales, and both shimmered whenever they caught the light. Its face had a single red splotch that glittered no matter the lighting, creating its own dim bioluminescence.

Four bloated sacs jiggled on its back.

"How is it floating?" I asked.

"Blub produces helium," Sawyer said. "When the sacs get too full, he releases some of the gas, and then descends."

The fish let out a quiet *toot, toot, toot* and fluttered in the air until it was at head-level with Sawyer. She stroked the animal's head, and it wiggled—was it happy?—and then it circled Sawyer, like a moon in orbit.

"So, it farts helium," I said.

"Yes. *He* farts helium."

"Creepy."

"Creepy?" Sawyer looked up from her work and frowned. "Blub is adorable. Everyone loves Blub."

"How is Blub even alive? It's a freak. Every educational vid I've ever seen says fish should stay in the water."

"If Blub could talk he would tell you he's a genetically-modified fish. And he's a step above regular fish, just like you when compared to normal people. He doesn't need water to maintain his existence."

"Is that so?"

I eyed the creature a second time, suddenly enthralled with its presence. Genetically-modified? It must have been produced by the superhumans. But was it a pet? Did they craft fish to swim through the air, simply for their amusement? I wouldn't have been surprised if the answer was yes.

A strange thought hit me.

"Is this the other genetically-modified crewmember?" I asked as I pointed to Blub. "It was all a joke, wasn't it? No one else on this rig is anything like me. The damn fish is the only other thing here with modifications."

"You've been looking for others?" Sawyer asked.

"Yeah. I've never met another like me. And I've been searching this starship for six months. The least anyone could have done was let me in on the punchline. Best enforcer ever—a flying fish."

"I guess that explains why you've been poking your head into every corner of the ship."

Sawyer jumped off the machine and walked over to the counter.

The scattered electronics—though chaotic at first glance—seemed to be laid out in a particular order. Sawyer picked through them at a quick rate, grabbing what she needed without disturbing any of the microtools or spare parts.

"Why all the machines?" I asked. "I thought you wrote code."

"I also play the part of Head Engineer. I use the machines here as test subjects before giving orders to the low-level engineers."

"I see."

Sawyer motioned me over.

When I got near, she took my right arm and turned it over. I gritted my teeth when I spotted the needle implanter used for identification chips. The device had a thick syringe, and the tip opened once inside the body to manhandle the chip located between the radius and ulna.

That was why she had summoned me. To change out my identification chip.

"What were you going to do when you found this other genetically-modified person?" Sawyer asked.

"Proposition them for a good time, of course."

"Of course," Sawyer repeated with unmitigated sarcasm.

She jabbed the needle into my arm, but it didn't take all the way. She wrestled with it for a bit, and a rivulet of blood poured from the puncture wound. It stung, but I had felt worse. I held back all commentary as the syringe dove past my muscle.

"What's wrong with my plan?" I asked, attempting to distract myself from the strange, twisting sensations under my skin. "I've got plenty of stamina. I'm good-looking."

Sawyer pulled back on the needle and removed my stolen chip. The process of yanking it out hurt more than putting it in, and I had to fight with my own urges to stop myself from grabbing at the injury.

The chip was nothing more than a fleck of electronics. Sawyer readied a new one, plugged it into the injector, and coated it with a goo-like medicine before lining it up with my arm a second time.

"You have a one-track mind," she said.

"Hey. It's been close to six months. Wanting companionship isn't unusual." I glanced over at the fish as it circled the room. "I don't think Blub will make for a good time, however."

"Blub is great companionship. He never complains. He doesn't take up much space. He's soft."

"That's everything I've ever wanted," I quipped. "A companion whose description could fit a fold-out bed."

Sawyer stifled a chuckle. "Fold-out beds are convenient."

She shoved the needle back into my arm, and I gritted my teeth, straining my jaw. It burned the second time, no doubt from the chemicals in the goo that helped the chip integrate into the system, so the body wouldn't reject the foreign object.

"You ever watch those old educational vids they show to kids?" I asked, recalling my first few days in a classroom. "They talked about space travel, and time dilation, and spatial fluctuation, and all the many ways you'd die if your rig got fucked-up."

"I didn't see those," Sawyer said as she adjusted the needle.

"There was a vid on the importance of companionship. It warned about deep-space delirium and the irrational thoughts that come with listlessness. Or the paranoia and severe depression that often lead to suicide. Even one relationship can cut the possibility of those outcomes in half."

"Let me translate. Something, something, something—justification for getting laid. Did I miss anything?"

What a smartass. But she had a point.

"That's about the gist of it," I said.

Sawyer grabbed a vial marked *Liquid Skin* and dropped a dot of it over the needle wound on my arm. The drop congealed within seconds, stopping the blood flow. While I examined the new skin, Sawyer patted my arm down with a clean rag, removing the last traces of evidence that she'd ever fucked with my identification chip.

Blub sailed over, and after another *toot, toot, toot,* he descended onto the countertop in front of Sawyer, demanding her attention by blocking her view. She appeased the creature and stroked its scales with a feather-light touch of her fingertips.

The damn fish was the size of my forearm, and its fins moved about as though caught in an invisible current. The longer I stared at Blub, the more I was tempted to touch him, but I restrained myself. I still didn't like the thing. I had never interacted with animals. The foreignness of the situation bothered me more than anything else.

"Your new identification chip is clean," Sawyer said as she continued to graze the scales of her fish. "Once we reach Vectin-14, you should be able to use it at any terminal without issue."

"Thank you."

I rotated my arm a few times before turning away. Sawyer held up a hand, and I paused.

"You don't have anything else?" she asked.

"Like what?"

"What about what you'll tell the other genetically-modified person? What else would you say? What would you discuss? Is there something only you two will understand?"

I hadn't thought about it. All I knew was that life had been different for me. Everyone was envious. Everyone who was impor-tant wanted me as their pawn. Was that how it always went? That's what I wanted to ask.

"I'd talk about life experiences," I said. "Maybe we went through similar hardships. You know how it goes. Humans tend to be tribal."

"Your mother must have been lucky. Most… people like you… are made by superhumans who craft individuals to specialize in a certain field. In essence, determining what they'll most excel at in life, be it fine-motor control for artists, or physical capability for bodyguards… or improving the beauty of fish for decoration."

Blub relaxed under Sawyer's touch.

"Mara said something similar," I muttered.

"It's true. The other genetically-altered individual on the *Star Marque* was constructed to better serve superhumans."

"So, there *is* someone? Not just the fish?"

"That's right."

"Who is it?" I asked. I thought I could find them myself, but I didn't want to wait any longer.

Sawyer didn't answer. Instead, she scooped Blub into her arms and held the fish like a baby. The creature didn't object, but it did offer a tiny *toot* as it blinked into a restful state. I had never seen a fish blink, but I supposed modifying the fish required tweaking its ability to survive above water.

Silent seconds ticked on.

The longer I stared, the more I realized Sawyer had similarities to the fish. Her red hair—a color I had never seen on Capital Station—matched the red of Blub's bioluminescence. The way her freckles covered the bridge of her nose in a splattered but controlled mess paralleled Blub's black spots. They were random only to an untrained eye and placed in an appealing pattern to highlight other aspects of her beauty.

"It's you," I said, more accusatory than I'd wanted.

"Took you long enough to piece that together," she said. "I could almost hear the motors in your brain, frying under the strain."

"What did they design you for?"

"Isn't it obvious?"

Sawyer motioned to the room with a wide sweep of her arm. I glanced around, taking in the horror show of machines and equipment. They'd crafted her to be a computer specialist and engineer? I supposed someone had to do the maintenance on their ships, and most superhumans wouldn't want to stoop to such a "dirty" level.

"I need a fourth the amount of sleep a normal human needs," Sawyer said. "I have an eidetic memory. I was meant to be a worker for computers and coding, working long hours. Endellion doesn't have many officers, so she asked me to also be the mechanic, fixing the starships and machines aboard the *Star Marque*. I can handle it all—thanks to my advantages—but I'll never be able to do anything else, really."

"Your parents let this happen?" I asked.

"What parents?"

It was my turn to be silent. She had to have parents. Didn't she?

"I was cloned, essentially," Sawyer said as she stared up at me.

I'd never noticed before, but even her eyes were an unusual shade of grayish-blue. Someone really had put in the time to design her the way they saw fit.

"They took the DNA of a human on record, pieced together the zygote, and then altered it from there," she said. "I don't have a mother or a father. Just a tube, a lab, and a fish for a brother."

Sawyer rocked Blub back and forth.

The screens on the back wall flashed red. I snapped my attention to the pulse-quickening color, my body tensing with a dump of adrenaline. Sawyer walked over, no haste in her step, and tapped through the various messages. There weren't any alarms, but I could practically hear the Capital Station sirens ringing in my ears. What was going on?

She jabbed the PAD mounted on her forearm. "Endellion. There's an arrest warrant for a group of rebellion corsairs. They've made off with half a hospital's worth of medical supplies and genetic material."

The comms in the room cracked to life, and Endellion's voice rang clear through them. "You're sure they're rebellion corsairs?"

"Positive. They have two light cruisers under their control, both designated United-Earth affiliation."

Rebellion, huh? I hadn't heard of them in a while.

The rebellion was the leftover United-Earth faction—Homo sapiens who disagreed with the reworked Federation constitution and argued against superhumans' control. There weren't many rebellion sympathizers on Capital Station, but the few I'd met had the same damn thing to say every time: *"Superhumans were a mistake. They're here to phase us out. A slow form of genocide they hide through laws, regulations, and control."*

I didn't know the rebellion still operated in groups large enough to have control over light cruisers. I heard rumors they still controlled a few asteroid mines and moons around a gas giant on the edge of the Cygnus Sector, but was that enough to do anything other than slowly wilt away? They were their own form of genocide.

"Who issued the warrant for their arrest?" Endellion asked.

Sawyer tapped through the screen. "It's from Minister Virri Ontwenty herself. Apparently, this is her personal property."

"Are we en route?"

"We're close. 30 minutes away, tops. Even with deceleration."

"Send the coordinates."

Sawyer let go of Blub and tapped at the screens a second time, sending the new route to the pilots. As she typed in the recommended speed, the screens reverted back to their default white, and she backed away with a curse.

Across each screen read the message: *You have entered Commodore Cho's zone of control and will be redirected to his command ship, the* Relentless Nova, *effective immediately.*

"Endellion," Sawyer said. "Do you want me to—"

"No. Join me on the bridge."

"Right away." Sawyer gave me a quick glance before motioning to the door.

"What's going on?" I asked.

"We're being forced to dock on Commodore Cho's dreadnaught-class carrier, the *Relentless Nova.*"

"Even though we should be going for the guy with his name on an arrest warrant?"

Sawyer walked past me and exited the room without answering. I jogged after her, curious and irritated that I didn't know what was going on. She hustled down the hall past the conference room where I'd first met Endellion, and all the way to the most intricate door on the vessel. The plate next to the entrance read: *Bridge.*

We entered together, but in the back of my mind, I knew I shouldn't be there.

The bridge, set up in a semi-circle of terminals and stations, was already manned by Endellion herself, along with a handful of pilots at their respective stations. Lysander stood at Endellion's side, as did Quinn. The main screen sat in the middle of the room for all to see —it was a flat, two-way hologram that could be viewed from any station in the room.

The screen pulsed to life with the same message: *You have entered Commodore Cho's zone of control and will be redirected to his command ship, the* Relentless Nova, *effective immediately.*

I glanced out the main window that made up one of the room's walls. The dreadnaught-class starship—a behemoth of metal alloys shaped like a diamond—floated in the void of space. Twenty other ships—all a fraction of its size—buzzed around it, each slowing to dock. The *Star Marque* turned in its direction, steadily decelerating.

"The *Relentless Nova* is forcing us to dock?" I asked.

Sawyer nodded, but Lysander turned on his heel and glared the moment he recognized who I was.

"You shouldn't be here," he said. "Return to your post."

Endellion stood with her hands clasped behind her back. "Clevon can stay. I want everyone else at their stations. Commodore Cho will hail us any moment."

"What is Cho doing?" Quinn asked, parroting my inner thoughts.

"He's controlling the situation. He'll assign an enforcer team to handle the warrant."

"Does he even have the authority to do that? You're a commodore as well."

"We've never been able to determine our pecking order."

The way Endellion spoke made me think Commodore Cho wasn't going to be happy to see us.

TEN

Corsairs

I lingered in the shadows around the edge of the room, observing the situation as Endellion waited patiently to be hailed. The screens pulsed a second time, and the hailing frequencies flashed on the main terminal.

A man appeared on screen, his black enviro-suit decorated with a star over the collarbone, the same as Endellion. The mark of a commodore.

His salt-and-pepper hair and small eyes gave him a worn-out appearance, but his muscled frame and straight stance told me he wouldn't be a chump in a fight. Still human, though. I thought there might be a chance he could be superhuman, but I supposed I would never get to see one—not when the universe liked to keep everything from me.

The moment Commodore Cho spotted Endellion, his lip twitched, and he narrowed his eyes. "Commodore Voight, I didn't expect you to return to Vectin-14 quite so quickly."

Endellion smiled. "Governor Felseven no longer requires my assistance."

"He sent word along the relays that he was displeased with your service. Said you were a little too concerned with your own glory.

126

You do the enlisted men a disservice when you prioritize your pride over the HSN Corps."

What a joke.

Endellion did everything Felseven asked—better than he could have hoped—but he said one negative thing about her attitude, and she needed to be reprimanded? I figured war hounds like Commodore Cho didn't have the time—or fucks to give—to investigate the issue themselves. All he wanted was praise from his super-human superiors, I would bet my life on it.

"I wasn't aware Felseven was so derisive with his comments," Endellion said.

"I figured you would have traveled to the edges of the Vectin Quadrant to bide your time in hiding before the governors held their hearing—especially given that so many find your presence unpalatable."

"I believe Minister Barten and Admiral Vanine would disagree with your assessment, Commodore, but I don't have time to talk ballroom politics. Release control of my ship. I have corsairs to apprehend."

While I could sense the tension in the room—especially from Lysander's stiff posture and Quinn's gritted teeth—Endellion remained calm, almost amused. Commodore Cho waved away the comment, mirroring Endellion's cool demeanor. The two were having fun with this.

"I'm afraid the situation is beyond your capability," he said. "These corsairs have seized a cargo vessel and have command of two light cruisers. A single vanguard ship will likely be destroyed. I would be negligent in sending the *Star Marque*."

"As the captain of my vessel, I alone know its capabilities. The *Star Marque* is capable of dealing with two light cruisers."

"That's not necessary. I'll be sending two of my frigates to deal with the situation. They'll escort the stolen cargo vessel back to the Vectin-14 station."

Endellion glanced at the readouts on the edge of the screen. "I see no frigates."

"They'll arrive in due time."

"Then you may send them to catch up to me."

Commodore Cho laughed aloud. "You forget yourself, Commodore Voight. Your honorary title holds little power here. You'll get no favors with that attitude."

He terminated the line of communication. A second after the screen went blank, a message pulsed to life. It read: *Your placement in the docking queue has been moved to the highest priority. Prepare for docking procedures.*

I didn't know the Federation Navy kept control over the enforcer ships that way. It made sense—considering enforcer captains and their crews weren't actually enlisted men, and the Federation would have wanted a failsafe to control enforcer actions—but I was still surprised. Commodore Cho's dreadnaught had total command over the *Star Marque*, ripping Endellion's authority away simply for flying too close.

"Sawyer," Endellion said. "I trust you've done as I asked."

Sawyer offered a hesitant nod. "Yes."

"Then disengage us from the *Relentless Nova*."

"Of course."

Focused, Sawyer exited the bridge. I wanted to go after her, but I held back and watched Endellion speak to the *Star Marque*'s pilots. They set a course in their star charts, and Endellion opened the intercoms for the whole ship.

"Enforcers of the *Star Marque*," she said. "This is your captain speaking. Regardless of what the computer terminals say, do not start docking procedures. You are to prepare for a hard jump and ready yourself for combat. That is all."

A "hard jump" was a nice way of saying the *Star Marque* would accelerate much faster than it did on a normal trip. It would jerk forward after an initial burst from the engines, much like how the starfighters operated their speedy acceleration. Sawyer said it wasn't the safest option, but I figured it would give us a good head start. I heard vanguard-class starships were the fastest in the Federation fleet. They were meant to dive in first and take the enemy by surprise, so I was sure this would be an experience.

Then again, I didn't know the protocols for a hard jump, and that hit me like a steel bar to the face. Should I be standing around when we made the leap forward? My gut answered with a solid *no*.

I exited the bridge and jogged down the hall until I got to Sawyer's little hideaway workspace. I caught her typing away at the computers, fiddling with things foreign to my comprehension. There was an anxious energy in the air, like the whole ship shuddered with anticipation. Even Sawyer seemed a little jittery, her hands trembling as she worked.

"Where are we supposed to go for the hard jump?" I asked.

Sawyer waved her hand around. "Buckle down my equipment, would you?"

I glanced over the dim room and noticed most of the large pieces of machinery had belts capable of being secured to the floor. Although I had never done anything like this before, it seemed simple enough. I strapped down the machines nearest to me.

"What's going on?" I asked.

"We're breaking Federation law by altering the control code."

"But why does Endellion have to answer to that asshole? Quinn is right. Endellion's also a commodore."

"Endellion was an enforcer captain first, and was then given the honorary title of commodore by Admiral Vanine—which isn't unheard of, but it's rare. Most traditionally promoted commodores don't care for that, and I think Cho is willing to take the reprimand for disregarding her authority."

Her typing never slowed, even while she explained.

I buckled a third piece of equipment. "Do you need me to stop talking? For concentration?"

"I told you—I was designed for this. Talking to you isn't the distraction it would be for an unaltered human."

I knew the feeling. So many things came easy to me, despite how difficult they were for others. Sawyer might well have been my genetic equal.

But amidst my nervous anticipation for the immediate future—and my admiration for Sawyer—my curiosity burned through. "Why?" I asked. "Why did she even become a commodore if she isn't going to command ships or act in a military capacity? Why stay an enforcer captain?"

"I'll explain later," Sawyer said. She turned to her PAD. "Endellion, you should be able to disengage."

The *Star Marque* quaked as I belted down an engine block.

"Thank you, Sawyer," Endellion said over the comms.

"How long until we leave?"

"You have thirty seconds."

Sawyer whipped around, her eyes searching the room. She dashed over and grabbed Blub out of the air. The fish squeaked in response as she rushed to the wall and opened a section of steel paneling to reveal an emergency storage space. The closet-shaped room wasn't spacious, but Sawyer motioned me over with a quick jerk of her head.

"Buckle up," she commanded.

I stepped into the room with her, and the door closed. By the time I was done securing myself to the wall, the *Star Marque* quaked, and the intense feeling of increased G-forces crashed upon me. The pressure kept my back flat against the wall. I glanced over to see Blub tucked into Sawyer's jumpsuit, his body flat against her stomach, his little eyes bulging.

I hadn't finished battening down Sawyer's machinery, and the moment I heard the crash beyond the door, I cringed. The room would be wrecked, but it was hard to think about that with the pressure crushing me against the wall.

Unlike the starfighter simulation, the pressure didn't last long. Within ten seconds, the ship eased into its new speed, allowing me to breathe easy.

"That was different," I said.

"Gravity dampeners," Sawyer muttered. "They help stabilize the G-force inside the ship."

"Why don't we have those on the starfighters?"

"The fighters are nothing more than eggshells made of thin, steel alloy around as much weaponry as possible. Even the life-support system is half of what it should be, barely better than an enviro-suit. A gravity dampener would take up too much space and add unnecessary weight."

Sawyer unbuckled herself from the wall and opened the door.

"Wait," I said. "Is that why the asteroid wrecked me in the simulation? Thin defenses?"

"Obviously."

She released Blub from her jumpsuit—the fish spun in the air like a confused balloon—and hustled to the many computer screens that lined the far wall. All her equipment had smashed into the opposite wall, leaving her workstation intact.

I unfastened my safety belt and walked into the room, my attention drawn to the screens. Each one displayed the cockpit of a starfighter. Quinn jumped into hers, followed by Lee, and then Mara.

"You should get to your fighter," Sawyer said.

"Won't it take thirty minutes to reach the corsairs?"

"More like twenty now, but you've got to be prepared. You'll launch once we get in range. It's now or never for a preliminary system check."

I nodded and exited the room, somewhat in a haze. The mounting mental pressure made it hard to focus. I was about to enter an actual fight. Not a fight with fists, but a fight in the dead of space, wrapped in an *eggshell*. One wrong move and it was all over.

When I looked up, I stood in front my starfighter. I opened the hatch and slid into the cockpit, my heartrate interfering with my breathing. I thought I was over this, but reality had a way of adding an extra edge of seriousness that couldn't be simulated, no matter how many practice runs I'd breezed through.

The hatch closed, sealing me in the darkness of the fighter. The interior gripped my lower legs and held me tight. When the lights flickered to life, I flipped the diagnostic switch and watched the numbers run across the main screen. A small piece of me hoped there was something wrong—something that couldn't be fixed—an excuse for me to avoid the situation.

Another piece of me hated that I would ever wish for something so craven.

The side of my screen flashed the pilot assignment. It read:

SF-1 [Captain]: Endellion Voight
SF-2 [Subcommander/Starboard Leader]: Quinn Lee
SF-3 [Starboard Fighter]: Adachi Mara
SF-4 [Starboard Fighter]: Nelya Advik
SF-5 [Port Leader]: Yuan Xun
SF-6 [Port Fighter]: Noah Jevons
SF-7 [Port Fighter]: Humphrey Lee
SF-8 [Support]: Clevon Demarco
SF-9 [Open]: Unlisted
SF-10 [Open]: Unlisted

EIGHT OF US. And I was in Starfighter Eight. I had never had a lucky number before, but right then I knew what it was going to be.

"Attention, starfighters," Endellion said across the comms, her voice cold and smooth. "Our scanners have detected the targets ahead. We're to incapacitate two rebellion light cruisers. Each battleship has point-defense systems that rival the *Star Marque*'s, and the distances have been programmed into your flight computers."

I took a deep breath, remembering my training.

Point-defense systems were torpedoes and lasers used in close quarters against smaller ships. At a far enough distance, anything could be dodged in a starfighter, but when up close, the torpedoes traveled so fast that a starfighter pilot wouldn't have the time to react. Not only that, but the point-defenses were automated, meaning they were triggered by proximity and not by the unreliable hands of people.

Get too close to a starship, get destroyed. Guaranteed.

Endellion continued, "Each cruiser has a missile-barrage weapons-hold. The *Star Marque* will get close, open fire, and then be forced to retreat."

I took another deep breath, trying to remember every detail we'd learned in our tactics training.

A missile barrage was meant to finish the fight the moment it began. A scatter burst of a few hundred warheads blanketed an area of space like a shotgun blast, inflicting as much damage as possible to a larger ship. Starfighters could weave through the barrage. In theory.

"While the *Star Marque* retreats to a safe distance, the starboard leader and their team will destroy Cruiser A, and the port leader and their team will destroy Cruiser B."

"Understood," Quinn said.

"Heard," Yuan replied.

"The enemy has starfighters of their own," Endellion said. "Clevon and I will handle the enemy fighters. Any questions?"

"No, Endellion," the others answered in unison.

I couldn't find my voice.

The diagnostics finished, clearing my starfighter for combat. All systems go.

"Ready?" Endellion asked me through the one-on-one comms.

"Let's do it," I said.

Every stressful minute we waited took a year off my life expectancy.

I closed my eyes and focused on regulating my breath. The haze persisted, clouding my mind no matter what I thought of. Time passed like a dream. I opened my eyes, and already we were within minutes of our target. It wouldn't be long now. I grabbed the two side-sticks and flexed my fingers.

"Thirty seconds 'til engagement," Endellion said.

"Disengaging," the computer intoned.

My starfighter detached from the *Star Marque*. With muscle-memory precision, I pulled away from the docking port. Five seconds after I departed, red dots filled my screen. I took in the information like only a genetically-modified human could.

Two enemy ships, one labeled A, the other B. 250 inbound warheads. A single cargo ship. 20 enemy starfighters.

Only seconds to make my decisions.

I hit the speed and charged toward the open battlefield of space. Waves of warheads—shells half the size of my fighter—rolled toward me, so numerous and scattershot that I had to maintain a steady hand to dodge everything. 3 degree tilt. 20 degree increase. 15 degree decrease. Each motion happened so fast it barely registered.

4Gs. 5Gs.

I had three hyperweapon bolts and twenty torpedoes. Not much, so I needed to make them count.

"Prepare to engage," Endellion said. "Overshoot them."

"Got it."

"Clevon."

"Yeah?"

"Let me see what you're capable of."

My display screen highlighted the 20 enemy starfighters, as well as the invisible line between safety and the point-defenses of the two enemy cruisers. Endellion thought we could stand against ten to one odds? I didn't like the numbers—and they messed with my resolve —but I found solace in having accelerated faster than everyone else in the training simulations. It would be my biggest advantage.

With gritted teeth, I punched the speed, ready to see what a real starfighter could handle.

At 6Gs, I closed in on a group of five enemy fighters. They spread out and whipped around, coming at me from different directions. They were going to flit around and strike, or they were going to corral me into another fighter, so I amped up the speed once again.

7Gs. 8Gs.

So much pressure. *Please, Lucky Number Eight, don't fail me now.*

My vision grayed at the edges, but the enemy fighters couldn't keep up—they accelerated at half my rate.

"Demarco," Sawyer said, her voice a sweet relief. "You can't maintain this. You'll pass out if you continue."

9Gs.

I looped around and opened fire on the enemy fighters. Five torpedoes shot, but only two enemies hit—the red dots vanished from my screen. Three enemy fighters fired at me, and I spun to avoid any collision, my body reacting to the information with near-instantaneous reflexes. I shot by them and curved back fast, no doubt taking them by surprise with my precision at such speeds.

I fired five more torpedoes as I streaked past, hitting another two enemy fighters. I clenched my teeth so hard I thought they would break.

The moment I flitted around, I spotted a cluster of debris heading my way. I dodged most of it, but a large, spinning piece of hull sailed into my path.

Noah's fighter swept from the side, launching torpedoes, blasting the clutter, and clearing my path.

"Don't die on the starter rock," he said over our personal comms.

The G-force pressure prevented me from giving him an adequate reply, but his comment got me chuckling, even if it hurt.

A second later, an enemy fighter flew into Noah's range. I launched in Noah's direction and fired one of my hyperweapon bolts accidentally. The radiance of the shot stunned me—a star fragment's worth of light—and it vaporized the enemy fighter without stopping. I never should have used something so powerful for a small fighter, but I barely gave my attack thought.

And the enemy fighter hadn't been fast enough to dodge. Nowhere *near* fast enough. He had turned slightly, like he had wanted to dodge but didn't have the reaction speed needed. I could see it now, like a fight in the death pits on Capital Station.

But I didn't have time to congratulate myself. All my attention was drawn to my flight path. Every obstacle came at me like a bullet, due to my continually-increasing speed. I dodged, tilted, swirled, looped, and turned. My screen lit up with two new targets.

"These are the enemy starfighter leaders," Endellion said. "They're keeping the Port Team from their target."

She raced after them, her celerity on display. I pushed to keep up, watching as the G-force increased at decimal points, like the plasma engines were struggling to add more acceleration. I almost matched Endellion, but she accelerated along with me.

9.5Gs. 9.6Gs. 9.8Gs.

No other fighter could touch us. But the longer I went, the worse it got.

I reached the enemy commanders, the gray at the edge of my vision closing in.

"*Demarco*," Sawyer shouted. "You have to decelerate soon!"

Although both enemy pilots shot in different directions, they were too slow. I overtook one, and Endellion took the other. One torpedo and I had reduced my target to cinders. Endellion did the same before curving wide and returning to the fray.

I jerked back on the controls and slowed my starfighter, pulling away from the enemy cruiser before I could destroy myself on the point-defense system. My breath became ragged as I gulped down air. Once my vision returned, I smiled. That was close.

The *Star Marque* returned to the battlefield, and another missile barrage from the enemy cruiser filled my screen with crimson dots. I slammed the side-sticks and raced away, slipping between warheads with all the grace of a dancer. Despite the myriad of dangers, my pulse ran hot with exhilaration. I didn't know when, but at some point, I'd started laughing, and now I couldn't stop.

Two enemy starfighters chased me through the maze of missiles, likely hoping to catch me while I was distracted.

They wanted to fight? I would give them a good fight.

I whipped my starfighter around and let loose another five torpedoes, targeting the closest fighter first. A second wave of warheads exploded from the nearby cruiser, and I rolled to avoid the bombardment. My attention was divided, but my heightened mental capacity took in every bit of detail as though in slow motion.

When the second fighter turned to avoid a warhead, I fired, catching him off-guard and scrubbing his existence from the stars.

"Clevon," Endellion said.

"Yeah?"

"New target—Cruiser B."

Cruiser B highlighted on my screen, the life-support systems marked for destruction. Once the life supports were down, most of the crew would follow. Those lucky enough to be wearing enviro-suits would continue, but the cruiser would be an easy target by then.

I headed straight for the cruiser, increasing my acceleration back to the 7Gs' worth of pressure, ensuring nothing would stop me from getting to my destination. At 8Gs, I was closing in, entering the mythical zone of *close enough for hyperweapons* but not so close that I would get destroyed by the point-defense. I fired once my targeting locked, taking pleasure in the brilliant flash of light as the hyper-weapon bolt smashed into the life-support systems and wasted everything—including the steel alloy—into a fine gas.

The hyperweapons were the most destructive weapons I had ever seen.

"Finish it," Endellion said as she flew off toward Cruiser A.

My computer highlighted the Cruiser B's bridge. To no one's surprise, the point-defense had the largest range around the bridge. It was the center of control. Even with the life support gone, the team in the bridge could fly the metal casket off toward a safer loca-tion, or maybe even rendezvous with an ally. But they weren't getting away.

I increased acceleration, reaching 9Gs, flitting into position, and then diving toward the cruiser. I fired my last hyperweapon bolt, watching with a smile as it disintegrated the bridge. The gaping hole in the ship reminded me of an open chest wound from a plasma rifle. The ship bled into the cold space around it, blood made of steel, plastic, and people.

I shot down eight enemy fighters and brought a cruiser to its knees.

Lucky Number Eight won the day.

With the cruiser down, I finally glanced at the condition of the battlefield. All enemy fighters were destroyed. The last cruiser was wrecked, but not defeated. The cargo ship we'd come to rescue sat idly, 100% intact.

And the *Star Marque* flew in, dominating the situation by spraying a missile barrage of its own across the remaining enemy cruiser. The warheads smashed along the side, destroying a majority of the cruiser's hull. The life support failed. The engines failed. It was only a matter of time before the crew ran out of oxygen.

A hail from the corsairs came through the open frequencies. I switched my comms over, curious what was being said.

"This is Alexei Pavlova," the man on the comms said. "Captain of the United-Earth Cruiser, *Rampart*. This is a formal declaration of surrender."

"I hear you, Captain Pavlova," Endellion replied. "This is Commodore Voight of the Federation Vanguard, *Star Marque*."

"Oh, shit."

I slowed my starfighter as I set my return course, my eyebrows raised. Did they know each other?

"Please, listen," Pavlova said. "We only stole medicine and genetic-research material. It's for the humans of Landing Station. They're suffering."

Endellion said, "That doesn't excuse grand theft, burglary, robbery, assaulting an enforcer starship, attempted murder of my crew—"

"They'll die, Commodore! You know the sickness! The deformities! Even half that shipment could save millions."

"I've heard your plea, Captain, but your crimes are too great. Perhaps if you surrendered immediately, this could have played out a different way. As it stands, I have a job to do. Minister Ontwenty wants her property back."

"The rumors are true. You're a traitor to your own kind."

"You can explain yourself to the justicars of Vectin-14."

"Never. We should be free from the superhumans, not serving them. You're hurting all of humanity with your actions."

"Honor your surrender, Captain."

Pavlova cursed under his breath. "I rescind my declaration."

ELEVEN

Medical Supplies

"Quinn," Endellion said over the starfighter comms. "Do you still have any hyperweapon bolts?"

"Yes, Endellion."

"Target the bridge."

"Of course, Endellion."

Before the enemy captain could take any action, Quinn fired, her hyperweapon blast lighting up the bridge like a pyre in space. And then, as fast as it had happened, the radiance disappeared, along with whoever was on the bridge. Painless way to go, really. One second Captain Pavlova existed, and the next, he didn't.

"All ships, return to your docking ports," Endellion said.

Everyone flooded the comms with their agreements.

I headed back to the ship, an odd calm settling over me now that the fight was over. The intensity of the struggle lingered in my system, and although I was drained, I knew I wouldn't be able to rest.

Hopefully, it was drinking time.

My starship latched onto the *Star Marque*, and I waited for the 30 seconds it took to seal the ships together. Once the hatch opened, and the starfighter released me, I stepped out and rotated my arms. All in a day's work, I supposed.

"That's how you do it!"

I turned in time to spot Lee jogging over. He didn't slow—if anything, he picked up speed—and then lunged, his arms wide. I gritted my teeth and stepped back, ready to clock this fool in the jaw, but I stopped myself when I took note of his laugh. Lee collided with me, squeezed his arms around me in a tight embrace, and patted my back. With conflicting emotions raging through my system, I offered him a few tentative pats in return.

But it went on too long.

"Get off me," I commanded.

He jumped back, still laughing, and slapped my arm, like he couldn't stop himself from touching me.

"You were amazing! I could never imagine accelerating that fast!"

Quinn, Advik, and Mara hurried over, with Yuan trailing behind, thanks to her limp. Everyone crowded around, smiling just as jovially as Lee was.

"You flew circles around those enemy fighters," Quinn said, going out of her way to tap my chest.

Yuan nodded. "Crazy. You're not sick? You didn't pass out? Are you even human?"

"I couldn't believe Endellion wanted you as her wingman, but you pulled it off. I guess I'm a pretty great training instructor, right?"

Everyone laughed at the end of Quinn's statement, and I couldn't help but chuckle along. Quinn held out her fist, and I stared, confusion growing with each passing second. She knocked her knuckles against my loose hand.

Ah. We were buddies now.

I balled my fist. She tapped it and slammed her shoulder into mine. Lee hugged and shook me, his spare energy enough to power the whole damn ship. I didn't stop him this time, however. Everyone wanted a piece of me, apparently—and who could blame them?—

so I let them have their fun. They joked and congratulated me over and over, until it almost lost meaning.

"Where's Noah?" I asked, glancing around.

Quinn shrugged. "I don't know."

"I'll go get him."

Out of all the fighter pilots, he and Endellion were the two I most wanted to celebrate with.

I walked away from the others and headed down the hall and around the corner. Noah's fighter was docked on the other side of the ship, but still on the same deck. It wouldn't take long to reach him, which meant it shouldn't have taken long for him to reach us.

When I strolled up to his fighter, I spotted the open hatch. Noah sat inside, barely moving. I leaned against the side and peered into the vehicle. Damn, those things were small. I supposed it was to maximize torpedo capacity, but what did I know?

"What're you doing?" I asked. "It's happy hour. We've earned the right to get wasted tonight."

He gripped his jumpsuit at the torso, his fingers twisting into the fabric. His breath came short and ragged. He avoided meeting my gaze. Lysander wasn't lying when he'd said Noah experienced pain.

"Go on without me," Noah said in a tiny voice. "I need... to sit here for a few minutes."

"Give me your hand. I'll take you to the infirmary."

"I can get there by myself."

So, he was ashamed. That took some of the stress away—I doubted a man on the verge of death would be worried about appearances. He was suffering, but I suspected the medics would have something for him. He probably didn't want me to see him like this. I didn't blame him. I wouldn't want people to see me struggling to stand, either.

"Hey," Quinn said as she walked up to the fighter. "What's going on? Us starfighters have done our job. Now it's time to relax and let the ground enforcers do their thing." She gave Noah a glance, and her eyebrows knitted together. "Everything okay?"

I grabbed her upper arm and turned her away. "He's got vertigo," I said. "Don't make a big deal of it."

"Oh?" she asked. "All right. I'll see you in the mess hall."

"Sure."

She walked away, offering Noah one last sideways glance before rounding the corner. I knew she was aware of his condition, but that didn't mean Noah wanted it to be his sole defining feature.

"Give me your hand," I said.

"I… don't think I can walk," Noah said.

"Then I'll carry you."

I didn't know why, but I didn't like the idea of him sitting around in silent agony as everyone went off and got their booze. If I took him to the infirmary, I knew I would be able to enjoy myself. At least then he would be in the hands of a medical professional. I had to help him, especially after the stunt he'd pulled when he shot the debris out of my path. The kid had been looking out for me.

Noah held up his arm, and I slid it over my shoulders. It was easy to lift him—I was already strong, but a few months of training had made a bigger difference than I'd imagined. When I went to scoop him out of the fighter, Noah shook his head.

"Let me… at least pretend to walk."

I helped him out and supported most of his weight on my shoulder. He used what little strength he had to "walk" alongside me, one arm clutched over his stomach, like he was holding in his intestines.

"Is it always this bad?" I asked.

"No. I just pushed myself a little too much…"

We reached the infirmary without running into anyone else, and I practically heard Noah sigh in relief. The sole medic on duty looked up from her computer terminal and rushed over—though she didn't appear to be panicked, which was a good sign. If she was confident she could handle the situation, I was sure Noah would be fine.

"Thank you," Noah said as he was led to a nearby magnetic gurney.

I nodded. "Don't mention it."

The *Star Marque* quaked, and it took me a second to regain my footing. Noah and the medic continued as if the tremor never happened, but I glanced around, curious about its source. Sure, things happened in space all the time, but the moment the *Star Marque* failed was the moment it would become an impromptu graveyard.

"We're docking with the cargo vessel," Noah said with a weak laugh. "That's what caused the shake. We've got to clear the starship of any corsairs that may be hiding."

I relaxed a bit, but I could still feel the adrenaline, thick in my veins. "So, we're going to kill all the rebellion pirates on the cargo ship, as well? Damn. Endellion's a lot more ruthless than I originally thought."

Everyone in the room got tense. I glanced between the medic and Noah, confused by their shift in attitude. They regarded each other with troubled looks before returning their attention to me.

"Endellion isn't like that," Noah said. "Those rebellion thugs are the ruthless ones."

The medic nodded. I didn't even know her, but she chimed in with, "They go to all sorts of places, killing everything that moves and stealing everything that doesn't."

"They just keep fighting the superhumans," Noah added, "even though the war is long over."

I chuckled. "I don't think you understand. I *like* that Endellion doesn't fuck around. If these guys are unstable, there's no reason to play nice."

The ship's intercoms crackled for a moment, silencing all conversation. Everyone glanced around.

"Clevon," Endellion said. "Suit up and report to the docking bay."

Then the intercom crackled a second time, ending the communication.

Noah lifted an eyebrow. "Suit up?"

"I don't know," I said. "But I'll be back. You just get your shit together and meet the others in the mess hall."

"You'd better be there."

"I'm looking forward to it."

The idle excitement in my system stirred as I ran to my capsule bunk. Why had Endellion summoned me? I didn't know, but I didn't want to keep her waiting. I ripped off my jumpsuit and pulled on my enviro-suit. Its claustrophobic tightness had become familiar, and I didn't mind the sensation as much as I had in the beginning.

Starfighter pilots didn't wear enviro-suits, due to complications. Apparently, the cockpit locked the pilot in place and messed with the enviro-suit's automated environment regulation. The pressure would cause the suit to engage in emergency-system procedures. Not only that, but the helmet—while programmable—didn't have the necessary information for the ship's system. Plus, if the helmet were left in the hoodie position, it would dig into the spine of the pilot at higher G-forces.

But the enviro-suit was a must for all other situations.

Once properly geared, I got into the lift and headed for Deck Five. The docking bay on Deck Five was the entrance and exit for the entire ship. It had the largest decontamination room and space lock, allowing the *Star Marque* to safely attach itself to space stations, ports, and other ships with ease.

When the lift door opened, I was surprised by the number of enforcers standing in formation. Lysander paced in front of them, waiting for the ship to complete its final scans before opening the connecting bridge to the cargo ship. Endellion waited off to the side, ready and vigilant. I made my way to her, ignoring the odds glances from the other enforcers.

Lysander spotted me and tapped the side of his helmet until I switched over to the channel with him and Endellion.

"What're you doing here?" he asked, louder than any reasonable person should be.

"I was summoned," I replied.

"Endellion?"

"It's fine," she said. "I asked Clevon to accompany me. You take the enforcers through a systematic sweep of every deck."

Lysander huffed. After a silent moment, he added, "There are a lot of valuable objects and information on that ship."

I almost offered a solid "fuck you" through the comms, but I bit my tongue. I wasn't going to steal anything. Once he got it through his fat head that I was dedicated to my new career, he would stop insinuating otherwise. At least, that was what I assumed.

"No need to fret," Endellion said. "Clevon and I will be together at all times."

"Very well."

I reached Endellion's side and gave her a quick nod. She returned it, and then motioned me closer. I stood right next to her, the two of us separated from Lysander and the other enforcers. I didn't know what Endellion wanted with me, but it was obvious that she wanted me close.

"The bridge is open," the computer announced with little enthusiasm.

The connecting door unlocked, and then slid apart, revealing the decontamination room and the long bridge over to the cargo vessel. Gravity shifted ever so slightly the moment the door opened. It got weaker, no doubt because the fields of effect didn't extend beyond the ship.

Sure enough, when the enforcers headed for the cargo vessel, they jumped and then floated across to the other door, traveling the 100 meters like they were in a suspended state of mid-leap. The cargo vessel opened and allowed them inside, each wave of enforcers hitting the bulkheads and righting themselves in the low gravity of the other starship.

Once everyone jumped across, Endellion and I leapt through the bridge. I had experienced 0Gs before—there were a handful of times when Capital Station lost gravity for a few hours—but it still brought a smile to my face. Nothing felt as liberating as the ability to glide in any direction, free of restraint.

I hit the cargo ship bulkhead and got back to my feet. Then I walked up to the entrance of the vessel and entered, the visor of my suit telling me that the atmosphere aboard was a good ten degrees cooler than it had been on the *Star Marque*.

Lysander sent squads of enforcers to all parts of the ship, ignoring me completely. That was fine. I turned my attention to Endellion, and she motioned for me to follow.

I switched my comms to a private channel with her.

"We're heading to the med bay," she said.

Endellion hefted her rifle. I did the same, but now I was on edge. Did she think we would be met with resistance? I doubted any sad sack on this hunk of space debris could stand against the both of us, but I couldn't get *too* cocky. Hubris was the leading killer of extraordinary individuals.

Then again, if there was any talent in these corsair lunatics, they would've given us a better starship rumble.

We started down a corridor, and Endellion picked up speed into a half-run. I kept up, curious about how she knew her away around the rig. Unlike the *Star Marque*—which had rough edges, visibly apparent weapon storage, and space management for hundreds of people—the little cargo vessel seemed to have its living quarters separate from its work areas. The clean walls, devoid of emergency weapon caches or exposed pipes, had a variety of cubby storage meant for blankets, pillows, and other such luxuries. The place felt like a home, and it probably was for the limited crew.

Or had been. Blast marks scorched the walls and blood stained the floor. The crew had put up a fight. And lost.

I caught sight of a deck map posted on the bulkhead as I ran by. I only got a quick glance at it, but that was more than enough time to process the information. This rig had two decks. Deck One— living quarters and lab. Deck Two—cargo hold. Made for easy navigation, I supposed.

Endellion stopped at a door and typed something into the computer terminal by the lock. I took my place at her side and got a good look at the surroundings. I hadn't seen anyone yet, outside of the *Star Marque* enforcers.

"Did you know the cruiser captain?" I asked, my thoughts wandering. "Sure sounded like *he* knew *you*."

"I was once a member of the rebellion," Endellion replied with a hint of disinterest.

"Really? When was that?"

"When I worked on Midway Station, before I became an enforcer."

I didn't give two shits about the rebellion or their United-Earth agenda. They took to pirating anything the Federation owned and controlled, and it looked like they would kill other humans to do it, too.

"You hate the superhumans?" I asked, antsy. "Is that why you joined the rebellion?" Why hadn't she opened the door yet?

"No," Endellion replied. "The rebellion was just a rung in the ladder I needed at the time. They served their purpose, and then I was done with them."

"Those chumps fought like they were rungs."

Endellion chortled. "Indeed."

She tapped the screen of the computer terminal one last time, and the door unlocked. Before she opened it, she turned to me. "There are four in the room. Two to the left, and two to the right. They're waiting for us."

"How do you know all that?"

"I can sense them."

I almost laughed aloud. Did she expect me to believe that? What was she? Psychic? Only gypsy defects who wanted to take advantage of someone's ignorance claimed to be something so stupid.

"You kill the two on the right," Endellion continued. "I'll get the other two."

Instead of arguing, I nodded. "All right."

She opened the door and stepped aside. We waited a few seconds before turning together and firing into the room from the cover of the doorframe. In the fraction of a moment, I saw the entire medical lab. I took note of the injured man in the corner—one of the men on the right side I was supposed to be killing—and the other was a guy in a white enviro-suit with a plasma pistol. I shot the pistol-toting thug through the chest, my plasma bolt digging into the bulkhead before frying out, but I refrained from shooting the other. The injured guy had his helmet down, his face and neck lacerated by shattered glass, and he cowered in the corner, his knees to his chest.

Endellion killed the others before I was done taking stock of the situation. She regarded the injured man with a quick glance, and then turned to face me. Neither of us said anything. After three heartbeats, she walked into the room and headed straight for the computer terminal, ignoring the man in the corner completely.

I also left him. It felt wrong to gun him down when he had already surrendered to fear.

Endellion peeled back her helmet. Her braid uncoiled and fell against her back. To my surprise and fascination, she unbuckled the fasteners of her suit and allowed the sleeve to slide off her left arm.

Most cyborgs had scars—tons of them, from all the surgeries and injuries that came from having metal under the skin—but Endellion had a smooth purity to her skin unlike even a normal individual. No scars. No tarnish. Somehow perfect, like the enviro-suit kept her fresh.

She held up the PAD on her forearm. The thin computer sucking the heat from her body could have easily fit under the snug confines of an enviro-suit, but why had she brought it? I stared, unmoving and without comment, as Endellion pulled out the connecters from the computer terminal and attached them to her PAD.

I ripped my helmet off and frowned. "What're you doing?"

"Copying the medical research the ship is carrying."

She said nothing else.

"Forgive me for sounding like an infant," I said, "but isn't that stealing?"

Endellion matched my gaze. "Yes."

"But—" I cut myself off and took a breath.

Didn't Lysander just say that I shouldn't be on this mission because I would steal something from the ship? Surely Endellion didn't have the authority to do this. I almost couldn't believe this was happening. Wasn't this superhuman research? Wasn't she risking everything by doing this?

"Do you have a problem with it?" Endellion asked.

"I thought *you* would," I said.

"And if I don't?"

"Well..." I glanced at the computer while I mulled over the situation. "Isn't this research about... genetic defects?"

"Yes."

"Can we use it to help Noah?" I shrugged. "And Lysander, I guess?"

"We could."

"Then fuck it. Copy all the information."

Endellion smiled and returned her attention to the computer. "I knew taking you aboard was the right decision. We see eye-to-eye, Clevon."

Well, she was tall enough to see eye-to-eye with me, that was for sure. But I hadn't known she'd wanted someone with flexible ethics. Maybe that was why she hadn't hesitated to bring a criminal into the fold.

"Can we use this right away?" I asked as I motioned to the computer terminal.

"I'll need a doctor. An *actual* doctor, not a medic I inherited from another crew. Someone who can expand upon complicated research and reach a logical conclusion."

"The *Star Marque* doesn't have a doctor like that?"

"Not yet. But soon."

Endellion sucked in her breath and grabbed at her forehead with her right hand. I lifted an eyebrow and took a step closer. She rubbed at her eyes, and then her temple, her brow furrowed.

"Another reason I need a competent doctor," she muttered.

From my peripheral, I noticed the attack, but didn't have enough time to deal with it. I leaned away, but the attacker's swing wasn't for me. He swiped at Endellion. Despite her closed eyes and the pain in her head, she managed to step to the side. But the PAD on her arm jerked her back—it was still connected to the computer, and she didn't pull it free in time to fully dodge.

The injured rebellion fighter clipped her shoulder with a knife-like fragment of glass. He drew a thin line into her skin, cutting enough to bleed but not enough to get down to the bone.

Endellion kicked him square in the gut. He sailed back, collided with a bench, and then vomited blood across his white enviro-suit. Guy wasn't getting up after that, but he did squirm across the floor, whimpering.

"Sorry about that," I said as I turned back to Endellion. "I should've kept a better——"

I stopped cold.

Endellion's hand shook as she reached for a pouch on her enviro-suit belt. She withdrew a small squeeze-tube of Liquid Skin and applied it straight to the injury in generous amounts. Although the computer beeped for further prompts, she ignored it in favor of dealing with the tiny wound.

"It's just a cut," I said.

She said nothing, her focus consumed by the scratch. She applied a second layer of the Liquid Skin and rubbed it in, her hand still trembling.

I forced a laugh. "I guess you're an old-school woman at heart, right? Worrying about your beauty?"

"Kill him," Endellion commanded. There was a cold seriousness in her tone unlike anything I had heard from her before.

The order took me by surprise. After a hesitant moment, I turned to the sad sack on the floor with a cocked eyebrow. He struggled to find his breath—and his stomach—after a kick like that. He had attacked us, though, and he was an enemy that killed the crew of this ship just to take their cargo. And I was sure he would strike again, if his body wasn't frozen in shock.

Plus, I had already given him his life. If he had stayed in the corner, he could've lived.

I took aim with my plasma rifle and fired, creating a hole through his skull, and a seared dent in the bulkhead behind him. He collapsed, unmoving.

When I glanced back, Endellion was still engrossed by the nick on her shoulder.

"Is it really that important?" I asked.

"Yes."

"Why?"

"Superhumans don't have scars."

"So?"

Endellion finished with her task—her injury coated and massaged to perfection—and then resumed her work at the computer terminal. "A superhuman never would've let that happen," she said in a low voice. "They never would've been caught off-guard. They never would've been wounded."

I slung my rifle over my shoulder and shook my head. "Don't be crazy. You can't hold yourself to superhuman standards."

"How can I think of them as my equals if I can't hold myself to the same standards?"

Her response stopped my line of questioning. She wanted to think of herself as their equal? Endellion really *was* ambitious. That was borderline insanity, or maybe unchecked narcissism. Or maybe she *wanted* to be seen as an equal. Was that her real goal? Not ruling a planet, but being seen as an equal to the members of Homo superior?

"That guy tried to kill you," I said, my thoughts piecing together a different mystery.

Endellion nodded. "That he did."

"Not me. *You*. And the captain of the Rampart knew you by name. Why do these guys care so much about who you are? You fuck them over or something before you left their ranks?"

"I sold the Federation hundreds of locations, passwords, encryptions, and personnel files from the rebellion," Endellion said. "I was a United-Earth officer. I had a fair amount of access to their confidential material, and I took advantage of it when I left."

I couldn't stop myself from laughing. No wonder they wanted her dead! Way to make enemies. Way to make a lot of enemies.

"Why?" I asked between bouts of mirth. "Just because you could? Did they fuck with you or something?"

"Buying a starship takes a lot of credits, Clevon. When you come from a backwater world, no one wants to loan you anything, and my parents were on the brink of starvation. Where else was I going to get the funding to start my own enforcer unit?"

I got my amusement under control and scratched at my chin. "Does anyone else know about it?"

"Some. Not many. I met most of my crew after the incident. I wouldn't hide it if they asked, just as I didn't hide it now. But the rebellion isn't an organization that deserves respect or reverence. They're terrorists and thugs. I don't regret my decision."

She finished copying the information, detached her PAD, and then glanced over at me. "You're only as good as the obstacle that stops you from achieving greatness," she said. "And I'm much better than the rebellion."

TWELVE

Midway Station

The mess hall wasn't as crowded when half the enforcers were stationed on the rescued cargo ship. It was almost as noisy, however. I supposed coming out on top of a fight had excited everyone, not just me.

Lee sat on top of the table, pink in the face, as he downed another brandy pouch. "We're unstoppable. The enemy didn't even touch us." He motioned for another drink, and Quinn passed it over with a cocked eyebrow. Lee cracked open the straw nozzle and gave her half a smirk. "I vote we get a vacation. Well-earned, I say."

"A vacation?" Quinn repeated. "You get hammered every evening, babe. How is that not a mini-vacation already?"

"I have to wake up for training the next day. We deserve to sleep in. Right, Yuan?"

Yuan shook her head. "Don't drag me into this."

"Oh, c'mon," Mara said, grabbing Yuan by the arm. "I want to sleep in. Vote. Do it for me."

Rolling her eyes, Yuan let out a long exhale. "Fine. I vote we should get a vacation. At least until we reach Midway Station. That's only a few days from now."

"See?" Lee said, pointing with his pouch. "Yuan knows what's up." Then he turned his drunken attention to me. "Do it for Demarco. Did you see the way that guy piloted? He deserves to sleep in."

"I don't need to sleep as long as the rest of you do," I said as I nursed my pouch. "I don't have a stake in this." And no matter what Quinn decided, I was going to stick to my training.

Mara leapt over Yuan, slid down the bench, and then shook my shoulder. "Us mere mortals would appreciate a few extra hours of sleep. Please vote for vacation, Demarco!"

"Knock it off," Quinn said as she shooed Mara away. "I swear you lose a few years of maturity for every sip you take."

"So, you'll give us the vacation?"

"Yes, all right? We all get a vacation. But only until Midway Station. Then it's back to our regular training regimen."

Lee did a fist pump before throwing back the rest of his brandy pouch. The guy drank like he had been genetically modified to handle alcohol—at least, for the first few hours. He was on the verge of sloppy, and everyone knew it. When he went to grab another pouch, Quinn crossed her arms and tilted her head to the side.

"I'll be fine," Lee replied with a laugh. "I don't have to wake up tomorrow."

That comment got everyone laughing. Everyone but Advik. She stared at me a little longer than was polite, and I returned the gesture with narrowed eyes. When she remained silent, I set my pouch down and frowned.

"You got a problem?"

Advik had a face and frame that was easy to forget. Her black hair and copper skin matched most everyone else's, and her voice was quiet as a mouse.

"I learned to pilot from someone like you," she said.

"Someone like me?"

"Genetically modified. He was the best pilot I ever met."

"But now I'm the best, right?" I asked as I stroked the collar of my enviro-suit.

Advik turned away, a slight blush on her face that got me

excited. "He was full of himself, too. I'm glad Endellion brought you aboard."

I sidled up to her, ready to ask if she wanted to play out some student-teacher fantasies when Noah came striding up to the table, his head high, and a smile on his face. The others noticed him a second later, each cheering his arrival with a whoop and a raised pouch.

"How're you feeling?" Lee asked. "Get over that vertigo?"

Noah rubbed the back of his neck. "Yeah. Got some medicine, and they fixed me right up."

"You'll get over it eventually! Everybody goes through it. Well, except this jackass." Lee halfheartedly punched my arm.

"It's okay to admit you're jealous," I said.

"As long as I have Quinn, there's nothing I need to be jealous of."

He took Quinn's hand and kissed her knuckles. Quinn laughed, but the adoration in her eyes was hard to mistake. She pulled him close, and the others at the table broke into *ahhhs* or eye rolls. Yuan motioned to Mara and nodded towards the exit, and they stood before anyone could protest.

Noah took a seat next to me. "You're back already? What did Endellion want?"

"She took me over to the cargo ship, and we killed some straggler rebellion soldiers."

"That's it?"

"That's it."

"Seems... like a waste of your talents," Noah said as he grabbed himself a brandy pouch from the table.

I sipped the last of my drink and mulled over the events. Endellion had surprised me. I'd thought she would be straight-laced, but I suppose that was foolish. No one was ever 100% clean. Everyone had some dirt—white lies, theft, cheating at a game. I had met men and women far worse than Endellion on Capital Station. What she did was child's play compared to the darkness of a depraved thug.

So why did it give me pause when I thought about her?

"You okay?" Noah asked.

I gave him a sideways glance. "Yeah."

He leaned closer and lowered his voice. "Are you sure nothing happened?"

I glanced around. Everyone continued their celebrations, some drunker than others, but everyone remained in high spirits.

"Nothing else happened," I said. "It was odd that Endellion wanted me to stick with her, but I did."

"Yeah. Odd. But I guess she really trusts you. She's never asked anyone else to join her on a mission away from the *Star Marque*."

Was that so? What happened on our outing was a dark little secret?

Really made me wonder.

I STARED at the ceiling of my capsule bunk, unseeing.

It was hard to sleep. An anxious energy *still* coursed through me, and I took deep, slow breaths to help quell the restlessness. We would reach Midway Station soon, and then we would get off this rig for the first time in six months. I'd technically left when I entered the cargo ship, but the entire event felt like work. It hadn't counted.

The credits we would pick up at the station would be substantial. Endellion took as much from the rebellion cruisers as the *Star Marque* could carry. We left the husks for salvage crews, but some of those computer components could fetch a high price, even when disconnected from their starship.

"Did you have fun celebrating?" Sawyer asked over the comms, breaking my thoughts with her unexpected communication.

I stretched and tucked both my hands under my head. "Always." I had never celebrated like that on Capital Station. It felt welcoming on the *Star Marque*. Almost wholesome. Hard not to get addicted to the company and good times.

"Everyone looked like they enjoyed themselves."

"Heh. Yeah. I guess they did." I exhaled. "What were you doing during the dogfight? Just watching me perform?"

"I was watching *everyone's* performance. It's my job to maintain the starfighter systems for each pilot, so they can focus on fighting. I'm everyone's navigator."

"All eight pilots?"

"Yes."

"You've got a legendary ability to multitask."

"That's what I was designed for."

I took in another deep breath. The way she'd said that last statement was so detached, like the thought bothered her on a deeper level. Maybe I needed to change the subject.

"Endellion do anything to celebrate?"

"She never celebrates things like this."

"Why not?" I asked with a laugh. Seemed like as good an event as any to celebrate. People on Capital Station would sometimes just celebrate the time of year, not necessarily an accomplishment.

"Endellion says hundreds of thousands of people have won simple space engagements. It's nothing noteworthy."

Goddamn. Even *she* failed to impress herself, apparently. "I think Endellion needs to loosen up."

"She likes to stay focused."

I closed my eyes and thought back to all my training. I had become more focused lately, that was for sure. Endellion's drive was admirable, and if I had a fraction of her willpower I would have been ten times the man I was now. I couldn't let her get too far ahead of me, not if I hoped to catch up.

"Do you know what happened on the cargo ship?" I asked.

"Of course," Sawyer drawled.

"About the medical research?"

"Yes."

Interesting. Sawyer knew we were stealing but never voiced an objection. At least, not to me.

"What do you think of it?" I asked.

"I think Endellion occasionally breaks the rules for the greater good."

I laughed. "Spoken like a true fanatic."

Sawyer huffed over the comms, crackling the speakers with her haughty dismissal. "Endellion rescued me and Blub, thank you very much. Breaking all sorts of laws to do so, I'll have you know."

I tried to say something, but Sawyer continued, heated, "And she's not supposed to take the genetically defective if they require medication to function, either. That goes against enforcer crew bylaws. And she's only supposed to pardon criminals who have done harm to her crew or starship in the line of duty, not random criminals she picks up from backwater space stations. Sometimes she bends the truth or goes against official conduct, but she's never failed us... so I'm willing to go along with it."

I waited while Sawyer took a few breaths of her own.

"If Endellion fails, we all fail," Sawyer intoned, shifting from agitated to serious. "I'm willing to follow Endellion to the end, even if she makes risky decisions. If that makes me a fanatic, so be it."

I asked, "She rescued you and Blub?"

"That's right."

"From what?"

"Our creator." Sawyer sighed. "Homo superior has no reason to think of Homo sapiens as equals. Let's just... leave it at that."

———————

I STEPPED off the *Star Marque* and froze in the middle of the walkway.

Midway Station was unlike anything I had imagined. It floated in orbit around Vectin-14, the capital planet for the whole quadrant, attached to the surface with a space elevator that led all the way to the surface. A quick glance upwards rewarded me with a sight far different than I had ever seen.

Large segments of Midway Station had been constructed with transparent metal alloys, allowing a hazy view of the planet far above us. Vectin-14 shimmered with an array of whites, reds, blues, and purples—a planet of color, unlike the dull grays and lifeless black seen on most starships. The system's star, Vectin, shone beyond the edge of the planet, creating a halo effect with the atmosphere.

"Remind you of Capital Station?" Quinn asked.

"Fuck no."

"It's a space station."

I chuckled. "I won't feel at home until I've got a knife against my throat and a group of gangsters attempting to rob me blind."

"That can be arranged," Quinn said with a laugh of her own. "I used to run with guys like you when I lived here. All thugs. Most of them addicted to chems. We made our money hustling defects."

"I remember you saying that," I said, still enthralled with the colors. It was almost like seeing the sky. Almost.

"You look like the cargo workers I stole from as a kid. It's real easy to pick someone's pocket when their head is craned upward."

"I feel sorry for the chump who tries to steal from me."

"I was pretty good back in the day. Only got caught when cameras were involved."

A piece of me wanted to ask, *Is that a challenge?* But I kept it to myself. Quinn was just bragging about her glory days, and I liked hearing about them. It really didn't matter if I could have caught her younger version pickpocketing, anyway. Instead, I enjoyed the moment a bit longer, before continuing my walk onto Midway Station.

"Where're you going?" Quinn asked.

I stopped and glanced over to her. "What do you mean? I'm going to look around. I'm not part of any ground crew."

"Endellion said you're with us for the meeting."

Me? For the meeting?

I understood why she'd wanted me in the meeting on Capital Station—I was the enforcer that busted the chem ring, after all—but why did she want me now? The question lingered without Quinn picking up on it. She motioned me over with a wave of her hand, and then headed for the overseer's administration office.

Although I was curious, I kept the questions to myself. I jogged to meet her, and then stepped into the office. It was like a building, considering the faux sky "outside." The administration office was nearly identical to the one on Capital Station. Cold. Unfeeling. Lacking color.

Endellion and Lysander waited for our arrival, both dressed in their enviro-suits with their helmets back. Federation soldiers lined the walls, standing at attention while Midway Station workers buzzed around their computer terminals. I didn't even have a second to greet Endellion before a hush fell over the room, quieting the workers. The soldiers stood a little taller, and a man entered from the far door, his enviro-suit decorated like Endellion's.

"Ah," Endellion said with a forced smile. "Commodore Cho. It's a pleasure to see you again."

The commodore—flanked by eight soldiers—strode up to Endellion and stopped with military precision.

"Commodore Voight," he said. "I'm surprised you have the gall to show your face here in person. I've got half a mind to call for your arrest."

"I suppose your arrest warrant would need to detail your attempt to inhibit a fellow commodore from carrying out the request of a Vectin minister," Endellion replied, cold and confident.

"We are not equals in authority."

"Our titles say otherwise."

"I have dedicated my life to the Federation and the HSN Corps. I was trained in a military academy. I command a squadron of warships. When you disregard my command, it is an act of insubordination. Even an enforcer mercenary—like yourself—should understand that my assessment of any given situation trumps your own."

"Is this how you always conduct a dressing-down of your fellow officers?" Endellion asked without a hint of irritation in her voice. "In front of your soldiers and a collection of station workers?"

"Would you rather the audience of Minister Ontwenty?"

"Is she here?"

"Yes. She's collecting all relevant data from the back and—"

"Very well," Endellion interjected. "We can continue this discussion in her presence."

She stepped around the commodore, her intense gaze set for the depths of the administration offices. Lysander and Quinn hurried after, and I jumped to their side, but only after a quick glance around. Sawyer wasn't here, and it bothered me. She had been quieter than usual the last few days.

The station workers cowered behind their terminals as we walked by. The soldiers, on the other hand, gave Commodore Cho concerned glances, almost like they were expecting an order, perhaps to stop Endellion. He never issued it.

We walked straight to the door. Endellion tapped at the computer terminal, and it opened, allowing us access to a long hall.

Commodore Cho and his personal soldiers followed behind us. I glanced back to catch a tight smirk across the commodore's stern face. The guy reminded me of Lysander in all the worst ways. He was the type of guy I would have loved to punch in the face. I was sure he was eager to see Endellion reprimanded.

Once we reached the end of the hall, Endellion opened the last door and strode through. I caught my breath as I entered, my attention drawn to an individual unlike anyone I had ever seen before.

A superhuman. I would have bet my life on it.

The superhuman woman stood taller than everyone else in the room, a good 30 centimeters taller than myself, with a physique so perfect, slender, and lithe that I could hardly believe she wasn't some sort of fantastical hologram. She turned to face us, and the slight movement had an elegance that shouldn't have even been possible —given the minimal effort—but I could tell the woman had an almost supernatural control over her muscles.

Unlike me, Endellion, Commodore Cho, and the rest of us, the woman wore an enviro-suit with a fine layer of metal chips, each linked together to allow for free movement. Some chips—scales, really—blinked with an inner pulse of light, betraying the tech woven within.

And her skin had a gradient effect, lighter on the front of her throat, gradually darkening on the side, and bronze across her face, up to her long, white hair. Black dots lined the side of her neck, and I couldn't help but think of pictures of animals I'd learned about when I was younger.

I had to stare up to get a good look at her face. She glanced between us for a few seconds, her expression changing from curious to neutral, as though she had come to a conclusion.

"Minister Ontwenty," Commodore Cho said.

He stepped forward and bowed his head.

Next to Ontwenty, he looked like a child. He was already a few centimeters shorter than Endellion and I, but it was laughable when compared to the minister.

"I dismissed you, Commodore Cho," Minister Ontwenty said, her voice lyrical and velvet to the ears. "Or have you brought me the captain of the *Star Marque*?"

"I am Commodore Voight," Endellion said, before Cho could interject.

"Welcome, Commodore. I am the Minister of Medical Research for Vectin-14. You may address me as Minister Ontwenty."

"Of course, Minister Ontwenty." Endellion stepped forward and bowed her head in a similar fashion to Cho.

Lysander and Quinn—as though snapped from a daze—followed Endellion's example. I was the last to pay my respects, and Ontwenty gave me an odd glance, her eyes shifting over me as I offered my bow.

"Thank you for seeing me," Endellion said. "I have disturbing news."

"Oh? Explain."

"A copy was made of your research."

I gritted my teeth at the mere mention of the copied data. Why would Endellion tell her that? Was she turning herself in?

Endellion continued, "My chief cyber operations officer discovered the copy transfer data around the time we engaged with the rebellion cruisers. No doubt they considered themselves close enough to risk a transmission to an ally vessel within the sector. While I've retrieved the genetic samples, your physical research, and the original data, I'm not certain I was in time to prevent a full transmission."

Was that true? Had the rebellion agents made a copy? Or was she referring to our own?

Commodore Cho cast a long glower in Endellion's direction, a bulging vein in his neck betraying his building ire and blood pressure.

"I would have gone after the corsairs faster," Endellion said, "but the route was under lockdown from the *Relentless Nova.*"

"I was following Vectin Fleet procedure," Commodore Cho said. "The corsairs were in my section of space, and I had two frigates under my command, as I already informed you."

Minister Ontwenty pivoted and walked back to a computer terminal. It was only then I removed my attention from the super-human and glanced around the room. Her guards—armed with plasma rifles—were dressed in the same high-tech enviro-suit she wore. And the guards… they were bulky and tall, not as tall as she was, but my height.

Like they, too, were genetically modified. They had to be.

Mara and Sawyer's comments rang in my ears. They'd talked about how superhumans made people for specific purposes—perfect bodyguards or engineers. It got my skin crawling. Like all these people were nothing more than flesh robots, programmed as if they were a computer designed for one task, and one task only.

"We appoint enforcers to carry out our arrest warrants," Minister Ontwenty said, "and to fill in the gaps of law enforcement for stations and colonies with an ever-increasing population of Homo sapiens. They act outside the Federation military and aren't tied to the rigors and standards set by our navy."

Commodore Cho held up a hand. "B-But she holds the title of commodore!"

"Commodore Voight continues her duties as an enforcer captain first. It was improper to hold the enforcers back for as long as you did, and I will send word of this to Rear Admiral Lone. My research is of the highest value."

As if trying to save face, Commodore Cho forced a tight smile. "I see. Perhaps I can make this right by shipping your research through the Federation Navy channels, rather than through untrust-worthy cargo ships."

I didn't know whether Commodore Cho was attempting to anger the minister or if he'd just gotten lucky, but the woman turned her full attention to him, her long, white hair flowing with the movement.

Before Minister Ontwenty could speak, Endellion took a step forward. "Allow me. The *Star Marque* will be responsible for your shipment."

"You?" the minister asked with a smile. "I've read Felseven's reports."

Endellion hesitated, but only for a second. "I'm aware he voted to have my petition to govern removed from consideration, but my quality work record still stands."

"Felseven praised you at every turn, and then spoke about your dubious methods to achieve your goals. I believe he described you as 'overreaching and ambitious,' likening you to 'an eager dog awaiting a treat.'"

"Felseven has a way with words."

The minister let out a single laugh and brushed her hair back, revealing more of her skin. More black dots—smaller than a fingernail—lined both sides of her neck and disappeared beneath the edge of her suit. There were even some behind her ear. What were they? Decoration?

"Commodore Cho can deliver my medical research," Minister Ontwenty said, "but I want the *Star Marque* to serve me here on Midway Station. We'll see if you're everything Felseven says you are."

THIRTEEN

Sapiens

I placed my hand on the space elevator door.

Midway Station was attached to Vectin-14 through the elevator—the gigantic transport stayed taut through the use of counterweights and centrifugal force. Cargo and manpower were taken from the surface to the station every couple of hours. That was all it took to experience the surface of a planet—a couple of hours.

And I had already been standing there, like a schmoe, for over an hour. The denizens of Midway Station gave me fleeting glances as they went by, and a couple repeat vendors offered me suspicious glares. Everyone had a purpose as they shuffled by. I was the only idiot gawking at the infrastructure.

Endellion and the minister wanted time to themselves. While everyone else returned to the *Star Marque* to prep for work on the station, I stayed to contemplate a myriad of possibilities. Life was so different than before, back when pit fights were common and I had no one to watch my six. I was going somewhere—becoming *someone* —and not just living life as a parasite on the belly of society.

I liked it.

Someone stepped up next to me, and their shadow blanketed

the area. I tensed and turned around, surprised to see a second superhuman, this one male. They were so... tall. Not gigantic, but lithe. His suit—just as high-tech and scaled as Ontwenty's—shimmered in the light, like oil on the surface of water. A second thing for me to gawk at.

He gave me a sidelong glance. "Step aside."

On instinct, I wanted to defy him. He didn't own the damn space station.

He was flanked on either side by men in similar enviro-suits—men like me, likely modified humans. But I wasn't intimidated.

The superhuman must have sensed my insubordination because he cracked half a smile. "The space elevator can be dangerous if not operated properly. Step aside, *sapiens*. For your own sake."

I almost laughed. "Is that some sort of slur?" I asked as the man tapped at the lift terminal. "You should be a little more creative. Calling me a 'sapien' is hardly an insult."

"*Sapiens*," he corrected, his voice a smooth baritone. "With an *S*. It's origin-world Latin for *wise*. And if you embodied the virtue, you would return to your own business."

"I'm admiring the scenery. I'll stand wherever I damn well please."

The superhuman gestured to our steel-on-steel alloy surroundings. "Simple minds are entertained by simple things, I suppose."

"Now you're just being an asshole."

"I've done nothing but state facts. If you have a contention with reality, I suggest alcoholism. Your kind has a knack for delusion."

Who the fuck did he think he was? I balled my hands into fists, tense and ready to fight, despite our size difference. The superhuman laughed, his short, white hair catching the light like some strands were aluminum, glittering with a metallic edge.

They said superhumans were superior to humans in every way —not swayed by their emotions, better at keeping control than humans were—but I was coming to realize some tales were mere propaganda. This guy reminded me of a few sad sacks on Capital Station, with all the personality of a douchebag and half the charm.

The lift door opened, but the superhuman didn't enter. Instead, he shifted his gaze to something past me and smiled. "Speaking of delusion…"

"Clevon."

I knew who it was even before I turned around. Endellion was the only one who called me Clevon.

"Good afternoon, Commodore Voight," the superhuman said. "Here for the ceremonies?"

Endellion walked to my side and offered a quick bow of her head. "Good day, Minister Felseven. I just returned from serving your uncle on Capital Station."

Two Felsevens? Could the universe handle that much insufferable?

"I heard of your work," Minster Felseven said. "My uncle sends me messages through the relays on a frequent basis."

"You must be the one who informed him of my petition."

"Someone had to warn him before you could get your cyborg claws into his business."

The silence that followed added a new level of tension. That Minister Felseven jackass was just as bad as the Governor Felseven who ran Capital Station and Galvis-4.

"Is there really such harm in allowing a human to govern for a single term?" Endellion asked. "Twenty years and the seat will be open again for voting."

"We have standards," Felseven replied. "Lowering them for the likes of you only invites a similar situation in the future."

"I don't require a handicap, Minister. I've passed all the mental and physical examinations many times over, and I qualify for the position, according to the minimum standards set for military personnel."

"The vote on your petition won't happen for another year. That's plenty of time to change the requirements for the position. You may think you're playing the game, Commodore, but I don't appreciate your blatant power-grab or your tendencies to find every loophole in our system. There are others far more suited to the position of governing than the likes of an enforcer captain."

Endellion forced a smile. "Have some perspective, Minister.

There are 102 planets within the Vectin Quadrant that require governors. One garden zone planet for one term is nothing more than the blink of an eye for superhumans. Perhaps your efforts would be better placed elsewhere."

Minister Felseven stepped up to the open lift. I backed away—not wanting to cause Endellion trouble—but Endellion didn't move, despite their close proximity.

"Careful," Felseven said under his breath as he walked by. "My suit is worth more than your life. How's that for perspective?"

Felseven and his bodyguards entered the lift and the doors closed, leaving Endellion and me with a cold farewell.

I let out a forced exhale and crossed my arms. I wasn't sure how I should have reacted to the conversation. Fighting the guy was out of the picture, and Endellion was playing with politics I didn't entirely understand. I understood the general picture—Homo superior didn't want Homo sapiens in the upper level of politics. And it sounded like the whole Felseven clan had it out for Endellion. Or perhaps humans in general.

Endellion said nothing. She didn't even look at me. Her eyes were filled with a pensive melancholy, and it was unlike anything I had seen from her before. But it was over before I could comment. She took a breath and returned to her composed self without a hint of hesitation.

"How'd your meeting with Minister Ontwenty go?" I asked.

"Minister Ontwenty is excited to have the *Star Marque* working for her directly."

"She's not worried about your dubious record?"

"It was because of my record that she was enthusiastic."

I couldn't help but chuckle. Minister Ontwenty wanted Endellion because she had questionable methods for getting shit done. That improved the chances that work on Midway Station would be interesting. What could a Minister of Medical Research want with a group of enforcers, anyway?

Endellion faced me with a new intensity as she panned her gaze from my head to my toes. The way she looked at me always made me nervous, but I smiled and let it slide from my thoughts.

"You got something you want to say?" I asked.

"Yes," she said. "I brought you aboard the *Star Marque* because I needed a pilot."

"Yeah, you said as much."

"But I also want someone I can rely on. Someone to help with tasks no one else can do. A confidant."

"Oh, yeah?"

"I wanted to wait until later, but I'm running out of time. You're the only one with the talents I need, and you're the only one who will understand what I'm going through."

I glanced around. Lysander and Quinn were nowhere to be seen. It was just Endellion and me, standing around the space elevator while groups of workers and merchants went about their business.

"What're you talking about?" I asked.

"Greatness competes with greatness, and I need someone to help me compete."

"With the superhumans?" Or maybe she just wanted to get back at Felseven. "You want to be the Minister of Medical Research now or something? I can't really help you with that. Not unless you want to know which chems work as the best painkillers."

To my surprise—shock, really—Endellion took my elbow and led me away from the space elevator. I glanced over to her, confused, but said nothing. Endellion returned my bemused expression with a look of confidence and amusement. I would have said she was having a laugh at my expense, but Endellion wasn't like that.

"I need a doctor for the *Star Marque*," she said.

"Look, I'm amazing, but I'm no doctor, no matter how many compliments you pass my way."

"While it's amusing to imagine your brash bedside manner, that's not what I meant. I spoke with Minister Ontwenty about a new and undiscovered talent in the medical field. Someone I think would be perfect for the *Star Marque*."

Endellion led me to a door, typed something into the computer screen next to the lock, and waited. After a few seconds, the door slid open, and we continued on our strange trek. We passed through a few security arches with x-rays and cybernetic detection before exiting out another door and entering a wonderland of plants and water.

I stopped dead in my tracks to take in the sight.

It was a garden. Lush green leaves and bright, yellow flowers contrasted in amazing ways, growing out of controlled beds. A wall of wondrous aromas hit me as I walked to the first fern in sight and marveled at its size. We didn't have plants like that on Capital Station. The most we had were bio-farms, and they were filled with the low-light mosses used in nutrient paste.

I had only seen plants like this in informative documentaries or entertainment vids.

I was half-tempted to rip off my enviro-suit so I could touch the leaves with my bare hands. Why didn't these damn suits have removable gloves? I opted instead to graze the tips of the leaves, worried I might damage something if I touched them too hard. The plants must have been delicate, what with their thin petals and tiny stems.

It wasn't hard to see Endellion was fascinated by my reaction—smirking the entire time while I marveled at my surroundings—but I couldn't help myself. When I glanced up and saw the beauty of Vectin-14 through the transparent aluminum skylight, it really was like standing planetside—or so, I'd imagined.

"Glad you joined the *Star Marque*?" Endellion asked.

"Yeah," I murmured. "Real glad."

"And this is only the beginning. In a couple of days, I'll be traveling down to Vectin-14 to meet with Ontwenty and the other ministers."

I turned to face her, but my thoughts lingered on my breath. The air, so fresh and wonderful, was distracting. "You're going down to the planet?"

"That's right."

"Take me with you."

"Of course."

"Really?" I asked. I half-expected her to make it contingent on something. Or maybe I still thought she was fucking with me. "Will the whole crew go?"

"They'll have the option, if they want. My crew means a great deal to me, and I'd like to show them I haven't forgotten my promise. Besides, I would hate to deny you something you've been waiting for your whole life. Your mother was from Vectin-14, after all."

I glanced back at the plants, my chest tight with eager anticipation. I had never felt that kind of excitement outside the arms of another, and I wondered how I would feel once I actually had my feet on the ground.

Endellion let out a long sigh. "I really do need someone I can trust at my side."

"Don't you have Lysander? Quinn? Sawyer?"

"Lysander is the type to adhere to the rules and can be rather judgmental, to his own detriment."

"Heh. You can say that again."

"And Quinn is responsible for my starfighters."

I nodded. "You're saying she doesn't have time."

"Sawyer is the backbone of my operation, and I wouldn't want to distract her."

Sawyer worked harder than anyone else I knew. Fueled by her love for Endellion, I supposed, but that meant she was in the same boat as Quinn.

"But none of them have my drive," Endellion said.

I lifted an eyebrow and turned my attention to her. "Your 'drive,' huh?"

"No. They don't understand that sometimes you have to risk everything. I saw you were different when I heard you'd entered the battle royale, forsaking everything you had to leave the station. It's what I admire about you. What I want from you."

All mirth was gone. Endellion had the same seriousness about her that I'd seen the first day we met. Cold. Precise.

"What do you want?" I asked in a gruff tone. I didn't like to fuck around, and it felt like she was holding something back.

"Some of my methods are unscrupulous," she said without hesitation or shame. "But I always keep the greater goal in mind."

"Unscrupulous? Like how you betrayed those rebellion scumbags?"

"Yes. Exactly like that."

"You do this all the time, I take it."

"Only when needed. Maintaining a professional reputation within the Federation is important, especially with ministers like Felseven breathing down my neck. I can't jeopardize that by playing fast and loose with everything. That being said, when I do need something done fast and loose, I want someone who can keep up. Am I making myself clear?"

It was all starting to come together.

Sawyer's statements. Endellion's actions on the cargo ship. The way she'd betrayed the rebellion. Even how she'd sent me to find those chem dealers on Dock Seven. The list probably went on and on, even if I wasn't aware of it all. But still, she had done right by her crew. They were taken care of—better than they'd been before—and someday, they would have a prize most people would never know. Living planetside would make for a great retirement.

"What do you want me to do?" I asked.

I wasn't above unscrupulous. I had done a lot worse, though I had morals I wouldn't compromise. Besides, it wasn't like the superhumans were playing fair—they made all the rules, rewrote them on a whim. They had all the advantages, and all the human military assholes wanted Endellion out of the picture. Evening the odds wasn't such a crime. And Felseven could go fuck himself.

"I need a doctor," Endellion said.

"You said that. So, what? You're going to kidnap one?"

"Never. They would make for a poor physician if I couldn't trust them with a knife. I need a *willing* doctor. An *excellent* doctor. And I need you to be charming on command."

"Charming, huh? And here I thought you were going to ask me to kill someone for you."

"I try to avoid that when possible."

I laughed. Was she serious? She sounded serious. She sounded like a cold unfeeling computer, actually. Her eyes had that intensity that had attracted me to her in the first place, and I took a step closer to marvel at her unnatural green irises.

"That's it?" I asked. "Do you even understand the meaning of the word *unscrupulous*? This doesn't sound like a questionable job."

Endellion smiled, took my elbow, and led me deeper into the station greenhouse. She said nothing until we reached a garden bed filled with fat ferns, their leaves as thick as human fingers. Then she let me go.

"I want to see how you can handle yourself with assignments."

Always testing me. Always challenging me.

"Wait here," she said. "There's someone in the garden I want you to meet. I just have to find her."

The click of her enviro-suit boots was all I heard until she disappeared around a bush covered in purple flowers. The label on the garden box read: *Cloned Earth Specimen #356-a, Rhododendron.* I walked over and examined the flowers, fascinated by how they grew in clumps, four to five tiny flowers all blending together as one.

Why was everything grown planetside so beautiful?

When one of the flowers fell, I caught it and held it in the palm of my hand. Out of instinct, I covertly tucked the tiny bit of plant life into a pouch of my enviro-suit. A souvenir. Maybe I could examine it closer, once I returned to the *Star Marque*.

"What're you doing here?"

I straightened my posture and turned around. A cute woman in a white enviro-suit and a lab coat gave me a harsh frown. She was short—maybe 40 centimeters shorter than I was—and I stared down at her with a cocked eyebrow.

"You should be with the minister," she said. "Ontwenty left ten minutes ago."

"I think you're confusing me with someone else."

The woman pursed her lips and glared. "This isn't funny. Go, or I'll report you myself."

"I'm an enforcer with the *Star Marque*, ya kook. Back off."

"O-Oh. I'm so sorry. My mistake, it's just… you look so much like the minister's bodyguards. You're so… large."

I scratched my chin and offered her a shrug. "All us genetically-modified people look the same, is that what you're saying?"

She cracked half a smile. "Well, yes. Of course. That's the point." Then she focused her attention on the thin-leafed milkweed, seemingly ignoring me altogether. She knelt down and examined the base of the plants.

My thoughts went to a dark place. All the minister's guards couldn't be the same, right? That would be ridiculous. They must have had free will and individual personalities. Even twins had their own desires, for fuck's sake. But I didn't know anything for sure. I would speak to Sawyer about it. She seemed to know everything there was to know about genetically-modified people.

The woman removed a pair of scissors from her lab coat. She cut a leaf, severing it from the stem, and a milky fluid gushed out of the slice. Then she snipped off another leaf. And another. The white ooze dripped down the plant and into the box of fertilizer.

"Will the plant be okay?" I asked, half-tempted to stop her from mutilating it further.

The woman gave me an odd look before cutting another leaf. "Yes, of course."

"It doesn't feel anything, right?" The liquid substance reminded me of blood.

She chuckled. "Plants don't have the same nervous system as humans. Don't worry. The milkweed will regrow any lost leaves. I've done this plenty of times, but your concern is refreshing." The woman motioned me over with a wave of her hand. "Did you want to use the sealant on the cuts? It'll stop the latex from seeping out. That's the white fluid."

I walked over, took a knee, and glared at the tiny bottle she handed over. It had a nozzle, and the sides were soft. I applied a small amount of force—for me, anyway—and the sealant shot out the nozzle like a fountain.

"Point it at the plant," she said through her laughter. "Right here. Where I took the leaves." Then she grabbed my forearm and guided my hand like I was an infant—or maybe she just wanted to initiate physical contact.

I smiled and played along, sealing the holes in the plant and allowing her to lead the way. I hadn't had much luck with anyone on the *Star Marque*, and it was nice to know I hadn't completely lost my appeal. Plus, the woman had a gentleness about her that was inviting. Even her guidance was provided with a soft touch.

"Clevon."

I got tense and stood. The woman stood as well, her brow furrowed. Endellion waited on the path between plants, her arms crossed, but she offered a tight smile.

"Commodore Voight," the woman said, her voice barely above a whisper. "Good day."

She gathered her leaves and hustled off without even a second glance back. It got me curious, but I didn't ask. Endellion's reputation preceded her.

"I see you found Dr. Rhodes," Endellion said. "Perfect. I was going to bring her to you, but it's obvious she wants little to do with me."

Dr. Rhodes? Ah. I saw where this was going.

"You want me to be charming with her, is that it?" I asked.

"Yes."

I laughed at the thought. *That* was what Endellion wanted me for? She hadn't needed to make such a big deal out of it—I would have been her stud, free of charge.

"Tell no one I asked you to do this," Endellion said. "No one."

"It'll be our secret."

"Good. Then I'll arrange for you to meet her again."

FOURTEEN

Doctor

"There are only two ways someone can be appointed to govern a planet," Sawyer said over the comms. "The first path is by becoming a civil servant, but before you can hold an official position within the Federation government, you need to pass several aptitude, political, and bureaucracy tests. And while the bureaucracy test can be studied for, the political test isn't about knowledge or expertise, but about opinion and culture, meant to keep the Federation values uniform across the Vectin Quadrant."

"So, you have to say the right things to pass," I said as I stretched out inside my capsule. "Like it's a secret little club that keeps out anyone they don't like."

"I would say that's accurate. Only superhumans who have interned with other government officials ever seem to pass the political portion of the civil-service exams. That can't be a coincidence."

What a bunch of bullshit. I knew stuff like that had to be rigged from the start. People in power never wanted to share power—why would they?—and they would do anything to keep hardworking schlubs from taking a piece of the pie.

"What's the second way?" I asked.

"Military officers are allowed to petition for governorship.

Normally, you would enroll in an officer academy and rise through the ranks. But—just like the civil-service exams—officer academies are rigorous in their testing, and most applicants never pass. They test you on so much information that you basically have to come from wealth to afford all the study materials and time needed to get in."

Goddamn. No one wonder humans never got those positions. They had to be born into it.

I smiled. "But Endellion found a loophole."

"Yes. She discovered several instances of honorary titles awarded to enforcers who showed exemplary dedication to the Federation. Endellion knew the minimum requirement to petition for governorship was holding the title of commodore, so when Admiral Vanine needed specific tasks handled, Endellion volunteered every time, working tirelessly for his benefit."

"She did some suspect things." It wasn't a question. I could see the pattern, and now I knew why Endellion took such risks.

"She did engage in a few unlawful activities," Sawyer said in a slow tone. "But it paid off in the end. Admiral Vanine asked her to... do something for him... and she asked for the rank of commodore in return. He accepted, and the rest is history."

The darkness of my capsule had the warmth of a black hole. I tossed to the side and wrestled with unwanted thoughts. I should have gone to sleep a few hours ago, but the allure of Vectin-14—as well as the fate of the *Star Marque*—weighed heavy on my mind.

"Sawyer," I intoned. "I want to ask you a couple questions."

"Plot twist: that's what you've been doing this entire time."

I sat up and huffed out a laugh. "Personal questions. Face-to-face."

No response. I waited.

Nothing.

"Well?" I asked.

"Well, what?"

"Is that all right?"

Sawyer sighed. "I suppose you can meet me in my workroom."

177

I wanted to ask her to come down to my capsule, but I supposed that worked, too.

I flipped on the light, glared at my clothing, and opted instead to grab a sheet and wrap it around my waist. I wasn't going to be out long, and my deck was currently on its night cycle. It would be fine.

I hopped out of my capsule. The dim lighting blanketed the room and halls, and I crept out of the sleeping quarters—though no one could hear me in their capsules, even if I yelled. Once in the lift, I hit the button for Deck One and waited.

The lift stopped at Deck Two, and the door opened. Yuan glanced up to meet my gaze.

She cocked an eyebrow as she ambled into the lift, her leg as stiff as ever. Then she smiled and hit my stomach with the back of her hand. "Finally found someone to hook up with, huh?"

"I wish," I said with a groan. "I'm heading over to see Sawyer."

The lift door closed, and we continued.

"Sawyer's odd," Yuan said. "Sticks to herself." Again, Yuan gave me the once-over. "I'm surprised a guy like you hasn't had any luck. I hear lots of people lamenting their cold bed while drowning in brandy."

"Yeah, I should take a break from training." I gave her a sideways glance. "How'd you and Mara meet, anyway? Fish for her at a bar?"

"I met her during one of my patrols. I was the enforcer on duty, and someone came screaming about a suicide attempt. I had to rip the laser pistol out of Mara's hand."

Fuck. Mara had attempted to kill herself? Fun-loving, happy-go-lucky Mara?

Yuan must have seen my surprise because she shook her head. "That was a long time ago. Endellion helped her. She got Mara a cybernetic implant that regulates her chemical imbalances. I really owe Endellion, ya know? Mara's all better now."

Chemical imbalances, huh? Seemed odd, but I wasn't a doctor.

"Good to hear everything worked out."

The lift doors opened.

"Get out of here," Yuan said, "before people see me and you like this."

I exited into the well-lit hallway of Deck One. Once the lift door closed, I shuffled toward the Central Communications and IT Logistics room. Sawyer was always there, doing something or another with the code and the core of the ship. Endellion must have had a lot of demands. She really needed to fill those other officer positions so that Sawyer could get some free time.

"What are you doing?"

The shock and indignation told me who'd spoken long before I turned around. Lysander had a stick so far up his ass, I swear it had changed his vocal chords.

I regretted not putting on proper clothes. Anything to save me from having to interact with the man.

"I'm going to see Sawyer," I said as I tilted my head to the side to get a better look at him.

His arms were crossed and his face flushed. I couldn't tell whether he was enraged or embarrassed. Probably a mixture of both.

"This is the officer's deck," Lysander said through clenched teeth. "And you're walking around like it's your personal bathroom. Have you no respect for anything?"

Oh, here we go.

"The other enforcers take note of you, Demarco! They're going to mimic your attitude and demeanor. You need to set a proper example."

"Nobody looks to me for jack shit," I said, rolling my eyes. "Save that speech for a role model."

"You're one of the *Star Marque*'s starfighters. It's because of you and Endellion that we defeated those light cruisers and saved the cargo vessel with such ease. And to add to your limelight, Endellion herself asked you to accompany her on a personal mission. Of course the other enforcers are going to idolize you!" Lysander motioned to me with both arms, his pent-up energy boiling over. "You don't live in a sweaty bag of garbage anymore! You can damn well dress and act with the newfound respect your station deserves."

I opened my mouth to retort, but I stopped before I said anything. A piece of me could sense his jealousy—Endellion had taken me on some assignment he knew nothing about—but another piece of me felt the sting of his words. I hadn't considered what the enforcers thought of me. Or how my actions could or couldn't reflect on Endellion. And she had been trying so fucking hard, in every sense of the word.

"You're right," I said with an exhale.

"I know I'm right," Lysander snapped.

Clearly, the words hadn't sunk in.

He took a moment to smooth his crewcut hair. Then he said, "I know you haven't had any official training, and I know this isn't a proper military vessel, but even a sliver of common sense should have told you this was unacceptable."

"I already said you were right. What else do you want? Thirty lashes?"

"I want you to get your shit together."

"All right. I'll get it together."

Lysander glared. "Don't play games with me. Just because you—"

"I'm serious," I stated, cutting him off before he went into a full-blown tirade. "You're right. I hadn't thought about my actions. I'll do better in the future."

He stared at me for a long moment. His eyebrows twitched. He started to say something, and then stopped. I would have killed to read minds, but instead, I could only speculate. Had he wanted to reprimand me? Or did he struggle with my admission that he was right?

Lysander threw up a hand in frustration. "Good. Don't let this happen again."

He stepped around me, but I reached out and took his arm. He whirled back around, tense.

"I've got a busy schedule," I said. "But maybe, if you've got room for me, I'll come by and go through the motions of your daily training."

Again, the quiet that fell between us lasted longer than I would have liked.

"I'll always have room," Lysander finally said. "And I think my training would do you good."

"Your brother said you were one of the best in the HSN Corps."

"He told you about that?"

"Is it true or not?"

"Well, I wasn't put in a Hall of Fame, if that's what you're asking, but I was praised for my instructional abilities on several occasions."

"Really? With your attitude?" I quipped.

Lysander ripped his arm from my grasp. "You're impossible. This kind of mockery wouldn't be allowed in the Corps. They knew how to respect their superior officers."

"I'm just getting my last kicks in before you beat it out of everyone, Officer Killjoy." I couldn't help myself. Fucking with him was too easy.

To my surprise, Lysander half-laughed. "There's a time and place for everything. We've been hired by the Minister of Medical Research, so now isn't the time to be unprofessional." He turned away and headed for the lift. "Keep that in mind, Demarco. And I look forward to seeing you in basic training."

I already had too much shit to do, but I supposed I could squeeze in a few sessions with Lysander and the ground enforcers. Well, as long as Endellion didn't have much for me.

With my path clear, I headed straight for Sawyer's workroom. I didn't even bother announcing my arrival—I just walked in and shut the door behind me.

Sawyer, seated at her computer terminal, turned her attention to me the moment I took a step into the room. Blub floated around my head, paddling the air and staring at me with giant fish eyes. I waved him away and walked to Sawyer's main work desk. Each screen mounted to the bulkhead appeared to have a different section of the ship on display.

"You wanted to ask me questions?" she asked as she typed away on a proper keyboard.

"Yeah, I did, but I'm not in the mood anymore."

"Have a headache?"

I cracked a smile. I loved her sense of humor. She got me, and I think I was one of the few people who got her, if Yuan's perspective was shared by the crew. She wasn't hideous or anything, quite the opposite. Cute. Unique. Why did she lock herself away in the workroom?

"Have you ever thought about us as a quaint little monogamous pairing?" I asked. "We'd make a great team, and we both know you're into me."

The red of her face matched her fiery hair. She pulled her knees up to her chest and pursed her lips. "I *have* seen you naked more than acquaintances should."

"I've heard worse excuses for getting together."

"But I can't," she said, terse. "I just… can't."

I said nothing. I'd heard worse excuses for staying apart, too. Why did she keep me at arm's length?

Damn. Maybe I came on too strong.

"But I'd like it if you stayed and chatted for a bit," she said without glancing in my direction. "Conversations with you are the highlight of my day."

Perfect. Mixed signals. We must have been a platonic thing. She wanted my company, but she didn't want *me*. Maybe she only wanted women—or maybe, she had a fetish, and I didn't tick the box—but whatever the reason, it was clear that physical interaction would not be part of the package.

While disappointing, I still enjoyed our musings. I'd rather be frustrated and talk to her than nothing at all.

I leaned against the bulkhead and slid down into a sitting position. "I wasn't sleeping well, anyway."

Blub circled close, and after a quiet *toot, toot, toot,* he sailed down to my head. His fish mouth opened and closed on my close-shaven hair, like he was nibbling me with the force of a tickle.

I wanted to ask Sawyer about genetic modification, but maybe I didn't really want to know. The more I heard and saw, the more goddamn questions I had, and at a certain point I stopped caring about existential bullshit. Instead, I stroked Blub and smiled when he shook his fins. "Tell me about your work, Sawyer."

She gave me half a smile. "Really? I thought you didn't like it when I talked too much about the specifics."

"I've got time to kill, and you've got a nice voice."

Sawyer laughed. "Admit it. You just want something that'll put you to sleep."

Damn. She knew me too well.

I NEVER GOT TIRED of seeing Vectin-14 through the clear, metal alloy on Midway Station.

The colors invigorated me, even though walking around the station could be a chore. Apparently, Midway Station was separated by decks. The top deck—the deck with the view—was reserved for government workers and high-rolling merchants. The lower decks were for the squalor. Humans. Defects. Deformed. The lower you get, the worse it became. They worked as maintenance crew for the elevator, or dockhands for loading and unloading, and their situation reminded me of Capital Station.

There was always a hierarchy. Someone was always going to be on top, and someone—a lot of someones—were going to populate the bottom.

I never got to experience the top until I joined Endellion. Now I was seeing a world I had only ever dreamed of. Two days on Midway Station and already I couldn't wait to move on to greater things. I wanted to see and do more than ever before.

The dock door opened with a hiss, and Endellion stepped off the *Star Marque*.

She was different in casual clothing—more human and less unapproachable perfection—even though she retained her poise. There was something about her I couldn't articulate. Like she was always in control of herself; every detail down to the wrinkle in her cargo pants had been planned out months in advance. The only time I had seen her flustered was with that stupid cut on her shoulder.

I couldn't even see traces of the wound anymore. And a tank top suited her. Her muscled arms shouldn't have been hidden under the sleeves of an enviro-suit. The PAD on her left arm shined when hit by the light.

Endellion lifted an eyebrow.

"You're striking," I said with a smile.

"Keep that level of engagement with Dr. Rhodes this afternoon, won't you?" Not even fazed by my comment.

Endellion walked toward the elevator, and I kept to her side. My casual clothing felt odd, now that I had gotten used to the jumpsuit-and-enviro-suit combo. I did like the ease of casual clothing, however.

"Are you so machine you don't feel the heat between your legs anymore?" I asked.

"I love your candid manner of speech, Clevon," she replied, smiling. "Always cutting to the heart of the issue, regardless of tact."

"You've only got so much space inside your body. I've seen cyborgs choose between having feeling in their left foot or being able to punch a guy like they have a rocket in their fist. And I haven't heard of you taking anyone to bed."

Endellion pulled a pair of gloves from her pants pocket. "I use only the latest in cybernetic technology. The kind reserved for super-humans. I refuse to tell them—any of them—that I had to lessen myself to reach their level." She jammed a hand into one glove, and then did the same with the other, covering her PAD so forcefully that I worried she would rip her clothing.

"You need to loosen up," I said.

She gave me a sidelong glance, and the harshness drained from her mannerisms. "Is that right?"

"I know plenty of methods. They'll take the tension right out of you."

"Do try to have more etiquette with Dr. Rhodes," Endellion said. "And if she mentions people are taking advantage of her, play that up. She's had a bad record with individuals who were only out for themselves."

We reached the lift, and Endellion opened the door. The lift had two rings: The outer ring was used for going between decks; while the inner ring—the larger of the two—was meant for going straight to the space elevator. Endellion entered the outer ring, and I joined her. She hit a button to take us up. We were already on the top deck, but apparently there were special lounges located near the clear ceiling, reserved for VIP personnel. I hadn't known she had access. I hadn't even known we would be going there.

"Anything you want to tell me about Dr. Rhodes?" I asked.

"The less you know about her, the better. Lastly, try to keep in a public area. The more people who see you, the easier it'll be for me to use it."

Public area, huh?

"What about things like politics?" I asked. "Disagreeing is a good way to turn people off."

"Do you know anything about the specifics of politics? Or even have an opinion on legislation?"

"Well, no."

"Then what's the problem? Agree with Dr. Rhodes on any given conversation you know nothing about." Endellion narrowed her eyes. "Don't second-guess yourself, Clevon. Sawyer tells me you're quite engaging and skilled at repartee."

"She said that? About me? What else did she say?"

"She assured me the two of you weren't intimate."

Well, that hadn't been what I wanted to hear. And somewhat awkward to bring up in a conversation. Unless Endellion had been asking Sawyer about it?

The lift door opened, revealing a cocktail lounge in whites and silvers. The whole place had the feel of an entertainment vid, too glitzy for anything in real life. People walked around in clothing I had never seen in person before. Dresses, military suits with pants and belts, and shiny, black shoes. They were so foreign, they almost looked like costumes.

"I think we got off at the wrong stop," I said as I motioned to our outfits.

Endellion walked into the cocktail lounge with a smile. "It's important you and I look the part of an enforcer crew." She motioned to the bar. "Have fun with Dr. Rhodes."

"Am I seducing her? Or am I—"

"I said, be charming. Whatever comes of it is fine, but seduction isn't a requirement. The only requirement is that others see you together."

Before I could ask any more questions, Endellion smiled to a nearby couple and joined them. They struck up a conversation, but I wasn't the type to schmooze with random, fancy jackasses in parade suits. I focused my attention on the bar. I liked drinking, and it appeared Dr. Rhodes had already started without me.

The lounge was sparsely populated, and it was easy to avoid the others as I sauntered over to the bar. Dr. Rhodes was the sole patron, sitting on a barstool, her attention on the room. Her white enviro-suit hugged her body to reveal every curve. She was young— I guessed early twenties—and she stared up at me with a youthful expression when I took a seat next to her.

"Oh," Dr. Rhodes said. "You're the man from the other day. Commodore Voight's bodyguard."

I was on the verge of correcting her, but I decided against it. "And you're Dr. Rhodes. You can call me Demarco."

She held her rum pouch close as she glanced around the lounge. Her gaze stopped on Endellion, who took to engaging in conversations on the opposite end of the room. Dr. Rhodes stared, and I could tell from her stiff posture she was on the verge of leaving.

The bartender showed up, and I motioned to Dr. Rhodes's drink. The guy produced another rum pouch, and I cracked it open right away. Alcohol made conversation easier for everyone.

After a sip, I said, "I didn't know people actually dressed like this. Looks like it's hard to move in those outfits. Not practical."

"They're waiting for the elevator down to the planet. It's less than half an hour before it arrives, and then they'll be participating in political ceremonies. Dress like that is required."

"Have you been down to Vectin-14?"

"Oh, yes. Many times."

I knew Endellion wanted me to focus on the doctor, but I couldn't help myself. "What's it like? Amazing? I imagine it's unlike anything else."

Dr. Rhodes faced me with a smile. "You were fascinated by the plants, weren't you?"

"I've never been planetside, and Capital Station doesn't have any greenhouse gardens."

"Surely the station showed regular educational vids on plant life."

I laughed aloud but settled down quick. "You haven't met the people on Capital Station. That's not the kind of vid they'd tune in to."

Dr. Rhodes swiveled on her stool until she fully faced me. "I'm curious, then. How was it? Seeing plant life for the first time in your life? Describe the experience."

"In a single word, fan-fucking-tastic. I wish I had touched them with the skin of my fingertips, but the scents and visuals were enough to sate me until I get planetside."

I leaned closer to her and smiled. She returned the look, and a piece of me wondered whether it was because I was an attractive guy, or because of her reaction to my pheromones. Not that pheromones replaced the need for banter and personality, but they were enough to shift someone's perception from neutral to favorable.

"The flowers were beautiful," I said. "But you're far more alluring than anything in the garden."

Dr. Rhodes stifled a laugh and looked away. "And here I thought you were being earnest with me."

"I'm being honest. Trust me—I never felt the urge to kiss one of the flowers."

"Okay, enough flattery. What do you want?"

"Want?" Damn. I must have been off my game if she knew I wanted something already. Then again, I wanted in her pants, and it wasn't like I was hiding that fact.

Dr. Rhodes placed her elbow on the bar and propped her hand on her palm. "I'm used to people coming to me for something. You don't have to play coy. What is it you want?"

"Well, you're a good-looking lady. That's probably why people approach you."

She rolled her eyes. "If you're going to deny it, I'm going to leave."

"Okay. I admit it. I want to flirt with you and see where it goes."

She didn't say anything for a moment, and I detected a low hum of music coming from behind the bar. It was a classy, slow-tempo piece, with sounds from instruments I didn't even know the names of.

Dr. Rhodes sat back and narrowed her eyes. "I suppose you aren't the usual type," she said. "You're not a scientist or a researcher, are you?"

"I research the best way to shoot people," I quipped. "Does that count?"

Dr. Rhodes lifted an eyebrow. "You don't know who I am?"

"You're Dr. Rhodes." I scratched my chin, trying to think back to our brief meeting. Even Endellion hadn't told me anything more. "That's all I got. Should I know who you are?"

"Do the names Simon and Marian Rhodes mean anything to you?"

"No."

"They were one of the families on the first mass transports." She stared at me for a second. "The mass transports were the ships that came from Earth."

"I know what they are," I said, holding back my sarcasm. "So, you're from an origin-world family?"

All those origin-world families had wealth and power. Even people on Capital Station knew it.

Technically we were all descended from origin-world humans, but those with strong inheritance and family ties kept their children from falling into the dregs like the rest of humanity. It was how Overseer Tobin Grank became the man who ran Capital Station in

Felseven's stead. And why some humans—like Commodore Cho—could afford to get into a military academy.

"My mother operates several laboratories for Minister Ontwenty," Dr. Rhodes said. "People approach me all the time to get to my mother. They want grants for their research, or they want sway within a university, or they want a career on Vectin-14. The list goes on. And trust me—they all flirt and say the nicest things. I've heard it all before."

"A lot of people taking advantage of you, huh?" I asked.

Endellion wanted me to mention it, and this was as good an opportunity as any.

Dr. Rhodes played with her rum pouch, moving it around the bar countertop with the tips of her fingers. "It's gotten to the point that a random bodyguard hitting on me at the bar is a highlight, actually." She let out a long sigh. "Thank you for confirming that I'm an individual, separate from my mother's estate."

I smiled. "Is that what you were doing here? Looking for a quick pick-up?"

"I was supposed to meet someone here," she said with a harsh bite to her words. "But *surprise, surprise*, after I introduced him to the researchers in my mother's labs, he's never around anymore. He's probably kissing the ass of every passerby with a title. Pardon my language."

I took a sip from my pouch and waved my hand in a circle, urging her to continue.

Dr. Rhodes shrugged. "I would say he misses four of every five outings. I understand he's busy, but aren't we all? I make sure my schedule is clear, yet he doesn't have the same respect for me?"

"Why even bother meeting with him?"

"He's intelligent. That's why we were introduced. He impresses everyone he meets, even though his formal education is questionable. Self-taught and a skilled apprentice, apparently. I'm always *impressed* when he talks to me about his work, but that's only *when* we're talking."

"I've known thugs who were more romantic."

"Right?" Dr. Rhodes forced a laugh, but it was clear to me the subject was depressing her. She stared at the rum pouch like she was going to drill a hole in it with her gaze. "Maybe I should be more understanding," she muttered.

"Or maybe,"—I reached out and took her hand—"you should be with someone who counts themselves lucky to be in your presence." When she didn't resist or object, I brought her hand closer and rubbed my thumb along her knuckles. "From where I'm sitting, I see a talented young woman with a degree and a future. Where's this sad sack you're waiting for? If he's so intelligent, he should know how to keep a schedule. It ought to be a crime to waste your time."

Dr. Rhodes stopped staring at her pouch and gave me a quick glance, a shade of pink across her cheeks and ears. Still, she didn't pull her hand away. Her heartbeat was hard enough for me to hear —maybe not for other humans, but I was a different story. I kissed the bridge of her fingers, and her heartbeat doubled. It excited her, and the reaction exhilarated me.

Damn. I loved flirting. Too bad Sawyer didn't want me. Nothing topped the rush of a first time.

Dr. Rhodes gave me an odd look, half confused. "You don't look like the romantic type."

I couldn't help myself. I shook my head. "I'm some enforcer on a random starship, devoid of etiquette. If I impress you with my wiles, your intelligent buddy has the personality of a hammer."

She laughed loud enough to break the quiet of the lounge, this time genuinely. It got me laughing, too, if only because we were bashing some asshole I had never even met.

But what I'd said was true. Dr. Rhodes had everything one could hope for in this quadrant of strife and suffering—a fancy life, a career that wasn't maintenance work, no genetic defects, and an inheritance of wealth. Someone risked their relationship with her to go suck metaphorical cock at a lab somewhere? He deserved a good mocking.

"I think you've made the choice easy for me," Dr. Rhodes said once her laughter died down. "I was going to give him another chance, but waiting for him has always been an embarrassment. And talking with you has given me a new perspective."

While she returned to staring at her rum pouch, I looked around the room. Although the other patrons were on the opposite side of the lounge, most stole glances in our direction. They pointed and muttered, and I wondered what they were so excited about.

"I take it you're going to cut ties with your friend?" I asked.

"It's overdue." When she returned her attention to me, all her depression seemed to have melted away. "How long will you be on Midway Station?"

"I'm not sure. Why?"

"I'd like to see you again. Perhaps away from prying eyes. I like that... you have no stake in all the old family drama. And I appreciate your practical advice."

I wasn't entirely sure what Endellion wanted me to do now. She'd sounded as though she wanted something big—like convincing Dr. Rhodes to go back to the *Star Marque* with me—but I got the feeling Dr. Rhodes just wanted time with someone who would treat her right. There wasn't really anything to keep her from leaving the *Star Marque*, once she'd had her fill.

Or perhaps Endellion had something else in mind.

"Sounds good," I said. "Maybe we can talk about your work in the garden, and I'll actually show up on time."

Her laughter made the conversation easy-going.

The other patrons in the lounge flocked to the lift. Dr. Rhodes slid off her stool, and while still holding my hand, she pulled me playfully close. I leaned forward, and she hesitated, like she didn't want to be the one to finish the motion, her warm breath on my chin. I wrapped my free hand around the back of her neck and guided her to me.

This was why I had missed being with women. Her lips were soft when I pressed mine against hers, and the gentle lap of her tongue excited me. I had been with enough men to know most liked it hard and rough—at least, the men on Capital Station had. Different than Dr. Rhodes. Pleasantly different.

When I broke away from her, I savored the taste of her lips. She had some sort of flavoring, something with a sugary aftertaste. That shit was addictive.

"Thank you for the company," she said as she headed for the lift.

I could already hear the murmurs from the peanut gallery. The crowd left together, however, resulting in a deserted lounge. Endellion and one other were the last patrons, and the soft music substituted for liveliness.

Endellion walked to my side. I leaned back against the bar and stretched.

"I like Dr. Rhodes," I said.

"And you did a good job. I would say your performance was nearly perfect."

"That's all you wanted? I think even Lysander could have pulled this off, and he's trying his damnedest to imitate a pile of rocks. Dr. Rhodes was craving company, I just happened to be the lucky guy sitting next to her." I was surprised one of the fancy jackasses hadn't tried. Then again, she was technically seeing someone. Perhaps I was the lout for hitting on her.

Endellion flipped her braid back. "Trust me when I say that Lysander wouldn't be suited for this line of work."

"Well, I'm glad I helped out. Not that this was strenuous. You can ask me to do this any time of the day."

"For now, I want you to stay close. When we get down to Vectin-14, you'll act as my personal bodyguard."

"Sure. That's what people think I am, anyway."

As long as I got to the planet's surface, I didn't care what I was doing.

FIFTEEN

Vectin-14

I had never ridden a space elevator.

I stood at the window made of transparent, aluminum alloy and watched the descent with rapt attention. According to Sawyer —who I just assumed knew something about everything—the ring-shaped elevator had four compartments. Three were for cargo, and one was for passengers. It cut the energy cost of life support and allowed the other three compartments to carry a total of 100,000 tons of material.

It still took three hours for the trip, but I wasn't complaining. I absorbed every second into my memory, like I would be tested on the event later.

The elevator shook as it entered Vectin-14's atmosphere. I didn't bother sitting, despite being told to before the trip. Instead, I kept my gaze glued to the view, my hand gripped to the safety rails. Once the shaking stopped and the elevator entered a thick layer of cloud cover, a robotic voice sounded over the speakers.

"Welcome to Vectin-14," it said. *"Vectin-14 is the capital planet for the Vectin Quadrant, one-fourth of the Cygnus Sector, and the first colony location for the mass transports over three centuries ago. The diligent workers of the mass transports spread from the Vectin System to the Galvis System, and then, finally,*

to the Romoni System, acquiring a total of 102 planets for the Vectin Quadrant, 11 of which sit in the garden zone around their respective stars.

"Vectin-14 was chosen to become the capital planet, thanks to the speed of its rotation, and the composition of its atmosphere, which allows for some cloned Earth vegetation to flourish. Because of this, research for the entire quadrant was conducted in the laboratories of Vectin-14, making it an important central point of progress. New technologies continue to flow from Vectin-14 to all Federation planets.

"Please enjoy your stay on Vectin-14," the computer concluded.

Well, now I felt like a tourist.

"What're you going to do with your piece of property once Endellion becomes governor?" Lee stood next to me, his gaze set on the clouds. I hadn't heard him approach, but I attributed that to the distractions.

I shrugged. "I don't know. At this point, it still feels like a dream."

"I know what *I'm* going to do."

"Oh?"

"Quinn and I are going to make the cutest damn babies you've ever seen. Tons of them."

I snorted back a laugh. "You're going to unleash a plague of children upon the land, is that it?"

"Once I'm dead, they're the system's problem." Lee leaned back and gave me a smile. "C'mon. You've got to have a goal. We're so close! I know you haven't been with us for as long as some of the others, but every day it seems like we're getting within spitting distance of living planetside. Nothing will stop Endellion. Mark my words."

I had a goal. I wanted to be like Endellion. Get a ship. Get a title. Have things I had never experienced. Ambitions beyond myself. I was about to set foot on a planet for the first time, and then my bucket list would be completely checked off. So I needed a new and better list.

Noah got up from his seat and walked over to me. Like Lee, he stared out into the clouds, transfixed. "What're you guys talking about?"

"Have you ever been planetside?" Lee asked.

"Never."

"Yeah, me neither. What're you going to do with your piece of land, huh?"

"I don't know. Probably live on it. See what it's like." Noah placed his hands on the railing and let out a long exhale.

I glanced around and counted about 100 of Endellion's crew among the passenger seats. They were easy to spot, considering their black enviro-suits. The other passengers wore jumpsuits or planetside clothes I still didn't consider to be real outfits.

Endellion, Yuan, and Quinn spoke in hushed voices by another window, their backs to the passengers. I stared for an unhealthy amount of time, no doubt looking like a creeper, but I couldn't help but wonder. Endellion always had something going on.

"Hey," I said, keeping my attention on Endellion. "Why didn't the whole crew join us on this little trip?"

"Most of the crew has admitted to high anxiety at the thought of open spaces," Sawyer answered, pulling me from my musing.

I turned around to see her and Lysander standing with me, Lee, and Noah. Since when had they gotten there? I needed to pay more attention.

"Anxiety about open spaces?" I asked.

"Yes. It's called agoraphobia. It's common among individuals born and raised in space stations and starships. Most have thoughts and nightmares about falling upwards, into the sky, especially given that they're accustomed to gravity malfunctions. That'll never happen on a planet, but the hallucinations can be so lifelike that it causes psychosis in a decent number of people."

"Is that why Advik didn't join us?" I asked with a huff.

"Yes."

"Tsk. I've had unsettling dreams about being planetside, but I stoned up."

"We'll see."

"What's that supposed to mean?"

Lysander crossed his arms and frowned. "You can't strong-arm a mental holdup. If you experience stress or unmanageable levels of anxiety, make sure to report it."

"You *can* strong-arm a mental holdup," Lee said with a laugh. "It's called 'alcohol.' Trust me. You'll break that mental holdup's will to live."

Lysander sneered. "You're proud of that answer?"

Lee slapped Lysander on the arm. "Alcohol bends reality over its knee and busts out the belt, let me tell you! I know you don't drink, but you should. Everyone would love to see you in the mess hall from time to time."

The elevator cleared the cloud layer, and I whipped my attention to the view. We were 4,000 meters above the ground, and the sight took my breath away—green plains, red foliage from the trees, purple fields, blue rivers, and an indigo sky beyond the clusters of clouds. Vectin-14 was a goddamn rainbow of life, and I placed my hand on the window to get some perspective.

And the Vectin star... it shone from on-high, casting pillars of light through the holes in the clouds. It was fucking beautiful.

Sawyer stood next to me and stared at the view with an indifferent expression written across her face.

"You ever been planetside?" I asked, breathless.

"I was born on Vectin-10 and lived there until I was in my teens."

"Is Vectin-10 anything like Vectin-14?"

"No. Vectin-10 is a lot hotter. They mine gases there, and it's... grittier than most places I've been."

I hit her shoulder with the back of my hand. "Not grittier than Capital Station."

Sawyer chuckled. "If Capital Station is a sweaty, diseased armpit, then Vectin-10 is an unwashed grundle. Both are places no man should go."

We shared a genuine laugh as the elevator got closer and closer to the ground. The speed decreased, allowing us a sparkling view of a controlled-irrigation river. The mass agriculture fields added a bit of order to the landscape with long, straight lines of food, a complete contrast to the chaotic nature of the forest in the distance.

Metal grating against metal screeched in the distance—odd, considering I had grown accustomed to the silence of space—but I knew the atmosphere allowed sound to travel. It was a new experience.

When the elevator connected with the ground, the industry of the area came into view. Warehouses. Roads. Shuttles. Mag-lev trains. Thousands of workers packing and unpacking goods to be shipped or loaded onto the elevator. Automated cranes and lifts made the work fast, but it was clear there was so much business that they didn't have a second's rest.

And they were dealing in all sorts of goods—food, weapons, medical supplies, and crates labeled with chemical warnings. Planets dealt in all sorts of resources, and it didn't surprise me to see so much trade.

The elevator shook. I grabbed the railings and waited until it locked into place. The passengers got up and headed for the decontamination room. Each passenger passed through it, getting scanned and sprayed with a cleansing gas. Anyone who failed the scan set by the Vectin-14 customs regulations was denied entry onto the planet.

I got in line and entered the decontamination room with Noah, Lysander, and Sawyer. Noah and Lysander gave each other nervous looks as the scan completed, and the gases washed over us. Vectin-14 didn't deny genetic defects, so both brothers were allowed planetside. Sawyer didn't seem surprised—if anything, she stood closer to me than before—and she was quiet. Well, quieter than usual.

When the door opened, the warmth of the sun washed over us. Sawyer cringed away, but I stepped into it, ready to experience raw light. I didn't even look at the workers as I walked straight from the elevator unloading zone to the grass beyond the gates.

I unfastened my enviro-suit and pulled at the collar until I got my arms out. I'd peeled the suit down to my waist by the time I reached the field. The sun—the wind!—against my skin delivered a shiver of excitement straight to my spine.

Goddamn.

I hit my knees and dragged my hands across the grass. The green blades scratched and tickled, but they were soft at the same time, and I loved the confusion of sensations. When I'd had my fill of the grass, I dug my fingers into the dirt and scooped up the brown-and-black soil. It had a distinct odor, and I inhaled deep to savor it.

This was what I'd wanted. I had it. It was all around me. Planet-side beauty beyond even my wildest imaginings.

Quinn's distinct laughter rang out behind me. "Are you going to kiss it, too?"

"I was thinking about rolling in it," I said. "Or should I buy it dinner first?"

"You've already gotten to second base. Why stop now?"

I glanced up at the indigo sky spotted with clouds. For a second, I got dizzy. The sky spanned forever. *Forever.* It was like looking out into the depths of space. I was so small. Then I turned my attention to the horizon. There were shades of mountains in the distance— tops coated in snow—and hills that rolled until they disappeared.

It was insane how much something changed when I got close to it. The planet was amazing from space, wondrous on the elevator, and now that I was on the surface, I was certain no one person could ever experience it all. It was that vast. It was that amazing.

Mara bounded up to me and Quinn, a smile plastered across her face. "Look at you! I didn't believe Yuan when she said you ran out to the grass, but you actually did!"

"Stay together," Lysander called out from the road. "We've yet to reach our destination."

Endellion's ground enforcers marched in squad formation toward the mag-lev trains. I could catch up to them in a heartbeat, if I wanted to. Instead of rushing, I took another deep breath.

Quinn tapped my arm. "C'mon. We're going to be here for a while. You'll get your fill, I swear."

"I don't know if I'll ever have my fill," I muttered.

"Good news—once Endellion becomes governor, you'll get to test that theory. But she's not going to get Minister Ontwenty's favor if you're worshipping the dirt."

MINISTER ONTWENTY HAD us watching a laboratory, but I had never seen anything like it before.

The lab sat in the center of an "enclosed" area. It wasn't like a starship or a space station, in terms of enclosure—it was protected by a fence, with the sky wide open above us. The lab workers, researchers, and scientists all lived and worked within the designated area. The company town had stores and food shops, all owned by Minister Ontwenty. The entire research crew was separated from everyone and everything. Something about corporate espionage or some shit, but I didn't understand it. All I knew was that Ontwenty wanted her research to remain hidden, and she went to great lengths to keep it that way.

I ran with the other ground enforcers as Lysander took us through some drills. First physical training, then formations, then gunmanship, and finally, maintenance. It was almost the same routine the starfighters went through, but there was a lot of attention paid to field practicality. If a starfighter went down, there was no survival situation—the pilot was dead. But Lysander took us through drills as though the ground enforcers might be on their own and needed to be able to think on their feet.

I didn't mind. Running didn't bother me. I could have done circles around every schmoe on the force. But I did enjoy taking in the air.

According to my enviro-suit, the air was 23% oxygen and 76% nitrogen. My suit thought that was on the high end of the oxygen ratio, but it also said it was technically breathable, so I kept my helmet down.

The buildings around the artificial company town were works of art. The walls stood tall, sleek, and curved, made of black solar-panel metal, flexi-glass, bioplastics, and redwood. Everything had a feather-light feel to it. Clean. Effortless. The labs sat underground, in facilities reminiscent of space stations, but with controlled environments and posh workrooms. Only the perimeter wall looked like something designed without comfort in mind. The damn thing hummed with high-voltage electricity, and guards armed with plasma rifles lined the top of it. And all the buildings had a detection system built onto the roofs to capture any surveillance activity. It caught drones, digital signals, radio signals, and even managed to detect people who weren't authorized to be on the premises.

I was certain Ontwenty was paranoid.

"I like this place," Noah said as he jogged up to my side.

Although I didn't feel the burn of the run, I could see the sweat pouring off Noah's forehead by the bucketful. If he'd worn his helmet, the suit could have regulated his temperature, but I assumed he was also enamored by the environment.

"I can't get enough of the sky," I said, keeping my gaze upward.

It changed color with the time of day. In the morning, it was orange. In the afternoon, it was indigo. In the evening, it was a dark purple with a hint of red. And the Vectin Star was so glorious I found myself glancing at it every once in a while—even though I had been yelled at nonstop to never do that.

But it was gorgeous.

"The gravity is different here," Noah said between huffs. "Stronger. Makes everything difficult…"

Sawyer had said the gravity would be a little higher. But only a little. It was 1.1 of the standard setting we used on the starships, which would make a difference, but I couldn't feel it yet.

I stopped at the end of our track, near the wall and straight under the sunlight. Noah placed his hands on his knees and posted his arms as he took in a few deep breaths. The other enforcers who'd kept my pace walked over and pulled back their helmets.

"Wow," one guy said through a wide smile. "You don't even look fazed."

A woman with a crewcut nodded. "You're that starfighter, right? Endellion's new right hand? Are you really part-superhuman?"

Lysander jogged up, breaking all conversation. Without taking off his helmet, he motioned to me, and then pointed to one of the distant buildings. "Sawyer wants to speak to you," he said. "She said you weren't answering your comms."

I hadn't been wearing my helmet as often as I should have. I nodded. "All right."

Noah watched me go, but ultimately stayed with his brother

and the other ground enforcers as they gathered into their formations. I left him knowing nothing would happen. Why were we even there? The walls had guards, the people seemed secured, and it wasn't like there was another facility close by. Everything on Vectin-14 had room to breathe, metaphorically and literally.

I opened the door to the building Lysander had indicated, my hand on the latch for several seconds. The hinges of the door and the wood it was made from made for a lightweight object. There was nothing quite like it on a space station.

And when I stepped inside, the floor was covered in a soft carpet of woven wool and synthetic fibers. Capital Station had cushioned walkways covered in rubber and padded plastics, but those didn't compare to the fluff of a carpet.

More and more, I associated "delicate" and "soft" with "expensive luxury." Vectin-14 seemed to be awash in decadence I hadn't even thought possible.

"There you are," Sawyer said as she walked into the front room with a cup in hand. "I've been trying to reach you."

"What for?" I asked, staring at my boots and marveling at how the carpet sprang back into position when I lifted my foot.

"I have a gift for you."

"Oh, yeah?"

Sawyer motioned me to another room, and I followed, bouncing along with every step. Carpets were amazing.

The posh little dwelling had four rooms, but they were bigger and more spacious than anything on the *Star Marque*.

"Where's Blub?" I asked.

"He's on the *Star Marque*. Don't worry, he's in good hands. I miss him, but he's an indoor fish that wouldn't take well to Vectin-14's environment."

We entered the back room—a study of some sort—and I eyed the couch, chairs, and wooden desk. To my surprise, Advik waited in the corner, her back against the wall, and her long, black hair dangling over her enviro-suit without any ties or headbands.

I lifted an eyebrow. "What're you doing here? I thought you

stayed behind with all the other sad sacks who have agoraphobia or whatever."

She replied with a half-lidded glare. "I didn't want to be left behind."

"Really? Could have fooled me."

"What's that supposed to mean?"

"I mean, if you wanted to be with us, you should have come. I've known shadows more assertive than you."

Sawyer raised a hand. "Enough. We have things to do."

"I'll wait in the other room," Advik said.

She pushed away from the wall but stuck close to it as she made her way across the room and out the door.

Once it clicked shut, Sawyer exhaled. "You could be a little less confrontational with your teammates."

"C'mon. Advik is a starfighter, for fuck's sake. She pilots a death weapon in space and kills fools on command. How is she afraid of something as pathetic as a wide-open sky?"

"If I remember correctly, a certain cocky someone got paralyzed with anxiety the first time they got into a starfighter. I think it might have been because they were afraid. Afraid of *space*, perhaps? That's pretty irrational and pathetic."

I walked over to Sawyer and huffed. "You're always bustin' my balls. I got over that, didn't I? I can pilot a starfighter with the best of them now."

"And Advik joined us planetside."

I opened my mouth but closed it before I said something stupid. Sawyer was right. Goddammit.

Sawyer took a seat at the desk and smirked, like she knew exactly what I was thinking. I should have been irritated, but I liked that she cut me down every once in a while. Her comments contained just enough truth to give me perspective.

"Here," she said. "I refurbished this for you."

She dragged a PAD across the top of the desk and pushed it toward me.

PADs were expensive. I'd had one once upon a time, but I'd ended up selling it to cover debts. They were great personal computers, they could be used to contact anyone, and they monitored the user's health. There was little downside, but they could easily break. The PADs kept their skin-like thickness, due to the computer components being made from graphene, a single layer of graphite with bonded carbon atoms, arranged in a hexagonal lattice.

And I only knew that because I'd sold a whole batch of knockoff PADs while on Capital Station. I'd given a speech to the buyers that I'd read straight from an MF PAD production sheet, knowing full well whatever the hell I was talking about did not describe my fake PADs.

I was a dick, but it paid the bills.

"I need to mount it to your arm," Sawyer said.

I unfastened my enviro-suit and pulled at the collar until I got my left arm out. The PADs drew power from the internal heat produced by warm-blooded humans. No need for recharging. No need for external power sources. But that meant a power cord had to be inserted straight into my body.

I waited, but Sawyer didn't move.

"What's wrong?" I asked.

"Oh, I thought you were going to take off more of your suit."

I let out a single laugh. "Do I need to?"

"Well, no. But I'd like you to."

"Sawyer," I said, smiling. "If you ever want to see me without my suit, I'm more than happy to oblige."

With a few quick motions, I got the enviro-suit off my other arm and down to my waist. I went to take the rest off, but Sawyer held up a hand.

"No, you can stop. There are windows here, after all."

Sure enough, the windows looked out onto the beautiful landscape of the company town. Not that I cared about my modesty, but I was sure Sawyer would be irritated if she had to explain my behavior to any of the others.

Sawyer held up the PAD and pulled a string-thin needle from the side. It didn't hurt when she inserted it into my arm, but I could tell she was distracted. She kept her eyes on me the entire time, a look of absentmindedness about her.

"You're a real tease, ya know that?" I asked.

She lifted an eyebrow. "Oh?"

"You had me thinking you didn't want me. Now here you are, asking me to strip."

"I never said I found you repulsive."

"But you *did* turn me down."

Sawyer fitted the needle deep into my arm, and then snapped the PAD shut. Once situated, it powered on and read the identification chip nestled between my radius and ulna. With all the information it needed, the PAD greeted me with the text: *Salutations, Clevon Demarco.*

"I can't be with you," Sawyer said, not bothering to meet my gaze. "But that doesn't mean I don't fantasize about it." She pointed to the PAD. "And I don't just give these to anyone. I could have kept it for my own use."

She was a real goddamn enigma.

"Why can't you be with me?" I asked.

"What was that?" Sawyer lifted a hand to her ear. "'Thank you, Sawyer, for the wonderful PAD'—is that what you said? I didn't quite hear."

"Sawyer."

"And you should keep it on at all times. The other starfighters all have PADs, but it's hit-or-miss whether they wear it."

"Does it have something to do with your genetics? Did the superhumans you talked about do something to you?"

My statement caused her to grimace. She swiveled her chair away from me and pulled her leg up to rest on the cushion of the seat. "Endellion needs you, Demarco. She told me to send you to her once I was done. Which is now."

She wasn't telling me something, but now wasn't the time, either.

"What does Endellion want?" I asked. "I haven't seen her in the last two days. Not since we got planetside. She up and vanished to spend all her time with the superhumans."

"She needs a bodyguard. Rebellion forces intend to kill her."

"Wait, what? How would she even know that?"

Sawyer swiveled back around. "I decode rebellion messages all the time. Their encryptions are never above my level."

"Why would they try to kill her? I know she fucked with them in the past, but—"

"She keeps in contact with rebellion turncoats. Men and women who expressed their displeasure before Endellion betrayed them. They contact her, she pays them or offers sanctuary, and a little more of the rebellion suffers every day. Since the rebellion knows of Endellion's actions, it's not hard for turncoats to reach out to her, you see."

"She keeps in contact with people who betray the rebellion?"

"If you think Endellion ever completely severs ties with something, you're sorely mistaken. She never passes up an advantage or opportunity. Trust me."

"So, you know there's a plot to kill her? Here on Vectin-14? I thought this place was superhuman central."

"Who do you think works the megafarms and moves all the goods off-planet?" Sawyer asked with a dismissive wave of her hand. "Superhumans are *above* such menial labor. They don't do service jobs, they don't do physical construction work, and they wouldn't be caught dead hauling foodstuffs. Humans and defects get those pleasures, and some of them get resentful when there's no way to escape such a thankless existence."

"Where is she?" I asked. "If Endellion needs a bodyguard, I'll be there." Though I felt sorry for the assassin who tried to take her life.

"I programed the information into your PAD. Goodbye, Demarco."

Again, Sawyer turned away from me, her stiff posture unusual. I could tell she wanted me to leave, but I took my time slipping my enviro-suit back on, hoping she would break down and talk to me. It must have had something to do with her past life, some reason she kept herself sequestered from the world.

But it was her business.

Once dressed, I left the study, still enjoying the carpet beneath my boots. Advik waited in the front room, her arms crossed over her chest.

"Forget what I said," I said as I walked to the front door. "I was being a jackass."

Advik smiled. "I heard everything."

I stopped with my hand on the latch. "Everything?"

"Unlike a space station, voices carry through these walls. I'll try to act more like a killer pilot in the future."

"No need to act like one," I said. "You *are* one. I just want you to remember that when you think the sky is going to eat you."

I opened the door, but Advik reached out and took my arm. She gave me an odd look, her brow furrowed. "Keep Endellion safe, all right?"

"Of course."

"A lot of us would have nowhere to go if it weren't for the *Star Marque*. Myself included." Advik tightened her grip before letting go.

I nodded. "I understand."

SIXTEEN

Operation

I could see why Endellion spent all her time with the superhumans. Everything they did was beyond compare. Sure, space stations were a marvel of human ingenuity—the height of science and technology from Earth—but as I stared at the superhuman-designed blueprints on the screen before me, I knew the space stations would one day be a joke in polite society.

"As you can see, preparations are already underway for the Stellar Engine," Minister Ontwenty said as she motioned to the diagram. "Construction will begin in less than a year."

The Stellar Engine was a megastructure built around a star in a chain-link fashion, closer than a planet in the garden zone, but far enough away not to be damaged by the star's blaze. The engine captured heat, radiation, and solar flares, and then converted it all to energy. *So much* fucking energy. More than any generator could ever create.

According to Ontwenty, a whole host of space stations could be built off the Stellar Engine, perhaps even an artificial planet—a type of "Dyson sphere," she'd called it—with enough power and room to accommodate the whole damn quadrant, and then some.

Trillions of people could live on it. Maybe quadrillions.

"You're sure it could generate that much power?" I asked, staring at the blueprints.

"Yes," Ontwenty said. "While I'm currently the Minister of Medical Research, I also received doctorate degrees in plasma physics, molecular science, and energy conversion while at university. I was a member of the research team that went over the numbers for the Stellar Engine."

"All those degrees?" I asked.

"Yes. Aerospace engineering is a hobby of mine, so I became well-versed in the matter."

Hobby, huh? And here I was, weightlifting in my spare time.

Ontwenty smiled. "Our collective forefathers did great work with fusion reactions and ionized gases. They mimicked the energy output of stars to power their starships and create better weaponry—that's what plasma rifles are, after all—but it was a fraction of what an actual star could produce. 'We will take it further'—that was the motto we worked under while in the developmental phases of the engine research."

"Sure. Whatever you say."

Endellion stared at the diagrams in quiet contemplation.

"My current research involves the radiation emitted from our quadrant's three stars," Ontwenty continued, her enthusiasm and excitement almost infectious. "It's a well-established hypothesis that the exposure to these stars is the cause of the frequent genetic defects found in Homo sapiens, especially given the high rate of defect occurrences compared to Earth's numbers. I don't have a simple picture of this research to show you, but rest assured my team and I are on the verge of creating a radiation treatment that will prevent defects in the future, for all organic, DNA-based life."

"Interesting," Endellion said.

Interesting? I could barely keep up with it.

"With the Stellar Engine and my medicine," Ontwenty said, "we could create a perfect utopia in our corner of space."

She motioned for us to follow.

Minister Ontwenty's home was among the palatial penthouses that made up the gleaming skyscraper in Torinova, the capital of

Vectin-14's northern hemisphere. Two whole floors were dedicated to Ontwenty's comfort and relaxation when she wasn't conducting medical research. She showed us everything with a smile and wave of her hand, including a greenhouse garden tended to by her house-keepers.

The place was a goddamn wonderland, mixing the convenience of technology with the glory of nature.

We arrived in a sitting room, everything so soft and clean it must have been worth more than the *Star Marque* itself. Ontwenty took a seat across a chaise lounge, and I fell back into a chair two times larger than anything I had ever sat in before. I felt a growing bit of embarrassment when I placed my arms on the armrests. It wasn't comfortable, and I looked like a child pretending to be an adult. The chair was clearly built with the larger superhumans in mind.

"How do you like the city, Clevon?" Minister Ontwenty asked.

"It's—" I glanced out the window to the blues, grays, and glints of sunlight sparkling off the sea of glass—"fascinating."

"Your mother worked here for a long while."

"You knew my mother?" I blurted out, shocked.

"No. But upon Endellion's request, I had her file pulled. She was an accountant for Dr. Hillvia Lone. Your mother lived a modest life, and I assume she saved a large sum for the genetic-modification procedure. You're a lucky child."

"R-Right."

I didn't want to talk about my mother. It was disconcerting that everyone seemed to be rummaging around my past and a little unnerving that Endellion was one of those individuals. Endellion's history made me think she hadn't investigated my mother out of the goodness of her heart.

Ontwenty leaned back on the lounge, her planetside outfit one of glamor, not practicality. The long robe hung loose on her sleek body, exposing skin I never would have seen if she had been in an enviro-suit. Her long legs, muscled arms, and the sliver of her ribcage showcased her multi-toned skin, ranging from pale to bronze. The black dots on her neck speckled the area above her collarbone.

Well, they weren't dots. They were holes. Smaller than a finger-nail. I wouldn't have even been able to see them if I hadn't been staring so intently.

"You haven't met many superhumans?" Ontwenty asked.

Endellion took a seat next to me. "Forgive his manners. He was raised on a space station."

"What's with all that?" I asked, motioning to my own neck and chest. "Are those holes? Are you ill?"

Ontwenty and Endellion shared a laugh. I waited, wondering if they would answer, but I knew Sawyer could always tell me if I remembered to ask when I got back to the company town.

"Members of Homo superior were designed," Ontwenty said with a smile. "Most human flaws were removed—when possible—while maintaining an overall humanoid appearance. For example, it's a design flaw that Homo sapiens can die when eating. A single piece of food lodged in the windpipe could be your undoing. Homo superior doesn't share its esophagus with its trachea. As a matter of fact, Homo superior breathes more oxygen than Homo sapiens, and our blood is richer for it." She motioned to the tiny holes.

"You breathe from them?" I asked.

"Yes. They also sense much of the atmosphere, and the airways are lined with filters that prevent most deadly gases from taking effect."

"What if someone strangled you?"

Endellion shot me a stern glare—like I should have shut the fuck up—but Ontwenty chuckled.

She turned her head and pulled back her white hair enough for me to see the backside of her ears. More breathing holes in a cres-cent line, like they were decoration.

"Homo superior have reworked vein structures, and our spines have been modified to protect two additional arteries. With plenty of blood and oxygen, strangulation is a near-impossibility."

"Is that so?"

"These additional airways also allow for Homo superior to make use of our ampullae of Lorenzini."

What? It took me a second to mull over the words. "What the

fuck is an ampullae of Lorenzini?" I asked, knowing I was being uncouth, but there was no easy way to ask without showcasing my ignorance.

Ontwenty didn't seem to mind—she actually seemed prepared for the reaction, like she'd assumed I wouldn't know even before she said it. "The ampullae of Lorenzini is an organ found in some fish. It's an electroreceptor that senses the flow of electricity, even weak signals produced by muscle movement. Sharks use this organ when hunting their prey to great effect. Homo superior uses it to better craft technology and regulate power flow. Our electronics are unrivaled, and it's due, in part, to being able to see these electrical currents with ease."

That must have been a superhuman's "sixth sense" that everyone always spoke about. Everything clicked into place. I glanced over at Endellion and narrowed my eyes. She had always been able to sense things around her. Things outside of her vision. People on the other side of a door.

Endellion matched my gaze and nodded. "I have a cybernetic ampullae of Lorenzini. But we didn't come here to get a lecture from the minister." Endellion returned her attention to the superhuman. "I was wondering if I could use your medical facility in Nogiwa. I've arranged to meet a doctor there."

"*My* medical facility?" Ontwenty asked.

"The one with genetic-defect research, yes."

Ontwenty mulled over the request before nodding. "You've already been so helpful in my research, I don't see why not. Let me make sure everything goes smoothly—I'll send a note right away." She got off her lounge and exited the room in a few quick strides.

Once Endellion and I were alone, I stared out the window. We were eight stories up, and the view took my breath away. Sawyer had said humans raised planetside had a fear of heights, which was an interesting contrast to humans raised in space, fearing the sky. One feared what was below, the other feared what was above.

Sawyer must have been right because the distance to the planet's surface didn't faze me. It was all so captivating.

"You've already done things for Ontwenty?" I asked, keeping my voice low.

Endellion leaned back in her chair. "I gave her blood samples from the genetically-defective criminals I've apprehended over the past seven years."

"Why?"

"She wanted defect samples from all over the Vectin Quadrant, and this way she didn't have to pay."

"She didn't want to pay the defects, you mean."

"Them, or the couriers, or the processing fees, or the taxes, or the licenses, or the containment costs. It may be minor, but now she has a resource her competitors don't."

I shifted in my seat and gave Endellion a half-smile. "You're not supposed to be selling that kind of stuff, I take it."

She returned my reserved smile. "I didn't sell it."

"But you got favors."

"Exactly."

"And, for some reason, you dug up my mother's information."

The follow-up left Endellion quiet. Her expression changed to something neutral—almost melancholy—but she kept her gaze fixed on mine. "And you think I plan to do something nefarious with it?" she asked.

"I think you plan to do *something* with it."

"Perhaps it was for your sole benefit."

"You're too cunning for altruism."

Endellion chuckled, but the melancholy remained. "Clevon, don't disappoint me. Not now."

"What's that supposed to mean?"

"Whenever individuals start to learn of my tenacity, they get anxious. Suspicious. Fearful. It's hard to find someone whom I can trust with my plans. Whom I can trust to be myself with. I figured with your skills and history, you wouldn't be so unnerved by my power plays and methods."

Learned of her tenacity, huh? That was one way to put it.

"I'm not afraid of you," I stated, a cold edge to my voice. "But I don't want lies, either. Tell me, straight up—why did you inquire about my family?"

"To show you my influence can be to your benefit. And because I want to ingratiate myself with you."

My smile returned. "I'm already your starfighter."

"I told you," Endellion said as she crossed her legs and leaned back. "It's hard to find individuals who aren't wary of me. You're one of the few whom I believe when you say you're not afraid. I want your company."

"Heh." I turned away and stared out the window. The gleam reflected off the spectacular architecture, causing me to squint. "I don't mind your secrets and games. Just don't use them on me, and we'll be fine."

"Is that so?"

Minister Ontwenty walked back into the room, the flow of her loose gown catching my attention over the scenery. She was alluring in every way, even if her aesthetics were something I had never considered. I wondered what it would be like to roll between the sheets with a superhuman. Were they really better at everything? It would have been fun to conduct some research.

"It's done," Ontwenty said. "Schedule an appointment with a doctor, if you need to."

"Thank you," Endellion said.

I scooted forward in my chair. "Hey, are there any places with modified animals around here?"

Ontwenty nodded. "We have museums, a safari park, and a menagerie."

"If we're handing out passes to places, can I get one to that menagerie?"

"Of course. I love to treat station humans to the wonders of Vectin-14."

I STEPPED off the mag-lev train and onto the station platform. The damn magnetic, levitating vehicle could reach some impressive land speeds. I knew the *Star Marque* traveled faster than light once it reached its top acceleration, but it wasn't the same as watching scenery zip by the windows. *Everything* felt fast.

Endellion, dressed in her casual cargo pants and tank top, walked straight from the station and onto the footpath. I followed at her side, taking in the sights. Every part of Vectin-14 seemed to have been designed long before construction. The roads were set in grid patterns, the trains were perfectly spaced for maximum efficiency between stations, and the trees were evenly spread along the walkways.

We passed through a security gate, and I eyed the mounted plasma guns and the modified guards. Endellion didn't give them the time of day. Our destination sat in the center of the enclosed compound, and she headed right for it.

The indigo sky reflected off the windows of Ontwenty's medical facility. *Nogiwa Med-Fac 284—R&D* was etched into the metal beside the front door, and I wondered just how many of these research facilities must have existed. Shuttle ships landed on the roof, four stories into the sky, unloading supplies by the crate.

To my surprise, Lysander, Yuan, Mara, Quinn, and Sawyer all stood outside the facility, waiting on the walkway to the front door. Everyone but Sawyer sported an enviro-suit, helmets down, and each carried a plasma rifle. I was in the same get-up, but I hadn't thought they would be there.

Endellion and I reached the group, and she acknowledged them with a curt nod.

"What're you doing here?" I asked Lysander.

He narrowed his eyes. "In case you forgot, *I* am Endellion's Subcommander of Ground Forces. The real question is: why are *you* here?"

"Oh, this is awkward. I thought you already knew, but… I'm the superior marksman and fighter."

Mara stifled a laugh.

"I have business here," Endellion said, ignoring our conversation. "And I want you all to stand guard while I'm with the doctor."

I turned to her. "And?"

"And while I'm in the middle of an operation, I don't want anything to happen."

"Operation? You never said anything about an operation."

Endellion smoothed her casual attire. "Occasionally, recalibration of cybernetic implants is required. In addition, I need another implant inserted into my spinal column, into the C6 and C7 spinal segment. It's a delicate procedure, one I would only trust to be done at a facility such as this."

I glanced around. The entire compound had its own security, and the place had a tranquil aura. No loud noises. No bustling crowds. It wasn't an environment I was familiar with. On Capital Station, I knew what the thugs looked like. Was Endellion worried one of the guards would attack her? One of the resident researchers?

Endellion led the others into the medical facility, and I followed. Advik's plea rung in my ears. She didn't want Endellion to die, and more and more, I understood why. Everyone on the *Star Marque* had shaped their lives around Endellion's promise. They planned to live planetside—that was the end goal, the dream—and nobody else on the ship had the drive to make it happen.

A piece of me wondered if I could ever rival Endellion's scheming. Maybe I would never need to find out, but I hated to come in second.

Once inside, I was greeted with windowless halls and plain gray walls. The building had all the charm of a space station, and already I yearned for the outside. Each door we passed through, Endellion scanned the identification chip buried in her arm. A few guards gave her questioning glances, but they didn't speak to her.

We rode the elevator up to the fourth floor.

"Lysander, take Yuan, Mara, and Quinn to secure the floor," Endellion said. "Clevon and Sawyer, you're with me."

The others did as they were commanded.

"Are we meeting our doctor?" I asked.

Endellion nodded. "That's right."

Heh. That would be awkward. "Is there something I should do?"

"You're my bodyguard. All I need you to do is stand watch."

I traveled with Endellion to a room labeled, *Operations 4/4*. She opened the door, and we stepped into a wonderland of technology and medicine. A capsule bed was mounted to the back wall, the cover glass and a few robotic tools were built into the headboard and footboard. The counters around the room displayed various types of medication, each set separated by a computer terminal. A single table held two cybernetic implants, each on a stand to keep them from touching the cold, metal surface.

It took me a second to notice the man by the capsule bed. He calibrated the robotic tools, adjusting them with a touchscreen read-out. Then he turned around, scowling.

Everything about the man screamed "stiff" and "serious." He stood straight, had a quick gait, and his black hair was slicked back and held in place with enough product to keep it looking wet.

I assumed he was a nurse. So, where was Dr. Rhodes?

"You must be Commodore Voight," the man said. "I'm Dr. Clay. You requested I meet you for an evaluation?"

Endellion walked up to the man and returned the nod. "Thank you for seeing me on such short notice."

Doctor? Him? But I'd thought...

Dr. Clay crossed his arms. "I'm sorry to say, but I won't be with this facility much longer. I would recommend you wait until another doctor can see you. That way, when you return, you'll be able to meet with the same team members."

"Don't worry," Endellion said with a smile. "I know your work contract was denied renewal."

The statement left the doctor speechless. He stared for a moment, and then took a deep breath. "I wasn't aware private professional information was shared so flippantly."

"I assure you, it isn't. I just so happen to know a great many researchers, including Ontwenty herself. They talk, you see."

Dr. Clay glared. "Of course they do." He turned on his heel and motioned to the capsule bed. "This rejuv-cell will run a complete scan of your body, mapping out bones, muscles, blood flow, cybernetic implants, organ structure, and key markers in your DNA. Once I have the scan, we can discuss your options from there."

He tapped the capsule's computer terminal, and the glass lid opened. Endellion stepped up to the side of the machine and ran her fingers along the edge.

"Assuming you find nothing out of place," Endellion said, "I intend to go through with a recalibration and insertion of the regulator into the spine."

"I think it best you have another doctor perform the surgery. Like I said, I won't be here much longer."

"And you want more time to apply to other facilities and laboratories," Endellion said. Not as a question, but as a statement.

By the look on Dr. Clay's face, she was right.

But why were we talking to him? Why had Endellion asked me to speak with Dr. Rhodes?

"You must know the other facilities won't take you," Endellion continued. "Not here on Vectin-14. At least, not any facility you would consider worthy."

"I have work to do," Dr. Clay said through clenched teeth. "Perhaps you should be on your way, rather than offering me insults."

"Hear me out, Dr. Clay. I think what's happened to you is a crime."

"And what do you know of it?"

"I know the entire Rhodes family is clan-like and obsessed with their own successes, never once reaching out to help mankind. They're infantile for turning away talent, especially for something as petty as the cancellation of an engagement. Even if you and Dr. Rhodes are no longer on good terms, they shouldn't have attempted to exclude you from much-needed research."

I caught my breath.

Endellion never wanted Dr. Rhodes. She'd wanted Dr. Rhodes's fiancé.

It changed everything I'd thought was happening back on Midway Station. My insistence that Dr. Rhodes leave her significant other haunted me for a prolonged moment as Dr. Clay digested Endellion's words.

"You know an awful lot," Dr. Clay said, slow and careful.

"Like I said, I'm good friends with Ontwenty herself."

Dr. Clay laughed, but he kept his stiff posture. "I see all those rumors about you are true. You really do keep high company. Now the question is: should I be worried or elated? Are you telling me all this because you can get me a position straight through Ontwenty?"

"I have a better deal for you."

"Oh?"

Endellion smiled, so sure of herself, like she was cornering the man in a trap he didn't even know he was in. "How about you join me on the *Star Marque* as the medical officer my crew so desperately needs?"

Dr. Clay laughed even harder, and then turned away. "On an enforcer ship? That's worse than working in a tiny, commercial lab. At least then I would still be in the community."

"Is that really what you want? Seeing your old associates at social gatherings and explaining your situation to them? How you've failed to achieve anything, like so many of them predicted? I've already heard some of the rumors. You were nothing without Dr. Rhodes—or so they'll say."

Dr. Clay whipped around. He waited a minute, taking calming breaths, before he said, "An enforcer ship has nothing for me."

"Sawyer," Endellion said with a motion of her hand. "Show the doctor all the research Ontwenty has given us."

Sawyer shuffled forward and held up her left arm, her PAD on display. The screen showed research, all right. Research stolen from Ontwenty's cargo ship. The same research Endellion had stolen herself.

I couldn't believe Endellion was getting away with this. She'd painted her relationship with Ontwenty as something more than it was. And Dr. Clay stared at the information with rapt interest, his eyes scanning the lines of text and examining each diagram. He ate it up.

I had to hold back a laugh. Endellion lied like a pro. No hesitation. No qualms. Damn, if I didn't know what was going on, I wouldn't have even suspected.

"Ontwenty gave this to you?" Dr. Clay asked. "An enforcer captain?"

"Future governor," Endellion corrected. "Ontwenty is helping me achieve greatness. And, once I'm appointed, everyone in my crew will be rewarded with a parcel of planetside property. While others intend to live on theirs, I'm sure a savvy individual could sell their allotment and make enough credits to publish their own research and start their own facility." Endellion let that sit before adding, "Can you imagine the look on your associates' faces if you came back from *this* to a man in charge of his own work and future?"

Holy shit. She was giving him a pitch, like she'd given *me* a pitch back on the ship. *"Work on the* Star Marque, *and I'll make all your dreams come true."* It might as well have been her fucking slogan.

"That's how much you need a doctor for your crew?" Dr. Clay asked, his eyebrows knit tight together.

Sawyer pulled her PAD away, and Dr. Clay almost reached out to hold her arm, but he stopped halfway.

"Maintaining my cybernetic enhancements is important to my success," Endellion said. Then she gave me a sideways glance before adding, "And a handful of my crew members are defects. I've seen your articles and research. With Ontwenty's notes, I'm sure you could help them immensely."

Dr. Clay rubbed at the black stubble across his chin. He was a thin man, but his eyes had a brightness and energy that betrayed his keen mind.

"You also employ defects?" he asked, more to himself than anyone else. "Interesting. And I assume you apprehend defective humans."

"Of course."

"I've heard mixed things about you, Commodore Voight, and I thought most of them impossible. But your access to this facility—coupled with your possession of Ontwenty's research—proves you're well on your way to becoming the first human governor since the reformation."

"So, you'll perform my operation and join me as a member of my crew?"

"I'll do the operation," he said. "But let me get my things in order before I accept your offer."

"Very well."

Endellion turned around and motioned for Sawyer and me to join her. We walked to the door, and she stopped. "Sawyer?" Endellion asked, keeping her voice low.

"They're here," Sawyer replied, staring down at the text across her PAD. "They've been here for a while. They're using short-range transmitters to communicate. I suspect it's to bypass security. Given the range, they're already inside the facility."

"Who?" I asked. "These wannabe assassins?"

"That's right. They're also here to acquire research. After decoding their messages, I can safely say one team plans on killing Endellion—and themselves—to act as a greater distraction. The defect research is important to them, but Endellion is a nice secondary."

Endellion grabbed my upper arm. "Take Sawyer and find them. Stop whatever attempts they plan to make. Alert the other security personnel, if needed. You accomplishing this alone won't impress me."

"Why go through with the surgery right now?" I asked. "Obviously we should wait until these guys are dealt with."

"I need to meet with the Vectin ministers, governor, and high governor in 12 hours from now at a pre-hearing for legislative process. After that, Ontwenty will assign me the task of suppressing a rebellion transport, which will require us to leave Vectin-14. Since recovery time for my surgery is eight hours—assuming no complications—I can't risk delay. Additionally, removing Dr. Clay from Vectin-14 as soon as possible cuts back on the chance that someone else will make him an offer."

Damn. She'd had a fucking dissertation prepared for that explanation.

"All right," I said. "We won't let anything happen."

"Good."

Endellion released me, but before she could move away, I took her arm instead. She gave me a cold stare, but I didn't mind. She was always intense, even if she tried to hide it.

"You never mentioned a plot of property when you recruited me," I whispered. "But you mentioned it to the doctor right out of the door."

Endellion nodded. "There are two types of people who work on an enforcer starship—the desperate, and those who take to the profession. Dr. Clay is desperate, thanks to you and Dr. Rhodes, and needs the extra push. You, Clevon, take to the profession. The property is a bonus for you, not a requirement."

I wanted to argue, but she was right. I hadn't needed the added incentive to join, but the doctor had been on the fence until she sweetened the deal.

The desperate, huh? Endellion seemed to have a lot of those in her crew.

"I have an operation to get to," she said. "Don't fail me."

SEVENTEEN

Assassination

"Where are they?" I asked.

Sawyer shrugged. "In the building. Perhaps outside. But close."

"You don't know where they are specifically? I thought you were on top of this."

"Tracking the communications of a bunch of would-be assassins isn't enough to impress you?" she sarcastically asked. "Next time I'll let you do it, and I'll be the one toting around the gun."

Now wasn't the time for playful bickering. "Do Lysander and the others know our targets are close?"

"Not yet."

I pulled my enviro-suit helmet over my head and waited as it suctioned into place. Once the screen pulsed to life, I switched through the comms until I had everyone in the nearby area.

This wasn't Capital Station. I didn't know my way around, I didn't know the procedures, and I didn't know the terrain. Devising a plan that involved catching a bunch of assholes who *did* have that information put me at a huge disadvantage. It wouldn't stop Endellion, though, so I couldn't let it hold me back, either.

"Lysander," I said. "If you were going to lead a team of rebels into this building, what would you do?"

For a second, he didn't answer. I got angry—thinking he was ignoring me—but the moment his comms line flickered onto my screen, I calmed down.

"Most research facilities on Vectin-14 have internal scanners to prevent corporate espionage," he said. "That means that prepping the place with explosives or an electromagnetic disturbance would be near-impossible. They would've gotten caught within the hour."

"The building does have internal scanners," Sawyer said to me, not through the comms.

How was she even hearing the conversation? She wasn't wearing an enviro-suit, and she was just standing around with her gaze glued to her PAD. Maybe she had some sort of cybernetic implants, as well, something that worked in tandem with her PAD, so she could listen in on communications.

Lysander continued, "The mag-lev trains go through security checkpoints, and walking in on foot is a long trek that requires passing several gates with guards. The quickest way into the building, avoiding the most obstacles, is through the landing pads on the roof. Those transport shuttles are checked and given clearance at other stations, but the clearance authentication could be faked—or the cargo tampered with afterwards—and no one would know until the shuttle arrived onsite."

"And then what?" I asked.

"Preparations would be made on the landing pad to avoid the internal scanners. Once inside, the alarms would likely trigger on any unauthorized weapons, but by then they would have the advantage."

I switched off my comms and turned to Sawyer. "And what would you do if you were on this assassination team?"

"I'd be manning the building's scanners," she said with a raised eyebrow. "That way, when the insurgency began, I could prevent the alarms until it was far too late for security to do anything about the problem."

"Wouldn't someone notice the scanners being tampered with?"

"Depends. But that's why I wouldn't risk long-term prep. However, a couple extra minutes can go a long way."

I reconnected my comms. "Lysander, Mara, you two should meet me on the landing pad."

"I'm already there," Lysander said.

"I'll head that way," Mara chimed in.

"Good. We'll search the place together. Quinn, Yuan, you two should get to the IT office and check on the people operating the internal scanners. Someone might attempt to tamper with them."

"Heard," Quinn replied.

"On it," Yuan said.

I glanced at Sawyer. She didn't look up, but she did say, "I'll stay close to Endellion's operating room and let you know if anything happens."

With a nod, I headed for the roof, my plasma rifle in hand. Mara met me when I rounded the corner to the stairwell. Although she was small, the black enviro-suit and rifle made up for any lack of natural intimidation, and she moved with the confidence of a fighter, which was all I really needed.

We jogged up the steps until we reached the roof. The tinted visor of my suit dimmed the intensity of the harsh sunlight. I didn't need to squint, and I took in my surroundings.

Lysander waited for us at the door, rifle against his chest. Before we headed toward the landing pads, he grabbed my arm and pulled me close. I switched my comms to private, and he pointed to the subcommander insignia embedded on the collarbone of his enviro-suit.

"We have a chain of command for a reason," he said. "It's so that subordinates don't get confused. So there aren't conflicting orders or goals."

"What of it?"

"Demarco," he said, strained. "Put one and two together. We can't both issue commands. Do you understand? Basic training would've helped you with this."

Fuck. He was right. I probably should have respected the whole chain-of-command thing more.

"I understand Endellion trusts you," he continued. "And we are a small team, so I'm not going to contradict your orders now that we're in the middle of the operation, but I'd appreciate your cooperation in the future."

I bet he wanted to yell, but he strove to be diplomatic. I could respect that. "I understand, Ground Commander Jevons," I said with a formal bow of my head.

Lysander pushed me toward the landing pads. "Don't give me any of your bullshit. Let's get this over with."

The roof of the medical facility had all the same structure and rigidity as the inside did. Fences surrounded the edge, a checkpoint office sat by the landing pads, and a small storage shed for incoming cargo all made me think it would be a quick job. Where could they have hidden?

Fifteen people hustled around, all dressed in jumpsuits. Workers. Two security guards stood near the checkpoint office. Unloaders gave me odd glances as I headed for the shuttles, and the guards got tense, each hefting their weapons.

We stopped one of the shuttle pilots. After we switched our comms to vocalize, Lysander pointed to the shuttles. "We have reason to believe these ships contain unauthorized weapons. We'll need to see your manifest."

The shuttle pilot straightened her jumpsuit and nodded. "Of course. Right this way."

Lysander walked to one shuttle, and Mara jumped to the other. The shuttles were small aircrafts meant to fly through the planet's atmosphere. They could carry 19 tons, along with four passengers, making them easy to search. Easy pickings.

While Lysander and Mara searched, I spotted guys moving crates from the storage shed to the elevator door. They moved in teams of two—one controlling a motorized dolly, and the other walking in front to kept the path clear.

I held up a hand. "What're you guys doing?"

"Working," one quipped.

"We're going to have to search those."

The unloaders gave the security guards questioning glances. The guards—two genetically-modified men as big as I was, perhaps bigger—wore similar enviro-suits to the enforcers of the *Star Marque*. They walked over with plasma rifles in hand and motioned for the unloaders to continue, despite my orders.

I slammed my hand on the motorized dolly to prevent them from leaving.

"We have a situation," I said. "I'm an enforcer with the *Star Marque*. There's a group of terrorists, or jackasses, or whatever you want to call them. They're here to steal research."

"Oh, yeah?" one security guard asked, baritone even through the comms of his suit. "Why wasn't this reported to main security?"

"Does it look like I know your special protocol around here? *You* call it in to main security. We have an emergency situation."

"We need a cause for concern. A reason, or evidence, that makes you suspect terrorists are on the premises."

"I've got a cause for concern," I said. "We've got messages. One sec and I'll have them sent."

I reached up to switch the comms, but then the guard moved. He slid one foot forward and twisted his hips ever so slightly, and while the motion wasn't overtly aggressive, I knew what was coming. My heart only beat once in the time it took for the guard to lift his rifle, and because we were so close, I pushed it to the side before he managed to pull the trigger, causing a bluish-white bolt of ionized gas to streak across the roof. It sliced through the fence and sailed off toward the horizon.

I was at a disadvantage. I didn't have my rifle up, and the second guard was readying his.

And they both moved as fast as I did.

During the second and third heartbeat, I lunged to the side and rolled behind one of the crates. The second guard fired and clipped my ribs, destroying a portion of my suit and burning a furrow straight through my bone and flesh. There was enough pain to see white, but the moment faded as survival adrenaline kicked in.

I planted my rifle against the side of the crate and fired. The plasma bolt seared through the lightweight aluminum alloy, streaked across the roof, and tunneled through the first guard's chest.

The other guard and I had a rapid-fire exchange that worked about as well as two blind guys trying to shoot a mouse. The crate sprouted holes at a frightening rate, and I shifted to the side to grab the dolly's steering handle. I pressed down on the accelerator, and the thing kicked up to a decent speed, perhaps 15 kilometers an hour. With a smile, I rode it toward the elevator, making sure to keep the crate between me and the trigger-happy guard.

I hadn't thought the genetically-modified personnel would have been in on the attack. I'd learned my goddamn lesson about assumptions.

More plasma fire lit up the area, and I chanced a peek at Lysander and Mara, who had joined the fray. A handful of unloaders pulled weapons from crates, but I gunned them down in a matter of seconds. Six shots, six bolts through the skulls of turncoat workers.

I caught sight of the injured guard crawling across the rooftop, blood gushing from his gaping chest wound, like he was creating a red carpet with his bodily fluid. Normal men would have gone straight into shock after taking a plasma bolt, but the guy had tenacity programmed into him.

I fired and clipped the side of his head, delivering a hot dose of mercy and creating a corpse.

Lysander and Mara weren't fast enough gunners to catch the other guard, however. The modified man leapt out of sight before tossing a clunky grenade. A pulse of electromagnetic energy—an EMP explosion—issued from the grenade, rocking the roof and wrecking simple electronics. The pulse stung my muscles, but it passed quickly, only to burn again when a second pulse washed out.

The motorized dolly fried and stopped functioning. The visor on my suit went on the fritz. The comms rang with bits of static. And then the trigger of my rifle ceased to function since the onboard computer was used to calculate the perfect ignition for the gas. It was required when firing, and without it, the gun was worthless.

The enviro-suit didn't stay down for long, much to my relief. As a backup safety, the suit had a protected battery cell that reset the systems. The visor returned to its normal function. Once back online, I jumped off the dolly and threw down my rifle. I would kill those assholes with my bare hands, if that was what they wanted.

One of the unloaders ran and leapt at me. I allowed him to collide with me—as stepping aside would have aggravated my rib injury—and he wrapped his arms around my torso. I activated the anti-grappling system of my enviro-suit without a second thought.

An extra-powerful jolt of electricity sparked from the seams of my suit. The unloader flew off and hit the roof on his back with a strained exhale, his body twitching. But the electricity didn't just hurt my attacker—the rip in my suit caused the system to shock me as well, though not as thoroughly.

I gritted my teeth and fell to one knee, struggling to maintain coherent thought.

Well, that was what I got for being fucking stupid.

As I forced myself to stand, I took note of the other unloaders. Most had taken cover or fled to the storage shed. Then my gaze landed on Mara. She was sprawled out on her back with no one else around her, one leg spasming. What happened? She hadn't been hit by a plasma bolt, and the only other weapon—

No, I knew. Sometimes those damn EMP grenades messed with internal cybernetic parts, especially the cheap ones. Hadn't Yuan said Mara had something in her brain? She needed to get out of the situation as fast as possible.

Controlling my breath and holding my rib injury, I ran for her, but the guard and Lysander caught my eye. Lysander had his plasma rifle's receiver open, exposing the cold gas bolts, along with the rifle's ignition. He was attempting to fire the thing manually. I knew it could be done, but I had never seen anyone do it without burning themselves in the process. And they weren't superficial burns, either.

The guard pulled out a simple knife and headed for Lysander. Sometimes the old-fashioned weapons were the best. With his strength, he could carve up a normal human in seconds. And without a working rifle, Lysander was no match for someone of my caliber.

A tremor beneath my feet got everyone wobbling.

"Demarco," Quinn said over the comms. "We have enemy combatants in the IT office."

I closed the distance between myself and Lysander, only switching over my comms in time to say, "Handle it. We're busy."

I tackled the guard, despite my wound, and we both hit the rooftop. The man jumped up faster than I did, but I kicked him and rolled to my feet. Again, the guard went for Lysander—because Lysander hadn't given up on fixing his rifle—and I didn't have the speed to adequately deal with the situation. In the fourth of a second that my mind took to race through the options, I leapt in the way and physically blocked the knife attack with my body.

The blade impacted on my enviro-suit, and the powerful mesh weaving warded off the steel weaponry with its dispersion of kinetic energy through micro-hexagonal structuring. But the guy was strong enough to force his way though. He grabbed my shoulder, tensed to thrust, but at the last fraction of a moment, slid the knife up to the hole in my suit and stabbed me between the ribs.

Fuck.

I grabbed him, kept him close, and tripped him while he focused on gutting me.

A searing sensation filled my chest, and each breath was harder than the last. Blood. It filled one lung. I coughed and half-choked, but I continued to wrestle the guard, keeping him from Lysander.

"Demarco, move!"

I released him and rolled away.

Lysander fired twice, burning two holes in the guard's chest and creating tiny divots in the roof. It seemed the reinforced alloy of the building had been designed to withstand standard plasma fire.

I didn't know how Lysander had done it, but he had managed to rig the ignition and fire the plasma rifle without hurting himself. I was impressed, but only for half a second. Then I got to my feet—keeping the knife in my side to prevent bleeding to death—and staggered over to Mara.

I picked her up, and she behaved no better than a corpse. I motioned Lysander to head for the elevator, the heat in my chest building.

"You need to stop," Lysander said. "You're badly wounded."

Again, I motioned to the elevator, biting back words because I didn't have the energy for conversation. I held my breath, knowing my genetically-modified body could handle 10 to 15 minutes without oxygen intake. After that, I would pass out—and after *that*, I would choke on my own blood.

Lysander complied with my demand and ran to the elevator door. Once open, he held it until I could get in. He gave me the once-over, his stare lingering on the knife buried to the hilt between my ribs. It was an odd sensation to have an object embedded in my body, perpendicular to my spine, but I was lucky I hadn't gotten stabbed in my heart.

Here was hoping that nothing vital had been struck.

The longer we went, the more my body grew numb with heat and ice. Holding my breath helped to keep the flare of additional pain low, but the agony persisted. It was hard to think of anything else. My visor flashed warnings about my fluctuating heartrate.

"You took that hit for me," Lysander muttered.

If I could have, I would have reminded him that he was a defect, and I wasn't. As long as we managed to get through this, I would have an easy recovery in the healing vat, but his rejuvenation would come with a hefty price. Taking the hit was the most efficient outcome for the whole of the *Star Marque*.

Before Lysander picked our destination, he shook his head. "You and Mara shouldn't be heading toward the fight. I'll take you both to the ground floor."

Sweat beaded across my flesh. I ripped off my helmet, needing to feel the air against my skin.

Lysander took us to the ground level, and while we traveled, he attempted to take Mara from me. I pushed him back and glared. I would take care of Mara. He needed to get his ass to Endellion as soon as possible. He seemed to understand and stopped offering to help.

The elevator doors opened, and I rushed out. Lysander headed back up after giving me a quick nod.

Medical personnel stopped in the hall and offered assistance. A few guards rushed over as well, and I got tense. How could I know who to trust? What if they attacked?

Nothing happened right away, so I handed Mara off and pulled my helmet back on. Once the comms reengaged, I forced myself to say, "The security's in on it."

"Demarco?" Sawyer replied. "Don't worry. Quinn and Yuan informed the rest of the facility through the IT office. Outside enforcers have been called in."

"Hm," I replied, more of a grunt than anything else.

"But I need your help. Come back to the operations room."

Sawyer's request struck me. I headed back to the elevator, despite the protests from the medical personnel. I shook them off and hit the fourth-story button. It was a quick ride to my destination. The first thing I noticed once the doors opened was the guy in the hall holding a plasma rifle. Not a security guard—an unloader from the landing pads.

He hefted his weapon, wide-eyed and shaky. I stepped forward, grabbed it, pointed the barrel away, and then reached out to seize his neck. His workmen's jumpsuit offered little protection from my grip, and it was easy to crush his windpipe. When he kicked, I turned to the side, offering my non-injured ribs up for a few soft strikes.

"Demarco."

I glanced over. Sawyer stood outside the operations door, one eyebrow up.

She pointed to the man in my grasp. "He's on our side. He fought the assassins when they came from the roof."

It didn't take long to strangle a man with a blood choke. Cut off the blood flow from the carotid arteries, and it led to unconsciousness within a matter of seconds. The man in my grip had already gone half-limp by the time I released him, and he staggered into the wall before falling on his ass.

Maybe he shouldn't have pointed a gun in my face.

Pain returned when I realized Sawyer wasn't in immediate danger. But she had said she needed help. I walked over, leaving a small trail of crimson droplets on the floor. She gave my injury a glance before motioning to the room.

"Talk to the doctor," she said. "And then get yourself some medical attention."

I would have joked about her lack of concern, but I was struggling to breathe. Not the time.

I entered the operating room. Dr. Clay stood next to the capsule bed, his arms crossed. Endellion rested inside, under the glass and lying on her stomach. The robotic arms tended to the gaping incision that ran the length of her spine, a cut wide enough to expose the metal, threaded wires fastened along her bone processes. Endellion didn't move, and a clean implant sat next to her body inside the capsule bed.

"What in the name of gossamer's rings is going on?" Dr. Clay asked.

Sawyer shuffled in after me. "The doctor refuses to finish the operation."

"Now isn't the time for a medical procedure," Dr. Clay snapped. "I've set the machine to seal her back up. We can reschedule this after we know the facility is secure."

With a hand on the bottom of my ribcage, I walked over to the doctor. He took a step back, bumped into the bed, and stared at me with a furrowed brow.

I switched the comms to vocalize. "Finish it."

"I'm putting her life at risk by operating during such conditions."

"She knew the risk."

"She *knew*? Are you saying she knew of an attack?"

I grabbed Dr. Clay by the collar of his coat and yanked him close, holding back a cough. "I said. Finish it."

His shaky breath coated my visor. When I did finally hack and wheeze, red spittle coated the inside of my suit.

"I won't be held responsible for her death," Dr. Clay said, holding his hands up. "If there's another tremor during—"

"The rest of the insurgents have been dealt with," Sawyer

stated. "You shouldn't have any further interruptions from explosions."

There was no way for her to know that, but she said it with a certain amount of confidence that came across as genuine. She must have taken lessons from the Endellion School of Subterfuge.

I released the man and pushed him toward the capsule, unable to speak without losing a lung. He must have sensed my desperation because he backed away and offered a slow nod.

"A-All right," Dr. Clay muttered. "I'll do it. It's obvious she wants it above all else, or she wouldn't have left her goons to strong-arm me."

Sawyer placed her hand on my back. "Demarco. You need medical attention. Right now."

I knew.

I turned, and the edge of my vision went black.

EIGHTEEN

Inner Demons

Thick mother-cell fluid swirled around me. The LED lights blinked red, giving me enough illumination to see the globs of blood and dead skin cells floating in the goo. I took deep breaths through the breathing tube and attempted to relax, but it was difficult considering the cramped confines of my healing vat.

I took solace in the fact that I wasn't in overwhelming agony.

A familiar clink echoed through the fluid. A small hole at the bottom of the vat opened, and the mother cells drained away, spinning the entire way. I didn't think I had fully recovered, not after seven-and-a-half hours. When I grazed my side, I felt a furrow through my flesh, and there was a sting to my touch. It wasn't an open wound, sure, but the healing vats typically restored someone to their full capacity.

One side of the vat slid down, creating an opening.

"Rejuvenation 87% complete," a feminine voice intoned. *"Right Rib Five has been reconstructed. The inferior lobe of the right lung has been mended, but dermis, epidermis, and intercostal muscles are still in recovery phase. Please speak to a physician or resume treatment immediately."*

I walked out of the vat and yanked the breathing tube from my esophagus. After a few quick snorts and a shake of my head, I felt a little better, but the mother-cell fluid stuck like jelly. It was hard to clear out of every crevice. I would be sticky all day.

The med-fac recovery room had 13 healing vats lined against two walls. A cluster of flowers and ferns filled the opposite corner, giving the place a livelier atmosphere than the *Star Marque*, but the room still had that sterile smell that accompanied all medical facilities.

Lysander waited by a desk stationed near the door. He poked around at the computer terminal, answering questions that popped up onscreen.

"What's going on?" I asked through a stressed wheeze.

"Endellion said you can either continue your treatment on the *Star Marque* or you can join her at the pre-hearing," Lysander said. He stopped his work at the computer terminal and tossed me a towel. "Either way, you should clean yourself up."

I lifted my arm and grimaced. My injury was definitely still raw and deep. If I let my body recover naturally, I was sure to have a scar, but I would live. The real question was: how long would it hurt to move my right arm?

Lysander leaned against the desk. "Thank you, Demarco."

I lowered my arm, slow and careful, before wiping off my face. "For what?"

"For your teamwork on the roof."

"You pulled your own weight. Nice work with the rifle."

"They taught us all kinds of field survival techniques in the HSN Corps."

I wiped off my neck, chest, and stomach while avoiding the injury. Maybe the leftover mother cells would help it recover faster.

Lysander sighed. "Listen. I misjudged you when you first arrived. I thought you would be more trouble than you're worth, and you wouldn't put the needs of the *Star Marque* before your own. And I thought you might be a bad influence on Noah, but he's been better than he ever has since you arrived."

"Is this an apology?" I asked, half-smiling.

"You made it easy for me to assume you'd be trouble," Lysander snapped. Then he inhaled and relaxed. "But you proved me wrong, and I'm glad you did. I'd rather this outcome than me telling Endellion, 'I told you so.'"

I had never bothered to get to know Lysander. He wasn't the type of guy I would have gotten along with back on Capital Station. But that was the past. Maybe he was even the companionship I had been killing myself for since I'd joined the *Star Marque*. He seemed like a decent guy right now.

"You miss the HSN Corps?" I asked as I continued wiping myself off.

Lysander nodded. "My parents both served in the navy. I wanted nothing more than to follow in their footsteps. My father knew how much it meant, and he got a line of doctors to vouch for me—to cover up my defect, basically. I still don't know how anyone found out, especially after eight years of service... but none of that matters anymore."

"Your training saved my ass back on the roof," I said. "I would say it still matters."

"Maybe you're right. Endellion does value my understanding of the navy and my ability to train her ground enforcers."

"Were you hooking up with anyone before you were discharged?"

Lysander narrowed his eyes and scowled.

I replied with a shrug. "C'mon. I already know your questionable past and status as a defect. Is telling me about your love life really worse than that?"

He huffed. "Yes. I was *hooking up* with someone, as you so eloquently put it. I had been with her for three years before I was discharged."

After I ran the towel down my shoulders, I asked, "Did she know about you? Your defect, I mean."

Lysander's gaze fell to the floor. "No. Once I was outed, she left me. I haven't been with anyone since."

It wasn't like someone could pass their genetic deficiencies to another—outside of having a biological child—so there was no need to disclose such information right upon meeting someone, but

I could understand people's concerns. Lysander had lied to his CO, after all. Maybe the woman had felt he lied to her, as well.

"Hey," I said, drawing Lysander's attention back to me, "that's messed up. But I'd never treat you that way."

He lifted an eyebrow and gave me a questioning stare.

I couldn't imagine Lysander being affectionate or flirty—or much fun, really—which were my favorite parts of a relationship, but I bet he would be loyal and dedicated to fulfilling a role. I might as well have *tried* to engage him and see if he was interested.

I motioned to myself. "I'm still pretty gooey, you wanna help wipe me off?"

A long second passed in silence.

Lysander grew red. He rubbed the bridge of his nose, a deep frown set into his face. "Oh, sweet, Holy Mother," he muttered into his palm, "what am I being punished for?"

"You don't know what you're missing out on," I said. "I've never had a complaint."

He replied with a guttural groan, the very definition of disgust. "I never want to hear you say anything like that again. Ever."

"What's wrong? Scared?"

"We're professionals in a professional environment!" Lysander exhaled. "How do you make everything between us so insufferable?"

How had I made everything insufferable? What warped reality did the guy live in? I was the life of the party.

Lysander turned on his heel, looking anywhere but at me, like he'd just realized I was naked. "Forget it. Keep your inappropriate comments and suggestions to yourself. Endellion is waiting down the hall. Finish up and meet with her."

Then he opened the door and huffed off without another word.

He probably would've reacted the same way no matter who hit on him. He really was a stick in the mud.

Goddammit. That was everyone. Every single person on our rig. Either they didn't want me, or they were already in a relationship. I had tried. I really had. I'd hit my limit.

Where was Dr. Rhodes when I needed her? We had been great.

I could have gotten along with her for days, yet everyone on the *Star Marque* treated me like I was their grandmother propositioning them for a good time.

Left alone, I finished up and walked over to the desk. My PAD and enviro-suit sat waiting, and while Sawyer had taken her time inserting the power cord into my arm, I took the PAD and jammed the wire in, regardless of the sharp pain or blood. I could handle it.

Suiting up required a bit of wiggling, thanks to my lingering injury, but I could also manage that.

I exited the recovery room and headed down the hall. A few researchers rushed past me—no doubt still dealing with the earlier event—but they said nothing. Each door had a label etched into the metal of the doorframe, and I stopped at the waiting room. I walked into an argument.

"—and there's nowhere else on Vectin-14 as equipped as this facility to take care of Mara," Yuan shouted.

Endellion shook her head. "I've recruited a doctor from this facility to join us on the *Star Marque*. He can handle Mara with the tools we have."

"There's no reason to wait. I want her back to normal."

"She's normal *now*."

Yuan stepped up to Endellion—despite being a third of a meter shorter—and glared with an intensity that twisted her features. "Don't you start with me. You know damn well what I mean."

Endellion stared down at the other woman, unfazed by her aggression. "The implant will be fixed in due time. Until then, she can wait in the infirmary. Sedated, of course. To prevent any self-harm."

"You'd better hold up your end of the deal. I haven't said anything, nothing at all, so you get Mara the help she needs. If you don't..." With that, Yuan stormed out of the room, her gait a little off, thanks to her stiff leg. I stepped out of the way, and she never acknowledged me. Once the door shut, I returned my gaze to Endellion.

The look on her face—so cold and contemplative—made me nervous.

"Everything okay?" I asked.

Endellion smiled, dispelling her previous expression. "Of course. If I broke down every time someone threatened me, I never would've been promoted to commodore."

"That's your secret to success, huh? Not buckling under threats?"

"No," Endellion intoned, her smile gone. "My secret to success is making sure anyone who threatens me regrets it."

I scratched at my chin and mulled over the comment. "But you're going to help Mara, right? You weren't lying about that?"

Endellion nodded. "Of course. It might not be as a fast as Yuan prefers, but Mara is a talented starfighter. I wouldn't leave her in her current state."

It seemed like I'd missed something. But I shook the thought away. Now wasn't the time. "Lysander said you wanted to see me," I said.

"I want you to accompany me to the pre-hearing."

"A pre-hearing?"

"It's a meeting of Vectin ministers before the official hearing. They discuss all propositions, changes, and laws that will be discussed in the day's open council. Most disputes are handled during the pre-hearing—out of the public eye—so that the ministers can appear to be uniform in their dealings when the time comes to debate them in the open council."

"And you want to talk about your petition."

Endellion smiled. "Minister Felseven will be there, and I'm certain he'll argue to change the laws regarding who can and cannot become a governor."

"Is it filled with procedure and rules?" I knew nothing of that.

"It's a casual meeting. Nothing with bureaucracy."

"All right. I'll join you."

She looked away, her expression distant, perhaps lost in thought. Although she had just been in surgery, Endellion didn't appear any different. She was still tall, strong, and capable. No one would have even known.

"You recovered pretty quick, huh?" I asked, impressed.

Endellion stared at the far wall, unseeing. "My head still hurts, and with each breath, I feel a sharp string along my spine, but both should clear up within a few days."

"You hide it well."

"Weakness isn't for the great. It's an excuse others use for their failings."

"Ever get tired of that mentality? Seems like it would wear a person down."

She shook her head. "I see the way you hold your arm to your side. Yet, you're not about to let it stop you from accompanying me. It's what I like about you, Clevon. You make me feel like I might not be alone anymore. Like someone else might share my aspirations."

I didn't say anything, but I appreciated the compliment. Every day I found myself striving to be more than I'd been the day before, and it was all thanks to Endellion. She didn't let anything stand in her way. I wanted that same kind of passion and drive.

"You can count on me," I said.

I WAS TOLD "WEATHER" was the state of a planet's atmosphere at a certain place and time. I had learned all about rain, hail, and snow. They were only words before I saw them for myself—things I thought I knew but could never understand.

Each drop of rain against my skin was a surprising sensation. Different than a shower, and with a unique odor that carried the scent of the dirt. The distant rumble of thunder added to the chorus of natural sound. Better than the groan of warped steel aboard a dilapidated space station.

I pulled on my helmet and watched the droplets splatter against the visor.

"Sawyer," I said into my comms. "You ever see weather like this?"

"Not often," she replied, bored. "Vectin-10 has a lot of dust storms, due to the barren megafarms."

"I'd like to see those."

"Trust me. No one wants to see that. Some days got so bad, it was a danger to step outside in anything less than a sealed enviro-suit."

"I want to see *everything*," I muttered, lost in my own wanderlust.

"I'm sure you'll change your tune after you witness a tropical cyclone."

I chuckled. "Is there anything that gets you excited about the outdoors?"

"The thought of going back indoors."

"Blub would like rain."

It was Sawyer's turn to laugh, and I joined in—just imagining the floating fish getting taken away by a strong breeze amused me. Poor thing would never stand a chance.

"All right," she said. "Endellion is waiting. Get on the mag-lev train already."

I turned and headed back into the station. I was surprised no one wanted to join me outdoors, but I supposed the novelty of plan-etside experiences would wear off eventually. Still, I enjoyed the feelings while they lasted, picturing the clouds and dreary skies with a smile.

We traveled fancy. A special mag-lev train reserved for diplomats and ministers arrived to transport Endellion and a few other military personnel to the pre-meeting garden party. Each commodore got their own train car, and I headed to the one labeled *MG-8*—Endellion's designated accommodations.

Once I stepped inside, I took note of the spacious atmosphere, the white-and-silver decor, and the lack of passengers. Endellion and I were the only ones aboard, and it took me a couple seconds to look away from her.

Endellion sported a black dress, similar to Ontwenty's. It flowed with her movements, covering, but not hiding, the form of her body. It exposed her long legs, ribcage, and shoulders, plunging deep enough to the curve of her breasts. Her skin had a healthy glow—pristine, despite her history of violence—and her auburn hair wasn't braided. It was pulled back and flowed in waves between her shoulder blades, stopping at her hip.

"Clevon," she said, motioning me to one of the cushioned couches.

I took a seat and continued to stare. Unlike everyone else on the *Star Marque*, I had never seen her in the showers or in a state of partial undress. Her outfit made me think it would be an amazing experience.

Endellion took a seat opposite me, her stiff posture likely a result of the surgery that had taken place hours before.

The mag-lev train started and headed out of the station. I motioned to our surroundings. "Only me?"

"Who else would you recommend I bring?"

"Sawyer, for one."

"She doesn't care for the company of superhumans."

That was true.

"Lysander," I said.

"He's a genetic defect," Endellion replied and shrugged. "And was dishonorably discharged from the Navy HSN Corps. It would be awkward to explain his presence, and most would see it as an oversight on my part."

"Quinn?"

"She has a criminal record on Midway Station. Technically I absolved it, but I'm sure one of the attendants would bring it up to spite me. Another *faux pas* I don't wish to deal with."

"They don't know about my Capital Station record?"

Endellion smiled. "Capital Station is far from here, and I doubt they'd be able to find your record, even if they looked."

That ended the conversation, and I returned to admiring her.

It occurred to me that femininity—like the plush environment of Vectin-14—was a luxury. Most women on Capital Station couldn't afford to be dolled-up and pampered. They were starving, or they were born with a misshapen limb, or they were criminals who needed to worry about the chems they were smuggling more than their appearance.

Seeing Endellion fit both the role of an enforcer captain and a beautiful woman worthy of Vectin-14 high-society was another accomplishment I hadn't even considered. Most would have had to pick one over the other, but Endellion seemed to consider sacrificing *anything* to be a failure on her part.

Despite the buildings that rushed by the window, the smooth flow of the mag-lev train made it impossible to detect any movement. I relaxed back on the couch, knowing we would arrive within a few minutes.

I returned my attention to Endellion. She rubbed at her neck, her hands trembling.

"You okay?" I asked.

"Yes."

"No, you're not."

Endellion didn't remove her hand from her neck. I got up and walked over to her. When she didn't protest, I placed my hand on her shoulder and rubbed my thumb along the grooves of her muscles. The harder I squeezed, the more of her cybernetic implants I could feel beneath the skin. Everything about her was tense.

I kneaded her flesh up to her neck and pushed her hair to the side. Her spine felt... jagged. I knew it was nothing like a natural spine, not anymore, but I was surprised by the asymmetry of it. When I rubbed down past the axis, Endellion shuddered.

"Painful?" I asked.

"Very."

I released her, but when I went to move away, she reached back and grabbed my hand.

"Continue," she said between shallow breaths. "I need it."

Torn, because I didn't want to hurt her, I placed my hands back on her neck and massaged softer. She didn't protest or complain, but I could feel the shivers and the trembling. Normally I would've been into rubbing down a beautiful woman, but it seemed more like torture than foreplay.

"Keep this between us," she said, her voice strained.

"Why? Afraid people will see you as weak?"

"Yes. They're always judging me. I can't let them see me as anything other than completely in control."

"*Them?*"

"Superhumans. My crew. Everyone."

Judging, huh?

I remembered the time her shoulder had gotten nicked by the rebellion fighter. The way she'd fretted about her appearance. She took that shit to heart.

"You think the superhumans will be harsh on you?" I asked. "You're a human. I thought they didn't think much of humans. Everything you do should be impressive."

"I have to be seen as an equal," she said, curt, "not as a child who presents her parents with a halfway-acceptable finger-painting. If they can maintain themselves—if they can flaunt their beauty, if they can lead massive organizations with ease—then so can I. And I'll prove it. When Felseven makes his claims that I can't handle the stresses of the Federation, I'll be there to dispel the doubts. I'll look the role, I'll speak the role, and I'll be everything and more."

"What if they deny you?"

"I'll make sure they won't."

I didn't think I had ever heard *that* amount of edge in her voice. I rubbed her spine a little harder, and she ground her teeth.

"Should I stop?" I asked.

"No. Continue."

I did as she said, despite my reluctance. Determined to take my mind off the situation, I asked, "Is it true you were born on Ucova?"

"Yes."

"What're your parents doing? Now that you're a commodore?"

"They're rotting in their grave, like they've been doing for the last decade."

I almost laughed. Pretty macabre answer. But I should have remembered. Mara had told me Endellion's parents had died.

"Think they'd be proud of you?" I asked.

Endellion shook her head. "They hated my very existence. My mother made that quite clear. She didn't want to support a child, and as soon as she could, she kicked me out. If they were alive, there's no doubt in my mind they'd beg me for credits and favors. They didn't value dignity."

"That's not like my mother," I said, my thoughts already warm with the memories I still carried of her. "Every stupid little accomplishment I had was the next greatest moment for her. A semi-decent grade from my instructor? That's a day to celebrate. A completed scale-model of Capital Station made of toothpicks? Another day to celebrate. My mother thought I was humanity's savior, made flesh."

I wondered what she'd think of me now.

Endellion leaned back into my hands. She stopped shaking and relaxed into my touch.

"Feel better?" I asked.

"Much. You work wonders with your hands."

"You're not the first woman to tell me that," I said with a smirk.

Again, I attempted to step away, but she stopped me.

"Continue," she commanded.

"Yes, ma'am."

I didn't mind putting my hands all over her, if that was what she wanted. Not that we had time for that, but still. Then again, I was more than willing to be late to the meeting.

"It might not hurt for others to see your more human side," I said, digging my thumb in deep along the edges of her spine. "Makes you more relatable."

Endellion exhaled, her muscles untwisting beneath my fingertips. When I grazed a cluster of wires, it was an odd sensation, but they followed the lines of her muscles, blending enough that no one would be able to notice. She'd made sure her cyborg nature couldn't be detected from sight alone.

"I find it hard to trust anyone," she said.

Yeah, that was obvious. People with a lot of secrets didn't tend to socialize well.

Endellion inhaled deep. "You really are quite skilled with your hands."

"You think this is impressive? You should see what else I can do."

She chuckled. "You're not the first man to tell me that."

"But I can be the last."

"Smooth," she replied, almost sardonic. "Sawyer was right. You're never at a loss for words."

"Yeah, well, it's not doing me any good." I gritted my teeth as I recalled my myriad of rejections. None of them were having it.

"I enjoy it."

A nice statement, but I doubted it would go anywhere. Endellion had just admitted she kept her distance. I was in another Sawyer situation all over again. Good for some flirting, but not much else. Women were complicated. Hell, *everyone* was complicated—even Lysander had rejected me.

When Endellion didn't offer anything more to the conversation, I decided to resume my questions. Anything was better than stewing in frustrations—especially while I had my hands all over her.

"You ever think you've accomplished enough in your life?" I asked. "You're a commodore, for fuck's sake. You could stop trying and still be more accomplished than anyone I know."

"You only think the title of commodore is significant because of your limited understanding of the situation."

"What does that mean?"

"There are currently 1,614 commodores serving the Federation in the Vectin Quadrant at this moment, with a 150 in reserves. While some wield a great amount of influence, many are like me—small. Assigned to tiny segments of the quadrant. I'm a joke in terms of power, especially when compared to even a midlevel commodore who serves a rear admiral directly."

"Ever get tired of comparing yourself to others?" I asked, more dismissive than I should have been.

"Never," Endellion said, the cold edge returning to her voice. "Anyone who doesn't is delusional. They want to fool themselves into thinking they've done an admirable job with their life—that their limited accomplishments are noteworthy—but the reality is, they're insignificant. Worthless in the grand scheme of an endless universe. Like my parents. Most people never amount to anything, because they can't compare themselves to greatness. Because there's nothing about them to compare."

"Is that you or your inner demons talking?"

"Perhaps we're one and the same."

I ran my knuckles down her back, half-smiling. Her fire never died. It never even waned. Could she handle failure? Someone like her, I worried it would break her. But then again, maybe people like her never failed.

"When is enough?" I asked. "Once you're governor... are you going to be satisfied then?"

"First, I have to *become* governor," she whispered. Then she smiled. "We're almost there. Clevon, I want you to pay attention to the topics discussed. You might not realize it now, but the legislation decided here will affect everything, including my future. Do you understand?"

"I'll pay attention."

"Good."

The mag-lev train came to a halt, and the doors opened. Endellion stood, and our therapy session concluded.

She turned to face me. "Now let's attend our pre-meeting, shall we?"

NINETEEN

Voting Bloc

I felt like a schlub. A ratty outcast who'd drunkenly staggered into a high-class gala.

Everything impressed me, from the lavish carpets to the high ceilings. Capital Station had none of it. Wasting space had been unthinkable when I'd lived in a tin can, floating in orbit. Only a planetside building could have had ceilings ten meters up with windows that created entire walls.

Lights floated above us in clouds, like hordes of distant stars. Endellion had said it was a utility fog. Swarms of nanomachines connected through a static wave—powered by room temperatures and moveable with ease—once collapsed together could fit into a container no larger than my hand. I'd never known such technologies existed, and it seemed like my life on Capital Station had been a time capsule, separated from the progress of the rest of the universe.

Commodores, admirals, ministers, and governors mingled in the open rooms, discussing politics and trade with an acute understanding of nuanced subjects. I knew after two or three conversations I couldn't participate. I opted instead to listen and admire the surroundings. Even the smells were beyond anything I had experienced before. Food was served, beverages followed. Each was a pleasant taste and a new experience.

Once, in my younger days, my mother had watered down three-year-old soup from a can to last us for four days. Now I was snacking on fat little animals—sweet and juicy—while downing it all with real wine, made from grapes grown in the dirt.

The humans outnumbered the superhumans. Given my company, I would have guessed the ratio was 20 to one, but each superhuman commanded attention. They were all tall, a head or two over the tallest Homo sapiens in the room. They spoke with perfect enunciation at a speed slightly faster. A hair of a difference, but it was enough to highlight their intelligence in a subtle but constant way. There was no stutter, there was no stammer, and there was no gap of time between complex thoughts and formulating words. They spoke with wit and confidence that couldn't be faked.

Ontwenty stood in a small group, discussing policy with politicians and lobbyists. "I've backed the Stellar Engine," she said with a smile. "It'll centralize the Vectin Quadrant like nothing before. It'll eliminate poverty and strife."

"Minister Felseven and his uncle have denounced the project," someone chimed in. "Their constituents will vote to block the construction. I wouldn't be surprised if the project gets stalled indefinitely."

Endellion had told me to pay attention, so I made a mental note.

Ontwenty and her voting bloc wanted to construct the Stellar Engine, centralizing power in the quadrant and eliminating the need for outer planet farming and mining. Surprise, surprise, Governor Felseven—who'd made his name and gained his power from an outer-planet farming empire—didn't want the Stellar Engine to be constructed. He and Minister Felseven, along with *their* voting bloc, were determined to make sure it never happened.

In theory, the Stellar Engine would have to be paid for by increased Federation taxes on each planet, which undoubtedly made it easy for Felseven to convince other planet governors not to vote for it.

Sounded like they were at a deadlock.

But no one spoke about Endellion's petition, and I wasn't sure how to participate. Instead, I milled about on the sidelines, listening to the conflict and thinking about issues I'd never known existed.

"Twice your research has been targeted, Minister Ontwenty," a woman said, her lithe, superhuman posture giving her a regal elegance. "Why these attacks?"

Ontwenty smiled. "They're disgruntled that the Federation refuses to treat or sell to United-Earth terrorists. If they want to bask in the progress of my research, they shouldn't call for my death, should they?"

"What do you think about Emissary Barten's attempt to establish commercial dealings with the United-Earth Homo sapiens?"

"He's a fool," Ontwenty replied with a wave of her hand. "The rebellion should be put down, and these attempts to treat them as a sovereign group will only give their cause a sense of legitimacy they don't deserve."

"You might be forced to sell your medical treatments to them if the emissary is successful," the superhuman woman said, a slight amusement about her.

Another fucking problem.

Ontwenty conducted medical research to solve the human-defect problem. The United-Earth rebellion hated all superhumans and wanted them ousted from power. Some even wanted all superhumans dead. But many of the rebellion humans were defects. In theory, Ontwenty's research could save them, but they were still fighting the federation.

If Emissary Barten established peaceful trades, Ontwenty would be forced to sell her research to a group of terrorists who wanted her dead.

The chatter grated on me. It wasn't that I didn't understand the subject matter—it was just that I didn't know what to do with it. I was an outsider, peering into a world I wasn't a part of, and it made me uneasy. When I had my bearings, I was confident, but new situations reminded me I was on someone else's turf.

I glanced around and caught sight of Endellion in another

crowd. Although she was shorter than the superhumans, and didn't share their striking features, she mimicked their quick speech and never faltered, not even when presented with esoteric questions. She smiled, gracious, and then moved to another group, no doubt making sure her presence was felt, despite the large crowd.

To my surprise, people approached Endellion at every turn, asking to speak with her, questioning her goals, and demanding answers. Some individuals—sycophant kiss-asses—clung to her every move, praising her for being a leader of the Homo sapiens. They wanted her ear and her time, discussing all the things she could do for humans, which also helped them, of course. *"Humans should stick together,"* they said. Translated: *"Let me ride your coattails."* I didn't know whether I should have been impressed or disgusted. Who could get angry at a cockroach for scavenging? At least they had chosen someone worth clinging to.

I would have elbowed a bitch midway through the party if I were Endellion. But she couldn't do that. I had already heard whispers about her behavior with Commodore Cho—*Brash. Rule breaker. Arrogant.* One incident and they'd extrapolated her entire personality and condensed it into in a single word. Anything negative they could attach to her, they would.

My breathing became ragged, probably from the strain of my untreated injury, and I wanted to experience the crisp, planetside air as much as possible before I left. Most of the attendants ignored me. I suspected they thought I was some unimportant nobody, so I slipped outside without trouble.

The garden surrounding the building was an architectural marvel of nature. Trees, bushes, ferns, and flowers had been planted and arranged with an obsessive-compulsive perfection. I ambled through the designated pathways until the hum of conversation disappeared in the distance. The night sky—with the stars clumped together in blackness—made it seem like space itself had come to enjoy the wonders of the planet.

But that didn't ease my loneliness.

I pulled my PAD arm out of the enviro-suit and stared down at the device.

"Sawyer," I said. "Talk to me."

"What're you doing outside of the pre-hearing?" she asked.

"Endellion has it handled. If anything, I look like a boob standing next to her and nodding along to every fourth word."

"You're bored."

"Yeah."

I sighed and waited for her to continue, but she said nothing. Sawyer had shit to do. I'd known she might turn me down for a conversation, though I had hoped she wouldn't.

A second later my PAD lit up with micro-vids—tiny little email messages from a handful of people. I stared at them for a moment and realized they were from the other starfighters. Sawyer must have had informed them I was bored. It made me smile.

Lee had a cup in his hand, drinking away at some low-end club for the megafarm workers. He blended right in with three guys hanging onto his shoulder and giving me the thumbs-up. Quinn's message showed her walking the narrow corridors on Midway Station, strolling through her old haunts, dressed down in casual-wear. Noah showed me his marksman percentage—83% accuracy. Not bad.

"Getting better," he said on the vid.

And then Advik sent me a picture of a mud puddle. Not even a micro-vid. I only knew it was from her thanks to the sender's tag. She wasn't in the photo. There was nothing else in the photo, actually. Just a puddle of mud.

What a fucking weirdo.

I was about to send that statement back to her, when I stopped and examined the puddle a second time. It had ripples along the edges, and the mud shimmered with a slight iridescent sheen, like there was oil mixed into it.

I liked it. It was kinda like Advik herself. She required a second glance.

She sent me a message, no audio:

. . .

I'VE BEEN TAKING photos of the planet all day. Sawyer said you were bored and I figured you might like to see my best shot.

"WHERE'S THE COLOR?" I asked, and my words converted to a simple text message.

Advik responded with a photo of Vectin-14's purple sky.

SAWYER SAID LOOKING at the sky would help get me over my phobia. Want me to send you my collection of photos? I know you're obsessed with this place.

SHE GOT ME. I should have been taking photos ever since Sawyer gave me the PAD. We were about to leave the planet, and I didn't know when I'd be back.

"Sure," I said. "Send me everything you've got."

Advik sent me hundreds of pictures. It was decent entertainment. With a half-smile, I flipped through each one, enjoying the myriad of planetside wonders that were denied to people living on the space stations.

I got lost in the images, enjoying the air with each deep breath.

But I never heard from Mara or Yuan. It didn't surprise me. Mara wasn't dead, but she *was* in the infirmary, waiting for treatment, and Yuan hadn't been in the mood to talk since the incident.

Time slipped away from me, and after some point, my neck hurt from staring down for so long. I rotated my shoulder and loosened up, but I caught my breath and froze when I spotted Endellion. She stood amid the garden, her eyes closed, and her hand on her temple. Her eyebrows knitted together.

I walked over and crossed my arms. "What're you doing out here?"

"It's time to go," she said, but her eyes remain scrunched shut.

"The meeting isn't over."

"It doesn't matter. I know what's needed to accomplish my goals. Lingering any longer would only cause a problem."

Endellion motioned to the far end of the garden, to a gate that led out of the estate. She took a deep breath and headed for it, recovering her normal, calm façade. I stayed at her side. I knew she must have been in pain.

"Why don't you relax?" I asked, my voice low. "You might be pushing yourself too hard."

"I'm so close to my goal, Clevon. Stopping now is an impossibility."

"The enforcers on the *Star Marque* are banking on your success. I just want to make sure it happens. If you tap out, what're the rest of us going to do?"

Endellion glowered. "You think I'll fail?"

"I never said that."

"But you think if I continue like this, I will."

"I think there's a possibility."

Endellion stared straight ahead, her green eyes displaying a mixture of thoughts that were too difficult to discern. Then she stopped a few meters from our destination and faced me. "Everyone underestimates me. I thought you would be the exception."

Her statement reminded me of my time on Capital Station. Those thugs and cutthroats had underestimated me too. Obviously, they had regretted it, but that didn't change the fact.

"I've never seen you at your fullest," I said. "I think you hide it from everyone."

Endellion offered me a forced smile. "Never play an ace when a two will do."

"That makes it hard to judge when you're at your limit. I have to guess."

"What're you saying?"

"I'm saying, if you want me to keep up, if you want me to be the guy in your corner who never lets you down, I need to know what I'm dealing with. I need to know when to be concerned. I need to know the cards in your hand. Or else all my advice is bunk."

Endellion brushed back a lock of her long, auburn hair. "You're right."

"I know."

She laughed at my statement. After she recovered, she said, "Then you should stop training with the others and join me instead. Starfighter training. Physical training. All of it. You and I are the only ones on the ship who can handle the toughest of obstacles."

"Fine. I look forward to it."

"Good," she said as she walked to the gate. "Because we have two difficult missions ahead. One of them is a private mission. Just for the two of us."

"Sounds like my kind of assignment."

"YOU KNOW we need to leave soon," Sawyer said.

She stepped off the mag-lev train and glanced around. There was a nervous tick about her, like she was afraid someone would jump out of the bushes at any second. When she stood closer to me, I smiled.

"I told you," I said. "You'll love this."

"If Endellion gets upset…"

"We're waiting for the doctor to get his shit together. We've got an hour before anyone rides us for being late."

The morning rays shimmered off the dewdrops hanging on each leaf of vegetation. It was almost better than the damn exhibit we were going to visit, but I knew Sawyer didn't appreciate the view as much as I did. She barely gave it a second glance as we walked along the designated walkways.

"This place is so organized," I said.

"You should see pictures of Vectin-14 from 150 years ago," Sawyer said. "The place was a mess. Changing governments, wars, mismanagement on the part of the United Earth Governance. It's a lot nicer now, but there are a lot of regulations."

We walked up to the front doors of the menagerie, and I

scanned my arm, allowing us access. Ontwenty had been serious when she said she could get me in.

"You seem to know a lot about everything," I said.

"I read a lot."

I laughed. "All I ever see you do is type."

"You're not with me all the time."

We stepped inside. The place had a sterile smell, but the results spoke for themselves. Everything shone with a pristine sleekness. The tiled floor. The marble walls. The glass windows.

"What is this place?" Sawyer asked, one eyebrow cocked.

"I guess you don't know everything, do you?" I tapped her shoulder and pointed to one of the many large arched doorways. "It's over here. C'mon. It's amazing."

The place might as well have been empty. It was the same when I'd visited earlier, and I had no idea why. Who wouldn't want to see a bunch of animals and plants in near-natural environments? The building had multiple biomes specially-made to house a group of compatible creatures and vegetation. The best part was, most of the biomes were open—people could walk right into them. That was probably why people needed an access code to get into the place.

I wondered how much an access code cost…

Sawyer tucked her hands under her armpits as she walked. "I'm not fond of surprises."

"You don't trust me?"

She groaned under her breath but didn't say anything else.

When we reached the designated biome, I jumped in front of the computer terminal, determined to keep our destination a secret. "All right. Inside you go."

"You know, I don't usually leave the ship," Sawyer said. "You should count yourself lucky I'm even here."

"I'm very lucky."

"So, why are you deliberately getting on my nerves?"

"Just get inside the damn biome. You'll see." I grabbed her by the upper arm and shoved her into the room.

The biomes were separated by refraction veils. They were harmless particle screens that stopped lasers, but they also irritated most animals who had eyeballs. It kept them all confined without actually harming them or requiring solid walls.

Giant ferns and trees wrapped in vines made up the majority of our biome. Although it was all inside, the roof had a screen which mimicked perfect weather. The temperature remained a constant 22 degrees Celsius, and the place couldn't have been any more idyllic, even if it tried.

"Okay," I said, pointing upward. "Here they come. Do you see it?"

A flock of floating fish swooshed around the tops of the trees, moving like any school underwater. Their helium sacs deflated slightly as they descended toward us. Unlike Blub, they didn't make a tooting noise—they almost didn't make any noise at all.

However, just like Blub, the fish resembled koi. Their markings, all unique, were made of orange, red, black, and white, mixing together and giving the illusion of the whole flock as one giant unit. When they sailed by, I reached out and grazed my fingertips along the side of a few, marveling at their scaly texture.

Once the flock continued, I glanced over to Sawyer and noticed she was livelier than she ever had been, a smile across her face.

"Like it?" I asked.

"They have so many," she said. "I counted 213."

"You counted them, huh? Why not sit back and enjoy the moment?"

"I've only ever seen them in the labs. Two, maybe three at a time. I didn't know they grouped together like that. What do you call a group of flying fish, anyway? Is it a school? Probably, but it would be amusing if they had some special title. Like a mob, or a team, or a congregation."

"I knew you'd enjoy it," I said with a smirk. "And I figured I should get you off the ship every now and again, before you really *do* turn into a space hermit."

Sawyer laughed, but it didn't last long. She brushed back her red hair and looked up at me. "Thank you."

I waved away the comment, almost embarrassed that she had been so genuine. Almost.

"I know a few better ways you can thank me," I said.

"Not the classiest pickup line I've ever heard, but I'll wait to hear the punchline."

I shrugged. "Well, considering you've preemptively said no to half my options, I'm going to say you can thank me by telling me more about genetically-engineered creatures." I gestured to our surroundings. "I bet everything here was made in a lab. It's like we've returned home. Two modified people in a modified world."

Sawyer lifted an eyebrow. "You're poetic sometimes."

"You avoid my questions sometimes."

She sighed. "Very well. What, specifically, do you want to know about genetically-engineered individuals?"

"I dunno. Surprise me."

"Hm. Let's see. Once upon a time——"

"Take it seriously," I interjected. "I really want to know."

She took a deep breath and started again. "When the Federation formed, there were talks about how to solve the defect problem. Genetic engineering was proposed as a solution. Most humans who are engineered never develop any defects, and their DNA is a lot more stable. So..." Sawyer chose a seat on a nearby bench and relaxed, kicking her feet up on the railing. "The Federation approved government-sanctioned modifications. You can see a doctor to have your child modified, and the government will foot the bill if you're someone who qualifies."

"Is that what happened to me?" I asked. It couldn't have been. My mother had paid for everything herself.

"No," Sawyer said. "You're special. A private investment. Most of those other guys are made with a purpose. You see, to get the modifications done to your kid, the Federation requires they select a role for them to fill, which guarantees they'll be a productive human in the future. The Federation banks on the modified humans reproducing with normal humans, thus resulting in a stronger gene pool that will solve the defect issue."

The floating fish came around again, and Sawyer stopped talking to lean forward.

"Tell me what makes them made for a purpose," I said. "How

are they different from me? And tell me about yourself. I want to know everything."

Sawyer waited until the flock moved away again, following the straggling fish with her eyes until she no longer could. The fish were faster than Blub and moved up and down with ease. Maybe they were improved versions of Blub. They had to be, considering they were so silent.

But then Sawyer sighed. "Look, those other guys are modified to have muscles and quick reflexes and not much else. They don't process information as well or as fast, and they tend to die early. Actually, *most* genetically-modified humans die early. It's a design flaw. Intentional, I think. Like most of their flaws. To ensure things don't get out of hand."

"What do you mean?"

"I mean... sometimes they're made with flaws to guarantee they fit certain molds. You want to know about me? Well, my endocrine system is underdeveloped. Those are the glands that make and secrete hormones. I... don't have intense emotions. And anytime I do, it doesn't last long. Because that's better for a solitary worker, you see. No panic. No depression. Just a need to work, and a fulfillment through accomplishment. But it also ensures I'll be smaller, less aggressive, and not the greatest public speaker. You see what I'm saying."

"That's a fucked-up method of control," I said, mulling over the information. "Limiting people's talents." Limiting their options, really. They didn't have any choice but to be the thing they were made to be.

"Yeah, well, what're you going to do about it? It's a failed experiment, anyway. The defect numbers get higher and higher, and human populations are so separated in some areas that they don't even mingle with anyone who is genetically modified. The Federation now puts its stock in people like Minister Ontwenty, and she's been shutting down most modification labs. Well, the human labs, anyway. Superhuman modification is alive and well."

I sat next to Sawyer and laced the fingers of my hands behind my head, grimacing at the movement—thanks to my injury—but the pain subsided, so I kept my arms up. "So, is your deficient endocrine system the reason we're not a thing?"

Sawyer smiled. "No. But it *is* the reason I haven't had many *things*. People find me off-putting."

"Because you creep around and spy on everyone."

"Not *everyone*. Just individuals I find amusing. I figured you and I would have things in common."

I leaned back and breathed deep. Even in an artificial environment, the air was still sweet.

"Oh, and how have we not talked about you hitting on Lysander?" Sawyer asked with a lifted eyebrow.

"You know about that, huh?"

"I would've paid to be there in person. You're Lysander's least favorite person."

"We were having a moment," I said with a shrug. "And I'd just stumbled out of the healing vat. And I was desperate. All the pieces lined up. But yeah, now that I think about it, not the best play I've ever made."

Sawyer laughed. She took a good, long time doing it, too. I waited because I liked her laugh, and she eventually said, "You really *are* a horndog at times, aren't you?"

"Well, I wouldn't have to be if *someone* had accepted my advances."

She settled down and looked away. "I'm sure you'll find company at some point."

In the quiet that came between us, I knew that Sawyer wouldn't answer my ultimate question—why wasn't she being honest with me? She was afraid of something. Some detail she wouldn't reveal, even after I'd showed her all those wonderful koi fish. Maybe I should have stopped trying. If she was that adamant about not telling me, then it was a wasted effort.

"Endellion said we have two missions to accomplish," I said, my gaze set on the vegetation. "But she hasn't told me the details. You know what they are, don't you?"

Sawyer nodded.

"Tell me."

She returned her gaze to me. "Would it be okay if I... touched you?"

Wait, what? That was an odd request—and phrasing. No wonder people thought she was weird.

I snorted and laughed. "You have *carte blanche* to touch me any way you see fit."

Sawyer pulled her knees up to her chest and rested her head on my side. I bit back a growl and stopped myself from grimacing. She'd placed her head right on my goddamn injury, but I didn't want to scare her away and risk breaking contact. I just soldiered through. I would be bleeding by the end of the conversation, but it was worth it.

I really *was* getting desperate. Even painful pressure on an injury was better than nothing at all.

"The *Star Marque* will be assigned to put down some rebellion thugs," Sawyer whispered. "And then you and Endellion are going to assassinate a superhuman. Emissary Barten, to be specific."

TWENTY

Vice-Captain

I t would take us four days to reach our destination—a section of space by Outpost Station. That was where we would find our rebellion smugglers and thugs.

Lysander yelled something to the enforcers, but I didn't catch his words. Instead, I focused on the girl in front of me. She was one of Endellion's ground enforcers, going through the training motions to develop muscle-memory. We were mock-sparring, training for when the enforcers had to physically brawl with someone while they were on duty. I liked sparring. It was a good distraction. Too bad those fruit loops weren't a challenge for me.

The girl swung with her left, and I leaned away, dodging the blow. We took things slow—because Lysander wanted everyone to learn the correct form, rather than power—but it made the matches so fucking boring. I could have read one of Sawyer's technical manuals in the time it took for one punch to follow the next.

"Am I doing this right?" the girl asked between heavy breaths.

"Pivot with your rear foot and rotate your hips," I said, trying not to reveal my boredom.

"All right."

She punched again, better this time, but still slow. I couldn't really tell her to get faster. Some things were just impossible. She would never be able to give me a challenge in a stand-up fight. Well, she could have pulled an Endellion and augmented her capabilities. Maybe I should have told her to do that.

Just thinking about Endellion reminded me of the assassination. Sawyer didn't know much about it, and I hadn't had a chance to ask Endellion, but something told me she wasn't going to say much. If we were caught murdering a Vectin council emissary, the whole crew of the *Star Marque* would be charged with treason or worse.

Why would Endellion do such a thing? She'd risk everything—and everyone—with one mission.

I dodged a few more strikes, barely seeing anything around me.

Who the fuck was Emissary Barten, anyway? I remembered hearing his name at the pre-hearing, but just once. Ontwenty had talked about him. Was he the man who was attempting to open trade deals with the rebellion? Yes. That was it. And Ontwenty loathed the idea of selling her medicine to a group of thugs who wanted her dead.

It all came together now. Ontwenty had asked Endellion to handle the situation, to make sure the deal never happened. In exchange, Endellion would solidify her place as one of the next planet governors.

"*Demarco*," Lysander shouted, an edge to his voice that betrayed his frustration.

"Yeah?" I asked.

"Are you paying attention to anything I'm saying?"

"No."

A round of chuckles washed through the other ground enforcers. We were in a group of 50, so the laughter spread quick, but it didn't amuse Lysander, not one bit. The man glared at me, his arms crossed.

"What is it?" I asked. "Am I not up to your standards or something?"

"We're moving on. You and—"

Lysander cut himself off, his gaze set on something behind me. I turned around and tensed. Endellion waited on the sidelines of the sparring mats, standing with the other enforcers waiting to take their turn. She was in her casual clothes again, dressed much like everyone else in the room.

"Clevon," she said. "I thought I told you all training will be done with me from now on."

What was I? A child being reprimanded? Silence followed her statement, like everyone else held their breath, waiting for me to reply.

"I didn't think you meant *this* kind of training," I said with a one-sided smile. "This is group tactics and procedures. Stuff you couldn't practice with just one other person."

Endellion glanced to the enforcers, then the mats, and then back to me. "Seems like you're sparring. That's something we can easily replicate."

"You want to spar?" I couldn't keep the excitement from my voice. Everyone in the room must have heard it, too, because murmurs started circulating.

I had been waiting for the offer. I wanted to see Endellion at her fullest. No holding back. My corded muscles versus her cybernetic implants. She talked a big game, and I'd never had interest in the other enforcers, anyway.

Endellion stepped onto the mat. My old sparring partner hustled into the crowd, leaving me alone with our captain. My pulse doubled.

"If this is what you want," Endellion said. "We have time for a quick match."

"Is this really a productive use of our time?" Lysander asked as he emerged from the crowd and onto the mat. "Demarco just got out of the healing vat."

The chuckles that followed the statement only spurred my desire to have the match.

"You think I can't handle this?" I asked.

"I think we shouldn't even find out. When I was in the HSN Corps, the superior officers never fought against new recruits or trainees because—"

"Everything is under control," Endellion interjected. "Clevon and I are both accustomed to fighting. It'll be a friendly match."

"How friendly?" I asked. I didn't want it to be too gentle.

"Until one of us yields."

Oh, so, not friendly at all. Not if our goal was to force each other to submit. No one wanted to lose in front of a crowd, and Endellion sure as fuck didn't want to look weak to her crew. She was *that* confident she would beat me? She would be surprised. I had been improving ever since I'd set foot on the starship.

Lysander opened his mouth, and then shut it, obviously torn between speaking and compliance. After a moment, he exhaled and backed off the mat, allowing the match to happen without further protest. Silence suffocated the room, but there was one last thing I needed to check before we got our party underway.

I stepped close to Endellion under the guise of shaking her hand, but in a whisper, I asked, "Are you sure? I might cut that pretty face of yours." It was more threatening than I'd wanted it to be, but given her history with even the tiniest of blemishes—and her fear of judgement—I just had to make sure.

She lifted an eyebrow. "We're on the *Star Marque* with a competent doctor under my employ. I think I can handle a few scrapes in this environment, should they happen."

We broke apart, and I took my side of the mat. There was no need for bells and whistles. The moment we locked eyes, I knew the match had begun. She stepped forward, and so did I.

Endellion swung with her right at speeds the others couldn't comprehend, but when I moved away, she backhanded with a left. Her knuckles caught me above the brow, and I lived through the moment in slow-motion, spotting the smirk on her face as she coiled for a second round.

Her hit hadn't hurt, but when I tensed to lunge, a steady flow of blood got into my eyes. Her knuckles must have been angled and sharp, and she'd used the force of her strike to slice open my forehead. Instinctively, I lifted my hand to stop the bleeding, which was just what she'd wanted.

Endellion kicked at my undefended side, bashing my ribs right where I had been stabbed previously. Too fast. I didn't see it in time to dodge. I was healed—thanks to the mother cells—but the memory of the agony was still fresh in my mind. Her shin had the sting of metal. I might as well have been hit by a girder.

Two seconds into the match, and I had blood weeping into my eyes and a cracked rib.

Fuck me. I hadn't realized she would play dirty.

When she kicked a second time, I lunged close, getting hit, but it wasn't at the end of the arc, and I used the fraction of a moment she was open to elbow her in the gut—the one place she didn't have reinforced steel bones. Sure enough, my elbow sunk into her abdomen and sent her tumbling back.

Unfortunately, the blood on my face was too much. I either had to fight blind or sacrifice a hand to keep my vision clear. And since I couldn't risk not seeing her, I kept one hand up.

Endellion didn't take long to recover. I rushed in, hoping to bring her to the ground. If we'd have grappled, being blind wouldn't have been as much of a disadvantage. But she pivoted, the force and speed enough to tear the mat. I clenched my jaw, over-thinking the situation, knowing she had the same mental zeal as I did.

Then she grabbed my shoulder. Her eyes widened as I whipped around, elbowing her again, this time to the side of the head. I pulled back on the force, fearing I would disrupt the cybernetics in her spine. She didn't let go of my shoulder, but blood spilled onto her neck from her shattered ear.

The gasps around the room invigorated me.

In one brutal motion, Endellion threw me down onto the mat, my back hitting it hard. She punched me across the face, her strength augmented by the machines. For a second, all I saw was white, my hearing flooded with a single sharp note.

She'd busted my nose. I would be smelling blood for a week.

But she'd made a mistake. I was strong enough to flip us both over, despite the fact she was twice my weight—thanks to all that internal metal—and I slammed her underneath me, my vision returning gradually.

I pressed down into her neck—my elbow digging deep into her

throat—and held one of her arms down with my knee. Endellion tightened her grip on my shoulder. Her fingers acted like knives, and her grip was stronger than any normal human's. She wasn't limited to the muscles of her hand and forearm, not with the cybernetics throughout her entire body. When she squeezed, she had the force necessary to pierce through my muscle and rip out a chunk of my shoulder.

But would she do that before I choked her out?

I guessed we were going to find out.

Her fingers penetrated my arm, gouging out holes and covering the mat in slick, vital fluid. Pain flared, but it faded into the background of my mind, washed away by pure adrenaline. I strangled back a yell, and it half-mixed into a chortle. Endellion smiled up at me, like she was ready to take it to the next level. I smiled back as she wrested her other arm free and grabbed my side—just under my ribs—her knife-like fingers right over my vulnerable kidney.

She could have taken me apart, doctor and healing vat be damned.

I knew it. The heat between us was real.

I loved it.

"Enough!"

Lysander jumped onto the mat and grabbed me by the arm. I was half-tempted to shake him off and continue, but a few more enforcers hustled in to separate us. I got off Endellion, and she stood with ease, taking only a moment to brush off her clothing and wipe the blood from her ear. Her hand looked like a gore zone, however. My shoulder might as well have been mauled by a rabid animal.

"You never disappoint," Endellion said.

I smile. "I aim to please." I rotated my good arm and held back a wince when agony ran down my spine.

The crowd of enforcers chanted Endellion's name. She smirked, seemingly unfazed by the match. I did look the part of the loser—and I was seconds from having my organs vivisected—but no one lasted forever without blood flow to the brain, and her neck wasn't designed like a superhuman's. I could have choked her out.

Lysander ran a hand over his face. "This is unacceptable. There's nothing to be gained from ripping each other apart. This didn't demonstrate any of the techniques we learned, nor did it—"

"Yeah, yeah," I said with a dismissive wave of my hand. "Save it for when I'm not losing so much blood. Shouldn't you take me to get some medical attention? That's what a proper overseeing officer would do."

The look on his face was like he wanted me to bleed out on the mat, but he couldn't bring himself to let it happen. Lysander was too easily riled.

But I hurt. Fire built beneath my skin, killing the rush I'd had previously. I was ready for the doctor.

"You can train with the enforcers before or after you're with me, Clevon," Endellion said as she headed for the door.

Her hand stayed up by her ear, and it trembled when she touched her hairline. No one else seemed to notice—or if they did, they gave no indication.

"HOW'RE YOU FEELING?" Dr. Clay asked.

He didn't even look me in the eye. He stared down at the PAD on his arm, typing away, like he was one of Sawyer's long-lost cousins. Not much happened in the infirmary, yet he acted like he was busy all the time.

"I'm better," I said as I rubbed my shoulder. "Can I go now?"

Dr. Clay ignored me and focused on his own work. If he were anything like Sawyer, he would have been able to hold a conversation and work, but he was just an unmodified human with a flair for medicine.

Plus, the guy had one speed, and that speed was "fuck you."

"Dr. Rhodes had a better bedside manner," I said with a smirk.

Dr. Clay snapped his attention to me, a glare set on his angled face, like he'd been born with it. "You were never treated by Dr. Rhodes," he said. "Her specialty is pharmaceuticals, specifically for use on defects. You're some brute modification, like every other."

Then he turned away and continued his work.

I wondered how he would have reacted if I told him I intended to hook up with Dr. Rhodes the moment we returned to Midway Station. It would have been a dick move, but it would have been a *satisfying* dick move.

Whatever. He couldn't keep me in the infirmary. I slid off the examination table, energized, despite my messed-up sleep schedule. Being planetside hadn't helped anything. I had stayed awake for long hours to watch the sky transform from day into dusk, then from night into dawn. Sights like that couldn't be taken for granted.

I was halfway to the door when a collection of plastic bottles clattered to the floor.

"Calm down," Yuan hissed. "You're not yourself."

Mara, dressed in a thin gown, stood on the opposite side of her gurney. She took in a deep breath and brandished a scalpel, her hand trembling.

"What's going on?" I asked.

Mara held up the impromptu weapon. "Stay back." Her weak voice didn't carry far. When Yuan attempted to grab her wrist, Mara slashed, cutting Yuan's fingers. Blood dripped onto the gurney and floor. Yuan took a step back, cradling her hand to her chest.

"Shouldn't you handle this?" Dr. Clay said, motioning me to Mara. "This is what you were made for."

I ignored his bullshit and leapt to intervene. Mara didn't move as fast as I did. I jumped over the gurney, grabbed her wrist, and twisted it backwards, forcing her to drop the scalpel. She struggled to free herself from my hold, but her weak efforts amounted to little.

"Stop," she said. "Get away from me! Get away!" Her frantic screaming put me on edge. That wasn't like Mara. At all.

Dr. Clay walked over with the leisurely pace of an afternoon stroll. He held up a syringe, and Mara jerked and thrashed, her eyes wild.

"Hold her still," Dr. Clay commanded.

I complied, but I had half a mind to release her. I pinned both of Mara's arms and kept her from lashing out with my superior strength. At one point she attempted to bite me, more like a psychopath than someone stricken with depression.

Dr. Clay stuck the syringe in her shoulder. It didn't take long—a few seconds, tops—and Mara exhaled, her energy leaving with her breath. She slouched, and her eyes fluttered closed.

"Stop," she pleaded. "I don't... want..."

Then she fell unconscious. I held her upright and placed her back on the gurney, her small body small and lightweight. Yuan rushed to her side.

"What's going on?" I asked.

Dr. Clay didn't answer. He returned his attention to his PAD.

Yuan stroked Mara's face with her uninjured hand. "This isn't her. She's not herself. Once her implant is fixed, she'll go back to being just right." Yuan glanced up. "Tell Endellion I'm getting tired of waiting."

"I don't tell Endellion what to do. *No one* does."

"You're with her often enough. Until Mara is back to normal, I'm not going to pilot that damn starfighter of hers."

The animosity washed from her in waves, but all I could focus on was Mara. She didn't look right. Her eyebrows were knit, and she tossed and turned, even while unconscious. Yuan shushed her and whispered sweet nothings. It didn't seem to work. Mara continued to move around in her sleep.

"What're you still doing here?" Dr. Clay asked. He motioned to the door. "She needs rest, and you're in the way."

I gave Mara one last glance before heading for the door. A part of me felt responsible for her wellbeing, but another part wanted to forget it entirely. People got hurt all the time. We were in an industry of death and violence, after all. We wouldn't all make it.

But Endellion would become governor soon, and it would be like we had crossed the finish line. If we could just hang on until then, everything would be okay. At least, that was what I wanted to believe.

Just a little bit longer.

"THESE ARE THE STAR MAPS," Endellion said, pointing to the screens and scrolling through vast amounts of information.

Everything had to be in three dimensions or else it wasn't accurate. Not only that, but celestial movement had to be taken into account, along with possible variations for asteroid impacts or planet collision. Learning the shorthand for each number sequence was tiring, but Endellion insisted I needed to know how to read the goddamn maps, so I committed the information to memory.

"Doesn't Sawyer know all this?" I asked.

"Of course."

"Then why do I need to know?"

Endellion turned to me, a perfect eyebrow lifted. "The station of vice-captain requires this knowledge set."

"Is that right?" I asked with a laugh. "Are you charting out my career path for me?"

"I thought my intentions for you were obvious."

"You're serious?" I glanced around the central database for the *Star Marque*. Empty computer terminals sat idle. Endellion really did need to fill her crew. "I can think of a few others who would be more suited to vice-captain long before me."

I didn't like the stillness that followed my statement. Endellion took a moment before facing me. "Must you always question your place at my side? How many times do I have to spell out my reasoning? I'd expect this from someone with half your intelligence."

Always blunt. Didn't matter. I could handle the criticism, though I wished she would explain the steps of her madness more than not at all.

"I'll happily become your vice-captain," I said. "I just figured you'd want me to be straight with you. I know nothing about the captain's duties."

Endellion returned her attention to the star map. She scrolled through the Vectin Quadrant, highlighting space stations and refueling outposts. "The duties of the captain are all-encompassing. Sure, I delegate responsibilities to my officers but to evaluate their work, I have to have a basic understanding of what they do."

"So, you've got to know everyone's job."

"I also have to crunch the numbers. Every job we take has to pay for everyone's salary, along with the ship's upkeep, any supplies we may need, any repairs that must be done, and any equipment that needs to be replaced. Financial responsibility is perhaps one of the most important elements of being a captain. Again, an officer can handle this, but I make the ultimate decision of what jobs we take."

"Gotta be good with numbers. All right."

"Knowing the laws also helps, especially since the *Star Marque* is hired to supplement station enforcers."

"Uh-huh. Laws. Check."

Endellion circled our destination on the star map. "Politics. Enforcer ships only get contracts from station overseers and others of comparable or higher authority. If an overseer doesn't like you on a personal level, they can deny every one of your requests for employment. Knowing who you can serve, and how you can forge beneficial relationships, is another important factor of being captain."

"All right. Knowing how to play politics. Got it."

"Have a long-term goal," Endellion intoned as she turned to face me. "Nothing matters in life unless you have an end game. Your existence doesn't matter unless it can stand above others."

I crossed my arms and cocked an eyebrow. "Know everyone's job. Keep the books. Understand the laws. Play politics. World domination. Anything I missed?"

She laughed. "Yes, well, now you're starting to understand. And we haven't even gotten into the importance of strategy or combat maneuvers, especially with rogues like those in the rebellion."

"So, let's back up," I said as I waved my hand in circles, "to laws and politics. How does assassination play into that equation?"

It was almost time. We would reach Outpost Station in less than two days. Endellion had yet to tell me her plans, and now seemed like a good time to discuss it, especially since the outcome could be dire beyond belief.

"Sawyer told you?" Endellion asked, unfazed.

"That's right. But she didn't talk about much."

"Make sure no one knows about this outside us three. Ever. Under any circumstance. Even talking about it is conspiracy of the second degree. We'll be charged and fined, and possibly even sent to Ucova."

"No one is going to hear us here," I said, motioning to the ghost town we called the Central Data Room. I doubted anyone outside of Sawyer even knew where we were.

"You're wrong," Endellion intoned. "Or, you would have been wrong, had I not handled the situation ahead of time. You see, the Federation operating system for all starships includes a recording subroutine that listens for keywords of insubordination. Words like 'murder,' or 'assassination,' or 'overthrow.' Then it records those conversations and sends them to the authorities without us being the wiser."

I scratched at my neck. Fucking creepy. Not only did those codes give the dreadnaughts power over our enforcer ships, but they also monitored each crew, like they were criminals waiting to happen. Then again, we *were* discussing the death of an emissary.

"Sawyer fixed it so that won't happen, right?" I asked.

Endellion nodded. "Of course. Sawyer has always been the wildcard in my corner. She's an invaluable resource."

Yeah, that was how I liked to talk about people, too. Like resources. I wondered sometimes whether Endellion even realized she was doing it. Sawyer had to be listening in on the conversation, but I figured she didn't have any objections because she didn't say anything.

Lost in my own thoughts, I didn't even realize Endellion had stopped talking until a few quiet seconds ticked by. She rubbed at her neck, her eyes scrunched, and I knew her pain had returned.

"Sorry about that," I said. "The sparring match, I mean."

"You held back."

"Yeah, because something's not right with your implants."

"I wanted to see how the cybernetics would hold up."

"No, you wanted to beat me in front of your crew so that they'd understand you're still the superior combatant."

I knew Endellion enough to understand appearances were paramount in her world. It was archaic, but enforcers—and thugs, really—still valued personal might, even if that wasn't as useful in a universe with devastating technology. I still did, and there was no doubt in my mind the crew thought even higher of Endellion for besting me in less than 30 seconds.

She smiled, almost cold. "Yes, well, that was a reason, as well. But knowing how much force the absorbers in my system can handle is also beneficial. You see, Emissary Barten will be staying on Outpost Station for a few more days, but his quarters are behind anti-violence perimeters, meaning the use of lasers and plasma guns will be impossible."

"We're going to kill him with our bare hands?" I asked. Well, that was a different picture than what I'd had imagined.

"Yes. But the two of us should be able to handle one superhuman."

She was probably right. I knew then why it had to be us. We were the only ones who were capable of it. But if we were caught… I didn't even want to think about it.

"You know what else we should do?" I asked. "We should have that sparring match again. In private. That way we can prepare for the emissary and determine which of us is really better."

Endellion didn't respond. Instead, she stepped away from the star maps and stood in front of me, her look challenging, even without a single word uttered.

I smiled. "I'd love to play just as dirty as you. And without Lysander around, I'm sure it could turn into an exhilarating time."

"Is that really what you want, Clevon? Or do you want the company of an intimate partner instead?"

Her question caught me off-guard. I didn't have a response before she slid her hand up my neck and along my jaw. The woman had an excellent command of nonverbal communication.

"Are you serious?" I asked, my voice low. "Or is this you fucking with me?"

Endellion pressed herself against me, her mouth against mine, her lips hot and soft. When I felt her tongue, I was ready to take things further, but I held back, still in a state of semi-disbelief. She tasted like sweet sweat, the raw kind you only get from sex.

After I recovered a bit, I ran my hands along her body, thankful for her casual clothing. Even though she was a cyborg—even though there was metal and machines embedded into her flesh—she was smooth and curved in all the right places. And she didn't stop me from exploring every millimeter of her. If anything, she gripped me tighter and sucked on my lower lip, obviously enjoying whatever she tasted.

She stopped and broke our kiss, but not our embrace, her ragged breath on my chin and neck.

"So, how's this going to go?" I asked, my voice husky and laced with excitement. "You want it right here, standing up? Your quarters? My capsule? I'll fuck you in the lift, if that's your fantasy."

Her laughing only added to my enjoyment. Endellion ran her lips along my jaw and licked my ear. "So crude, yet so accommodating."

I sucked on her neck, rapt by the way she shuddered. "Gotta make the girl happy," I breathed into her skin. "Rule Number One for getting laid."

"And the second rule?" she asked in my ear, but her hand traveled to the top of my cargo pants. She unfastened my belt before I could remember what we were talking about.

"Don't argue with her," I said with a chuckle. "There are only two ways to argue with a woman, and neither work, so there's no point in doing it."

"And the third?"

I couldn't remember. I could barely recall my name. Instead, I grabbed at the buttons on her pants and ripped them open, ready to christen that forgotten room several times over. I hadn't been with anyone other than my hand in over a year. *A fucking year*. And now that it was so close to ending, I didn't want to think about anything else.

"You're quickly losing your options for how this plays out," I said as I slid her shirt up over her taut stomach.

"We could've studied star maps on the bridge, Clevon. The Central Data Room wasn't an arbitrary location."

Of course it wasn't.

TWENTY-ONE

By Design

E ndellion's quarters weren't as luxurious as I'd thought they would be.

The room had the space of 20 capsules, sure, but besides the bed, everything was a flat surface made of plastic or metal. The ceiling hung low—not *too* low, I could still stand—but after having experienced the planetside accommodations, I didn't think the interior of a starship would ever impress me again.

A few more hours, and we would reach our destination. We hadn't used our time wisely—not when we had rebellion fighters to kill and an assassination to complete—but I wasn't about to complain, either. After we returned to Vectin-14, I would be made vice-captain. Endellion used what little extra time we had to instruct me on all the tasks a vice-captain had to undertake. In between rolling through the sheets, of course. Best part of the job, really.

Funny how much life brightened after I got laid. The *Star Marque* could have imploded in a dark corner of space, and I might have been satisfied with how my life had played out at that point.

I was sure I would feel different in a few hours, but still.

Endellion walked out of her personal shower room wearing

nothing but a towel on her head. Her smooth skin, fresh with the scent of soap, didn't have a single blemish. I knew. I'd looked. Her obsession with perfection had lots of benefits, and not just in appearance.

I had been with lots of people, but not many had kept up with my stamina. She liked to be on top—which didn't surprise me—but I was fine with it considering the vise grip of pleasure from her well-toned body. And when she stared down at me with greener-than-possible eyes, nobody else even compared.

Endellion threw off the towel, freed her long hair, and took a moment to comb everything straight.

"You ready for round three?" I asked as I stretched out on her bed. I wore as much as she did. We could have made it a quick session.

She glanced over, and then returned to her brushing. "*You* don't look ready."

"You know it won't take me long."

"As appealing as that offer sounds, we'll be needed soon," Endellion said. "You and I will fight the rebellion light cruisers, and once the battle is over, we'll be taking the starfighters to Outpost Station."

"Without the *Star Marque*?" I asked, lifting an eyebrow. "Can the starfighters even make it that far on the fuel they'll have?"

"We're taking one less bolt for the hyperweapons to accommodate a larger fuel capacity. Emissary Barten is on Outpost Station currently. If we're to kill him, I don't want any chance that it'll be linked back to the *Star Marque*."

"Won't the station have a record of us docking?"

"They'll have a record of rebellion starfighters docking," she said as she braided her own hair into a tight coil. "But not *Star Marque* starfighters."

Ah. I understood now. Our starfighters were somehow going to register as rebellion instead of as the *Star Marque*'s. Another advantage Sawyer had brought to the table.

As if my thoughts summoned her, Sawyer spoke over the intercom. "Endellion, enemy light cruisers have appeared on the scanner. They're farther away from Outpost Station than I'd originally anticipated."

"Have they detected us?" Endellion asked.

"It seems so. They've altered course."

"Damn."

Endellion finished her braid, and then jogged over to grab her casual outfit from the drawers mounted to the bulkhead. It didn't take her long to slip into it, but I enjoyed every second. Then she turned to me, her expression as calm as ever. "Suit up."

I slid off Endellion's bed and grabbed my discarded clothing off the floor. I didn't know why, because Sawyer and I had never been a thing, but guilt ate at the edge of my thoughts. It was something about Sawyer's tone. She hadn't sounded happy, that was for sure.

And we hadn't spoken in the last few days.

I pulled my pants on, slipped into my shirt, and secured everything in place. Before I could say anything, the lights dimmed, and a red hue shined along the bulkheads, indicating the *Star Marque* had engaged combat systems. Endellion motioned to the door, and we left, running down the corridors and heading straight for the lift.

When we arrived, Yuan was waiting for us. She turned on her heel, glaring. "Endellion," she said. "We need to talk."

"Not now," Endellion replied as she motioned for Yuan to step aside. "You should be in your starfighter."

"I won't do it."

And then silence. Endellion said nothing, and Yuan gritted her teeth. I wasn't sure what was going on, but I *did* know that Mara was still out of commission. Seemed bizarre, considering we had a doctor and the tools, but I hadn't been in the right mind to ask Endellion the circumstances of Mara's condition.

"You promised me she'd be back to normal," Yuan said. "It's been four days! You're delaying this. Fix her."

"She'll be back to her usual, happy self, once this fight is over."

"Did you intentionally make Dr. Clay alter her implant? Is that it?"

"*He* altered it because of his own medical standards. I will simply have it returned to its prior settings, once we're done."

Yuan stepped forward, centimeters from Endellion, her whole body tense. "I won't fight. I refuse. Not until you fix Mara."

"You will fight, or Mara will remain as she is."

I barely had any understanding of what was going on between them, but I was already furious. Mara wasn't *a thing*, but the way they talked about her, no one would have known. I remained quiet, my focus on the red lights. We were supposed to be engaging the enemy, goddammit.

"You can't do that," Yuan said, strained. "You have to fix her."

Endellion grabbed her by the upper arm and shoved her against the lift door. "You know I can do whatever I want. The doctor won't alter anything without my command, not when it's against standard protocol. So, you can threaten to expose me and lose the Mara you want forever, or you can collect yourself and get into a starfighter."

Yuan didn't reply. Endellion pushed her aside and stepped into the lift. I followed after, giving Yuan a quick glance, but she didn't return it. She reeked of anger.

The lift door closed.

"Explain," I demanded. "What's happening to Mara?"

"She's suicidal," Endellion said, not a hint of emotion about her.

The lift sped to our desired deck. We didn't have much time.

"Is she? I'm starting to think this is all bullshit. What else is happening?"

"Mara has an implant that regulates hormone levels. Years ago, Yuan wanted to help Mara cope with the depression—and have Mara for herself—but normal levels of medication still left Mara dissatisfied with life. She hurt herself and others around her."

"So?"

"So Mara came to me, and I got a doctor to increase the level of hormone dumps, preventing Mara from ever feeling anything negative, to put it in simple terms. No anger. No depression. No anxiety. But such a procedure is technically illegal. I agreed to keep quiet and help maintain the implant, so long as Yuan continued to help me. She knows most of my past dealings—one wrong testimony and I could lose my title as commodore."

"For what?"

"For things like taking genetically-defective crewmembers or covering up the crimes of felons." Endellion narrowed her eyes. "You're aware I bend the rules. But if I lose my title, I lose everything. Do you understand?"

The story didn't quell my anger. If anything, it was worse than before. No one seemed to give a shit about Mara. Endellion just wanted her end goal, and Yuan apparently just wanted a happy-go-lucky playmate.

"Can Mara even think for herself?" I asked. "How can she? If she's deliriously happy all the time?" And she was, too. I'd known it was unnatural, I just thought she was a weirdo.

"What does it matter?" Endellion asked.

The lift door opened, but I slammed the button and shut it once again. Endellion met my gaze with cold anger.

"It's fucking disturbing," I said. "It's like Yuan is controlling her thoughts. Can Mara even say no? To *anything*? And you just let this happen?"

"What would you rather I do?"

"Fuck Yuan. I know you've broken the law, but I'm sure you can keep Yuan in check with something else. Don't let her overset Mara's implant."

"Then Mara's a risk to herself and deeply unhappy with life."

I gritted my teeth. Before I could formulate a response, Endellion narrowed her eyes. "What's best for Mara?" Endellion asked, almost a little too icily for the situation. "With this outcome, she'll enjoy life, have a relationship, and be a productive member of society. If we do things your way, she'll cut and bleed herself dry, wallowing in depression she can't shake. Tell me, which one of us is doing her a disservice?"

"But my way, she gets to choose," I said, fixated on the things Mara had lost to gain such an outcome. Surely there was another way for her to find happiness. There had to be.

"So, you're saying that allowing people to choose poorly is a benefit to them?" Endellion asked, almost laughing. "Design is always a better outcome. You were designed, and you're better than most. Superhumans were designed, and they're clearly superior. Society is designed, and it's better than chaos. Even *I've* designed myself to be better than I was before."

"But—"

"I never heard you complain that you were made physically fit without exercise. Your mother chose that for you. Shouldn't you have been allowed to be a fat slob, unable to move? Now think of Mara. Perhaps eliminating all negative choice is what's objectively best. And there's no benefit to Mara's unhappiness or her death."

I stood in front of the lift door, grappling with ethics I hadn't known I would ever have to deal with. How could Endellion be so confident her analysis was right? Or was she just manipulating me?

"You designed yourself," I said. "It's not a fair comparison. You made decisions."

"Some people can't make those decisions. They're stupid, or weak-willed, or born to a chem whore, or whatever reason you wish to attribute to their failings. Is it not benevolence to rig the game in their favor? To make sure they have no wrong choices?"

"And this coincidently works out for you, doesn't it?" I asked. "Because now you have two starfighters. Your reasoning isn't contingent on that, is it?"

"Endellion, Demarco," Sawyer said over the comms. "You don't even have time to do a systems check on your starfighters at this point. You have to get to your stations. We're engaging the enemy."

Endellion motioned to the lift door. "Perhaps we can talk about this a different time."

I stepped aside, still uncertain. She was right. Now wasn't the time. I should've investigated the situation earlier.

We made our way down the hall and stopped at our starfighters. Endellion jumped into hers, and I got into mine, hoping nothing was wrong with the systems. The cockpit closed, suffocating me in darkness and suctioning around my legs. I grabbed the two side-sticks and took a deep breath. The computer screens lit up, but the user interface was different than it had been before. It was clunky, took up more space, and didn't display the information I was used to.

"What is this?" I asked.

"An operating system used by most rebellion starfighters," Sawyer responded over the comms.

"I have to fight with this?"

"Yes. If you had been at your station earlier, I could've gone over it, but as it stands, you need to detach from the *Star Marque* immediately."

My starfighter quaked, and I shook back and forth, my shoulders bruised. "What was that?"

"The *Star Marque* is under attack. We've taken heavy fire."

What? Already?

Using the *Star Marque*'s main comms line, Endellion said, "Noah and Yuan, disable Cruiser A."

Noah and Yuan? Noah was the weakest pilot, and Yuan was distraught. Should they be a team? What was Endellion thinking?

"Lee, Quinn, and Advik, disable Cruiser B," Endellion continued. "Clevon and I will target the enemy fighters."

I didn't wait to hear confirmations. I performed my undocking procedures and pulled away from the *Star Marque* as fast as possible. Typically, I would have gotten a readout of everyone else's status. I would have been Starfighter Eight, Endellion would have been Starfighter One... but in this situation, Endellion and I were separate, and I couldn't see anyone else's information. When I glanced at the navigation I saw dots—the *Star Marque* fighters were in green, the rebellion fighters were in red—but no direct communication. I had lost the *Star Marque*'s main comms line the moment I detached.

"I have to go," Sawyer said. "Don't die, because I won't be able to whisper those sweet nothings if you do."

"Wait. I—"

"I can't. I'm sorry."

Her transmission ended. I had only one communication channel, and it was straight to Endellion's fighter.

"Clevon," Endellion said. "Focus. Destroy the enemy fighters as fast as possible."

I counted the red dots. 37. And that wasn't including the two light cruisers. The *Star Marque* started to engage, but the opening round went to the enemy, that was for sure. The cruisers must've headed straight for us the moment they'd spotted the *Star Marque* on their long-range scanners.

I had two hyperweapon bolts, and 20 torpedoes. Not enough to handle every enemy.

Without another moment of hesitation, I punched my starfighter forward.

5Gs. 7Gs. 9Gs.

The acceleration crushed me back into my seat, but I had developed a sick enjoyment of it. The thrill of fighting in space. Kill or be killed. Nothing compared.

I overtook three enemy fighters within a couple seconds. I fired three torpedoes while breathing down their necks. No possibility of dodging, but the debris from the impact registered on my scanners, warning me of possible collision. I tilted the side-stick and got by, but the narrow window for success made me sweat more than I should have at that point.

I needed to watch that.

There was nothing to hide behind. Our fighting arena consisted of nothing but open space, devoid of asteroids and scrap metal.

9.5Gs. 9.6Gs.

Gray seeped into my vision as I looped around and overtook two more enemy fighters. I fired four torpedoes, missing with two, but ultimately clearing two enemies off the battlefield. If Sawyer had been with me, I was sure she would have urged me to decelerate, but I couldn't.

My screen lit up, warning me that the docking port I'd left had been destroyed. Sure enough, when I looked at the information I had on the *Star Marque*, a large section on its side had been decimated by the enemy. My only solace came from a light cruiser's bridge going up in a blazing pyre of glory. Someone had gotten a fantastic hit with their hyperweapons, taking one light cruiser from the battle.

I whipped around and dove toward another enemy starfighter. My single-minded focus almost prevented me from keeping track of all the dots, but my mind was fast enough to take everything in.

One green dot disappeared—destroyed.

Five more red dots—destroyed.

Another hit to the *Star Marque*.

I gritted my teeth. Unlike the last battle—which we had planned out in advance—this time, we were slipping. I fired off five more torpedoes, taking out two more enemy fighters. I wasn't worried for my safety, despite my impaired vision. My heart seized the moment I thought of the others.

Lee, Quinn, Advik, Noah, Yuan…

Another green dot vanished from my screen. Two of them were dead.

9.7Gs. 9.8Gs.

I had never felt so frustrated, so powerless. I would rather it have been me versus 37 enemies than have to watch another starfighter from the *Star Marque* disappear. I fired four more torpedoes, destroying three rebellion fighters.

"Clevon," Endellion said, her voice icy. "Increase your acceleration and take out the last cruiser. It's turning for a second barrage on the *Star Marque*."

I was already at my limit. Everything in my cockpit flashed red, and the burn in my system came from the lack of proper blood flow. Didn't matter. Those rebellion assholes would be wiped from the universe in a matter of minutes.

I headed in, aware of the cruiser's point-defense systems. If I got too close, they would destroy me, so I flew in at an angle, my breathing weak. I knew what Sawyer would have said. *Breathe deep.* So, I did that. I forced myself to.

At the last moment—before I collided with the invisible wall of destruction that surrounded the cruiser—I fired my hyperweapon and pulled up. The blinding light of plasma flared for a few seconds as the bolt melted through the enemy bridge, killing everyone at the helm.

Another five red dots disappeared.

My grip slipped off the side-sticks. On the ragged edge of unconsciousness, I released the throttle. I couldn't handle the G-force any longer. An enemy fighter locked onto my position, and my screen flashed a warning. I didn't have the reflexes to move in time.

But the enemy starfighter exploded in a bright flash. Endellion had fired one of her own hyperweapons to remove the threat. She streaked by, and I tightened my grip on my side-sticks.

"Focus," she commanded.

I accelerated to match her. Four red dots remained, but one by one, they disappeared—undoubtedly handled by the last of the *Star Marque* fighters—as I circled around our combat zone. I breathed easier, though it didn't relax me. Two *Star Marque* starfighters had died, and who knew what had happened to everyone on the main ship?

"We're heading for Outpost Station," Endellion said, dragging my thoughts back to the immediate moment. "Keep close."

I exhaled and did as I was instructed. Still, the doubt and worry wouldn't leave me. I had never experienced anything like it before. I had never been so shaken. Tons of people had died on Capital Station. *Tons.* People I'd known. People I'd run guns with. I hadn't cared. Maybe I'd thought about them once or twice, when I got bored. It had never been like this. My chest and gut hurt, like they were twisted in on each other. It was so hard to articulate.

"Endellion," I said, needing someone to talk to. "Two of the *Star Marque* starfighters were destroyed."

"I saw." She was terse, but at least there was some emotion.

I took a deep breath. "I fucked up. I'm better than that."

"Enough."

"I should've acted faster."

"You'll never be fast enough for everything," she said with a hint of softness—but only a hint. "But we made it through. That's all that matters. Do you understand me? If you get caught up in the middle, if you lose sight of your goal or wallow in the decisions you make in between, you'll unravel."

"This isn't helping."

"The only thing that will help is getting better."

Maybe. But I hated thinking about it. All I wanted was a stiff drink. Or some sleep. Anything to stop my thoughts. What about the *Star Marque*? Was everyone safe? We wouldn't know for a while.

"It'll be a few hours before we reach Outpost Station," Endellion said. "Try not to dwell until then."

TWENTY-TWO

Emissary Barten

The trek left me with nothing but time.

Pensive and uncertain about the future, I stared at the screens of my starfighter. I thought about Sawyer, and I missed her voice in my ear. Endellion refused to speak, even when I asked questions.

We had almost reached Outpost Station. Fuel would be at half, giving us just enough to make it back to the *Star Marque*, once everything was said and done. That was *if* we could get it done.

The comms on my screen lit up a half-second before Endellion spoke. "We're almost at our destination."

"I know," I said.

"When we dock at Outpost Station, you'll change your attire. An enviro-suit has been stored in the compartment behind your chair. From there, we'll limit our communication to the bare minimum. Under no circumstance can you mention our names, the *Star Marque*, or the purpose of our visit."

"I take it all communication will be monitored once we're there?"

"When the inevitable investigation begins, I would rather not leave any evidence which can tie this back to us."

I agreed, but each second spent in silence killed a little more of me. I had never had that problem before. I hated the feeling of isolation. All I could think about was the *Star Marque* and its crew, and I yearned to return. Even Lysander's company would have been better than the dark starfighter floating through the void of lifeless space.

"Clevon," Endellion said. "You understand that we cannot get caught, correct? No witnesses. You can't let a man wallow in the corner of the room because you feel sorry for him."

"I won't make the same mistake twice."

The rebellion bastard that had cut Endellion was the last bit of mercy I'd had for any of them.

"Clevon." Her voice was somber.

"Yeah?" I asked.

"This will likely be the last dirty assignment I'll need completed before I become governor."

"Good."

"I can tell you're worried about the others, but just get through this for me, and their futures will be secure. We can't afford failure."

"This'll be over quick?"

"That's the plan. In and out in less than ten minutes."

No room for error. In and out. It would be for the best.

"Why this guy?" I asked, needing to know the answer. I thought I had figured it out, but confirmation would help my troubled thoughts.

"Felseven has threatened to change the requirements for planet governor so that I'll never qualify. Minister Ontwenty has promised me she'll keep the requirements the same, so long as the emissary is eliminated. If we kill him and escape without a trail, the rebellion will be blamed for Barten's death. Ontwenty wants this most of all. After this, she'll never be forced to sell her medical research to the United-Earth faction."

"And if the requirements stay the same, you'll get your planet?"

"Almost every piece of the puzzle is in place, Clevon. Once the emissary is gone, all I'll have to do is wait for the vote. I've secured enough favor from other planet governors to assure my victory. This step is crucial."

Then there was no getting around it. We had to off the guy.

Outpost Station flashed on my screen. The starfighter high-lighted open ports, and I set a course. It would have been hard to miss Outpost Station. The entire facility was built into a C-type asteroid, one with hydrated minerals present throughout its dark and porous core. The asteroid itself could have been a small moon.

Sawyer had told me all about it.

Although starfighters didn't typically dock outside a starship, they were still equipped to do so for emergencies. Endellion and I sent in our requests, and we were granted access. The moment my ship hooked to the dock, I released the seal on my legs and pulled out my new enviro-suit.

It was white. The same low-quality bullshit the rebellion guys wore. They were the cheapest enviro-suits on the market, mass-produced and easily torn. And they looked stiff as fuck. Nothing about them seemed comfortable. I had been spoiled by the *Star Marque*'s advanced suits.

Didn't matter. I ripped off my clothing and shimmied into my new suit. Before I exited my starfighter, I pulled the hood-helmet over my head and secured it into place. The visor flickered to life and gave me readouts of the area, but the information wasn't as detailed as my old suit, and it half-blocked my sight. Not the best design, that was for sure.

The hatch opened, and I jumped out, my muscles tense for a fight.

Some dockhand walked up to my starfighter and motioned to it with a jut of his chin.

"What's this?" he asked. "Why aren't you with a carrier ship?"

Endellion hadn't gone over the procedure for this. I didn't know what to say, so I didn't even bother trying to fumble out an excuse. The dockhand—dressed in an olive jumpsuit, his face smeared with sweat and dust—gave me a glare.

Endellion exited her ship, her perfectly-curved body accentuated by her tight enviro-suit. She got the dockhand's attention with zero effort.

"Excuse me, ma'am," he said. "But why are you two separate from your carrier ship?"

Funny how his tone changed in the presence of a beautiful woman.

"We're docking between rendezvous," Endellion said. "We'll be leaving within an hour."

The dockhand hemmed and hawed, but then replied, "Fine, but be quick. You're taking up valuable dock space with your tiny fighters."

I followed Endellion off our dock and into the general loading area. Hundreds of people pushed and shoved their way from one place to the next, their jumpsuits stained with more than grease from the machines. Outpost Station was built for a smaller number of people. I guessed it was a tenth of the size of Capital Station, and it showed.

Although the area swarmed with bodies, I stood a third of a meter taller than the rest. I shuffled between them, my eyes glued to Endellion. An easy target, considering we were about the same height.

"All the information you need is stored in your suit's files," Endellion said to me over the personal comms.

I switched away from vocalized communication and said, "Access stored files." The enviro-suit brought up two pictures and a few notes. One was labeled: *Emissary Barten.* The superhuman looked remarkably similar to the others, and I wondered if they were designed to be homogeneous. I hadn't seen any that were fat, or extremely short, or pudgy, or even balding. Their whitish-silver hair even had the same shine.

But I could see enough of a difference to tell him apart. He was my target.

The last picture was a layout of the docking deck for Outpost Station. I could use it as a map, and already I felt more secure in my mission. Endellion and I headed for the diplomats and regulations offices.

My notes explained Emissary Barten's visit. He was there to negotiate with representatives from the United-Earth faction. He resided in the diplomat's quarters, beyond a security gate. We wouldn't have weapons when we confronted him, and he might have guards of his own.

Endellion said nothing.

I took in the environment. Gray, chrome, rust, and exposed wires made up the walls. Grates—some dented, others open—made up the floors. My suit said the air had 20% oxygen and 78% nitrogen. The last 2%—rather high—was carbon dioxide, and my suit advised I shouldn't breathe it in. Didn't matter because I couldn't risk taking off my suit, but the air quality explained the myriad of coughs all around me. Some even struggled to breathe. The place might have been worse than Capital Station, especially given the number of hunchbacks and deformed defects mixed throughout the crowd.

It didn't take long to reach the security gate. Two men in similar white enviro-suits stood waiting, rifles on their shoulders. The gate sat before the door, an obstacle meant to scan anyone who passed through it. Weapons would be detected damn near instantaneously, which was why Endellion and I had come with nothing. No plasma rifles, no lasers.

The two men did and said nothing as Endellion strode forward.

The gate flashed red the moment she stepped between the posts. Both men hefted their rifles and motioned her out.

One guy glanced to the computer terminal and did a double-take.

"What the...?" he asked aloud, his suit's comms crackling his voice.

"What is it?" the other asked.

"Says here she's a cyborg. Over 65% of her is artificial."

Both men returned their gaze to Endellion, glancing over her body. I didn't blame them. The cyborgs around here didn't compare to the level at which she had hidden her augmentations.

"I'm sorry," the first guard said. "But no one is allowed beyond this point with more than 20% alterations. You're gonna have to stand back."

Endellion complied with their demands. She stepped up next to me and said over our personal comms, "You need to go in. I'll play support from out here."

"You want me to go alone?" I asked.

"It's the only way."

I didn't like it because I wasn't certain if I could handle a super-human, but making a fuss about entering would draw unwanted attention. I had to go in alone.

I walked through the security gate, and nothing happened. The two guards waved me on and pointed to the door. I strolled in, my heartrate high enough that my suit recommended taking a seat. My suit could go fuck itself. Not even a coma would quell my anxiety. First the fight, then the damage to the *Star Marque*. Now a solo assas-sination.

Had Endellion known we would be split up? Was this her way of avoiding culpability? I wouldn't be surprised if it were, but it seemed impossible for her to have known they would've restricted cyborgs. Or maybe I had become paranoid. She did a few things with exact planning, and now I suspected every move she made must have been calculated. I shouldn't have doubted her. Not at a time like that. Not when we were so close to her final goal.

She'd said this was the last corrupt move. I just had to make it through.

The cramped diplomat's offices had tasteful décor, including potted plants, but I didn't admire them. I traveled down the long corridor, doors on either side of me. Some were the living quarters for specific individuals, while others were labeled *Conference Room* or *Station Intercoms*. A computer terminal lit up and asked the reason for my visit. I ignored the computer and headed forward. The map in my suit's stored files gave me Barten's personal room. It wasn't far.

Another guard waited outside his door, but this guy wasn't like the schlubs by the security gate. He was like me. Modified. He had a plasma rifle, not to mention a sleek enviro-suit much like the kind we had on the *Star Marque*. We regarded each other for a moment—

I needed to get past him, and my mind spun through a million possibilities—and then he broke the silence between us.

"What're you doing here?" he asked.

"I'm running errands," I said over the suit's external speaker. "You know how it goes. Everyone thinks they're hot shit. Too important to deliver their own messages."

The guy chuckled. "Messages, huh?"

"For the emissary. Hush-hush bullshit. I thought I had left this stuff behind me when I escaped Vectin-14. Now I'm running on an hour of sleep. Everyone's so high-strung about this meeting."

"Right. I feel that." He motioned to the door. "The emissary should be in the middle of a meal. Don't take long or he'll get pissy."

I smirked and tapped the door console. It slid open, and I stepped inside, but I was taken aback by the surroundings. I'd thought it would be a study, or an office. Instead, there was a couch, and a screen for entertainment vids, and another door that led deeper into the office. It was a small living space, but clean and crisp compared to the docks.

With a deep breath, I crossed the room and opened the next door. I was greeted by a sparse kitchen, complete with a table and a couple of chairs. Another door sat across the room—I assumed it to be a bedroom. But my gaze fell on the single superhuman sitting at the table, his posture stiff, his clothing open and flowing, unsuited for space. Like the attire superhumans wore on Vectin-14.

It was Emissary Barten.

"What're you doing here?" he asked as he stood. "What have I said about interrupting mealtime?"

There was no one else there. No guards. No other witnesses.

This was where I needed to do it.

"I came to deliver a message," I said. "Sorry about the interruption."

Barten exhaled and retook his seat, though he glowered. "Very well. Have the final delegates of the United-Earth faction arrived yet? Or are you here to relay a personal correspondence?"

He didn't touch his food—vegetables and bread, fancy shit for a space station—but I could tell it was nothing compared to the food on Vectin-14. Barten held his bowl close, however, and never took his eyes from me. He had cutlery on the table, the steel knife and a fork caught the fluorescent lighting.

I stepped forward, and Barten tensed in anticipation, like he knew something wasn't right. I was reminded of my time with Ontwenty and how she'd explained that superhumans were designed to be superior to humans in every way. Perhaps Barten could sense my coiled muscles with his weird, electroreceptor organ —the ampullae of Lorenzini.

"Well?" Barten asked. "What have you come to say?"

Normally words came quick for me, but with each new breath, my throat grew tighter.

Barten stood, and I knew from his wide stance that it was a fight.

I grabbed a knife from the table in a split-second. His eyes tracked me—he even took a step back, before I turned to strike— but he wasn't as fast as he should have been. I lunged, putting everything I had into that one attack. I slammed Barten to the floor, mounted him, and stabbed the knife between his ribs.

I knew how fucking painful that could be.

But he didn't react. Instead, he damn near coldcocked me in the side of the head, his corded muscles capable of exerting a tremendous amount of force, even from a prone position. But I still had the advantage, and I stabbed again, ready to pepper the guy with a million open holes.

He wasn't wearing an enviro-suit. He didn't have a weapon. I didn't even think he had trained a day in his life for this. But he still had an immense amount of raw capability. When he thrashed, he almost sent me flying. Plus, he was larger than me—his legs long enough to lift his body off the floor when he arched his back —and it took all my concentration to maintain my position over him.

Barten slammed a chair and a table leg, sending his food and bowl to the floor. It echoed, but the duralumin walls and dense construction of the station prevented sound from carrying far. This wasn't like Vectin-14, where sound travelled long distances with little effort—we could have been playing the drums, and I doubted anyone would have heard a damn thing.

Barten punched my gut, and I grimaced. When he did it again, I coiled in on the bruised area, but after two more stabs, the guy finally bit back a yell.

I didn't care if superhumans had three extra kidneys, and a cheat code to resurrect themselves written into their DNA. The guy was dead. Each beat of his heart sent his blood gushing from the puncture wounds I riddled down his side. He tried to speak, and while most men would have drowned in their own vital fluid, Barten breathed through the tiny holes in his body, getting air, and sustaining his life much longer than a human could have. Too bad it wouldn't save him.

I stopped stabbing.

Barten spit a line of blood onto the floor and wheezed. His legs gave out. He crumpled underneath me, his body trembling.

Not bad for a defenseless guy in the middle of a meal. I'd thought it would have been difficult to kill a superhuman, but Barten had held himself like a scholar. I should have realized he wouldn't have been too hard to handle. And maybe he'd been designed better. Maybe he'd been smarter and faster. But in the end, he'd still had limitations. He was just a guy.

Superhumans still had *some* of humanity's flaws.

Barten stared up at me, fear etched into every line of his face. "Don't—" he choked out.

I kept him pinned to the floor, and I was ready to end it. No point in making him suffer.

"—don't hurt her," he murmured. "Anything but… anything but that."

His last request shook me. *Her?* Who was he talking about? I didn't come for any girl. But I couldn't inquire. Barten went limp, the back of his head hitting the kitchen floor. He was still breathing, and his blood continued to gush out with every beat of his over-worked heart, but there was nothing anyone could do for him now.

I stood. I had no desire to see his final moments.

"Dad?"

I stopped breathing. My mind locked. It was the voice of a child. A little girl.

After a long second, I glanced over my shoulder. A child stood in the frame of the open bedroom door, her hands on the wall, and her gaze set to her father. I didn't know superhuman ages—because I had never seen a happy family, and I hadn't grown up interacting with any—but I knew the child hadn't yet hit puberty. She was short, her cheeks still puffy with residual baby fat, and her glittering silver hair fell to her waist.

She stared, unblinking, and it took me a second to regain my breath.

The girl didn't run. She backed away and hit the opposite side of the doorframe, her arms wrapped tight across her chest. I hadn't noticed before, but she wore a planetside outfit. A long dress and leggings.

Her abject terror wasn't something I was used to. I walked over with no energy in my step. The girl didn't say anything.

Then she looked up at me.

Endellion would've wanted her dead. She would have insisted I kill the girl—to avoid a disaster.

I still had the knife. I could make it quick.

The girl didn't blink, and I waited for my anxiety to wane, but nothing changed. I had never killed a child before. I wished she would try to escape, but perhaps she knew it was futile. My mouth tasted of cotton and dust.

I backhanded her harder than I should've, but I wasn't in any condition to control myself. The girl hit the floor hard, and unmoving. I threw the knife down and left it.

I could have taken her life, but I settled for her consciousness.

I didn't care what Endellion would've done. I couldn't do it. Maybe I didn't have the same kind of ambition Endellion did— maybe I was weaker for it, maybe this was why I needed her to push me to do something with myself—but there were certain lines I couldn't bring myself to cross. Again, all I yearned for was the company aboard the *Star Marque*.

I had done this all for them. Myself included, but still. Once Endellion had her dream, everyone else would have theirs.

I needed to get out of here as fast as possible, but crimson splatters marked my white enviro-suit. I wouldn't be able to leave without questions.

I walked to the sink and splashed some water over my body. To my surprise, the blood washed away without trouble. A disturbing fact I would no doubt remember forever. Enviro-suits made cleaning up after a cold-blooded murder a simple task.

Once free of any damning evidence, I exited the kitchen, crossed the front room, and walked back into the diplomat's corridor.

"Was he pissy?"

I turned to the guard, my thoughts frayed. "What?"

"Was he pissy?" the guard repeated. "I told you, he hates being interrupted."

I nodded. "Yeah. He was upset."

Without another word, I walked away, my gaze set to the floor. I hustled out the security gate and made my way back to the docks, inconspicuous but dreading the passage of time. I had almost gotten away with everything. No one knew yet. If Endellion and I left in our starfighters before any alarms went off, we would make it.

"Well?" Endellion said over our personal comms. "Did you find him?"

I switched to her frequency and continued forward. "It's done."

"And there were no witnesses?"

It was almost like she knew.

"No witnesses," I said.

But she didn't protest my confirmation. It was better that way. I didn't care if the kid saw me. I had been covered by an enviro-suit, anyway.

Endellion met me at the entrance to the docks. I walked over to her and flinched the moment red lights flooded the area. An alarm sounded, and station enforcers rushed from their posts.

"Someone must've found the body," Endellion murmured. "We need to get back to our ships."

"Will they even let us leave?"

"We'll find a way."

The crowd on the docks stirred, agitated under the harsh, red security lights. They yelled and shoved and pushed, fighting to stay clear of the enforcers. I glanced over my shoulder and watched the security walls slam down, preventing anyone from leaving the diplomat's area. Perhaps they thought they would trap the assassin inside. But it was too late. I was already at the docks.

We reached our starfighters, but the docking ports had been locked down thanks to the alarm. The dockhands fought with the captains about schedules and order, but Endellion went straight for the guy who'd signed us in.

"We're heading out," she said. Not a question, but a statement.

"Not right now," the dockhand replied, motioning to the horror-show lighting. "We've got to go through procedures first."

"What're you going to do? Search my cargo?"

Starfighters had a single compartment, at most. Even the dockhand got a chuckle out of the comment.

"We were here five minutes ago," Endellion said. "We have a rendezvous to make, I told you that. We don't have time for station drama."

The dockhand rolled his eyes and pointed to our fighters. "Fine. Get in the cockpit, and I'll see you two out. I need the space anyway."

TWENTY-THREE

Lost To The Black Tide

The flight back to the *Star Marque* left me drowning in darkness. Space. My thoughts. I was still anxious about getting caught, even though we'd made it from Outpost Station without a hold-up. I wished the *Star Marque* would've flown closer to meet us, but the distance between the station and the ship served to hide our destination from the dockmasters. The space stations only tracked ships out to a certain distance before their scanners cut off and recorded other trivial details.

When the *Star Marque* showed up on my screen, I breathed easy. Once we were in range of communications, Endellion activated the comms. "Sawyer," she said. "Report."

"The *Star Marque* took structural damage to the starboard side," Sawyer replied, "but nothing that will prevent us from returning to Vectin-14."

"Good. Clevon and I will dock portside."

"I've already made space."

The navigation on my screen sprang to life, showing me the path to my new docking port. I allowed Sawyer to control the fighter, uninterested in where or when I docked.

"What were the causalities?" I asked.

"44 dead, 30 injured."

So cold. I knew Sawyer wasn't the most emotional person I had ever met, but there was something off about her.

"What about the starfighters?" I asked. "Who didn't make it?"

"Yuan and Advik. Noah is in the infirmary."

I gritted my teeth, my blood hot all over again. "Will Noah be all right?"

"Dr. Clay says he'll be back on his feet in no time," Sawyer said, softer than before.

Then the communications cut out. I rested my head back, my eyes scrunched shut. I would've given anything for a drink. Several drinks. A whole week of drinking.

"You're upset," Endellion said to me over a private channel.

Of course. How could everyone else be so calm? I was an adjusted individual, but the lack of reaction made me feel unstable.

"It's because of you that everything was a success," she continued. "I knew I could count on you."

"Just don't let the crew down," I said.

Our starfighters pulled into their docks, and I took in deep breaths the entire time. Once situated, I jumped out and hesitated, wondering whether I should head for my capsule or go to see the other starfighters. I wasn't sure what would soothe the parade of terrible thoughts marching through my mind.

Fortunately, Quinn rounded the corner of the corridor, her eyes lighting up the moment she spotted me. I ripped off my helmet when she drew near. "Demarco," she said as she placed a hand on my shoulder. "You've finally returned. What're you wearing?"

"Ask Sawyer," I snapped.

"You've heard about the others?"

"Yeah. I've heard."

"Come with us to the mess hall. You're just in time. We're having a celebration."

I jerked my shoulder out of her grip. "How can you be celebrating at a time like this? There's not much to fucking celebrate."

Quinn brushed her braided hair to the side and gave me a long stare. Unlike Sawyer and Endellion—who might as well have been bricks—Quinn had a melancholy that drew me in.

She patted my shoulder and smiled. "I've lost a fair number of friends over the years. It hurts, but a life like ours has no guarantees. The celebration is in their honor. You know. Like that poem."

"What're you talking about?" I asked.

"The poem. You know the one. About the first mass transports —the ones that weren't successful. It's called 'Lost to the Black Tide.' It's about everyone who's ever died in space. You have to honor their life, ya know? It's already bleak and cold out here. No reason to add to the misery with a funeral."

I was vaguely aware of the saying, *"Memories are the tombstones for those lost to the black tide"*—and I knew it came from a poem or some bullshit—but it wasn't like I'd stayed in school that long. The poem had something to do with a mass transport that was destroyed on its voyage. Hundreds of thousands of people died, their bodies lost to the darkness. It was a failure of humanity, but we had tenacity, because those origin-world bastards tried the transports again, anyway.

"This is what we do for everyone who dies," Quinn said, pulling me from my musings. "You should join us. It's important we do this together. We're brothers-in-arms."

Although I was uncertain about the gesture, I nodded anyway. If everyone wanted to do it, I might as well, too. I yearned for their company. I needed to be reminded why I'd done all that shit in the first place.

"Lead the way," I said.

———

I'D NEVER KNOWN such traditions existed. I wished I'd known sooner. Any reason to drink like I was trying to drown myself was perfect.

Lee, Noah, Quinn, and 30 other guys whose names I didn't even know sat around in an unused room of the *Star Marque*, a whole crateful of rum pouches open in the corner. Music blared over the comms, filling the atmosphere with energy. The lights remained low, but the laugher remained at an all-time high.

"—and she sneezed funny," one guy said. "That's what I loved about Wisner. You always knew when she was on the comms, 'cuz of all her weird noises."

A round of, "That's right," echoed between individuals.

Everyone took turns talking about what they'd loved most about the deceased. We all got a laugh at the good times, and then we moved on to the next one. It might have become depressing if it weren't for the jovial spirit in the room. No one seemed to linger on the *Star Marque* being smaller than before.

Forty people had died. That was 20% of the whole crew. Two out of every ten people had died on a single mission. Those kinds of numbers were hard to let go. And when I looked around, I knew they'd hit the starfighters the most of all. Mara, Yuan, Advik, and Endellion weren't there. It was hard not to notice, and I took another drink. Quinn threw an arm over my shoulders.

"You want to say anything about Advik?" she asked.

The room quieted a bit, but not much. Everyone still had to yell to be heard.

"She sent me a picture of a puddle once," I said with a single laugh. "I still have it on my PAD. One of the best pictures I ever saw."

Lee threw back a swing of rum. "She sent me a picture of a nest. You know, like the kind sky-bound animals make? Vectin-14 has a lot. But the nest didn't have any animals in it. Just broken eggshells. She thought it was symbolic. Advik really was unique."

Another round of, "That's right."

The music soothed my depression. I was sure Advik would have appreciated the celebration.

They talked about someone else, but I ignored that when Noah slid over to me. The benches around the edges of the room were probably meant for storage—especially since they had belt hooks and fasteners spaced out every meter—but they made for great seating. Everyone chilled around the edge of the room, facing the center, several smaller crates operating as makeshift tables.

"Demarco," Noah said. "I've got to thank you."

"For what?"

"All that training. I never would've made it without that."

"You insisted on training, remember? Thank your damn self."

"No, you don't understand. It was the attitude. I—" Noah stopped himself for a minute, his eyes falling to his lap.

The kid did look different. Muscular. Put-together. Even if he had to go to the infirmary after the fight, he didn't show it. He almost looked like he could have given Lysander a challenge if they sparred, and Lysander had been a ground enforcer for over a decade. Funny how much effort will change a person.

Noah sighed. "I had a problem before. I don't think I had it out there, during the dogfight. Yuan and I, well… we were the fighters assigned to the starboard side. There were so many missiles and enemy fighters. Yuan wasn't herself. I could tell. I figured I had to be the strong one, to pull through, and maybe she'd get her confidence back."

Obviously, it hadn't happened. Yuan really hadn't been in the mindset to fight. Should Endellion have kept her from the fray? I didn't know. I wasn't sure what I would've done as captain.

A dark thought struck me.

Maybe Endellion had wanted her to die.

But I shook my head. No. She wanted all the starfighters she could get.

"So, thank you," Noah said again. He leaned back against the bulkhead and took another drink from his pouch.

I threw back a mouthful of rum and listened to the words of my fellow *Star Marque* enforcers. Everything mixed together into a white noise that eased my depression. I grabbed another pouch and downed it as quick as the last. The laughter did me good.

CELEBRATING death for five hours straight had taken a toll on my stamina.

Half-drunk and completely exhausted, I ambled my way to the

lift. Noah accompanied me, nowhere near as inebriated, but just as tired. We were a few days from Midway Station. Soon we would return to Vectin-14, and until then we had no responsibilities. We had to rest while we still could.

Noah patted my shoulder. "I'm glad you made it."

"I was worried you'd died in the fight," I said.

"Honestly?"

"You *are* the worst pilot."

Noah cocked an eyebrow, and I laughed. Before he could say anything, I punched him in the shoulder. He joined in the laughter. "You don't have to be a dick about it," he said.

"Ah. You're fine. Unlike your brother, you have a sense of humor."

"I can't hold liquor like he can, though." Noah rubbed at his gut. "I might go vomit before I go to sleep." His blanched face and shaky hands told me he wasn't lying.

"I didn't know you had *two* defects," I said with a smirk.

"Ha, ha," Noah replied. "How can you drink three times more than me? *And* you're still standing? Gross." Before I could respond, Noah stumbled down the corridor in the opposite direction. "I'll see you tomorrow."

"Yeah. See you then."

Once he was gone, I entered the lift and stared at the options. Maybe I was just a drunk slob, but I contemplated them longer than I should have. Deck Three would take me to my capsule. Deck One would take me to Endellion. I had been shacking up with her before the assassination—just for a few days—but did that mean I had an open invitation to return to her?

I wanted someone right now. Not just for a hookup. Someone who knew me.

I hit the Deck One button and waited while the lift took me to my destination.

Deck One had the comfort of a walk-in freezer. The entire deck had a hollow feeling—undoubtedly, from the lack of personnel—but I pushed that from my thoughts until I reached Endellion's quarters. The door to her room blended with the ship's bulkhead, and it took me a moment of fucking around to find the door's controls. I buzzed for entrance.

Endellion answered a few seconds later, dressed down in casuals. She gave me the once-over. "You've been drinking."

"Nah," I said with a dismissive wave of my hand. "I was *celebrating*. Big difference, apparently."

Endellion stepped aside before I could even ask to enter. "I've been waiting for you."

"Have you?"

Her statement eased some of my doubt. I walked in and shed my enviro-suit, desperate to return to a state of normalcy. Once undressed, I threw myself onto her bed and stretched, my attention set on the ceiling. Endellion stripped and got on the bed. She was warm, and I enjoyed the way she crawled on top of me, but it was hard to focus.

"What have you been thinking about?" she asked.

"What's going to happen to Mara?"

The issue remained, but now Yuan wasn't here to contest anything. I wanted the remaining starfighters to make it, and not just through a technicality. I wanted their safety. I wanted to know they would have everything they'd ever wanted in the end.

"You're still concerned about her," Endellion said, more of an observation than a question.

"I don't want to lose anyone else."

"You want her returned to normal?"

"I hate the idea of taking away her choice."

Endellion lay across my chest. While most of her was firm with muscle, her breasts remained as soft and wonderful as any unaltered woman's. It wasn't the first thing I noticed, but it lingered in my thoughts, even as we continued our discussion.

"If you feel so passionately about Mara's fate, you can decide," Endellion said.

I glanced at her with narrowed eyes. "Why?"

"Why what? I just explained myself. Or are you too intoxicated to understand simple statements?"

"I thought this would be more of a fight. You were so adamant before."

Endellion chuckled. "I try to give you the things you want, Clevon. I thought I made that obvious. And you haven't been yourself since our successful operation. Perhaps this will ease your guilt."

"And you don't care about Mara's fate?"

Endellion had argued from a rigid position before. What was I missing?

"You're the vice-captain now," she said in a low voice. "I'm delegating the decision to you. Either way, I'll need to find more starfighters. And perhaps Mara won't suffer as much as she did before."

I wanted to question her further, but Endellion moved up my body and locked her lips with mine. Although part of me contemplated Mara's recovery, the rest of my body responded to Endellion's advances. I ran my hands along her back, enjoying every millimeter of her. I closed my eyes and relaxed.

That was what I needed.

DR. CLAY POINTED to the infirmary screen, his finger following the graph of Mara's chemical imbalances. "These represent Mara's serotonin, noradrenaline, and dopamine levels. And these lines over here represent an average woman's levels, according to Mara's age and genetic makeup. See how her serotonin levels are low? And how her—"

"I get it," I said, holding back my frustration with his matter-of-fact, patronizing tone. "Her numbers aren't the same as normal people's. I'm saying, you should wake her up, so I can talk to her."

Dr. Clay exhaled. "Endellion ordered me to alter her implant."

"Now I'm telling you—as the vice-captain—to wake her up. How many times do I need to explain it?"

The infirmary never had much in the way of personnel. Two medics, and now the doctor. All three of them stopped what they were doing to stare. Even Noah, who stood by the door, perked up and lifted both eyebrows.

"*You're* the vice-captain?" Noah asked. "Since when?"

"It'll be announced later today," I said.

Dr. Clay scoffed. "I never should've joined this rig if some brute is the best we have for the position of vice-captain."

Noah pushed off the bulkhead and stomped over. "Hey. You watch your tone. Demarco risked life and limb for this starship."

"So does every ground enforcer when they're deployed for a mission. Do they all get turns at being vice-captain?"

"Demarco isn't like the guys you know on Vectin-14. He's—"

I grabbed Noah's shoulder, my fingers digging deep into his muscle. He stopped speaking and took a step back, but I could tell he was still angry just from the way he held himself. How had Dr. Clay ever hooked up with Dr. Rhodes in the first place? He had the charisma of a wet towel.

"Wake her," I commanded.

Dr. Clay replied with a curt nod, and then prepared a small syringe. He stuck Mara in the arm and injected the clear fluid at a slow rate. Noah and I waited in silence. It took only a few moments for Mara's eyes to flutter open.

"Adachi Mara," Dr. Clay said, his tone formal. "I am your primary physician aboard the *Star Marque*, Dr. Clay. Can you understand me? A simple nod will suffice."

Mara blinked and turned her head from side to side. When she spotted me, she squinted, her eyes wet and red from prolonged sleep. "Demarco?" she muttered. "Demarco…"

With a long sigh, Dr. Clay poked at the PAD on his arm. "Apparently no one on the *Star Marque* can follow simple instructions. Yet another clue the crew may be suffering from a contagious delusion."

"Get out of here," Noah snapped. "If we need a doctor, we'll call."

Dr. Clay left without protest. Endellion had said he was a researcher back on Vectin-14, and I could see why.

The two medics finished their cataloguing and hustled from the room, though I didn't have a problem with their presence. Still, I was sure Mara's case had given them stress. Mara had attacked Yuan, after all. She was unstable.

"Are you okay?" I asked as I reached out to take Mara's hand. Her palm was coated in a thick layer of sweat, but I didn't break the contact.

"Where's Yuan?" she asked, her voice raspy.

"Yuan isn't here."

Mara rolled to her side and groaned. "Get away. I don't want to be touched."

I let go of her hand. "Listen, I have something I need to discuss with you. Can you sit up?"

She complied with my request, moving at a slow pace. Once upright, Mara rubbed at her face and hair, combing it back. I had never seen her so disheveled, but it was to be expected after days of inactivity and comatose sleep.

"I don't feel right," she muttered. "I don't want to be here. I just... want to be alone. I don't want to see Yuan. Not now. Not ever."

"The doctor says you're depressed."

Mara didn't answer. She rubbed at her temples and bit her bottom lip, her whole body trembling. The lightweight gown they'd provided her didn't seem to offer much warmth. I grabbed her blankets and tossed them over her shoulders.

I took a deep breath. "You know you have a cybernetic implant, right?"

"Yes," she said.

"Did you know it was being misused? That you were being doped-up to remain happy?"

Mara scrunched her eyes shut and pressed her palms against her face. "I... didn't know."

"Well, what do you want to do about it?"

Again, silence. Mara barely moved.

Noah took my elbow and pulled me to the side. "Wait, Mara. We'll be right back." He dragged me to the other end of the room, a look of disbelief written across his face.

"What?" I asked.

"She just woke up. What're you going to tell her next? How Advik died? That she's been sleeping for days on end?"

"She's got to stone up and deal with this. What? You want to leave her in a coma? Or are you like Endellion? You think we should force this on her, one way or another?"

"I'm saying, don't be fucking callous."

I glared at the kid, and he glared right back.

"Don't you remember?" Noah asked. "Remember the first day Sawyer evaluated us? Lysander thought I should have a similar implant to Mara's. He thought I was too stressed and it was affecting my performance as a soldier. But I dealt with it. Slow, sure, and with limited medication, but without an implant. Federation-standard treatments—along with focus—made the difference."

"Yeah, but I helped you," I said. "And I helped you by yelling at you, basically."

"But Mara's situation is different. She's lost everything, Demarco. She doesn't have a brother looking out for her, or a family to impress."

And it was obvious her relationship with Yuan hadn't been everything I'd thought it was. Mara didn't even want to see her— perhaps Yuan had known Mara disagreed with her.

"She doesn't need anyone yelling at her," Noah continued. "You heard the doctor. She becomes depressed easily."

Maybe Endellion was right. Mara would most likely hurt herself, and it would be my fault. Perhaps Dr. Clay *should* have tampered with her implant a second time.

"Let me stay with her a while," Noah said, his voice filled with conviction. "I know what she's going through. I'll explain it to her at a slow pace. I'll stay here and make sure she doesn't hurt herself. And then she can decide what level of medication she wants."

"Why?" I asked.

Noah took in a breath, and then shrugged. He looked away and stared at the infirmary bulkhead. "Mara's a fellow starfighter. I should have her back, and I think I'm the only one who will understand her situation. I want to pay it forward. She should be in charge of her own fate."

Noah wanted to help Mara? Because of me?

"I'll be here," I said. "Endellion thinks this will harm Mara, but… I just want her to have the choice." I glared at Noah, needing to hear the truth. "Did *you* prefer having a choice? Or would you have preferred it if Lysander altered you without your knowledge?"

"I like that I don't let it define me," Noah said. "I feel better than before. Different. I *did* something. I chose to do this. To seek help, medication, and betterment. No one else. If I didn't have the choice, I wouldn't have…" He shook his head. "Am I making any sense? I don't think I am."

"You're fine," I said. "I get it."

I was conflicted, even still. If Mara had been genetically modi-fied—like myself—her choices would have been removed. In that situation, I wouldn't have been as bothered. Maybe it was because I couldn't change her genetics, or maybe it was because the implant had been installed after her failings—or, her *perceived* failings—but it wasn't the same as starting with a higher baseline through genetic manipulation.

Success changed people—it bred confidence and contentment. Success couldn't be had in a system with no failure, because there would also be no achievement. A life devoid of recognition would lead to resentment, but recognition had to be earned—there was no shortcut for it. Maybe Noah could help Mara. He had learned his ultimate life lesson, after all. And he *did* seem to have his shit together.

"All right," I said with a sigh. "You can explain what's happened, but I'll be here, just in case."

Noah offered me half a smile. "Thank you, Demarco. I swear I'll help her through this."

TWENTY-FOUR

Requirements

"**A**s of 24 hours ago, Clevon is officially my vice-captain," Endellion said.

The officer conference room remained quiet. Quinn and Lysander each regarded me with a raised eyebrow, but Dr. Clay and Sawyer didn't even bother glancing in my direction. The table between us seemed like a gap, and I feared they would have objections. Or were they waiting for me to give them a speech? They would be waiting a long damn time.

Lysander returned his attention to Endellion. "Why?"

"Clevon has proven time and again he's a trustworthy and talented individual."

"He's undereducated."

"Really?" I asked. "You want to start this?"

Lysander let out a long exhale. "I'm not trying to irritate you. I'm being serious. You obviously don't know your way around a starship. You still stumble with the basics. Why would you—of all people—be qualified to take the position of vice-captain? It's a legitimate question. I'm surprised you didn't ask the same thing when you were promoted."

I supposed he was right. I didn't have a formal education, and I did have to play catch-up most of the time when Endellion trained me. Still, I couldn't help but get defensive. I hated when people underestimated me.

"I can handle it," I said. "I've been learning. That's how I spend most of my time—you know that."

Lysander shrugged. "I concede the point. You do try to educate yourself, and you are usually busy when I see you. But do you really think that's enough? In the HSN Corps, it takes a minimum of five years' experience before someone is promoted to the position of vice-captain."

"We're not in the HSN Corps."

Endellion held up a hand, ending our conversation. "It doesn't matter. I've made my decision. We're woefully understaffed, and more officers will only be a benefit, even if they need additional training."

"This is all just for shits and giggles, right?" Quinn asked. She leaned back in her seat. "In less than a year's time, Endellion will be a planet governor. Then it won't matter who has what position because we'll all be living planetside."

I had wondered about that. Why bother with formalities when everything would come to an end soon, anyway? But that didn't mean I didn't appreciate the confidence or the responsibilities.

"Of course, this is all a jest," Dr. Clay said, rolling his eyes. "Anyone with the title of commodore could find a better candidate for their vice-captain. I would venture a guess that Commodore Voight wants Demarco for a specific reason or simply as a project until she leaves the enforcer game for good."

"Clevon has displayed and cited urges to explore the quadrant further," Endellion said. She sat with a straight posture, calm like always, but now that we had been intimate, it was hard to see her the same way as before. I wondered what her inner thoughts were. "I might need an enforcer crew when I'm governor," she continued. "When that time comes, perhaps I can call on Clevon to assist me."

I hadn't known she wanted that. I mulled the information over and replied with a slow nod. "I do want to see more of the quadrant," I said.

Quinn tilted her head to the side and gave me a half-smile. "Well, don't expect me to be your starfighter officer. Lee and I have plans."

"I heard. A million babies."

She laughed. "Not *that* many, but a couple, at least. I've seen enough starship battles to warrant retirement."

Dr. Clay didn't need to chime in, but he added, "And my agreement ends the moment Commodore Voight becomes governor. I won't be staying on this ship a second longer."

"As governor, I'll have more resources to find crewmembers," Endellion said, ignoring the comments from the others. "It shouldn't be a problem."

Again, the officer conference room fell silent. Everyone had voiced an opinion—except for Sawyer. She stared at the table with a blank expression. The others must have taken note of her demeanor because Lysander cleared his throat, drawing Sawyer's attention.

"Do you have anything to say?" he asked.

Sawyer shook her head. "No. I think Demarco would make a fine vice-captain. He's dedicated to the *Star Marque*, and he's more than willing to learn the procedures."

"I always thought *you* would be vice-captain."

"No." She returned her gaze to the table. "I'd rather work alone in my room. The position of vice-captain requires too much interaction."

"One last thing," Endellion said, steering the conversation back to business territory. "When we reach Midway Station, I'll be attending the hearing for final deliberations regarding planet governorship. All requirements for the position should be finalized then. Afterward, we'll be leaving to cover tasks for Ontwenty until the final vote for my rulership. This is it. The final few months of our voyage together."

The others nodded and muttered statements of understanding.

Endellion stood. Instinctively, I did, too.

"If there are no further comments, this meeting is adjourned," she said.

Lysander, Dr. Clay, and Quinn pushed away from the table and shadowed Endellion out of the room. I ambled behind them, lingering back to watch Sawyer. With the enthusiasm of a slug, she got out of her chair and shoved her hands into her jumpsuit pockets. I waited by the door and stopped her when she came near.

"We haven't spoken in a few days," I said.

"I've been busy."

"When *aren't* you busy? That's never stopped you from speaking to me before."

"I'm busier now." Sawyer didn't glance up at me. She kept her focus on the door, her shoulders slumped.

"What happened?" I asked. "Don't give me bullshit. I know when you're upset."

"I'm not upset."

I almost laughed aloud. "Fuck you, Sawyer. Maybe you don't see it, but you might as well be on fire, that's how obvious your depression is. Tell me what's going on. You know you can trust me."

"This is the most emotion I've felt in a long time." She finally met my gaze, her gray eyes searching mine. I loved her freckled face, but not when it was twisted with worry.

"Yeah," I said. "I can see that."

Most of the time she had fleeting expressions. Sure, I could get her to blush or laugh, but a few seconds later, she'd be back to normal. All a part of her intentional flaw, but that made any prolonged emotional state something to take extreme note of.

"No one has noticed I've been depressed," she said.

"You stick to yourself."

"Hm."

I stepped up to her and narrowed my eyes. "You going to tell me what's bothering you? If someone's been harassing you, I'll kick their ass."

Sawyer shook her head. "No. It's Blub."

All mirth left the conversation. "What about Blub?"

"He got injured during the fighting."

I followed Sawyer out of the officer conference room and into the corridor of Deck One. She hustled toward her workspace, faster than I had seen her move in a while. I walked in after her. A portion of her desk space had been cleared to accommodate a small, cloth bed. Blub sat nestled on top of the blanket, his fish body resting flat on one side. His mouth opened and closed, and his fins spun in place at a slow rate.

Fuck. The sight of the sad little fish being grounded disturbed me more than blood and mayhem. What was wrong with me?

I leaned over the fish to get a better look. Blub's helium sacs had been ruptured on one side, preventing him from floating. I touched the injured area, and the fish grimaced. If he could have made noise, I swear he would have squeaked.

"He's been like this since the combat with the rebellion?" I asked.

Sawyer nodded. "I've been trying to take care of him, but he's not getting any better."

"Have you taken him to the infirmary?"

"No. Dr. Clay said he wasn't a veterinarian."

"Dr. Clay is a jackass. I'll get him to look at Blub."

I went to pick up the fish, but Sawyer grabbed my wrist and pulled at my arm. I glared at her—why had she stopped me?—but I could feel her trembling, so I said nothing.

"What if Dr. Clay says he's dying?" Sawyer whispered. "I don't know how long... I'm not sure of Blub's life expectancy, and he's been like this for several days."

What did she want me to say? Shit happens? Things die, get over it? I could have lied. I could have told her everything would be all right and Blub would pull through, even though I had no basis for that whatsoever. None of those options seemed good enough. She thought of Blub as a brother. What could be said about some-one's dying brother?

I placed a hand on her shoulder. "Whatever happens, I'll be here for you, Sawyer. Besides, either Blub will be in the loving arms of his sister until he's better, or we'll throw him the best damn funeral a fish has ever had. He's one of the crew. He deserves nothing less."

Sawyer's lower lip quavered. I tensed. I had never seen her so distraught. Silent tears ran down her face. She wrapped her arms around me and dug her fingers into my enviro-suit. Every breath she took, every beat of her heart—she held tight enough for me to feel it all.

"What's wrong?" I asked. What had I fucked up now?

Sawyer shook her head. She didn't sniff or sob, she just kept our embrace tight, her tears sliding down the exterior of my suit. I patted her back, uncertain what she wanted from me. I wasn't the kind of guy who handled weeping well. I hadn't dealt with it much, but every so often, someone had broken down on Capital Station and talked suicide. I opted to vacate the room during those occasions, but I couldn't imagine leaving Sawyer.

"Look," I said. "Whatever I've done, I'll make it right, okay? I didn't mean to upset you."

"You didn't upset me," she whispered.

"Uh-huh. Bullshit. You've never done this before."

"It's a lot of things, Demarco. Not just Blub." Somehow, she squeezed me tighter. "But you're not the problem."

Sawyer broke away and rubbed her eyes. Although red in the face, she returned to her muted expression and offered me a shrug. I was surprised. Most people didn't wrangle their emotions so quick, but hers weren't like the others. "Thank you," she said.

"What can I do to make this better?"

"Stay with me," she blurted out. "F-For a short period. A night. Or at least while Dr. Clay looks over Blub. I know I said I wanted to be alone, but that's not the case right now."

"Fine. I'll stay."

Sawyer exhaled and looked away. "Not too long. Maybe not even a whole night. Just a few hours."

"I already said fine."

"I…" She shook her head. "Endellion won't be upset?"

"Nothing upsets that woman. It'll be fine."

"Thank you, Demarco."

THE CORE SYMPOSIUM was the main parliament building for the

Vectin Quadrant. According to the computer on the mag-lev train, it was the first government building to be constructed after the mass transports and the first building to get annihilated during the United-Earth war. Superhuman architects rebuilt the place, and there was no doubt in my mind they were trying to send a statement.

The dome of the building could be seen from space. I exaggerate, but not much. The superstructure held meeting halls, conference rooms, and delegates from all over the Vectin Quadrant. The building had its own goddamn residential district inside, and many of the emissaries and diplomats called it home.

Technology made up every millimeter of the place, from the computer terminal doors to the windows that detected the weather and functioned accordingly without intervention to keep the entire place a comfortable temperature. There was even more utility fog—the twinkling starlight that kept every corner of the building awash in the warm glow of a perfect afternoon.

And time had gone into decorating the place so that it felt alive. Plants, even trees, grew inside, and maintenance kept the indoor gardens lush. Banners adorned the walls, some with pictures of Earth and others with pictures of planets from around the sector. I could have tilted my head back all day, glancing from image to image, and I never would have gotten tired.

I loved the Core Symposium.

Endellion and I waited in the Great Hall behind the last row of seats in the farthest nook away from the main podium. The half-dome room seated thousands. We lingered away from the others. The air tasted of cleaning products and cologne. Speeches from superhuman ministers echoed off the walls. Screens displayed the speakers from every angle, and I didn't have to squint to get a good view.

"Who're we waiting for?" I asked.

Endellion motioned to the next speaker. "He'll be giving the announcement."

"We could've waited to hear word aboard the *Star Marque*."

Although the building impressed me, I hated the droning of

politicians discussing legislation that had nothing to do with me. I would have rather spent my free time with Mara and Noah, or Sawyer and Blub.

My thoughts focused on the fish. Dr. Clay had said he would look into it and he didn't think Blub would die, but I still worried. He wasn't the gentlest of doctors.

"I need to speak to Minister Ontwenty," Endellion said. She glanced over at me. "You look troubled. Worried about what we've done?"

I was surprised she would even mention it, but there was no way anyone here would know what she'd meant.

I shrugged. "No. I'm not a fan of Dr. Clay."

"He's talented."

"He said he was busy, but since Mara has left the infirmary, there's nothing for him to do. What the fuck is wrong with that guy?"

"He's conducting his research, Clevon. I've told him to take as much time and resources as he needs."

"Defect research?" I asked.

"Yes."

Anything for the defects in our crew, I supposed.

The chime of a faux bell signified the end of the speaker's term. Murmured discussion filled the room as the next super-human took the podium. Endellion gave the man her full attention. I leaned against the wall, already bored with the spectacle. I wasn't in the mood for the pomp and circumstance of formal talks.

A second chime and silence blanketed the audience. A well-trained routine. It made sense. Their garden party was the time for actual discussion. This was all a formality—announcements and the like.

"Our first order of business regards planet governorship," the superhuman said. "The requirements for the position of planet governor have been updated to reflect our changing times and to ensure the role of planet governor goes to an individual who is qualified for the rigors of the position."

Although there wasn't much reaction from the room, I heard a couple gasps.

They'd changed the requirements? I thought that was the reason Endellion and I had assassinated the emissary. Hadn't Ontwenty promised Endellion she would prevent this from happening?

I glanced over at Endellion. She waited, her face set in an unreadable expression, but I had known her too long to think she was unaffected by the news. She didn't even blink. I returned my gaze to the speaker.

The superhuman continued, "In addition to the previous requirements, all neonate candidates for the position of planet governor will require a majority vote of approval from the acting members of the senate. Only once a majority vote has been reached may the neonate candidate receive the title of planet governor. All returning governors who have served their post without reprimand are excluded from this requirement."

Again, there were whispers.

Endellion turned on her heel and strode for the exit, not even bothering to hear the rest of the announcements. I followed after her, curious about her thoughts, but her hard-set glare warned me she was seething. It reminded me of the time that rebellion thug had cut her arm.

"We're going to speak to Ontwenty," she said as she slammed her hand on a door computer terminal.

"Yes, ma'am."

"THIS WASN'T how it was supposed to play out," Endellion said. Her volume doubled. "We had an agreement. I upheld my end. Why didn't you deliver?"

Minister Ontwenty's fancy, two-floor home in the massive skyscraper shook with the heat of their argument. I stood off to the side, just as angry, but I didn't think I should get involved. Endellion wanted to discuss our options, but I would've gone straight to blackmail or extortion. Ontwenty wouldn't have a career if Endellion exposed their plans.

Minster Ontwenty—dressed down and showcasing much of her flesh—rested back in her seat. She sipped from a clear glass and smiled. "Trust me, this was a better outcome than what Felseven had originally proposed. He attempted to up the requirement of title, which would've been impossible for you to overcome by the next election. Obtaining approval from the senate shouldn't be difficult."

"I shouldn't have any more hurdles to overcome," Endellion snapped. "This was supposed to be the last step. Gaining majority approval from 140 individuals could cost me everything. I don't have time to play games with each and every one of them!" She got louder and louder with every word. When Ontwenty didn't respond, Endellion paced the length of the room, her gait slow, her green eyes fixed to the floor.

The acting members of the senate included 102 planet governors, 30 ministers, and 8 undersecretaries to the high governor. Speaking to each one and gaining their approval would be a nightmare, especially given that Endellion would need their approval in less than a year. Not only that, each one was a superhuman, and they could always have a bias against her or ask for something outrageous in return for their support. The obstacles were limitless.

"You know I would voice my approval on your behalf," Ontwenty said. "My constituents and I would net you nearly enough. We have a substantial voting bloc."

"But it's not enough," Endellion said. "You already failed to stop Felseven from changing the requirements. How many votes went in Felseven's direction?"

"64 voted with me, and 76 voted with Felseven."

A six vote difference. That must have been hard for Endellion to swallow. It would come down to the wire. She might not become a planet governor at that rate. What would she do then? Everything she had done had been for this one, singular goal.

"You're overreacting," Ontwenty said with a smile.

"After everything I've done, I wouldn't say I'm *overreacting*,"

Endellion replied. "Who knows how many more of the requirements Felseven will attempt to change before the next vote? It's now
or never, and I question whether we can work together after this."

"Felseven is an opponent to both of us. I want you as a planet
governor, I made that clear. You've made friends with individuals I
would love to have connections with. We can still benefit from a
working relationship."

Their sly game of back-and-forth didn't sit right. Endellion had
been underhanded, but it was like we were diving deep into a
wormhole of complications, and we were not getting out anytime
soon.

Then again, what other option did Endellion have? How would
she explain to her crew that she wouldn't be able to keep her promise? They could quit and leave her stranded without a means to
complete any work. And who would fill her ship after that? She had
a reputation for getting shit done—if she lost that, she would have
nothing.

"Do you have ideas to solve this?" Endellion asked.

Ontwenty sipped from her glass. "I do. It might require more of
your *hard work*, but in the end, it would guarantee both you and I
come out on top."

Endellion stopped her pacing. She offered Ontwenty a glare.
"You've given this thought."

"Felseven intends to stop the Stellar Engine, and I refuse to see
that happen. It seems you also refuse to see your position as planet
governor slip from your fingers, which means we have everything to
lose if we give up now. Desperation spurs even a child to confront a
madman."

Endellion had gotten played. Ontwenty had done this on
purpose to get the emissary out of her hair, but also, to keep Endellion on a leash.

TWENTY-FIVE

Desperation

The purple skies of Vectin-14 took my mind off the situation.
Lines of defects made their way to Ontwenty's med-fac outpost. They waited for treatment, each signing away their right to sue before reaching the door. Each experimental chem had the potential for life-saving repairs to their warped DNA, but I suspected more than half would either see no benefit or a worsening of their condition. That was what happened on Capital Station. Free chems, but they had to roll the dice for them. If they got anything but a seven, they were fucked.

The *Star Marque*'s enforcers kept the peace around the medical facility. We also watched the line and acted as muscle in case any defects got uppity. It was an easy job while we waited for Endellion to decide on a course of action, but the longer we waited, the antsier I became.

Two men pushed each other in line. One had a lump of flesh hanging from his neck, a grouping of tumors trapped in the flesh sac of his skin. The other stood on a misshapen leg—too small to work well with his other leg—and he toppled over the moment the fight got aggressive.

People in line shouted.

I walked over and grabbed Lump-Neck by the collar of his jumpsuit.

"Keep it to yourself," I growled.

"That guy was cuttin'," Lump-Neck said.

I picked up the guy with mismatched legs and stationed him in line right where he needed to be. "Either of you assholes start any more trouble and I'll throw you both at the end of the line."

The wobbly guy frowned. "You can't do that. I need this medicine."

I hefted my plasma rifle and jutted my chin in the direction of the facility. "I'm in charge here until you get inside, got it? Stay in line like good little children and it won't be a problem."

Neither of them said anything else.

Good.

The roads around the facility carried the lifeblood of Okoga City. Vehicles of all shapes and sizes transported the workings of industry. Refined metal, food, bio waste, and even sad sacks heading to work. The place felt busier than anywhere else I had been on Vectin-14, except for the space elevator.

I returned to my post. Lee trotted over to me, bouncing with each step, like he had music in his blood.

"What're you doing?" I asked him through the comms.

"Listening to the local entertainment. Good stuff."

"Entertainment?"

"Yeah. Vectin-14 music plays over the satellite channels. Your suit can pick it up. Doesn't interfere with your comms, either. Well, it's harder to hear, but that's about it."

"Isn't that against the rules?" I asked, knowing damn well it was. All that ground-enforcer training included a laundry list of what not to do while working. I was sure if Lysander were there, he would have had a little hissy fit.

"C'mon," Lee said, a smile in his voice. "Just because you're some over-glorified vice-captain now doesn't mean you have to get stern with me. I'm not even a ground enforcer. I'm doing this because there's nothing for an amazing pilot to do."

He tapped the collarbone of my suit, and I rubbed the newly-added decorations. A few gold stripes set me apart from the rest. Vice-Captain—I liked the title.

"Fine," I said. "Just stop dancing like a lunatic."

"Aye, aye, Vice-Captain, sir." He gave me a sarcastic salute.

I turned to walk away, but Lee jogged up to my side and tapped my shoulder. His enviro-suit helmet was up, so all I saw was the reflection of my own helmet in his visor, but his body language spoke volumes. He got in close, as if to whisper, but our comms were set to one-on-one communications, so there was no need for nervous mannerisms.

"Hey," he said. "What's going on? We've been on Vectin longer than we should have, and Endellion hasn't been seen for the last couple of days."

"She's deciding our next course of action."

"Something else is up. I know it. Even Quinn has been acting strange. Did something happen in the Core Symposium?"

The information wasn't hidden. The public could have accessed the Core Symposium records from any all-access computer terminal stationed around the cities. Not only that, but the updates to legislation had been announced in public forums. I'd even heard news about Emissary Barten's assassination while wandering around Okoga City. Sure enough, the news reported rebellion involvement and that they may have used the peace talks as a false pretense to meet with the emissary.

Better than the reality. And the news would blow over soon. Barten wasn't popular, or so it seemed. Most didn't want to acknowledge the United-Earth faction because they were warmongers who hated superhumans, and any reason to see a pro United-Earth emissary gone was a reason to celebrate.

"Demarco?" Lee asked. "Did you hear me?"

"What?"

"Did something happen at the Core Symposium?"

"They changed the requirements for incoming planet governors," I said. "Don't worry. It's nothing Endellion can't handle. She's overcome worse."

Lee exhaled, and his whole body deflated a bit. "Why couldn't

Quinn tell me that? She said everything was fine, but no specifics. Thanks for keeping me in the loop."

I was surprised Quinn hadn't said anything, but perhaps Endellion had told her not to. Made me think I shouldn't have said anything, but it was too late to change it.

"Lee," I said over the comms as I headed to the mag-lev train. "I'm heading back to our company town. Let me know if anything happens while I'm away."

"Can do."

I needed to speak to Endellion, and I knew she was there. Every day she spoke with Ontwenty in private, and then returned to her room in the quaint little house Ontwenty had provided us for our planet stay.

Maybe she needed company as much as I did.

I switched my comms and exhaled. "Sawyer. Endellion is still on the planet's surface, correct?"

"Yes," she replied, her old tone back in full force.

"Blub okay?"

"I took him to a Vectin-14 veterinarian specialist."

"You did? Really?"

"Well, no. I had Lysander go for me. The superhuman in charge of the genetically-modified animals at the menagerie isn't someone I want to interact with."

"Heh," I said with a huff. "I knew it."

"Yeah, yeah. You know me so well. Do you want an award? I think I have some gold-star stickers I could put on your enviro-suit."

Sawyer's good mood did wonders for my own. I had felt off since the fight and assassination, but even a few interactions with the crew had repaired the damage from the mental fray. I wished I could say the same about Endellion.

I entered the mag-lev train with a group of random passengers. The trains ran so frequently and so fast, there was no waiting time. We got on, and then the train exited the station, zipping across Vectin-14. In a few minutes, I stepped off the transport and headed for the company town. The walls stood out against the lush landscape, which made getting lost impossible.

I could have used my comms to speak to Endellion—being face-to-face with her wasn't required—but I wanted our communication to be personal. I'd killed a man in cold blood for her. She'd promoted me to vice-captain and wanted me to pilot the *Star Marque* once she was a governor. And every night, when I was deep inside her, and we were breathing heavy, I knew we had tangled ourselves together in success. Speaking face-to-face would do us both good.

With a few quick nods to the guards, I headed in. The Vectin star had set in the distance by the time I reached Endellion's dwelling. I didn't bother knocking. I stepped in, switched on the lights, and froze.

For a brief second, the sight coated my veins in ice. The entire front room had been turned upside-down. The couch lay on its side, the cushions torn open. The side table had so many splintered pieces it might as well have been a jigsaw puzzle. A computer terminal—normally mounted to the wall—had been cracked in half.

I ripped off my helmet and ran a hand through my short hair.

"Endellion," I shouted. "Are you here?"

I jumped over the destruction and rushed straight for her bedroom.

Every millimeter of the building was the same. Destruction and mayhem.

I threw open the bedroom door and took stock of the situation. My gaze landed on Endellion—she stood in one piece—but then I took note of the smashed bedframe, and the ripped carpet. Splatters of blood pulled the whole room together, painting a story of murder, rather than comfort.

"Endellion?"

She stood in front of the mirror, her back to me, her hands flat on the glass. Her standard braid spilled over her shoulder, its tip crested in blood. Although I had the cold focus for a fight in my system, I forced myself to relax. I didn't see any intruders. Her tank-top and pants weren't torn.

Endellion glared at her own reflection, her green eyes unblinking.

"What happened?" I asked as I stepped over the debris.

She didn't answer.

It wasn't destruction from a brawl. The longer I stared, the more I saw the imprints of fingernails. Endellion had torn this place apart with her cyborg strength. She must have cut herself on a sharp edge of shattered metal or glass, but that hadn't stopped her.

I stood behind her and ran my hands along the muscles of her back. "You've got anger issues."

"I'm perfectly composed," she replied, no emotion in her voice, but her eyes screamed a different story.

"Tell that to your room." I kneaded her shoulders. The tense muscles underneath didn't ease up. I circled my thumb along her jagged spine, and then I kissed her neck, my panic gone and long replaced with hot lust. "There are better ways to relieve stress," I said.

Endellion didn't move. "I spoke to Ontwenty."

"And?"

"She wants me to dispose of Felseven."

I chuckled. "Which one?"

"The man who runs Capital Station."

I stopped my massage. "Wait, does she mean—"

"Yes," Endellion said, cutting me off. "But keep your words to yourself, Clevon. We're not on the *Star Marque*."

I gritted my teeth. "We just got done… doing something similar. We can't do it again."

I couldn't believe Endellion would have even suggested that. We couldn't assassinate another member of the Federation Government. Maybe we were capable, but there was an adage I'd learned when I ran with gangs: *"Sooner or later, if you do it long enough, you will get caught."* Even the smartest punks run afoul of bad luck. They couldn't account for that. We would've failed with Barten, had there been even the slightest of slip-ups. We'd almost failed outright when Endellion was prevented from seeing the man. What if I had been prevented, as well? What if Barten had beaten me in the fight? What if the guard in the hall had come in to say something as I was finishing the deed?

For every plan, there were 15 ways it could have been fucked up.

"We can't," I repeated. "Tell Ontwenty it has to stop."

"No. I've made my decision. We're heading to Capital Station."

"And what if we're caught?" I stepped away from her, my movements stiff with tension. "There won't be any trial, let me tell you. Capital Station has its own form of justice, and it's called 'taking the bitch out back and silencing her yourself.'"

"We won't get caught."

"You don't know that."

"I take risks. *Calculated* risks. I've done it forever, and I'm not going to stop now, even if you fear we might not make it." Endellion pushed away from the mirror and turned to face me. She was serious. *Always* serious. Even when risking it all, there was no backing down.

"Felseven won't operate like Emissary Barten," I said. "He's got hundreds of guards. He lives planetside on Galvis-4. He runs that whole fucking show. We'll never get close to the man, and even if we do, we'll never make it back to the *Star Marque*. Some things are impossible. We should focus on getting six other votes, for fuck's sake, not this."

"It's impossible for a poor girl born on Ucova to become a starship captain," Endellion stated, rigid and icy in every regard. "It's impossible for that same girl to become commodore. It's impossible for a human to ever gain standing within a Federation government run entirely by superhumans. Clevon, I've built my career on impossibilities. This won't be the one to stop me."

Where did her drive come from?

"It doesn't have to be all or nothing," I said. "Why not take a safer path? Getting the votes won't end in disaster. We can keep trying even if we fail, but not if we fail doing it your way."

"I won't fail." She didn't flinch or hesitate. There was no room for another interpretation.

I rubbed my neck and exhaled. She hadn't failed yet. How could I even argue? Endellion had made it clear—not even God himself would stop her plans.

"This will be the last time," she said.

"You said that about Emissary Barten."

"This is different. It *will* be the last time."

"All right," I said. "We'll do it your way. But this has to be the last time."

"Good. Now leave me."

I glanced around the room. "You're going to stay here? Alone?"

"I need to focus." Endellion turned around and faced the mirror. "And I'd rather there were no distractions."

"When will we head out for Capital Station?"

"Two days from now. Inform the others."

I WATCHED the defects mill about in line, but my mind couldn't have been further away.

With each breath, I felt my insides tightening. I never wanted to return to Capital Station. I couldn't believe I would play a part in its owner's death. A year ago, I never would've imagined such a fate.

While I walked around the med-fac building, my gaze honed in on Mara and Noah. They stood together near a long line, both watching over the crowds. I sauntered over, pleased to see Mara had recovered enough to work.

"What're you two doing?" I asked over the personal comms.

Noah turned his attention to me. "Demarco. How're you?"

"Good."

Mara glanced between me and Noah, but didn't say anything. I couldn't see her face—not with the helmet up—and I wondered about her emotional state. Was it rude to ask? Probably. But who gave a fuck, really?

"You feeling better, Mara?" I asked. "I didn't know you were back on the job."

"Noah said taking my mind off things would help," she said. What an odd tone she had with limited medication. Calm. Even. I did miss her ability to make me smile with just a single statement. But it was what she had chosen. I wouldn't have forced her to be something she didn't want to be.

330

Noah pointed with his rifle, motioning to the far end of the line. "This line doesn't let up. I thought about going inside myself to see if there were any low-risk options, but everyone says those are taken first."

"We've got a doctor now," I said. "Don't risk it."

"You're right. I was nervous until I talked to Lee."

"Nervous about what?"

"About the *Star Marque*. I thought Endellion might not meet the requirements, and who knows what would happen after that? But Lee told me everything. It's frustrating that the superhumans yank Endellion around like this. Although, it never really stops her."

"Hm."

Noah shrugged.

Unwilling to continue the conversation, I patted both of them on the arm. "Glad to see you're doing better, Mara," I said. "Keep up the good work." I started to walk past them, but she held out a hand.

"Demarco," she whispered. "At some point I need to speak with you. In private."

"What for?"

"I wanna talk to you about Yuan. And Endellion."

I gritted my teeth. "Later. I can't hear this right now."

"On the *Star Marque*?"

"Fine."

I knew Endellion had done a million questionable things. I didn't need my thoughts mired under yet another bombardment of facts. I already regretted agreeing to her plan. I wondered what Noah and Mara would have thought if they knew why we were returning to Capital Station. I doubted either of them would have been ecstatic to hear the news.

"Demarco," Sawyer said in my ear. "You should calm down."

"I am calm."

"You suit provides readings of your physical condition. You know that, right?"

"In theory. What do you want?"

"You're anxious."

I stopped walking and held my plasma rifle close. "You know what's going on, Sawyer. How can you be so calm? Did you hear Mara and Noah? They think this shit is locked down. They think Endellion has already won."

"She has."

"Don't give me that. Why do you suck her dick so hard, Sawyer? You know killing Felseven is a terrible idea. You must. Tell me you think it's terrible."

"I think it's a fine idea. I know Endellion will pull it off, and then she'll become governor."

"Why?"

"Why do you have to question her?" Sawyer snapped. "You know what she's capable of. She's not going to lose now." Sawyer only got that heated when she talked about Endellion. I hated her fanaticism.

"Forget it," I said. "I don't need this." I switched off my comms and marched around the defects, my blood at its boiling point. We had six months before we reached Capital Station. Maybe I could convince them to change course. Or maybe I was just kidding myself.

TWENTY-SIX

Dead Drop

D rinking with the others took my mind off the present.

We lounged around the mess hall, testing out the new stock we'd gotten from Vectin-14. I'd had no idea alcohol could come in so many varieties. The guys on Capital Station had claimed their synthesized shit tasted as good as any brewed beverage found planetside.

They were wrong.

"This has a hint of ranberry to it," Lee said, staring at his pouch like he was going to make out with it.

"What's a ranberry?" I asked.

"A fruit they have on Vectin-14. Real good. Sweet. You can taste it. C'mon, try." He handed over the pouch, and I gulped down the rest. I had no idea if it had ranberry in it or not, but I liked it. Sweet and potent, though it didn't burn like the powerful stuff. Seemed like something I could drink for a long while and not even realize I was getting drunk.

Quinn cracked open another pouch—her fourth, more than usual for her—and she gave me a sidelong glance. "How long have you and Endellion been hooking up?"

Everyone at the table stopped their side conversations, not sly about their curiosity in the least. Lee leaned heavy on his elbow, Noah widened his eyes, and Mara knitted her eyebrows together.

"We've been at it for a bit," I said with a shrug. "Long enough."

"No wonder she promoted you to vice-captain," Lee said, lifting his pouch in a toast. "Sleeping with my boss hasn't gotten me any perks. Yet." He and Quinn laughed before lightly pressing their lips together for a quick kiss. Then another. They didn't keep at it for long. After a few seconds, they both resumed their drinking. We had a lot of pouches to test out.

The PAD on my arm lit up with a message: *Clevon Demarco to the bridge.* I tapped it away and stood, drawing the attention of the others.

"Leaving?" Noah asked. "We haven't gotten to the expensive flavors Quinn bought us."

"Save some for me," I said. "I'll be back."

Although I'd had a decent amount of alcohol, I knew I was capable. I exited the mess hall, walked through the narrow corridors of the *Star Marque*, and headed straight for the lift. The enforcers I passed greeted me with enthusiasm and a quick nod or exchange. I took the time to answer each one, but the more recognition I got, the more I had to keep up pleasantries to maintain it. And I was just on an enforcer starship. I could only imagine what Endellion went through. She was famous enough to have assassins on her tail, after all.

I reached the bridge, my mind returning to everything I was trying to ignore. Endellion stood in the center of the room, the screens and monitoring systems displaying a Federation cargo ship. She motioned me to her, and I complied.

"We found our target faster than I expected," she said.

"One of Ontwenty's assignments?" I asked, knowing the answer to my question already.

"Yes."

After seeing the shape of Endellion's room planetside, I knew she didn't appreciate Ontwenty's games. Ontwenty had played her; I was willing to bet my life on it. If I were Endellion, I wouldn't have continued to run errands for the woman, but there we were.

Ontwenty wanted us to shake down a few starships suspected of smuggling goods or leaking information to competing companies. Maybe even the rebellion.

Ontwenty could have gone through official channels to get that cleared up, which made our involvement suspect. Ontwenty wanted us to do something unorthodox.

A screen flashed and revealed the face of a haggard woman. Her non-military-grade jumpsuit told me she was a civilian, but the cross insignia by her collar let the universe know she was still a captain.

"This is Captain Tavilla," she said, "of the cargo vessel, *Pegasus Star*. Is there a reason you've detained my ship? I have clearance. I'm transmitting the codes to you now."

"Thank you, Captain Tavilla," Endellion said with a smile. "But we'll be boarding your starship and searching the cargo."

"You can't do that."

"I can and will. I've already included the authorization in the information I've sent. Any resistance will be taken as an act of aggression toward the Federation."

Captain Tavilla tightened her mouth into a straight line. The screen flickered off. No farewell or end statement of any kind.

"Sawyer," Endellion said. "Have you finished scanning the area?"

"No," she replied over the comms.

"*No?*"

I lifted an eyebrow.

"The asteroids in the area create massive ambipolar fields," Sawyer said. "These electric fields interfere with standard mapping and scanning technologies. It's probably why they chose this location to do their dead drops. I need more time to narrow down the possibilities."

"Very well."

"Dead drops?" I asked.

"Locations at which to pass on valuable information. By leaving it in a physical location, there's no risk of leaving an electronic trail.

335

One person drops off their illegal information, and another person picks it up at some point in the future."

"Ontwenty suspects they're passing her research on to others?" I asked. The woman might have been paranoid.

Endellion said nothing.

I stood at her side while the *Star Marque* maneuvered into a docking position. It didn't take much, but everything had to be exact. The seals and latches were important for stability while making bridges, and no one wanted to find themselves lost in space. It seemed longer when watching the process, however. Lysander and his ground enforcers needed to cross over and check the ship.

"Not going this time?" I asked Endellion, quiet enough for her, and her alone.

"There's no prize to be had on the starship," she said.

The *Star Marque* made contact with the *Pegasus Star*, and I wondered if anyone would cause any trouble. I doubted they would, but I was still worried. Endellion showed no sign of anxiety, not a bead of sweat. Although it had taken me days to reconcile Yuan and Advik's death, she'd never mentioned them again. Was I the weak one?

From the bridge we could monitor the number of enforcers on the *Pegasus Star*, along with the decks they had searched. Lysander provided copious amounts of information, and the ground enforcers operated in a quick and efficient manner. I had trained with Lysander a handful of times—no more than ten sessions—but I could already see how his methods paid off. Everyone had a place. Everyone knew their place. The squads completed their jobs without delay.

However, on the second deck, a squad requested backup. Lysander and 20 others converged at the location, and even though I wasn't watching a video feed, the numbers and diagrams got my blood pressure up. I wasn't even that fond of Lysander, but the thought of the event turning bloody did make me agitated.

The confrontation lasted longer than I liked. The computers and scans said no rifles or lasers were involved. Whatever had happened couldn't have been too bad.

"Commodore Voight," Lysander said over the comms. "We've apprehended four individuals. Their ID chips match records we have for criminal activity. Although not linked to the rebellion, they have surrendered and confessed to aiding them."

"Take them to the brig," Endellion commanded.

"They claim starfighters are out in the ambipolar fields. From what they said, the people piloting the fighters are their associates. They had a falling-out. Half went to complete a dead drop, and the other half stayed on the cargo vessel. They're asking us to show the fighters mercy."

"And the people you have in custody—they're also starfighter pilots?"

"Yes, Commodore."

"Tell them I'll offer their fellows mercy if they surrender, but I can't make any guarantees."

"Yes, Commodore."

Endellion stared at the screen, her gaze distant. "Sawyer. Give me the information for the four that Lysander apprehended."

"Melba Bennett, Hattie Andler, Jermaine Chun, and Haruto Asahi," Sawyer replied. "I don't have much because they don't have a long list of crimes, but three of them worked for Garton Metals as transport guards. The company went under, and that's the last known date of employment. Jermaine is the only one who seems to have had multiple jobs, everything from pilot to miner. He killed a few people in a workplace accident. Since then, he's received two counts of terrorism in relation to the rebellion."

"And what about the area? Have you finished scanning it yet?"

"I've narrowed down the location. It's small, but if they only have a shuttle and a few starfighters, I think it's the place."

Sawyer still impressed me with her ability to multitask. Reading four people's personal history *and* scanning the area for potential hideaways wasn't a problem for her. I couldn't imagine Endellion running the rig without Sawyer's help.

Endellion turned on her heel and motioned for me to follow her. "Send me the coordinates," she said to Sawyer as we exited the bridge. Once in the corridor with the door shut, she glanced at me.

"Send our starfighters to dispatch anyone they find at Sawyer's location."

"You're not going to hail them first? Show them mercy?"

"We can't hail them if they're in a patch of electrical disturbance."

"You didn't even try," I said. "It might work."

Endellion stopped walking and locked her hard eyes with mine. "We couldn't hail them."

It only took me half a second to understand, but I was still surprised. "All right. What if they try to surrender when they see a bunch of enemy starfighters?"

"They won't surrender. They'll attack, and we'll destroy them. Understand?"

Oh, I understood. No mercy. It was all for show. "Whatever you say. But I'll handle it."

Endellion glowered. "Not you. Send the others."

"I'm a better pilot."

"I know. That's why you should send the others."

I cocked an eyebrow. "Oh, yeah?"

Endellion started walking again, her gait fast and powerful. I kept up, but her anger came across in each hard tap of her boot on the metal flooring. "Don't start with me, Clevon. I play with risks all the time. I risk losing a starfighter here. If I had to lose one, I wouldn't want it to be you. You're talented beyond the cockpit, and I need those talents for the future. There are others—less talented, more focused on a single skill—whom I can replace if they fail me on this mission. I'll risk them instead." Endellion waved her hand, like the conversation had ended, but I took a few steps and blocked her path, forcing her to stop and meet my gaze.

"There's no risk if I go," I said. "Because I won't fail."

She said nothing.

"The others have been drinking, and I can handle a couple starfighters and a shuttle."

Instead of waiting for her response, I walked away and headed for my starfighter. If she could pull that shit, then so could I. Talking about the others like tools didn't sit right with me. Perhaps that made me a poor candidate for leader. I might have been selfish—because a good crew didn't operate without knowing they could die in the line of duty—or maybe, it was just the timing. Right then, I didn't want to see anyone else lost to the black tide.

I jumped into the cockpit of my fighter and settled in.

"Demarco," Sawyer said over the comms as the screens flickered to life.

"Yeah?"

"You don't want to take someone else with you?"

"I've got you, don't I?'

Sawyer snorted back a laugh. "Be careful."

Once the starfighter suctioned me in, I broke away from the *Star Marque* and headed toward the coordinates on my screen. Asteroids floated in the nearby area, many without spin or much motion at all. My screen indicated the dark sides had electrical fields created by the solar winds. If I stayed out of the charged areas, there wouldn't a problem.

I zipped toward the largest in the area, the one with the most disturbance and energy. Since my scanners couldn't detect the ships, I switched my attention to the screen displaying the outside. My naked eye would have to pick up the slack.

Sure enough—just as Sawyer had predicted—a shuttle and three starfighters were attached to the dark side of the asteroid, at the bottom of a sizable crater. I kept clear of the electrical tail floating off the back of the asteroid, but I circled around enough for them to see me. If they left their spot, it would be easier to shoot them as the asteroid and its electricity made it difficult for all my targeting instruments.

But they didn't move.

The crater must have been their dead drop.

"What're you waiting for?" Sawyer asked.

I had no love for the rebellion or their associates, but I did prefer a fair fight. I circled around, and this time I fired a torpedo at one of the smaller asteroids. The resulting impact sent millions of fragmented rocks in every direction, filling the area with obstacles and debris.

I'd gotten my message across. Their starfighters took off from the asteroid's surface.

Sawyer sighed. "You gave them time to prepare?"

"I like it better this way."

"Endellion made it clear she didn't want you to die."

"I won't die."

The two starfighters flew in opposite directions. At first, I thought they would try to escape, but then I saw they were wrapping around for a pincer attack.

I sped toward one fighter like we were playing a game of chicken, accelerating faster than my target. Before we collided, he fired a torpedo, but I twitched my side-stick and dodged. Centimeters from the enemy ship, I streaked over and twisted back around, freeing myself from an attack on both sides. I fired my torpedoes, catching the fighter and destroying it instantly.

The second guy unloaded everything he had.

Fifteen torpedoes filled my screen. The move shocked me, but I twisted in time to avoid the barrage and sailed around the light side of the asteroid. I worried the other guy might have hyperweapons, so when I whipped around, I opened fire, giving the asshole no time to breathe.

He flew sideways and sailed around a cluster of porous rocks. My two torpedoes trailed off, missing him, and when he came back around, I knew I would have problems. I preemptively moved to the side, accelerating for cover, when a blinding flash of light filled the area. His hyperweapon had cut a hole through the asteroid I was flying behind, damn near clipping the side of my U-shaped fighter.

With my teeth gritted, I looped back around. The moment I exited cover, I launched a series of torpedoes. Two to get him to dodge in a specific direction, one to follow through, and a fourth to finish the job, once I was a few meters from him. The fourth torpedo caught him before he could turn away, and I sailed by his wreckage, sad to see a talented fighter go, but exhilarated I had come out on top.

Nothing beat the rush of living through a dogfight.

The passenger shuttle never left the asteroid, not even during the fight. I used two torpedoes and destroyed the damn space rock, crushing the shuttle with the resulting explosion and debris.

"Not bad," Sawyer said. "A needless risk to fight them, so I'm not sure you deserve credit, but I'm still impressed."

Hearing her voice relaxed me. "Sawyer. Join me and the others for a drink sometime."

"I don't drink."

"Don't worry, I'll drink enough for the both of us."

She laughed.

I flew my fighter back to the *Star Marque* and went through the docking procedures without the need for conscious thought. Once in place, I relaxed against my seat and waited for the cockpit to release my legs. "C'mon," I said. "You never socialize, but you've got the wit for it."

She half-groaned.

"How about this? You try it once. If you like it, great. If you don't, I'll hang with you for a few days in your workroom."

"Fine. I'll try it."

"Good."

The starfighter released my legs, and I leapt out of the cockpit. Again, my PAD lit up with a message: *Clevon Demarco to the bridge.* I tapped the message off my screen and exhaled.

"Anything happen aboard the cargo ship?" I asked, knowing Sawyer would hear me, no matter what.

"No. They've been cooperative."

"What're we doing with the criminals in our brig?"

"We've separated them. I don't have much information, so Endellion will question them before we attempt anything else."

"Attempt anything else?" I asked with a laugh. "We're not going to fly them straight to Ucova? Or back to Vectin-14 for some swift punishment?"

"Endellion wants more starfighters. She needs to know more about the people in our brig if she's going to recruit them."

The information filled my thoughts and slowed my pace. Endellion would recruit old rebellion sympathizers as starfighters? I was surprised. A little angry, actually. She didn't draw lines?

They'd tried to kill her. Several times. And what about Yuan and Advik?

I headed to the bridge, shaking off my doubt. I used to be a criminal, and I'd left that behind me, though the last few missions had felt more like my time on Capital Station. Maybe Endellion liked taking people and turning them around. Seemed a lot of people in her crew had a terrible circumstance in their past that she'd helped them out of.

TWENTY-SEVEN

Circumstances

Jermaine Chun reminded me of Capital Station. He had the look and smell of a guy who'd clawed his way out of the sewer. His long, oily hair hung forward, coating his face in a glossy layer of human grease. My standards for company had gone up since my time on the station. Maybe I would have associated with men like Jermaine before, but now he disgusted me.

Separated from the other starfighters we had in custody, Jermaine waited behind the bars of our brig, his ankles locked in place, allowing him to sit but not move around. He leered at Endellion, looking her up and down without a hint of shame. A part of me wanted to punch him in the dick. I wondered how well he would see, then.

"Can I help you?" Jermaine asked and cocked half a smile, his hands resting between his legs.

"Do you know who I am?" Endellion asked.

"You're a damn fine lady-captain."

"I'm Commodore Voight of the enforcer starship, *Star Marque*."

"So?"

I'd practically said the same thing when I met Endellion. The guy reminded me too much of my past self.

"I'm well aware of your history," Endellion said. "There's a warrant for your arrest and a bounty for turning you in."

Jermaine huffed but said nothing.

"Are you prepared to answer before a justicar?"

"Fuck you, bitch. If you came to taunt me, you got another think comin'. I've been to all sorts of rehab facilities. They don't scare me."

"Ucova has gravity far more intense than anything generated by a starship. Surely you've heard the rumors."

"You're taking me to Ucova?" Jermaine frowned and crossed his arms, his demeanor becoming tenser and tenser as he spoke. "That's not the closest place to here."

"I can choose the facility at which to check in criminals in my custody. Even if they don't keep you for the entire sentence, it'll be months before you leave."

Jermaine licked his lips and stared at the floor.

Before he could offer another thoughtful comment, Endellion continued, "Are you aware that commodores can pardon crimes? Perhaps you'd like to leave this place with your freedom, rather than shackled to another man and led away to a cell."

The statement got Jermaine sitting straight up in his seat. "Oh, yeah? Pardon my crimes? Whaddya want?"

Endellion had given me a similar speech back when we met. She'd pardoned my crimes and allowed me to join her enforcer crew. Now I waited by her side, silent. Would Jermaine one day work alongside me? I loathed the idea.

"We have three of your friends in custody," Endellion said. "And they've refused to talk. We know you were all involved in multiple crimes, but they deny any involvement. If at least one person testifies, it'll make it easier for my reports."

Jermaine mulled over the statements with twisted contemplation. Then it dawned on him. He smiled. "So, if I talk, you'll let me go, is that it? Collect three bounties for the price of one? How do I know you'll follow through?"

"If no one talks, I might not get *any* bounties. If one person talks, I'll get three. Either you or one of the others will eventually say something. Ucova will take us a few weeks to reach, after all. Do you want one of them to out you? Or would you rather be the one sitting pretty?"

The coldness in her voice and the way she played on his opportunistic personality, were the very definition of manipulation. Jermaine had jumped ship at every turn—at least, according to Sawyer's research. From one job to the next, the man chased money without a real plan. And now when he smiled, I knew he was ready to do it again.

"All right," Jermaine says. "I'll talk. Those other three are rebellion couriers. Neck-deep in corporate fuckery. You know. Selling stolen ideas, information. I've got an ass-load of specific incidents. I'll name the contacts."

"And when the four of you stayed on the *Pegasus Star*, was it because you didn't want to participate anymore, or were you acting as a safety net? A last resort, should something go wrong?"

"Yeah. That. Those other three were waitin' to do their part the entire time. They would've flown out, if we had enough fighters."

What a terrible leading question. And Jermaine had played right into it.

Endellion returned Jermaine's smile with one of her own. "Good. I'll have someone here to take the rest of your statements, and then we'll send you off with the *Pegasus Star* to the nearest space station."

"Fine by me."

Without another word, Endellion turned on her heel. I followed her out, giving Jermaine one last glance. The man sat smug in his holding cell, adjusting the crotch of his pants, a sly smirk clear on his face.

Once we exited into the corridor, I gave Endellion a quick glance. "I thought we were recruiting him."

"Not him. *Never* people like him. He's not sufficiently talented, nor can I trust him. The moment an opportunity presented itself, he would betray me."

"I could see that. But then why talk to him? There's no reason. The bounty on the other three is tiny. We'd waste more on fuel getting to Ucova then we'd make for turning them in. I thought you said being captain was about managing finances."

"This dilemma is by design," Endellion said. "The outcome is all that matters. If I have starfighters, everything we've done here will be worth it."

I still didn't understand how turning three people in and letting some asshole walk free would net us starfighters, but I said nothing and allowed Endellion to weave her reality. It felt like the situation with Dr. Rhodes all over again.

We walked to the next room in the brig and entered to find a woman in a similar position as Jermaine. Melba Bennett. Sawyer gave me all her information before I joined Endellion in the brig. Technically I had the information for all our prisoners, but Melba stood out. She was the oldest, the most educated, and the one who'd spoken to Lysander when his enforcers apprehended her on the *Pegasus Star*.

Unlike Jermaine, she had short hair, held back with a couple of pins. She remained calm with her posture straight and looked up the moment we got close.

"I'm Commodore Voight of the enforcer starship, *Star Marque*," Endellion said.

Melba nodded. "I've heard of you. You're the human running for the position of planet governor."

"That's right."

"What happened to the others?" Melba asked. "Did they surrender?"

"No," Endellion replied. "They opened fire, and we responded in kind. They were destroyed."

"All of them?"

"Yes."

Melba grew still and silent. Her gaze fell to the floor grating, her shoulders stiff.

"We're taking you all to Ucova," Endellion said, the only sound in the dreary room. "Once there, you'll be charged with terrorism and corporate espionage."

"We didn't do it," Melba said. "We backed out."

"Not according to your associate. According to him, you waited on the *Pegasus Star* as backup. Actions like that are tantamount to piloting the starfighters yourself."

"It's not true. Who said that? Ask anyone else. They'll tell you the truth."

The panic in her voice got under my skin. No one wanted to end up in Ucova, especially not for a crime they didn't commit. But I'd seen what was happening long before Endellion even explained. Melba didn't have any options. The people who could corroborate her story had died when I gunned them down in their starfighters, and now it was her word versus Jermaine's, and it didn't look good for her side of the story. Melba already had a record, and she had no proof to substantiate her claim of innocence.

"Sawyer," Endellion said. "Play back Jermaine's statements."

The comms in the room flared to life. *"Those other three are rebellion couriers,"* Jermaine's recording said, just as irritating over the speakers. *"Neck-deep in corporate fuckery. You know. Selling stolen ideas, information. They would've flown out, if we had enough fighters."*

The spliced together statement gave me pause. All of Endellion's questions had been edited away. Now it was just a testimony—a *damning* testimony that would send Melba and her cohorts straight to the mines of Ucova.

She knew it, too, because the color drained from her tan complexion.

"I've seen your records," Endellion said. "When were you going to learn that fanatics and outlaws will always throw away the bottom rungs to save themselves? There's no stability when you deal with individuals powered by delusion."

Melba didn't reply.

"You value stability, it's obvious from your long years at Garton Metals. Why would you choose such an unpredictable career?"

"We didn't have a choice," Melba said. "We lost our jobs, and nobody cares about pilots out on the edge of the quadrant. We... we took jobs with questionable people, and then it's a loop. You have to keep doing it, or they report you. Soon you're so deep you don't even realize you're circling the drain."

"Sounds like you've learned your lesson."

Melba glared, her fingers tightly gripping the edge of the harsh, steel seat. "What do you want? You've obviously got something to say. Out with it."

"I'm a commodore. I can pardon crimes within my jurisdiction and recruit whomever I want to serve as a member of my enforcers."

I had heard that line. Same one she'd said to me, but this time, the whole problem was fabricated from the ground up.

Endellion had gotten Jermaine to confess to crimes that weren't real. He was desperate—she knew that, *everyone* knew that—and he was a liar. Then with the other starfighters dead, there was no one to deny Jermaine's stories. Endellion could have let them all go. She could have let the starfighters in the electric fields surrender. She could have called Jermaine on his bullshit and realized the other three had nothing to do with the situation.

But that wouldn't have suited her needs.

"Why would you pardon us?" Melba asked. "What do you want?"

"I need more starfighters. Perhaps you could serve me on the *Star Marque* and regain your lost sense of stability. Trust me, I won't allow any old contacts to threaten you with exposure. There'll be nothing to expose."

Melba took in a ragged breath and exhaled.

"Think about it," Endellion said as she turned for the door. "I'll be back in a few hours to hear your thoughts."

Again, we walked out of the holding cell. Endellion offered me a smile. I crossed my arms as we entered the corridor, my mind anywhere but on my actions. I knew in my gut that Melba would say yes to the offer. I had. I didn't regret it, but if Melba knew the circumstances for her recruitment, would she still be willing? I doubted it. I wouldn't have been.

"You look troubled," Endellion said.

"Hm."

She ran a hand up my neck and grabbed the base of my chin,

turning me to face her. I stared into her eyes, conflicted by her intensity.

And then she kissed me, her soft lips a promise of relaxation. When Endellion broke away, she smirked. "This went perfectly. You've no reason to be tense."

"It doesn't sit right."

"Don't get soft on me, Clevon. You know as well as I do that working on the *Star Marque* is better than anything they would've achieved on their own. Obviously, they needed help."

"Aren't you just going to give the crew a bunch of land once this is all over? Less than nine months now. Do we really need starfighters that badly?"

"They can serve you," she said, "once you inherit the *Star Marque*. I never promised them anything. It's not unreasonable to say they joined too late for my retirement bonus, and I may need pilots when we reach Capital Station. Any excuse to get Felseven to meet with me, after all."

"Hm."

Endellion grazed her knuckles along the edge of my jaw. "You've seen the way others play the game. If I didn't do this, these starfighters would turn back to the rebellion or worse. This is what I need to win."

"You mean against the superhumans," I said, not a question, but a statement.

"Yes. And I told you, I wouldn't let anything stop me."

"I remember."

"You should feel the same passion," Endellion said, heated. "That's what it takes to succeed, Clevon. You can't be satisfied with being good enough or just doing your best. You have to focus on the results and the results alone. That's all that matters. That's all anyone cares about. It's all they'll remember you for. As it should be. And in the end, I'll get three new starfighters today. Do you understand?"

"Yeah," I said. "I get it. You won."

She was right, I figured. I kept feeling weak compared to her— inferior, almost—and now I knew why. Endellion wanted to win, and I just wanted goals. She didn't second-guess victory. It was the ultimate prize. Her ambition demanded a steep payment, but she was more than willing to meet the cost.

I should have been, too.

I leaned forward and kissed her again, uncertain but willing to accept her wisdom on the matter. Endellion had done more with her life than I had with mine. Perhaps she was right. I should emulate her behavior. I shouldn't have felt guilty about our course of action.

She smiled against my lips. "I'm glad you understand," she muttered, her hot breath mixing with mine. "I knew you would."

I HIT the computer terminal outside of Lysander's door.

It was the night cycle for the deck. Endellion had fallen asleep an hour ago. I couldn't rest. A part of me dwelled on the three starfighters, wondering what would change if they knew what had transpired. Why was I so obsessed? It wasn't like me. I didn't feel... right.

Endellion had made a good point. Who cared how they got there? We would treat them right, so the path they'd stumbled across didn't matter, even if Endellion had fucked with them beforehand to make it possible. If they were happy with the results and would become upset knowing the truth, was the truth even required?

Fuck. I overthought everything. Just like with Mara.

I flinched the second Lysander's door slid open. I'd thought I would have to buzz him a few times before he woke.

"Come in," Lysander shouted from inside his quarters.

I walked in and glanced around. His room—like all the officers' quarters—was larger than a capsule, but still cramped. I stopped in my tracks, caught by the sight.

Dr. Clay stood on one side of Lysander's bed, administering a shot to Lysander's bare arm. I would have made a comment—some quip to get on Lysander's nerves—but I held back when I noticed the dark purple-and-yellow bruises across his skin. They were circular, like spots, marking his body along the grooves of his muscles.

"Noah," Lysander said, staring at the floor, never bothering to glance up. "What have I told you about visiting me like this? I'll be fine."

Dr. Clay lifted an eyebrow, but he didn't bother to correct Lysander.

"I'm changing the medications you need to take," Dr. Clay said. "One shot in the morning, one at night. And when we make it back to a planet or station with a proper medical facility, I'll request something more potent." Once he was finished with the injection, Dr. Clay collapsed the syringe and placed it inside a biohazard bottle.

"What's going on?" I asked.

Lysander whipped his attention to me and glared. "Demarco? What're you doing here? Get out of my damn quarters. I'm visiting with the doctor."

"You invited me in, remember? And it sounds like Dr. Clay just finished."

Dr. Clay stepped away from the bed. "Quite right. I need to get some sleep." He walked past me and exited the room, no pleasantries about him.

Lysander stood and pulled up his enviro-suit, quickly tucking his arms into the sleeves. He never looked at me. He glared at the floor, staring a goddamn hole through it.

"How long do you have to live?" I quipped.

"Five years," he intoned. "Maybe a little more, if I find the right treatment."

I caught my breath. I had been joking—I didn't think he had a timeframe, and it took me a moment to recover. "I didn't know," I said. "I shouldn't have asked."

"Forget it," Lysander said with a sigh. "I've known for some time now."

"Still. Sorry about that."

"What do you want, Demarco?"

"I came here to talk."

"About what? I should be sleeping."

We didn't have much room, so I leaned back against the door and rested my head against the metal surface. "I have a question. What if you were playing dice and—"

"I don't play dice."

"It's hypothetical, jackass. Just listen."

Lysander pursed his lips and waited.

"What if you were playing dice, but I cheated to help your opponent? You lose all your credits, but I give you some of mine and tell you to bet big on the next roll. Then you do, and win it huge, because I secretly knew what the outcome would be the whole time. How would you feel about that?"

The look on his face reminded me of an irritated parent. Lysander took in a deep breath before saying, "Is this really what you wanted to discuss?"

"Yeah. It is."

"Have you been drinking? Are you on chems?"

"I *have* been drinking—a lot, actually—but I don't take chems. Look. That's not the point. I came to you because... I feel like you're the type of guy who wouldn't question how he felt about the situation."

Lysander rotated his shoulder and rubbed the portion where Dr. Clay had administered the shot. "Why wouldn't you just tell me you were helping me at dice?"

"I don't know. Pretend you can't talk to me about it. How do you feel about the situation after the fact?"

"I'd distrust you," Lysander said. "And I would be upset. You can't always know the future, and assuming you're doing me a favor because you suspect I'll fail isn't an excuse. Virtue comes from conducting yourself properly. All officers in the HSN Corps are taught that very lesson."

"So, you'd be rolling in credits but still upset with me?"

Lysander forced an exhale. "Did you hear a word I said? I'd rather we both play by the rules than have someone cheat for the jackpot. If you told me you'd cheated, I'd return the credits."

"Really? You're on death's door—you got fucked over by fate

itself when you were born a defect—and you'd be worried about the rules? Fuck the rules, Sander. You don't owe anyone anything."

"Sander?" he repeated, sardonic.

"Life cheated you first," I said, ignoring him. "What's the harm in cheating it back?"

For a long moment, he said nothing. I wondered if I had insulted him, but Lysander took a deep breath and allowed his gaze to shift to the wall in pensive reflection. "Being an officer—a leader of *any* sort—is the oldest of the honorable professions," he said, distant. "That's what my father said. And that's what *his* father told him. Discipline, etiquette, honor. They have their own rewards, different than credits and gin."

I didn't say anything. This was what I had come for. I wanted his advice.

"You have no idea how others will watch you. If you curse, so will they. If you cheat, they will, too. Not everyone. But if you influence even one other person…" Lysander threw a hand up in the air and huffed. "It's about *the whole*. It's about caring for something greater than yourself. An ideal. I don't know if you'll understand, but my father did. I want to as well."

I should've known. He was so focused on the rules and honor, he almost didn't care about the outcome. He might have been the exact opposite of Endellion in every way. Why had I even come to see him? I could have guessed Lysander's answers.

But I wanted to hear them.

At least Lysander wasn't questioning himself. Maybe I should have quit the introspection and dropped the issue. If I wanted to be like Endellion, I had to adopt her way of thinking, not Lysander's. After all, Endellion would walk away from the dice table with credits and an ally, and Lysander would walk away broke and with an enemy.

Despite my conflicted thoughts, results were all that mattered.

TWENTY-EIGHT

Return To Capital Station

1 00 days until we reached Capital Station.

I exited the lift on Deck One with Noah in tow. Free time came at odd moments, so I had to make the best of it. Between training with Lysander and learning everything Endellion wanted me to know—including weight training, starfighter training, and tactics discussions with Endellion herself—time flew.

"You sure this will be okay?" Noah asked. "Sawyer doesn't usually have company."

"I want her to see what she's missing out on."

Noah ran a hand through his short hair. "So, you brought me?"

"You're nonconfrontational and articulate. Those were the only requirements."

"That's it? I hit bare minimum?"

"Basically."

Noah crossed his arms over his chest and sighed. "And with that ringing endorsement..."

Although Deck One housed the officers of the *Star Marque*, the lack of people gave the corridors enough gloom for a horror vid. Noah and I walked in silence, the boots of our enviro-suits clicking against the steel grate floors, echoing around us. I stopped only once I reached Sawyer's workroom.

"Hey, Sawyer," I said as I opened the door. "I've brought company!"

She sat hunched over her keyboard, a video playing of the corridor outside her room right in the center of her main screen. She'd known we were coming. I ignored her silence and sauntered in. Blub—almost as good as new—floated over, reminding me of a child rushing to greet their favorite relative.

The fish moved in the air with lopsided balance. *Toot, toot.* He didn't move as fast, and when he dropped, it was in chunks, like he was stepping down an invisible staircase, instead of gliding.

"Hey, buddy," I said as I stroked the little guy. "How's my favorite fish?"

Noah walked in and widened his eyes. "Wow. Did you steal that from Vectin-14?"

I glared. "Of course not. This is Blub. He's been on the rig this entire time."

"He has?"

How could Noah not have known about Blub? Did Sawyer keep herself shut in *that* much? The situation was worse than I thought. I should've brought her company long before.

"Hello, Noah," Sawyer intoned.

Noah replied with a nervous chuckle and then said, "Hello."

Sawyer acted as every starfighter's navigator. I knew they knew each other, yet the tension in the room remained thick and awkward. I left Blub and walked to Sawyer's side. She didn't type or do anything on her computer terminal, but she did give me an odd glance.

"Why did you bring a friend?" Sawyer asked.

"You still haven't gone with me to the mess hall." I leaned against her countertop and offered her a smile. "I figured, since you aren't fond of crowds, I'd have to ease you into it."

"How considerate of you."

"Don't worry. I'm always gentle on a girl's first time."

Sawyer turned to face me, a slight pink to her face. "Sometimes I wonder where you get the confidence to say such things."

Noah laughed. Sawyer and I glanced over at him. "I wonder that same thing," Noah said as he attempted to pet Blub. The fish avoided Noah's touch and floated back over to me. Noah crossed his arms again, but his face lit up when he asked, "Hey, can I get advice from you, Sawyer?"

"Me?" she said. "What about?"

"Women."

Sawyer turned away, grabbed her keyboard, and went straight to typing. Her computer screen filled with... something. Code for a program, I knew that, but I wasn't sure what she was working on. It seemed isolated, like she'd removed a chunk of something bigger and decided to fiddle.

"Do you mind?" Noah asked as he walked over to join us.

"You can ask," Sawyer said, disinterested.

"All right, so, we're stuck on the *Star Marque* until we reach Capital Station. What would impress a girl here on the ship? If you were seeing someone, where would you want them to take you?"

Sawyer continued typing at a furious rate. "The *Star Marque* is a vanguard-class starship. It's not made with luxuries in mind."

"I know. That's why I need advice."

"Very well. Take her to a dark closet. I've seen enough of Demarco's entertainment vids to know that's where all the action starts."

I bit my tongue to hold back both my laughter and my embarrassment. I'd almost forgotten she'd watched those with me.

"Aren't you with Endellion now?" Noah asked. "Do you even need that anymore?"

"Sometimes our schedules don't line up," I said with a shrug. "But that's beside the point. Don't take a lady to a dark closet. None of them want that."

"The ones in the entertainment vids seem excited," Sawyer said with a hint of mischief.

"Oh, they're excited—for credits. Trust me, girls in real life aren't into plumbers, either, but if you trusted those entertainment vids, you'd think women get hot and bothered watching a guy clean out pipes."

Sawyer snorted back a laugh. "Well, Demarco, you're the expert. *You* tell Noah where to take a girl."

"I want to be respectful," Noah said before I got a chance to answer. "And proper. So, no joke answers, okay?"

"Well, if I were trying to impress a girl while stuck on this rig, I'd probably spend most of my free time with her," I said with a shrug. Blub circled my head. *Toot, toot.* I rubbed his little fins and continued with, "I'd try to get her to laugh, too. You want people to enjoy your company—don't give them reasons to avoid you. Make each inter-action memorable, that's the key. And if she has friends or family, make sure they like you. They're the ones she's going to talk to when she wants to discuss you, and you'd better make sure they have nothing but good things to say."

Noah focused his gaze on me and offered a slow nod. "That makes sense."

"I'd make sure she knew I was thinking about her by calling or sending a message," I said, thinking back to tactics that had worked in the past. "Maybe bring my friends over to meet her, just to make sure everything went smooth."

Sawyer stuttered in her typing, her fingers slowing for only a fraction of a second before she resumed her impeccable standard. She didn't comment or say anything, however.

"Sawyer," Noah said. "Do you think that would work? I mean, would you appreciate a guy who did all that?"

Sawyer gritted her teeth. "No."

"R-Really?"

"I'm not interested. In anybody. Ever. So, this is a moot discussion. You would be better off asking the bulkhead for advice."

"Oh."

"Who is this for?" I asked.

"Mara," Noah admitted.

Sawyer snorted. "She isn't into men. Even the bulkhead could have told you that."

"W-Well, I spoke to her about that. She said she would consider men, if she enjoyed their company."

"Hm."

Noah stepped around the machinery of the room, leaping over bits and pieces, until he reached the opposite end. Sawyer didn't glance over or engage. I waited, curious about her thoughts, but I doubted she would tell me, even if I asked.

"Sawyer," Noah said, staring at the junk on the floor. "I thought you did coding and stuff. Why all the machines? Aren't those two separate skills?"

"Yes," she said. "But we don't have a proper mechanical engineer, so I took over the duties."

"Is it true that you're as a smart as a superhuman?"

"Why?" she asked, curt.

Noah turned to me, like he wanted me to help him out.

"I think you're smart," I said, interjecting myself into the conversation.

Sawyer nodded. "I am. But I don't like being compared to superhumans."

Before I could say anything else, Noah chortled. "I understand. Lysander and I are from Ares Military Base, near Vectin-10. A lot of superhumans there are complete assholes. Most are government workers or high-ranking officers, so they've got egos the size of the Vectin Star."

Sawyer caught her breath and stopped typing. "You were... born at the Ares Military Base?"

"Yeah. Why?"

"I was—I mean, I come from Vectin-10. I traveled to the Ares Military Base on a few occasions. That's where I met Endellion."

Noah's eyebrows shot up. "Really? That's where Lysander and I met her, too. Funny, right? Sometimes it's a small universe."

They both shared a chuckle. Then Sawyer turned her swivel seat around and stared at Noah, like she saw him for the first time. "Lysander never mentioned that before," she said.

"He says you never talk to him," Noah replied. "And he said I should leave you alone, because you hate interruptions, but Demarco insisted. Sorry if I'm bothering you."

"No," Sawyer muttered. "Don't worry about it. I'm glad you came." She swiveled her seat back around and resumed typing.

I gave Noah a quick nod, pleased everything had worked out so well. I couldn't believe Sawyer had kept herself sequestered from the crew for so long.

---

59 DAYS.

I lifted weights, falling back into a routine while my PAD read me information about starships. Endellion wanted me to learn as much as possible, and it seemed like the best use of my time.

"Plasma engines contain ionized gas through use of magnetic and electric fields," the PAD said, robotic and feminine. I could have chosen something masculine, but I'd opted for the slightly softer interface.

Noah and Mara exercised on the machines next to mine. Both glanced over at my weight machine, their eyebrows lifted.

My weight limit had been restricted to 220 kilograms before. Not because I *couldn't*, but because none of the officers would change the damn restrictions on the machines. Now that I was vice-captain, I'd set my personal cap to 270 kilograms, much to everyone's shock and amazement. I was sure I could have handled more, but I didn't want to strain myself too bad before reaching Capital Station.

We had a superhuman to kill, after all.

"Smaller starships—corvette-class and below—can enter the atmosphere of garden-zone planets with a G-force of 3.5 or lower for a limited period of time," the PAD continued.

My thoughts drifted occasionally, but I was able to absorb the information well enough. Sawyer had created quizzes for me. Where did she get the time? Still, I appreciated it. She seemed to know everything in the damn information packets, anyway.

"So, Mara," Noah said between casual sit-ups. "I was thinking about visiting my brother after training. Did you want to accompany me?"

She nodded, but otherwise said nothing.

"Great. Whenever we're alone, he asks me about my visits to the infirmary, so you'll save me from that."

Mara barely lifted her weights, her gaze glued to the floor. "I'm glad to help."

"Hey, if you have anyone you want to distance yourself from by having company, I'm more than happy to return the favor." Noah punctuated his offer with an awkward laugh.

I ignored the teachings on my PAD to chuckle at Noah's failed attempts at humor. The kid didn't have the talent to become a comedian, but I suspected his willingness to try was all that was required.

Mara smiled, even though the "joke" was far from stellar. She had been better since she'd started taking the recommended amount of medication. Dr. Clay and Noah had kept her focused. She'd chosen the treatment, the company, and the activities. That was all that mattered.

Mara stopped lifting and turned to me. "Demarco."

"Yeah?" I asked.

"—starships of the cruiser-class and higher must—"

I tapped my PAD and stopped the information. Noah also stopped his workout and listened, though he didn't say anything. I rotated my shoulders, feeling the burn from my forearm to my lower back.

"Yuan worked with Endellion for years," Mara said with no preface whatsoever.

I wiped the sweat out of my eyes and steadied my breathing.

Mara continued, "Yuan did all sorts of dirty work for Endellion. And she was there when Endellion helped Admiral Vanine. Back when Endellion got her title as commodore."

"What about it?"

"Endellion asked Yuan to run false messages to the rebellion and act as a spy. Yuan even killed a few rebellion officers to make trouble. Admiral Vanine wanted conflict within the rebellion ranks. That's why Endellion had Yuan do all the things she did."

Yuan had killed for Endellion? My thoughts wandering to dark places.

Noah didn't react to the statements. He must have known.

"What else?" I asked.

"You heard about the *Orbit Cruiser*?"

The name rang a bell. It didn't take me long to recall. The *Orbit Cruiser* had been the old starship Mara, Lee, Yuan, and Advik served on. Their captain had gotten drunk at Midway Station and killed a couple of people. Afterward, his ship had been seized to pay for damages, leaving Mara and the others stranded and without a job.

"Endellion paid Yuan to slip something into our captain's food," Mara intoned. "Captain Dominic had a bad habit of getting wasted, but he never went wild like that before."

Endellion had planned everything? Of course. She'd wanted Captain Dominic's starfighters.

Before I could ask any other questions, Mara exhaled. "I… I'm glad you helped me, Demarco. I was with Yuan for so long, I thought I would always be like that. You know. Not myself. She… wanted to be with me, but…"

Noah held out a hand. "You don't have to talk about it again, if it'll upset you."

"No. It's fine. I want Demarco to know."

"O-Okay."

Mara ran her hand through her short hair. "I was with this girl, but… she died. That's when I got depressed. Really bad. Yuan wanted to 'make it better,' that's what she said, but I… well, I didn't want to. I just wanted to end it. I cut myself, and when she tried to stop me, I cut her, too. Yuan never walked right again after the incident. She didn't get medical attention in time. And after that, I never thought right again. Like living a dream. A forever-happy dream."

"Are you okay now?" I asked.

"Yeah," she said. "I'm fine. Noah has been with me. But I wanted to talk to you specifically. I wanted you to know that I appreciated you giving me the option. Yuan never did. Endellion never did. They didn't care. They knew what was best, and they decided for me."

"Don't mention it."

"Demarco," Sawyer said over my PAD, jerking me from my thoughts. "Can I speak with you?"

I tapped my PAD. "I'll be there in a second."

Mara regarded me with a slight smile. "I just wanted to tell you. Thank you, Demarco."

"Like I said, don't mention it."

I left Noah and Mara with the exercise equipment. Noah hovered close to Mara—a little protectively, anyone could see it— and Mara stared at him with a more genuine smile than she'd offered me.

I got two steps into the corridor when my PAD lit up.

"Demarco," Sawyer said, her voice low. "Mara doesn't understand."

I stopped walking and leaned against the bulkhead. "Understand what?"

"Those things about Endellion. Mara doesn't understand what she had to do."

I understood. Endellion had needed that commodore title, and Admiral Vanine had been willing to provide one. For a price. And Yuan had been a rung in that ladder. Endellion had paid her off and altered Mara, all to keep a pair of starfighters. All to have pawns in her game.

I understood all too well.

"Don't worry," I said. "I know."

Sawyer remained quiet.

"Is that all?" I asked.

"Yes."

"You just didn't want me to think poorly of Endellion?"

"I..."

"Forget it," I said. "I'm doing things Endellion's way. She gets results. And the crew needs her. They're relying on her."

Again, Sawyer said nothing.

"If that's everything, I'm going back to my training."

"R-Right," Sawyer said. "Right."

I walked back to the weight machine and resumed lifting. Noah and Mara remained nearby, happier than before.

---

20 DAYS LEFT, and a miracle happened.

Lysander and Sawyer sat with us in the mess hall.

Normally, Lysander ate and drank with the ground enforcers, but when he saw me coaxing Sawyer into the lift, he came along. I'd never thought I would want him at the table with us—since he was the human equivalent of a wet blanket—but Quinn had mentioned playing Pirate's Gambit, and I knew it would be interesting with him around.

"Sawyer," Quinn said. "I'm surprised you're here. You aren't busy?"

"I finished my work for the day," Sawyer said as she picked up a rum pouch and examined it with a sneer. "I don't think I need this." She pushed it to the center of the steel table.

Noah turned to his brother. "I thought you didn't drink?"

"I don't," Lysander replied.

"We have something in common," Sawyer said. She scooted closer to him, and every muscle in my body tensed.

Lysander smiled. "I've always been impressed by your work ethic. I'd say we have a *lot* in common."

"Noah *did* say you came from the Ares Military Base. I used to frequent that place when I was younger."

"Really? We should exchange stories at some point. It's been years since I returned home."

I hated the way they spoke to each other, like burgeoning lovers. I kept my thoughts to myself—because they were insane—but I was half-tempted to sit between them. It shouldn't have mattered. I wanted Sawyer to join us, no matter what. But since when did Lysander fraternize with *anyone?* Sawyer was out of his league.

Enforcers throughout the mess hall gave our table more attention than I was used to. I understood why. Four officers—two of whom were absent half the time—made up our ranks. And although I considered myself approachable, since most enforcers on this rig had no problem chatting with me, Sawyer and Lysander conducted themselves with closed-off postures. Even now, Sawyer hunched forward, her knees to her chest, glaring at the key drives we passed out for Pirate's Gambit.

Noah and Mara sat on one end of the table—both laughing and drinking—while Quinn explained the rules. Mara didn't seem as woebegone as before, and I turned away, satisfied she would be fine for the time being.

Lee flipped his key drive in the air and then offered me a smirk. "I don't think you're going to be successful this time around."

"Oh, yeah?" I asked. "Big talk coming from a guy who lost last time."

"Well, everyone here remembers your simplistic strategy, so I doubt you'll get very far."

I gestured to Sawyer and Lysander with a quick jut of my thumb. "We got fresh meat, and a lot has happened since the last time we played. I'm vice-captain now. Things are different."

Lee gulped back a mouthful of rum. He wiped his mouth with the back of his arm. "We'll see."

"I'll sit this one out," Quinn said. "We need an even number of people. Pair up."

I slid over to Lysander and smirked. "C'mon, Sander. Me and you." I didn't want him pairing with Sawyer straight out the door.

He rubbed at his temple. "In the HSN Corps, we would address our commanding officers by their title and last name, even when off-duty."

"When I ran with gunrunners, we would make up names so that passersby wouldn't know jack shit about what we were talking about. So, how about you call me Vice-Captain Demarco, and I'll call you Chronic Pain? Or we can stay casual while we play a stupid flip-chip game."

"Fine. Let's do this."

"We're going two rounds," Quinn said. "Two times with each possible pairing. Go."

Lysander and I revealed our choices long before the others did. I knew what he would do, and I knew what I wanted to do.

His key drive said *trust*, and so did mine. We both got negative-one point, but it wasn't as bad as both of us betraying, or one of us trusting while the other betrayed.

Lysander cocked an eyebrow. "You surprise me, Demarco."

The others pointed and murmured. I waved away their comments. "I said, you don't know me. I'm a new man."

Sawyer glared at my key drive. "I told you the game theory behind this."

"I know what you said."

She rolled her eyes.

Quinn snapped her fingers. "One more time. Go."

Lysander and I flipped. Just like before, we both chose *trust*. He stared at the key drives for a long moment, and I smiled. I could tell I was demanding everyone's attention. Good.

At negative-two points, I wasn't first, but I wasn't last, either. Noah already had negative-six. Mara didn't dick around.

Next round, and I faced him. Noah regarded me with a questioning glance before we revealed. We both picked *trust*. He sighed, and we went again. *Trust* both ways. The table took it better than they had last time. I wasn't surprised Lysander had never betrayed, but I *was* surprised Noah had decided not to betray, like he had last time.

Maybe Lysander was right. Maybe people *did* mimic the actions of their superiors.

But that was what I had banked on. While I knew Sawyer would betray both rounds—she'd told me as much and had done just that—the others played a little nicer. I stayed in the middle of the pack, until I reached Mara. People had played dirty with her. She was still in the lead—thanks to Noah and Lysander—but not by much.

Our first round together, I stared into her eyes. She returned my gaze with something I couldn't decipher.

We both flipped over our key drives.

She picked *trust*. I picked *betray*, ruining her score and solidifying my win.

"Really?" she said. "But I thought…"

"It's just a game," I said.

Our last round, we both betrayed, making me the winner.

The others nodded and patted my back. Everyone but Lysander —who was betrayed the most—though neither Noah nor I had ever done him wrong.

Everyone at the table trusted me because of my mannerisms and opening moves. They'd seen that I trusted Lysander both times, and they'd developed a false sense of security and loyalty. But I knew Lysander was a safe bet to take my gambit on. He wouldn't betray, not even in a stupid flip-chip game. It was a character flaw. But it worked for me. He'd set me up as a good guy, and I'd knocked down the leader to take the top position.

But Mara didn't take it so well. She left the table, and Noah followed after her. Was she upset I'd beaten her or upset I hadn't trusted her the first round? Weird either way—but she *was* prone to depression. Perhaps I should've allowed her to win. But that wouldn't have been in line with Endellion's philosophy of "winning no matter the circumstances." I'd based my tactics on her machinations, but I supposed a drinking game might not have been the place to test it.

Still, it had worked, even if it was just a stupid game.

NO MORE DAYS LEFT. We arrived right on schedule.

Capital Station showed up on the main screen of the bridge, ending the long wait. I stood at Endellion's side, ready to dock and revisit the place of my youth. It felt like a lifetime ago when I'd lived in the station, but in reality, it was a little under two years.

Time had a way of changing everything.

Capital Station still orbited Galvis-4, the outside white and pristine, despite the dregs of humanity dwelling within. I could already smell Dock Seven and taste the foul nutrient paste. I didn't miss it.

"Send a request to dock," Endellion commanded.

The bridge pilots punched in the coordinates and the message, hailing the station and requesting a space. I waited, my muscles twitching in nervous anticipation. Assassinating Felseven wouldn't be a simple task, and Endellion still hadn't discussed her plan. There was a possibility that she didn't even have one yet.

The picture of Capital Station disappeared from the screen as everything in the bridge flickered and blinked. Then all the screens reverted to a blank white. Across each read the message: *You have entered Capital Station's zone of control and will be redirected to a docking port under the authority of Governor Felseven and Admiral Gaeleven.*

My heartrate increased, worried Felseven knew the purpose of our visit.

Endellion waited, stone-faced, her hands clasped behind her back. "Sawyer," she said. "Give me a status report."

"Endellion. This isn't right."

"What's wrong?"

"The operating program being used to take control of the ship isn't Federation standard. It's custom... like my code to break away from Commodore Cho. I don't have a workaround for this."

"How long would it take you to make one?" Endellion asked.

The main screen blinked with a hail. Sawyer and the others calmed down as Endellion took the call, her eyes narrowed. From her reaction, I knew who it was right away.

It was Governor Maccarus Felseven.

TWENTY-NINE

Trapped

———

S ome superhumans stood in a league of their own. Governor Felseven had the menace and muscle of a bruiser, but the cunning behind his narrowed gaze reminded me of Endellion. His green eyes matched hers both in intensity and confidence. The half-smile he offered put me on edge.

"Commodore Voight," he said. "Welcome to Capital Station."

"What's the meaning of this?" Endellion asked. "Emergency seizures are for military-controlled space."

"My nephew didn't lie when he described you as impertinent. But if you must know, this *is* military-controlled space. Admiral Gaeleven has come to discuss politics with me on Galvis-4. A handful of planet governors and I will be discussing the upcoming elections and how best to proceed with the future."

"I request you release the *Star Marque* from this hold. We mean the delegates of your conference no harm. My history of serving you and Capital Station proves that."

I kept my gaze neutral, but I laughed on the inside. We'd come there to murder the man, and Endellion had the audacity to say we meant him no harm. The irony was thick, but the tension was thicker.

Felseven hadn't stopped smiling. "Commodore Cho reported that you tampered with the Federation-regulation operating system. A terrible mark on your history. These codes are meant to maintain order. I think it would be wise on your part not to fight the procedures."

"This stunt of yours won't go unnoticed," Endellion stated.

"I have friends in high places, too, Commodore. You think Admiral Gaeleven and my fellow planet governors are afraid of your threats? You'll be lucky to walk away from this space station with your title, once I'm through."

"You have no right to strip away military titles."

"But the admiral does."

The conversation stopped, though the screen remained active. My blood grew colder with each second. We were in a fight. Maybe we weren't throwing punches, but Felseven meant to win, just as much as Endellion did. He wouldn't let himself be cornered in a room all alone, like Emissary Barten had. He would destroy Endellion without ever having to lay a finger on her.

Felseven smirked. "I'll see you on Capital Station, Commodore Voight. Until then."

The screen flickered off, and the same message played from before: *You have entered Capital Station's zone of control and will be redirected to a docking port under the authority of Governor Felseven and Admiral Gaeleven.*

Endellion said nothing. She continued to stare at the screen, but I knew that stiff posture of hers. Most people couldn't recognize her seething, but I could. "Sawyer," Endellion said, half-shouting. "Why didn't I know about Admiral Gaeleven's visit?"

"No Federation records say he'll be in this portion of space at this time. I had no idea he'd be here."

"I want you to examine this homebrew code of theirs, and I want the *Star Marque* free of it, do you understand? I can't allow him to have control of our starship. We'll be trapped here."

"Yes, Endellion. I'll start working on it now."

The *Star Marque* turned on its own, controlled by the Federation's operating system, and headed for Dock One. I hadn't run with any gangs on Dock One, mostly because it was reserved for official business and special personnel. Unlike the other docks, Dock One housed only two starships. The odd dock protruded from the main portion of the station like a tentacle that reached into space, giving the starships an easier time of detaching and latching.

The other docks had hundreds of starships. Unlike Midway Station—which had been built with a space elevator in mind—Capital Station floated in orbit. Maccarus Felseven's grain empire, built from the megafarms on Galvis-4's surface, had to get its produce up somehow, so the planet-hopper vessels made runs back and forth, delivering tons of raw products.

Felseven didn't want to lose his importance. His massive, planet-wide grain operation supplied the planets and space station of the Galvis star system and beyond. Everything outside of the Vectin star system, basically. Which was why he didn't want Ontwenty's Stellar Engine to pass through legislation. The Stellar Engine would replace the need for Galvis-4's food production, and it would make the outlying planets obsolete. Felseven would lose everything. And since Endellion was Ontwenty's dog, Felseven had every reason and desire to make sure the *Star Marque* failed.

Even if he had no idea of our true goal.

We glided into Dock One and attached to the docking port. The starship rumbled slightly under our feet. The rotation of the station provided much of the artificial gravity, and the transfer from our gravity engines to the station's outdated system took a few minutes of adjustment.

With a quick nod, Endellion motioned for me to follow. We exited the bridge and headed straight for the docking port. Her silence unnerved me, and I took shallow breaths, but we hadn't lost yet.

"I haven't heard of Admiral Gaeleven," I said. "Do you know him?"

"He's an admiral like I'm a commodore—low on the scale influence. Once, he commanded great influence, but his time passed a while ago. Now he acts more as an instructor for the major academies, and while Gaeleven is respected, he doesn't do much."

"But he retained his authority?"

"Superhumans aren't susceptible to dementia or Alzheimer's or other mental diseases common in Homo sapiens. Although he's old, and his body is weaker, he retains much of his former self."

Endellion and I waited as the hydraulics for the outer door hissed and strained. I wondered if we should have brought any of the other officers before disembarking, but my thoughts veered away from the mundane when I spotted our welcoming party.

Forty guards waited on the dock, their plasma rifles in hand, their black enviro-suits up and secured. Felseven himself waited in the group, another superhuman at his side, no doubt Admiral Gaeleven. The admiral stood tall—almost as tall as Felseven's three meters—but his wrinkled skin hung loose, and his eyes were half-sunken into their sockets.

Superhumans were designed to live several centuries. Gaeleven could have been one of the first ones out of the tubes.

I didn't know if Endellion was caught off-guard by the soldiers and superhumans, but she made no indication of it as she stepped forward. I kept to her side, but I regretted not taking my plasma rifle. I couldn't fight the whole room if they opened fire, but I wanted to at least kill a few of them before they got me. I doubted they would do it, simply because mass murder would have been hard to cover up or explain, even with the backing of an admiral. No—they weren't there to kill us—they were there to intimidate.

"Commodore Voight," Felseven said as he stepped forward, his arms outstretched. "It's so nice of you to join us."

Endellion said nothing, nor did she return his gesture. Felseven allowed his arms to fall back to his side, his scale-covered enviro-suit a marvel of technology, no doubt capable of refracting lasers and heightening his electroreceptors. It moved with fluid grace as he stepped up to Endellion and towered over her.

"I'm ordering all ships to be searched," Felseven continued. "You understand the precautions I need to take to ensure my safety. Enforcers like you make safety a business, isn't that right?"

"I don't grant you permission to search my ship," Endellion said.

"I don't *need* your permission."

"Governors don't have the direct authority to authorize the search of a commodore's vessel."

"You already know the answer. Admiral Gaeleven has all the authority he needs."

"I'd rather leave Capital Station than be subjected to this treatment."

Felseven laughed. "No. This isn't a general inspection—these are the first steps towards a court-martial. Admiral Gaeleven and I have reason to believe you or some of your crew members are in violation of Federation protocol." He snapped his fingers and motioned to the *Star Marque*. "The entire starship will be swept from top to bottom."

The armed men—soldiers under the admiral's command—walked to the *Star Marque* in pairs. Endellion tightened her hands into fists, but she said nothing. What could she say? Felseven had her by the metaphorical balls.

He hadn't been this brazen before. He hadn't even bothered to see her when we were here last. I blamed Minister Felseven back on Vectin-14. That asshole must have said something that got under Governor Felseven's skin.

"If we find even one violation, you could be through," Felseven said. "Will we find anything?"

Endellion narrowed her eyes.

"Will we?" Felseven pressed. "I do hope so."

I wanted to say something—no, I wanted to get this assassination underway *right then*—but I kept my anger in check. Knowing Endellion, she was already plotting his death four stages in advance.

The soldiers marched by, leaving ten on the dock while 30 got to scouring the ship. We had broken lots of regulations, and I was certain they would find over half of them. The real question was: could they strip Endellion's title for minor infractions? Or would they uncover something deeper?

"Commodore," Lysander said, his voice audible through Endellion's enviro-suit comms. "Men from the station have come to search the ship. Should we stop them?"

Resisting was tantamount to attacking Felseven. We would be arrested, and then our problems would double.

"Don't interfere," Endellion said. "Allow the admiral's men to search the ship as they please."

"Yes, Commodore Voight."

The communication ended, leaving us in strained silence.

Felseven patted Endellion on the shoulder, his elongated smile showing his sharp, white teeth. I hated that he'd touched her. Every move he made dared me to lose control.

"You're quiet," Felseven said, his voice low. "My nephew said you made quite the impression on Vectin-14. What's wrong? You aren't as marvelous or composed as the other ministers thought you were." He brought his hand up and patted her cheek. "You should stay quiet. It's a better look for you."

Endellion clenched her jaw, but forced a smile. "Better men than you have tried to silence me. This won't have any effect on my governorship." She stepped back, distancing herself from Felseven.

"Oh, I'm certain it'll determine your governorship, actually. Once you lose the title of commodore, it won't matter what else happens. And then I'll win. Ontwenty and her constituents will fail. You'll go back to being an enforcer captain, so long as you aren't harboring something abhorrent on your starship. Because if you are, I'll see you imprisoned. Either way, you'll be right where you belong."

"Or I'll report this gross misuse of power, and everything you do here will be overturned," Endellion said, her voice just as calm as always.

"We both know you can't move faster than the information passed along the relays. By the time you make it back to Vectin-14, it'll be too late. You'll have been removed from the list of potential governors, and the votes will be cast."

The timing was tight, like all Endellion's plans. The more I thought about the situation, the more I realized there was a real possibility that we wouldn't be able to prevent her from losing her title or her capacity to become a planet governor. I hadn't seen the situation coming, and I doubted Endellion had seen it, either. Felseven had gone far out of his way to fuck her.

Admiral Gaeleven spoke with the ten remaining soldiers, a look of disinterest set in the shallow wrinkles of his face. When he walked over, he ignored Endellion and me completely. "Are we done here, Governor?" Gaeleven asked, a slow and deep tone about his voice. "We should be down planetside, meeting with our peers."

Endellion gave him a quick nod. "Admiral Gaeleven. Surely you don't share Governor Felseven's perverse pleasure in this game of politics? I've worked tirelessly for the Federation. You can confirm that with Admiral Vanine."

"She's pleading with you," Felseven said with a chuckle.

Admiral Gaeleven didn't smile or share in Felseven's mirth. Instead, he sneered and turned his attention to Endellion. "I remember the times when the United-Earth Homo sapiens misman-aged this quadrant, Commodore Voight. I also remember why we're here in the first place—to settle the edge of space, to improve and cultivate our civilization throughout the stars. Consolidating power into a single location with the Stellar Engine, and extending ruler-ship back to the failed Homo sapiens, are the exact mistakes history has taught us to avoid."

His sentence had a finality that killed all conversation. Gaeleven offered Felseven a glare, turned on his heel, and strode off, his mili-tary background so ingrained into his person that it showed through the disciplined snap of his enviro-suit's boots.

"I've followed your career," Felseven said. "Ambitious upstarts like yourself always turn to desperation. Undoubtedly, you came here at Ontwenty's behest, thinking she would be your ticket to governorship. I see right through your plans, and I'll have none of it. You're out of your league."

Then he walked off, smug and confident in his assessments.

Endellion could get desperate, but I didn't blame her. Every-thing was cutthroat, especially on Capital Station. That didn't change the reality, however. If Felseven stripped her title, what would Endellion do to recover?

I didn't think she would be able to.

"HAVE YOU HEARD ANYTHING?" Lysander asked.

I paced the front of the officer's conference room and shook my head. Capital Station would be the end of me. I thought I had escaped it forever, but it was like a goddamn black hole—not even light escaped it. Without the ability to leave the dock, we were stuck until Felseven and his admiral buddy concluded their investigation.

"Why hasn't Endellion made any statements?" Quinn asked.

I shook my head. "She and Sawyer have been *in discussions* for the last three hours. They refuse to speak to anyone."

Discussions, my ass. Endellion made demands, and Sawyer answered them. They were trying to think of something, but I wished they would do so in front of the other officers.

Quinn, Lysander, Dr. Clay, and I didn't occupy even ten percent of the room. Our voices echoed, and the numerous empty chairs made our conversation feel like we were playing pretend. We needed more crew members, but that was a problem we would have to deal with later.

Dr. Clay leaned back, his bony fingers laced together over his chest. "What're the chances Endellion will have the political pull to escape this mire we've found ourselves in?"

"She'll figure something out," Quinn said. "She always does. The problem will be when and how. And there's another issue."

"The defects," Lysander intoned. "I already know."

"Exactly. I don't think we'll be able to keep any of them if Felseven discovers their presence."

I didn't even need to ask why. Sawyer had told me a while back that defects who required medication to function weren't legally capable of being enforcers. Lysander, Noah, and Mara would be forced to resign. Even imagining it brought me to the edge of rage. Those three didn't deserve any more shit, not after the ordeals they had gone through. Felseven's trap couldn't have come at a worse time.

"What should I tell the ground enforcers?" Lysander asked.

"Nothing," I said. "For right now we don't know what's going on. There's no need to worry everyone by twisting their panties. Endellion will think of something or Sawyer will find a loophole in the laws, we just need to wait."

Dr. Clay narrowed his eyes. "What if Endellion is arrested? How will you—the new captain of the *Star Marque*—uphold her promises?"

"What the fuck did I just say?" I asked, damn near shouting. "We're not going to worry about that. Endellion isn't going to be arrested. And even if she is, it won't be for long."

"But *what if?*"

"Then I'll fulfill her promises, okay? That's what I'll do. Satisfied?"

"Look," he said. "I didn't join this starship because I wanted to. I joined because of those promises. If you can't keep them, tell me now, so I'll know to leave your crew if you become the captain."

I slammed my hand down on the conference table, enjoying the bite of metal against my palm. It fueled my anger but somehow calmed me at the same time, like it reassured my mind that I had control of something, even if it was as insignificant as destroying my surroundings or causing myself harm.

"Get out of here," I said. "You got your answer."

Dr. Clay stood and headed for the door. He said nothing as he exited, but I didn't care. While Endellion had wanted him, and he'd helped out the crew, I would have been content dumping him and finding someone else to fill his jumpsuit.

Quinn and Lysander stared at me. I looked away, a little shaken by their furrowed brows and searching eyes. They wanted *me* to come up with a solution? Both of them had been on this rig longer than I had. They knew the drill. But making decisions came with the territory of vice-captain.

"Continue as normal," I said. "I'll speak with Endellion and relay any information I think you'll find interesting."

They replied with nods.

I ENTERED Endellion's quarters in the middle of a night cycle. I hadn't been able to sleep, and we were pushing the 30 hour mark. None of the soldiers would allow the enforcers to leave the dock. Restless energy filled the corridors, and half the crew spent their day either going through the motions or getting wasted in the mess hall. The morale hit an all-time low at hour 24. Apparently an investigation that ran longer than 24 hours meant genetic testing had been ordered. No one wanted to hear that.

Although the lights were off when I entered, I knew immediately that Endellion was in the room. I couldn't see her, but her breathing betrayed her presence.

"I thought you were with Sawyer," I whispered.

She walked to my side and ran a hand along my jaw. "Take off your suit."

I complied with her command. Endellion had a bitter scent to her—it matched the atmosphere. Once I was undressed, she pushed me toward the bed. I was prepared to get on my back and let her run the show, but she stopped me.

"Touch me," she said.

She was already undressed, but my shock lasted half a second at most. I ran both hands over her body, enjoying the smooth feeling of warm flesh. Part of me wanted to pound this out—to get the relief from a long day of stress—but when Endellion pressed her lips against mine, everything became slow and gentle.

Not like the other times. We had never done anything so *romantic*, for lack of a better term. Our sex had been athletic and fulfilling, sating us both in carnal ways, not emotional ones. I supposed some emotions were always involved, but not like this.

Endellion tumbled with me onto the bed and pulled me on top of her. We had done this position before, but rough and animalistic. Again, she took her time, her tongue in my mouth, her legs wrapped around my hips. I kept my eyes closed and enjoyed the taste of her.

But then Endellion broke away, her breath on my chin.

"Tell me everything will be fine," she said.

I caught my breath, taken aback by her comment.

I recovered enough to say, "Everything will be fine."

"You'll stay by my side after this, won't you?"

"Of course." I kissed her neck and shoulder.

Endellion and I locked together, falling into a comfortable rhythm, but I could tell her mind wasn't in the situation.

"Sawyer and I discussed a few options," she whispered into my ear. "Some of them will cost me a great deal, but I refuse to lose here. Do you understand? I refuse to be beaten."

"I know."

"I don't think you understand. I won't let anything stop me. Ever."

"I understand. Trust me. I do."

She dropped the conversation, and we returned to kissing, connected at two points, heated at every surface. I couldn't take the gentleness of it any longer. I sped up, lust fueling me, and she didn't protest. Endellion moaned like she never had before—sensual and promising, like she was telling me she had waited a lifetime for this moment. It was enough to push me over the edge.

Breathing deep and satisfied, I stroked her arm and nibbled her flesh. "I'll be ready again in a moment," I said between heavy pants.

"I contacted another commodore in the area," she said as she untwisted her legs from my hips. "And Sawyer has discovered that the starfighters we used at Outpost Station—the ones using the rebellion's operating system—aren't affected by the Capital Station holding program."

"So, we can leave?" I asked, unmoving.

"We can use the starfighters, yes."

"Can they make it to the commodore's ship?"

"Yes. And we may need to make the journey, if Felseven wishes to push this situation."

I knew she would think of something. I exhaled and rested on top of her, though I propped myself up on my elbows. The distance in her voice gave me pause, however.

"What's wrong?" I asked. "What do you think will happen?"

"I don't know."

She said nothing else.

It was bullshit. She knew. Endellion would never sit around

without a contingency plan. I wondered if I should push the issue, then decided I would wait and see what she had in mind instead.

"Endellion," Sawyer said over the comms. "Felseven has requested your presence on Capital Station."

Endellion stroked the back of my neck. "It's time we settled this."

"All right," I said, hesitant.

Settle what? Did she still intend to kill the man? It would be suspicious if it happened right after Felseven had threatened her. There would be no denying her motives or opportunity. No. Endellion wouldn't be that brash or brazen. She must have had some other idea in mind.

She must have.

THIRTY

Eleventh Hour

Endellion and I stood in a courtroom on Capital Station, the audience empty, and the walls lined with Gaeleven's soldiers. I had seen a fair number of courtrooms on Capital Station. Section Six had the chem courts—the colloquial term for "courts that dealt with gangs and repeat offenders"—and Section Two had the zoning courts for businesses, new homes, and the switching of room designations.

But I had never seen the courtroom we were in before.

Unlike most areas in the space station, the ceiling curved upward, like two sheets of metal had been posted together to form an upside-down V. It gave the room an open feeling, but the hard lines reminded me that we weren't planetside. Everything from the Federation codes etched into the duralumin walls to the cold convict box screamed high-level authority. I would have bet my life the courtroom operated four days out of the year. It was a special courtroom, meant for political figures, infamous felons, and military tribunals.

Admiral Gaeleven stood at the center computer terminal. His screen projected in front of him but also on the back wall, displaying the charges and penalties for the whole room to see. The list scrolled for some time as he spoke.

"—and after a thorough investigation of the vanguard-class star-ship, *Star Marque*, we have discovered the following misconduct." Gaeleven cleared his throat. "18 counts of defect employment, one count of stolen intellectual property, 53 counts of digital tampering, and three counts of abuse of power."

Governor Felseven waited on the side, as did two other superhumans I had never met, no doubt planet governors themselves, considering their fancy enviro-suits and smug smiles. Strands of their silver hair reflected the artificial lighting like polished metal. The opposition against Ontwenty must have been high.

Gaeleven lifted an eyebrow. "You've used your position as commodore to pardon crimes you had no business pardoning. And to make the matter infinitely worse, you've hidden your own defect status from the Federation. How do you plead?"

The last bit shook me. I snapped my attention to Endellion, but she didn't meet my gaze.

She was a defect? Impossible. There was no way. I had never seen her—

But then a million tiny details made sense. Why had she wanted a doctor who specialized in defect procedures? It wasn't for the members of her crew. Why had she been so worried about scars, when healing vats could remove almost any damage? I had never seen her use one. Because she couldn't. And her cyborg implants caused her trouble from time to time. Some must have functioned to negate whatever troubles she had. The entire time—from the moment she was born, to the cusp of governorship—she'd made it all the way from the lowest ranks of circumstance and society.

Defects couldn't have titles.

No matter what Ontwenty or her constituents said, once that fact got out, Endellion would never be able to become a planet governor. Ever.

"I contest the findings," Endellion said, cold and unfeeling.

My heart beat hard enough for the both us. Anger and indignation burned at my core, but what could I do about it? What *was* there to do about it?

"We'll log your complaint," Gaeleven said. "And we'll order a second set of investigations to verify the first. In the meantime, you are suspended from duty until further notice. Should your title and position be revoked, I will have two of my frigates escort you back to Vectin-14 for final confirmation."

Endellion nodded. "You're too kind."

"If there are no further comments?" Gaeleven turned to the others in the room.

The governors, court recorders, and soldiers remained still and quiet. No one said anything. I wouldn't have been surprised if they'd said they could hear my pulse run hot from across the room.

"Then this hearing is adjourned."

ENDELLION HAD NEVER TOLD me about her genetic defect.

I stood in front of my starfighter, staring at the open door, my mind unable to move forward. It changed a lot. I'd thought she could recover her title and position—so long as she called in a few favors from her superhuman buddies—but nothing would make her defect go away. Endellion should have told me about the problem, but she'd banked on exiting the enforcer business as soon as possible. Six more months, and it wouldn't have been an issue. No one would've ever found out.

"Sawyer," I said. "Did you know?"

"Know what?" she asked over the ship's comms.

"About Endellion."

"Yes."

"You never mentioned anything."

"It never became relevant."

I placed my hand on the starfighter and exhaled. "What're we doing?"

"Your starfighter, Endellion's starfighter, and a third starfighter have the rebellion's operating system. They aren't affected by Felseven's hold. We'll fly out of the dock, but first we're waiting for the doors to open."

Admiral Gaeleven had ships docked at the station, but he and Felseven had left for the planet hours ago. By the time he ordered anything, we would be well on our way.

"What're we doing?" I asked. "Meeting our commodore friend?"

Sawyer waited for a long moment before replying, "We're going to dock at the central port for Capital Station. Endellion and I will take control of the station's main computer terminal. After that, we'll rendezvous with the commodore."

"Why fuck around with the main computer terminal?" I asked.

"We'll have control over the relays."

The information relays transmitted information ten times faster than any starship. Once Admiral Gaeleven sent his reports, the relays would get them to Vectin-14 in a matter of days. But if Endellion interrupted the relays… maybe she could get to Midway Station first.

Was that her plan?

"Does Endellion still plan to win?" I asked. "After everything that's happened?"

"Yes."

I gritted my teeth. "What about you? Do you still think it's possible for her to achieve her dream? For her to become a planet governor?"

"I think Endellion will find a way."

Fanatic to the end. I wasn't surprised, but I *was* worried. Taking control of the main computer terminal for all of Capital Station? Was it even possible? I never would've considered it as an option. Endellion hadn't ruled anything out. But what was her long-term goal? How could using the relays help her overcome the situation?

I climbed into my starfighter and allowed the cockpit to secure me into place. With a deep breath, I placed my hands on the side-sticks and waited while the screens powered up and displayed the various points of information. The map of Capital Station had a highlighted section—our destination—and I studied it with a keen eye.

The main computer terminal for the station was at the core. The heart of all operations. And the core had such an odd position that access seemed limited to one lift from the main station or six access ports near the base. The ports had acted as landing stations for the construction bots back in the day, allowing for the easy transport of material while the station was initially constructed.

My flight plan headed straight for one such access dock. Endellion's led her to the one next to mine, but a third path led off to the opposite end of the core computer terminal.

"Who else is coming with us?" I asked.

"I am," Sawyer replied.

"Why?"

"The main computer system has safeguards in place to prevent disaster. The central computer requires a dual-unlocking system: one person at one end, and another person at the other. These two key terminals are separated completely."

"Why so many safeguards?"

"The main computer system controls everything for the station, not just the relays."

"Wait, you know how to fly a starfighter?" I asked, my mind still twisted by the recent bombardment of knowledge. "Since when?"

"I always have, but Endellion has prohibited me from fighting."

"Yeah, I can understand."

Without Sawyer, the *Star Marque* wouldn't have been half the ship it was.

"So, you'll be unlocking the main computer, and Endellion will be unlocking it on her side?" I asked.

"No," Sawyer replied. "*You'll* be unlocking it with me. Endellion will be at the main computer terminal, downloading my alterations. The old code for the core computer is centuries out-of-date, but that also means it's easy to mess with. This operation shouldn't take much time."

"It's a three-man unlocking system?"

"Yes."

That didn't surprise me. Access to the whole station's main computer systems? Of course you would want a triple-secure locking method. Although, I doubted anyone had accessed the core terminal in some time. Capital Station's operating system was meant to maintain the baseline functions, such as the engines, relays, and power converters. Disrupting any of those processes would cause havoc for everyone on Capital Station.

My starfighter hadn't been resupplied since the last fight. Low fuel, and only two hyperweapon bolts.

"What's this commodore going to do for us?" I asked.

"He'll take us back to Vectin-14."

"And leave everyone here? Why?"

"Endellion believes she needs to speak to the other ministers directly."

Perhaps she would change the rules back in her favor. Keeping defects from the military had made sense back in the day, because they broke easier than healthy men and women. But obviously, Endellion had overcome her weakness, and her cyborg body could withstand more rigors than a whole troop of soldiers could. Maybe she had a plan after all, but the daunting number of variables made everything uncertain and foggy.

The doors to Dock One opened.

"Go," Sawyer said. "And follow the flight path exactly."

I detached from the *Star Marque*. My screen displayed two other ships leaving the *Star Marque* as well, and I focused on Endellion. She hadn't spoken to us. She hadn't even opened her comms line. I ignored the dread seeping into my system and focused on controlling my starfighter.

The outside of Capital Station didn't have the amount of traffic I had seen in the past. The other starships must have been held down by Felseven's trap program as well. He might have been trying to catch more than just Endellion, but it didn't matter. My starship didn't register anything out of the ordinary.

I sailed the starfighter straight into the access port at the bottom of the space station. It was small—my starfighter was almost too big to fit—but I managed well enough. Once latched in and attached, I pulled a plasma rifle out of my fighter's storage and stepped out of the cockpit. In an ideal world, I would have had my enviro-suit—since it offered the most protection—but I hadn't thought to pack it.

Endellion docked in the access port next to mine, and I waited as she jumped out, her own rifle in hand. She also hadn't packed an enviro-suit, but she was capable without it.

The landing zone, clear of any objects, had more color than the rest of Capital Station put together. Red, yellow, and black strips marked the area, along with an assortment of instructions for loading and unloading. The metal and paint had seen better days, all scuffed and faded. The place looked untouched by time, like the whole area had stepped out of a documentary vid about how origin-world humans built the first space stations.

Endellion motioned to the far door. "We don't have much time."

"Why?"

"Once they figure out my starfighters have left Dock One, they'll come searching. Act quickly, Clevon. This is where I need you the most."

I replied with a curt nod.

We opened the door and stepped into an engineering corridor. Grate floors, a mezzanine level above our own, and huge data-processing computer terminals shaped like towers made up the whole control room. The place smelled of oil, dust, and neglect. The forever-running central computer let off steam as though it were too hot for the environment, but I suspected it was from a coolant system that long needed to be replaced.

I turned my attention to the two guards stationed by the one access hatch that led to the lift. They stood a good 30 meters away, chatting to themselves, their guns at their side, casual in all regards. They hadn't seen us. And they had likely never gotten any action in a remote and forgotten location, such as the center control room.

I hefted my rifle, but Endellion grabbed the end of it.

"The discharge of plasma will register on the sensors," she said. "You kill the one on the left, I'll take the other."

I pulled a knife from the belt of my cargo pants and nodded. The room had an abundance of nooks and crannies, allowing

Endellion and me to jump from one darkened corner to the next without trouble. Memories of my criminal days came rushing back. I had done this before—easy to fall back into.

Endellion and I were too fast for the common man. By the time we got close, they were already dead. We both jumped out and took the men by surprise. My target—some schmoe with a lazy eye—attempted to lift his rifle, but I stabbed him clean in the throat, the blade stopping against his spine. He stumbled back, and I yanked my blade free in time to stab him again before he hit the grate flooring, my mind processing everything four times faster than my victim ever could.

Endellion stabbed her target under the chin, planting the blade of her weapon deep into the guy's noggin. What a way to go. She left her knife embedded in his head and continued.

"There," she said. "The key terminal."

She tossed me a stick drive—antiquated tech compared to things like PADs—and pointed to the insert slot. I walked over to the computer terminal and examined the many plugins for the computer tower.

"Wait for Sawyer's commands," Endellion said.

I frowned. "Did Sawyer have to deal with guards?"

"No. Her room only houses the key terminal. They don't station guards there until access has been scheduled."

Her answer betrayed the research she and Sawyer must have done. Yet Endellion had told me nothing. How was it that we could be so close, yet so far away? Every step of every plan felt like I stumbled behind her in the dark while she ran ahead with the only flashlight.

I waited at the computer terminal, the stick drive poised over the only slot that matched. Endellion ambled up the stairs to the central computer on the mezzanine level and ran her fingers over the controls. Her gaze locked on the screen, unseeing. She'd had that same intensity when I met her, that same hard look of someone willing to do anything. I shuddered and turned away. Her determination shook me sometimes.

"Demarco," Sawyer said over my PAD. "I'm ready."

"All right."

I plugged the stick drive in and waited. The computer terminal lit up, showing a total of three lights, all red. After a few painful seconds—like the machine needed extra time to process the information—one light flashed green. Then, another. Finally, Endellion tapped at her computer terminal, triggering the last green light.

"Welcome to the space habitat control systems," a feminine voice said from the computers, greeting us like we were tourists. *"This terminal monitors and—"*

Endellion plugged in her own stick drive—no doubt with Sawyer's workaround code on it—and then typed away at a furious pace, cutting the computer off before it could get any momentum.

I started to head up the stairs, but Endellion glared. "Stay there. I'll need you to input a few commands at your key terminal."

"All right," I said.

I walked back to the terminal and tapped my fingers along the edge. We didn't have much time, and each second that crawled by added to my blood pressure. The two dead guards bled out, but their blood dropped between the openings of the grates and fell into a pit of darkness below our feet.

"Are you sure you want to remove the first failsafe?" the computer asked.

Endellion tapped at the keys, her focus unflinching. "Clevon, confirm each action."

My screen asked whether or not I wanted to confirm the removal of the first failsafe system. I confirmed, and the computer reported Sawyer as having done the same. Sawyer must have been manning her terminal without direction.

"Are you sure you want to remove the second failsafe?" the computer asked.

I waited and confirmed Endellion's actions the moment the computer allowed me to.

"Are you sure you want to remove the third failsafe? Life-sustaining operations could be at risk if the failsafes are removed and the code is tampered with beyond immediate repair."

Again, I confirmed Endellion's actions. I wasn't surprised there were so many failsafes and warnings. The main computer could have been used in all sorts of inappropriate ways, and the level of security, though archaic, had likely been put into place to ward off as many troublemakers as possible.

"Are you sure you want to remove the fourth failsafe?"

So many failsafes. How many would we have to confirm? It ate time faster than a glutton in a slop pit.

"Are you sure you want to remove the fifth failsafe?"

I gritted my teeth and confirmed every time it asked. This was what we needed to do to interfere with the relays? Damn. I knew communication was important, and disrupting the flow from one source to another could be a felony, but the precautions bordered on the ludicrous.

I stopped paying attention for a few seconds, my thoughts returning to the future. What would Noah and Lysander do after everything was said and done? After Lysander had been discharged, he'd nearly fallen apart. I wondered if something like this was what had gotten him caught in the first place—a random check. No, that wasn't it. He'd said someone betrayed his secret.

Someone.

"Endellion," I called out, my chest tight, and my muscles tense.

"Yes?" she asked.

"Are you sure you want to remove the twenty-second failsafe?" the computer continued.

I balled my hands into fists, understanding now that everything had been planned out from the beginning. "It was you, wasn't it? The one who revealed Lysander's defect to the HSN Corp officials? You wanted him as your ground commander."

"Yes," she replied, no remorse in her voice.

"And Mara was right. You got her old captain wasted beyond reason and pushed him into a situation where he lost control. All so you could take his team of starfighters."

She said nothing, but I knew the answer from her tense posture.

"And me…" I had never considered it until just that moment. "You helped my old associates fuck me over, did you? Someone had to sell them those new ID chips, and Sawyer… she has so many."

Endellion had said she had been watching me. She'd admitted

without flinching that she had wanted someone genetically modified to be her starfighter and right-hand man.

I bet there were a hundred more stories, from her funding, to her contacts, to her suppliers. Mara and Yuan. She'd made every deal, manipulated every situation, bending reality to her favor. It was a smart move, considering that when reality had dealt the cards, it had given her one joker and that card with all the rules on it. How could you win a game with that hand?

Endellion had decided to burn down the card house and claim the insurance money.

"Well?" I asked. "You did, didn't you?"

"You know the answer, Clevon," she said.

"Are you sure you want to remove the thirty-first failsafe?" the computer asked, oblivious to our conversation. *"Life-sustaining operations could be at risk if the failsafes are removed and the code is tampered with beyond immediate repair."*

I almost couldn't believe Endellion's past actions. But I had decided to let go. I had to. There was no point to holding onto it. She'd made it clear that her methods worked the best. She wouldn't be stopped.

"Are you sure you want to remove the final failsafe?"

I confirmed the action, ready to leave and make the long trek back to Vectin-14. Maybe with enough time, I would see how everything was for the better. How the ends justified all the struggle and manipulation.

Endellion continued to type away, faster and faster, almost as if she couldn't wait to end our time there, either.

I stepped away from my terminal and exhaled. "You done yet?"

"Almost."

"Warning," the computer announced, no longer feminine or cheery, but harsh, like metal on metal, jarring in every regard. *"Course alteration detected. Speed corrections required."*

"What's going on?" I shouted.

Tremors filled the room. Grime and dust fell from every surface, and the steam from the central computer increased. Rumbling mixed with the strain of the girders and the twisting of the grates.

Capital Station had rotated with the same speed and orbit for three centuries—changing anything could cause structural damage.

Endellion didn't answer me.

"Warning," the computer announced as a pulse-increasing siren blared across the station's comms. Red lights flooded the area, blanketing everything in crimson and darkness. *"Planet collision detected."*

THIRTY-ONE

Victory At All Costs

E ndellion turned to face me, her expression hard and set.
"Planet collision?" I asked between the shrieks of the siren. "Endellion, what the fuck is going on?"

"Get to your starfighter," she said. "We're leaving."

"What's happening to Capital Station?"

"It will collide with Galvis-4 in a matter of minutes. Radioactive particles from the station's core will break away into the sky, polluting the atmosphere, destroying most of the grain operations. The resulting impact will leave a crater where Felseven makes his base of operations, destroying everything he's ever worked toward and killing him in the process."

Sirens continued their terrible wail. I shook, not with fear, but with mounting outrage. Endellion planned to send all of Capital Station to the planet's surface, destroying everything and everyone in one brutal strike. The sheer magnitude of such a decision didn't seem to faze her. She walked down the stairs, one step at a time, her green eyes focused on mine. Even in the red hue of the emergency lights, her gaze had an inner light that demanded attention.

"Capital Station has over a million inhabitants," I said, almost stunned into silence, but my heart and mind knew I didn't have time to flounder.

"Scum. The worst of the worst, and more than 70% defects."

Capital Station had more criminals and cutthroats than any place I knew, but did that mean their lives were forfeit?

"The *Star Marque*," I said, grasping at the details, trying to make sense of it. "What about the *Star Marque*?"

"What about it?"

"You'll just leave? It's stuck in Dock One!"

Sirens. Sirens. Sirens.

The screeching kept my pulse high and my blood hot. I stepped close to Endellion, and she waited a few steps up from the bottom, her expression unchanging.

"The *Star Marque* has served its purpose," she said.

"What about the people onboard?" I yelled loud enough to grate my throat, but it was still not as loud as the sirens.

"I have you and Sawyer. The rest are leeches. They've always been leeches, suckling at my success, attaching themselves to me because their own ambitions and dreams amount to nothing. They want my power, and they want my determination, but they're not willing to pay the prices I pay for it."

"*This*? This is the price? Have you lost your mind?"

"I told you," she said with finality. "The results are all that matters. Felseven, the admiral, all their supporting governors— they'll all be dead. Every last one of them."

"But what about…"

"They've yet to send their reports, and now it won't matter. Once we leave, they'll be corpses, my history buried with them, and without Felseven's vote or his supporters, my victory is guaranteed. I win, Clevon. Always. You're only as good as the obstacle that stands in your way to success. And I'm better than Felseven and all his scheming."

Millions of deaths? Her own crew killed? Was there no price she wouldn't pay for success?

I guessed not. I should have known. She'd made it clear from day one she refused to be stopped. Why had I ever thought Felseven and his goons had a chance? But this? The lack of remorse? It was too much. Too damn costly. Too fucking insane.

I shook my head. "We'll find another way. There has to be some other plan we can attempt, some other scheme that doesn't require *this*."

"Don't get soft on me, Clevon," she said as she walked off the last step. "There won't be any evidence after the dust settles. Capital Station was old, after all. A malfunction isn't outside the realm of possibility. Now let's go. We need to break clear of the station and return to Vectin-14."

"We should save the *Star Marque*, at the very least."

"There's no way to save them."

The floor rumbled, and the artificial gravity shifted and distorted. The room tilted—or it *seemed* like it tilted—and both Endellion and I had to stand at a slant to prevent ourselves from falling.

"Stop this," I commanded. "Change the course back."

"It's impossible. I've finalized the command."

"Fuck you! I know you can change it. Do it!"

Sirens. More sirens.

"This is the only way," Endellion whispered, her voice almost drowned out by the blaring warnings. "Don't pretend you care about the nameless filth on Capital Station or the superhumans who would have us in prison."

She went to step around me, but I posted my arm and prevented her from walking any farther. The room tilted again by another ten degrees, creating a harsh slant toward the far wall. Endellion and I kept our ground, our balance supreme.

"The *Star Marque*," I said. "I won't leave without it."

"Then you'll die with it."

We stared at each other. Her icy statement was a promise.

I realized then, maybe too late, that this was what it came down to. The result, the ultimate goal, was all she wanted, and anything that had to be destroyed to achieve success… so be it. Endellion's eyes, her posture, her aura—they screamed desperation and determination. She would let me die to win. Fuck—she would *kill* me to win. But in her world—the one where I protected the *Star Marque*, and she didn't—I was dead and she was a planet governor.

The results spoke for themselves.

Endellion must have understood I had processed the information, because she offered me a tight smile. "Come, Clevon. You know this is for the best. Could you imagine me handing out hundreds of planetside estates once I became governor? I'd be accused of favoritism and corruption, and it would've been a dark mark on my political career. In a way, this is serendipity. The perfect end to a good run."

When she went to walk around me, I lifted my rifle and buried the barrel in her gut. She tensed and stared at me, both shock and rage clear on her face.

"If you're only as good as the obstacle standing in your way," I said, "then you're no better than me. Turn around and fix this, or we're both dying right here."

Endellion took a moment, her eyes narrowing, sweat coating her pristine skin.

The crimson lighting. My trigger finger itching to fire. My heart pounding hard enough to deafen the sounds of the siren. Her deep breathing.

One of us was going to kill the other.

The station tilted again, the jolt of movement providing the opportunity Endellion wanted. She turned as I pulled the trigger, and I fired the plasma bolt into the grate stairway, burning a hole through the thin steel. She lifted her rifle, but I grabbed the end of it and thrust it upward. The tremor knocked us both sideways. We fell toward the wall—our new floor—but that didn't stop our fighting.

I landed hard on my back, but I ripped the rifle from Endellion's grasp. She answered in kind, striking my dominant shoulder with her metal knuckles, bruising flesh and cracking bone. She went to punch again—no doubt to dislocate something—but I rolled away and jumped to my feet. When I went to fire, she kicked at the rifle, catching my hand and knocking the weapon from my grasp.

Endellion swung with her right, but I recognized her dirty tactics. Instead of backing away and getting my forehead cut open, I lunged forward and tackled her to the ground. She jabbed my side, smashing my kidney and wrenching a shout out of me. Anger and bloodlust masked the pain within a fraction of a second.

She wanted to hinder me, like she had in our sparring match when blood dripped into my eyes. But this wouldn't be a drawn-out fight. I would make sure of that.

I pulled my knife and slashed down. I wanted to open her throat to ensure she died, but Endellion kicked upward, causing us to both tumble across the jagged surfaces of the ancient computer terminals. Bits of steel from the machines pierced my clothes and skin. My knife connected with Endellion's face during the scuffle, and the blade sank to the bone. She threw me off—her strength in a league of its own—and I crashed into a sharp edge of equipment, a terrible flash of agony ripping through my spine.

Endellion stood and staggered away, the station's shaking hindering her movement. She brought a hand to the slash that ran from her forehead down to her chin, just over her left eye, so wide open that it exposed bone and muscle and wept blood like a red waterfall. Her exposed eye socket had chips missing from where the blade had hit hard. Probably one of the few places she had bone left.

I got to my feet, knife still in hand.

The red lights flickered in and out until they died, blanketing the room in impenetrable darkness. Awash in the space-like void, I attempted to get my bearings, but Endellion punched me hard in the side. For a moment, all I could do was scream—I knew she had shattered an organ.

She grabbed my neck with her vise grip, and my imagination filled in the blanks. She planned to rip my throat out.

I slashed wide, hoping to hit her in the face a second time, and Endellion jumped back to avoid me. I knew she would. Stumbling blindly, I kept my blade up.

Endellion dashed away from me, despite the constant shaking of the floor. The scraping of metal against metal told me she had picked something up.

Her rifle.

I threw myself to the side, reconstructing the environment in my mind's eye with what little I could remember of the room. Endellion could see in the dark thanks to her ampullae of Lorenzini. I concentrated, my breathing loud, but the harsh clang of metal was distinct and easy to detect over all other sounds. When the station tilted again, I ascertained Endellion's location, as well as loose objects colliding with stationary ones. I jumped from one position of cover to another—or, at least, what I *hoped* was cover—and narrowly avoided a bright flash of plasma as Endellion opened fire.

She could sense me, but her aim wasn't what it would have been if she could have seen me.

My side refused to straighten. I hobbled, hunched over my crippled kidney, and groped around in the darkness. Endellion fired four times, her bolts slicing through steel and lighting up the area in short bursts. During the last two shots, we spotted each other. But I also spotted my rifle.

Endellion fired again, catching my right calf and burning half of it clean from my body. I hit the floor and rolled with the next tilt of the station until I reached my weapon. Once armed, I turned the rifle upward and fired in her general direction, forcing her to take cover.

I wanted to keep fighting—to finish it—but Endellion ran back toward the starfighters.

My heart stopped, and I couldn't breathe.

"Sawyer," I said, strained, jabbing my fingers onto my PAD. "*Sawyer!* Help me stop this!"

She didn't answer. I slammed my hand on the floor and forced myself to stand. I had to make it back to the starfighter. If Endellion and Sawyer wouldn't help me, I would use my last fucking breath to make sure Endellion paid for what she had done.

I would gun her down with her own fighter.

I half-ran, half-stumbled forward, Endellion's boots echoing throughout the main computer terminal. I fired in her direction, hoping to catch her, but all I managed to do was slow her down. She took careful steps and jumped behind objects while I jogged to catch up.

Although the room was half-upside-down, Endellion slammed her hand on the computer terminal for the access dock. The door opened, and she ran inside. Seconds behind, I froze at the door and waited, keeping myself on the other side of the wall and out of sight. After another tremor, I heard a starfighter hatch open— Endellion had been waiting to shoot me if I entered too hastily— but the moment she climbed into her fighter, I ran to mine.

The cockpit opened, and I lunged inside.

"*Sawyer*," I shouted. "I need your help!"

"Sawyer," Endellion said over the comms. "Disable Clevon's fighter."

The following second took a lifetime. I held my breath, my heart on the verge of exploding, my body protesting, and my mind soaked in so much hate I was ready to incinerate the whole fucking place to ash.

Who would Sawyer answer to?

My screens powered down.

"Sawyer!" I yelled, my throat already raw from the force of my shouting. "*Sawyer!* She's going to destroy the *Star Marque!* She's *killing* them!"

No. No, this couldn't be happening. Sawyer wouldn't do that. She wouldn't kill everyone on the *Star Marque* for Endellion.

I grabbed the side-sticks of my starfighter and jerked them around. Nothing responded. I yanked and thrusted, straining the steel they were made of, certain I could rip them clean from the fighter if I applied full force. Not even the cockpit hatch would open anymore.

I punched the side of the starfighter. The rumbling became constant, shaking every bit of machinery around me. I slammed my fist into the wall a second time until I felt a bone break, and blood exploded from my knuckles.

"Sawyer," I said, my teeth gritted so tight I tasted the copper from my split tongue and slashed cheeks.

She didn't answer.

I pulled my hand back, shaking. I had a fast mind. I could put everything together. I knew Endellion had left already, leaving me alone on the failing station, trapped in an area with no hope of escape.

I was already dead.

"Sawyer," I said again, unable to think of anything else to add.

She'd made her decision. I always knew. Sawyer followed Endellion no matter what. I was a fool to think she would stray from Endellion's commands.

"Sawyer."

I couldn't help it. Pain entered my thoughts and my body. I closed my eyes.

"Sawyer," I muttered, an edge of pleading in my voice. "Please. I'm begging you. You have to see this is insane. I want to save the *Star Marque*. I can't do it alone."

But I *was* alone.

Sawyer said nothing. She might not even have been listening.

Swallowed by the blackness of my cockpit, I leaned back, taking in the details of my future coffin. I had failed. As a person, as a man, as a vice-captain. I cared about the *Star Marque* and her crew, but I was too weak and incompetent to save them. I was the loser Endellion talked about in her speeches, the man incapable of protecting the few things in life he valued more than his own.

I hadn't cried since I was a child—when I'd cut my palm open on a shredded can top—but now silent tears streamed down my face.

All the shortcuts, all the dealings, all the cheating—it was in that moment I wished I hadn't done any of it. I wished I was with the others on the *Star Marque*, developing something greater than myself. Maybe Lysander had been right. Maybe I should've focused on the whole. Then I wouldn't have been in such a situation. I would have people I could count on. People I could *genuinely* count on. Lysander wouldn't have left me to my death. Noah wouldn't have. Quinn and Lee wouldn't have, either.

"Sawyer," I said, my breathing shallow but steady. "If you're going to do me like this—if you're going to kill me—at least whisper those sweet nothings you promised."

She didn't say anything.

I smiled to myself, caught up in pleasant memories. "Spending time with you, it was what I looked forward to. Every day, after training. Me, you, Blub. C'mon, Sawyer. One more round. For old time's sake."

Silence was my only answer. It stung more than heated words or denial.

This was it.

"Demarco," Sawyer said.

I caught my breath and snapped my eyes open. "Sawyer?"

"If you go after Endellion, I'll do it again."

My screens pulsed back to life, and I sat up straight as the starfighter fitted around me. Anticipation filled me with renewed energy. I jerked the controls and flew through the undocking procedure. Once free from the access hatch, I stared at my screen, taking note of the two green dots.

One for Sawyer. One for Endellion.

I wiped the blood and tears from my face, ready for a second chance at life.

The urge to fire off a hyperweapon in Endellion's direction consumed my thoughts, even though it was a long shot and I knew it would miss. Endellion had to pay for her crimes. But that had to wait. What could be done about the station? What could I do to change the situation?

When I backed far enough away from the station, I could see it entering the exosphere layer of Galvis-4's atmosphere. Red-and-yellow waves of heat washed off the white surface of the space station, lighting up space with its destructive brilliance. The *Star Marque* remained in Dock One, but how could I save them?

What should I do? Kill Endellion or head back to Capital Station?

I chose the *Star Marque*. I headed for the plummeting space station, aware I could be destroyed in the process, but I wouldn't let them die without a fight.

THIRTY-TWO

Fires Of A Falling Star

I punched my starfighter forward and rushed to the station.

"Demarco," Sawyer said over the comms. "You can't. The debris and burnup will destroy you."

"I don't care," I said through clenched teeth, the pressure from the mounting G-force messing with my already-injured body.

"It's too late."

"Help me or leave with Endellion. I don't have time for distractions."

I flew my starfighter straight for Dock One. My screens flashed with warnings. The heat, the particles from the breaking station, the gravitational pull—everything could kill me. But flying close enough wouldn't help anything. I needed to do something. Maybe I could land in the dock and force the attachments off the *Star Marque*. Maybe I could find another starship that wasn't immobilized. Anything. I had to try.

"Demarco."

I didn't answer. I wasn't lying when I said I didn't have time for her. Sawyer could go—my anger rested with Endellion, even if Sawyer had complied with her—but I couldn't deal with her situation while wrapping my thoughts around the plummeting problem before me.

"Demarco... I've come to help."

When I entered the exosphere, my starfighter shook, rattling my teeth against each other. "Sawyer. Can I blast them free?"

I had two hyperweapons. The bolts could vaporize metal. Could I use them to free the *Star Marque* from the constraints of the dock? It would be the fastest way to free them, but I couldn't do the calculations. I had no idea what would need to be destroyed.

Her green dot flew back toward me, heading for the edge of Dock One.

"I've highlighted the target shots for you," she said. "If you break that section of the dock and I land back on the *Star Marque*, I can get it out into space. Felseven's hold is no longer operational."

"Do it."

The coordinates on my screen showed the points Sawyer believed would destroy the dock. I accelerated into the atmosphere, the starship tremoring with such force. It was a struggle to keep my hands on the side-sticks. Bits of Capital Station's outer walls broke away, creating a duralumin trail that caught the light of the Galvis star. I dodged the fragments, my movements precise and my eyes unblinking.

Turn. Twist. Two-degree tilt.

The slightest of changes made a world of difference. I processed the information with unwavering attention, knowing full well that a single shard of metal could pierce the hull of my starfighter and kill me in an instant. Hundreds of obstacles filled my screen, almost hindering the path of my target, and sweat streamed down my face.

The moment I lined up my first shot, I fired.

Light from the hyperweapon matched the intensity of the flames all around the space station. The bolt sliced through Dock One, carving out a hole, weakening the structural integrity. I flew past the dock as a solid, metal beam broke away from the station.

"Demarco!"

I rolled around it, half a millimeter from clipping its side. I passed through a wave of heat trailing off the side of the station. It shook my fighter, threatening to tear it apart, but I burst through the opposite side and prepared for another run.

"Wait," Sawyer said. "I need to be aboard. Don't fire until I've docked to the ship."

The knowledge hindered my actions. Capital Station tore apart at a fearsome rate. A chunk of Dock Seven rose into the flames and burst into a flare of light, exploding and sending debris in all directions.

Sawyer flew toward Dock One, and my chest tightened until I could no longer breathe. It was hard to watch her dot on my screen —even after everything that had happened. I had never seen her pilot a starfighter before, and each obstacle shot at her faster than the last.

Her speed and acceleration remained minimal, but she moved with precision. When a cluster of metal chunks spiraled out of control, she dove into them, saving time by making a straight line for her destination. I ground my teeth, waiting for her dot to disappear from my screen, but it never happened.

Sawyer had made it.

Capital Station entered the thermosphere, a pyre of massive proportions.

I dove back in, knowing it could be the last of me. My starfighter protested the action, flashing warnings like a strobe light. I held the side-sticks tight, the muscles in my arms and hands strained from the grip, more so than any workout I had ever done. A lesser man might've been shaken or rendered unconscious from the fluctuating G-forces, but I was no ordinary man.

"Now, Demarco. Do it now!"

Time wasn't an ally. I rushed in.

My target appeared in front of me, along with a wall of atmospheric fire. I continued, aiming with the computer readout alone, picturing my target in my mind's eye. The flames and debris blocked my path, and my starfighter's computer told me they would destroy the hull. When I was certain I was lined up, I fired.

The hyperweapon pierced through the veil of searing heat, and I traveled through as soon as there was a semi-clear path. My blinding bolt smashed into Dock One, blasting it free from Capital Station.

I decelerated, my starship caught between turbulence and breaking apart. If I didn't dock right then, I never would.

The *Star Marque* moved away from the crumbling mass of Capital Station, a section of Dock One still clinging to its hull, like a spider of metal and wires. Unlike starfighters—which had the speed, size, and mobility to avoid objects—the *Star Marque* took strike after strike of debris as it pulled away from the planet.

Struggling to maintain my focus, I followed the starship, my navigation advising me to wait until it docked before I rejoined the ship. Impossible. I couldn't wait any longer.

To my relief and surprise, a navigation course appeared on my screen, detailing the speed and angle at which I needed to dock. It was Sawyer's doing; there was no doubt in my mind. I accepted her assistance and maintained my speed straight to my docking port.

The *Star Marque* lifted upward, shadowed by fractured pipes, bits of generators, and a hailstorm of metal. I landed at my port, my fighter scratched but not punctured. Once my ship locked into place, I breathed again, though I didn't remember when I had stopped in the first place.

Rumbling filled my ears as the *Star Marque* broke free from the outer atmosphere and sped away from Galvis-4. I didn't need to see the outside of the ship to know we were still carrying a section of the dock with us. It would be there until we landed again, until we could get a crew to wrench it off.

I stepped out of my cockpit and almost tumbled to the ground.

My left leg wouldn't support me. My calf hung limp, and my body rebelled against every action I took. I held onto the bulkhead as I dragged myself forward. White noise clouded my thoughts. The reality had yet to settle in.

"This is Ground Commander Lysander Jevons," Lysander said over the ship's comms. "All non-flight enforcers are to return to their capsules and remain there until further notice. I repeat, all non-flight enforcers are to return to their capsules and remain there until further notice."

My breath became ragged. Although there was a hole in my calf, the plasma bolt had cauterized the wound, preventing me from bleeding out. I stumbled forward, my destination set.

"Demarco?"

Quinn ran to my side. She grabbed my arm, attempting to help me, but I pushed her away.

"What's going on?" she asked as she reached to support my weight again.

I shoved her off. "Leave me. Take care of the others."

"Demarco... I have no idea what's happened."

"Where's Sawyer?" I asked, ignoring her question.

"She's in the officer's conference room. She's been distraught since she returned. Where's Endellion?"

I pressed forward, glaring down the narrow corridor but seeing nothing. A handful of enforcers ran past me, their breathing frantic and their hands shaking.

"It's Capital Station," one shouted.

Another added, "This can't be happening!"

Quinn hesitated. She shifted her weight, a visible debate etched into her face—would she follow me or deal with the enforcers? Quinn opted to rush after the enforcers, leaving me to my trek.

I reached the lift, entered with unsteady feet, and slammed my fist onto the controls, hitting Deck One. The travel didn't quell my troubled mind. Each second heightened my anger and frustration. Endellion had left. She'd *left*. We'd barely made it out alive, but she hadn't even been interested in our safety. The *Star Marque* had *"served its purpose"*—that was what she had said.

Endellion didn't want or need the *Star Marque* any longer. It had been another rung on her ladder. Another pawn in her game.

Like me.

I exited onto Deck One, my pulse high. The bulkhead supported my weak body as I made my way to the officer's conference room. Halfway there, I reached a room with transparent, metal alloy, providing a window into space.

I stopped, transfixed by the sight of Capital Station hitting the surface of Galvis-4. In my mind, there would have been a deafening boom to follow the visuals of the massive explosion, but the event played out in silence, like God Himself had muted the world. The destruction lasted for several seconds. Flares of light, followed by plumes of blackness. The black spot in the atmosphere didn't fade. It lingered, a pockmark across the planet, a crematorium for a million incinerated corpses.

Unable to stare at the devastation any longer, I turned away and finished my journey. When I reached the conference room, I opened the door, my gaze turning to Sawyer. She paced near the back computer terminal, running both hands through her red hair.

She stopped and looked up at me.

I had never seen her look so frantic or fearful. She exuded both emotions, so much so that I could smell them. Sweat clung to her jumpsuit, and she took a step back when I entered the room. If her weakened endocrine system meant she couldn't feel emotions as well as the standard schmoe, then it must have taken an extra amount of feeling to actually rile her. If she were normal, I'd bet she would have been on the verge of hysteria.

When the door shut behind me, silence settled between us.

Sawyer backed up into the bulkhead, her legs shaking. "Demarco," she muttered. "I…"

I hobbled over, my body broken in more places than one. Despite that, I steeled myself. Rage poisoned my blood, driving me to think unspeakable things.

I continued until I stood a few centimeters in front of her, my gaze neutral, but my muscles tense. Sawyer stared up at me, her grayish-blue eyes searching mine, like she wanted to read the answer to her unspoken questions.

"You helped her," I murmured.

Sawyer shook her head. "No. I didn't know."

"Don't fuck with me, Sawyer," I said, my volume rising, and my throat rasping out each word. "You helped her. You made all this possible."

"She never told me she was going to do this. I thought—I mean —I just didn't know."

I grabbed her by the collar of her jumpsuit and pulled her

close. Sawyer held my forearm for support but didn't struggle. Her trembling hands and watery eyes cut at me, but I pushed my pity aside.

"You made it possible for her to alter Capital Station's course."

"I swear, I didn't know," she whispered. "You were there, too. Did *you* know before it happened?"

I didn't, and for a moment, I reflected on my own outrage. Endellion must've known no one would support her mass genocide, but she'd banked on us following her once she'd pulled the trigger. And Sawyer had.

"You were going to go with her," I said. "You didn't even protest."

Sawyer knitted her eyebrows together, her breath shaky. "I owe Endellion everything."

"Explain."

"She saved me from General Lone, even though he offered a reward for my return. I… I told Endellion I would be with her to the end, so long as she took me on the ship, away from Vectin-10. I couldn't… I didn't think to say anything… but I couldn't leave you, either. I abandoned her after I had time to think. I came back, but I didn't know what she'd do ahead of time."

"Endellion saved you from one superhuman, and you were willing to let a whole space station die for it?"

"You don't understand!" Sawyer looked away, tears streaming down her cheeks and connecting at her chin. I didn't let go of her, and she tightened her grip on my wrist. "I wasn't his first," she said through stuttered breathing. "He had so many others before me. N-No one knew. He had them made just like he wanted, and then he threw them away when he was done. I was—I was next. If Endellion hadn't been there—if I had stayed one more day—I would've been shredded down for genetic scrap."

I narrowed my eyes, piecing together her broken story. Some superhumans had made people in test tubes. They'd made them just the way they wanted them. And then they fucked with them—literally and metaphorically. General Lone would've killed Sawyer and moved on to the next thing he'd made for his amusement. Apparently, when humanity created better versions of themselves, they couldn't design away their cruelty.

"I'm sorry," Sawyer said, strained but more in control. "I... I understand what I've done, I just never thought... I didn't think it would be like this." She wiped at her eyes, and then returned her gaze to mine. "I understand if you hate me... if you don't trust me. You... you're the only person I've ever connected with outside of Endellion. I couldn't leave you. I knew I wanted to be with you more than her, even if I owe her a duty I can't repay. So, please... If you're going to send me away, just kill me."

Her request struck me at my core. Kill her? She had acted as Endellion's tool. She'd helped bring about the death of over a million people. But were tools ultimately to blame?

"Make it quick," Sawyer whispered, never breaking her gaze from me. "P-Please. General Lone would drag out the pain for hours... I don't want to live through it again, Demarco. Please."

I eased my grip on her collar, knowing what she meant without needing her to spell out the details. General Lone was a sadist. If he went through multiple people, throwing them away when he was done, then he had a specific fetish most would never speak of.

I grabbed the zipper of Sawyer's jumpsuit and opened it past her collarbone.

Her eyes went wide, and she dug her fingernails into the skin of my arm, her whole body trembling. "Anything but this," Sawyer pleaded.

I wasn't going to touch her, but I opened the jumpsuit to gaze at her skin—to see the parts she always hid. It was just a thought.

Scars.

So many gnarled, terrible scars.

And I hadn't seen much—just the patch of skin under her neck and above her breasts—but I knew they were all over. She never sat right in her chair, and she hugged herself at points, hiding away. He'd tortured her. That was what General Lone had done.

Sawyer waited through my silent staring, her shaking form difficult to watch.

I zipped her jumpsuit back up and released her. "I helped her destroy Capital Station," I said. "I was there, confirming each step. If I were going to kill you, I might as well put a plasma bolt through my head as well."

Sawyer crossed her arms tight over her chest. "You won't send me away?"

"No. You helped me save the *Star Marque*. And I owe you my life."

She closed her eyes. "But what will we do now, Demarco? Endellion is en route to meet with Ontwenty's commodore associate, and the *Star Marque* is in no condition to follow—not when part of Dock One is still attached to the hull."

"We let her go," I said. "For now. When everything settles, when we've got our bearings—then we'll find her."

And she would answer for what she had done.

THIRTY-THREE

Star Marque Rising

"— And when the station became caught in Galvis-4's gravitational pull, Vice-Captain Clevon Demarco and Chief Cyber Operations Officer Sawyer Coda risked life and limb to wrench the *Star Marque* from the jaws of death," Lysander said, his voice carrying a regal tone.

Although he addressed the enforcers in the largest training room on Deck Three, I watched with Sawyer in her workroom, away from the others.

Cheers, clapping, and the stomping of feet sounded over the speakers. Lysander called for everyone to remain quiet, and the crew complied.

"The cause of the disaster is still unknown," Lysander continued, "but we will be at the heart of the investigation. Upon reaching the dreadnaught *Sagittarius*, everyone will be subjected to questioning. Please, comply with their demands until we've returned to Midway Station and rendezvoused with Commodore Voight."

None of them knew the truth. Everyone on the *Star Marque* believed Capital Station had fallen out of orbit due to a malfunction. As far as the crew was concerned, Endellion had chosen to "get help" while Sawyer and I saved them from imminent destruction. That had to be the story. If I'd told them what Endellion had done, it would have been the same as condemning them all to imprisonment. The entire *Star Marque* crew could have been held accountable for the number of atrocities she had committed, even if they were technically unaware of them.

It would've been the same for me and Sawyer.

And Endellion would find a way to squirm out of it, no matter whom I reported her to. She always found a loophole, some contact, some "scum" to help her out of the situation. I was sure she had already covered her ass for her crimes against humanity. Endellion knew the rules of the system so well, they acted as both her sword and her shield.

If I wanted Endellion to face justice, I would have to do it myself.

"What are you going to do?" Sawyer asked, her eyes glued to the screen as she turned the volume off.

"What do you mean?"

"When we get to Midway Station. What will you do, then?"

"It depends," I said, "on what we find there."

"We're two months behind Endellion. She'll have done something to protect herself."

Of course. I knew that. Attacking her straightaway might not have been an option. But maybe she was desperate. Maybe something had happened.

"I need more information," I said. "Then I'll decide."

"All right. And what about the others? When are you going to tell them the truth?"

"You and I will tell them when we get close. After we've found Endellion's location."

"If that's what you think is best."

I SAT in my vice-captain's quarters. The room didn't hold any fondness for me. I primarily slept in my capsule or Endellion's quarters. I kept the lighting dim to help me sleep, but I hadn't managed to get more than two hours of rest since returning from Capital Station.

My PAD lit up, filling the space with a bluish hue. I tapped at the screen and removed the notifications. More messages from the crew. They sent thanks and declarations of loyalty at any opportunity they could get. Most talked to me about friends and family—the people they couldn't wait to see again—and reminded me that I was the reason they would be reunited with them.

Half the crew had barely known of Sawyer's existence until Lysander's announcement. Now she got visitors and messages just as frequently as I did. Despite her antisocial and sarcastic nature, I had yet to meet someone who didn't think the world of her. Blub had become a celebrity. Everyone wanted a picture with the floating fish.

I wished those realities would have eased my anxiety and dread, but nothing did.

A beep at my door told me someone had come to visit. I got off my bed and tapped the computer terminal on the wall to answer. To my surprise, Lysander and Noah stood in the corridor.

Noah stepped forward and smiled. "Demarco. Hey. Are you okay?"

I exhaled. "Yeah."

"You haven't answered any of my messages."

I hadn't answered *anyone's* messages. What was I supposed to say? I was partially to blame for their near-death experience?

"You haven't been drinking with us," Noah continued. "And Lee says you don't talk to him anymore. You've been holed away."

"Endellion isn't here. I have to pick up her slack."

That was a lie. The reason the *Star Marque* didn't have all its officers was because the crew was small enough to get away with it. Sawyer handled maintenance, Lysander took care of the ground enforcers, Quinn handled the pilots, and Dr. Clay handled the infirmary. I could have stayed in my room for the next 60 days, and no one would have known the difference.

"You should be excited," Noah said as he tapped my arm. "You saved the day. Endellion's about to become a planet governor. We've won. You shouldn't even worry about the *Star Marque* right now."

I nodded, but said nothing. I wondered if Endellion would even bother keeping her promise.

Noah furrowed his brow. "Demarco… you sure there's nothing? Is it because you're worried about Endellion?"

"No."

"You sure? Everyone knows you two were a thing."

"Trust me. I don't miss it."

The moment stretched on, and Noah tucked his hands into his armpits. "All right," he muttered. "But let me know if I can do anything for you." He turned to his brother, but Lysander motioned to the door with a tilt of his head.

Noah left, giving me one last look over his shoulder before the door shut.

Lysander and I stood in the dimly-lit room, neither of us moving or speaking. I wanted him to yell. Anything to take my mind off reality.

"You've been like this since Capital Station," Lysander said, his eyes narrowed. "No bravado. No interactions with the crew. Something happened, and you're not telling the officers."

"If I have an official statement, I'll call everyone together," I snapped.

"I'm not here for your official statement. Noah says you're recovering—he thinks you need time—but I know Endellion well enough to see that something happened to her, and you, and perhaps the whole of the *Star Marque*. We could signal the other commodore and retrieve Endellion from the other ship, but obviously we're not doing that. Why?"

We had tried to signal the ship, but to no one's surprise, it had refused to answer. Endellion didn't want us to interfere with her trek to Vectin-14. She wanted to beat us there.

Lysander said, "You have more arrogance and confidence than everyone on the ship combined. If something shook *you*, it must have been catastrophic. What happened?"

"You wouldn't believe me," I said.

"Maybe I wouldn't have a few years ago, but that's not the case anymore, Demarco. Perhaps you're not military trained, but you're dedicated to the *Star Marque*. I've seen what you've done with Noah, and I know risking your life to get the ship away from Capital Station was no small task. You could've saved yourself. A man who would risk everything is a man I can trust."

His words sank into my thoughts. Lysander really *was* Endellion's opposite.

"What do you know about Endellion?" I asked.

"She's a calculating commander with a goal, and she keeps it in sight at all times."

"Her only goal is power. She says she wants to be a planet governor, but has she ever said why? She doesn't give a shit about ruling a planet. She wants something else. Something bigger."

Lysander lifted an eyebrow. He mulled over my comments before saying, "I don't know where you're going with this, but perhaps she just wants the success."

"No amount of success will quell the demons that fuel her ambition." I couldn't keep the hate out of my voice, and I knew Lysander must have sensed it.

"What's this about?" he asked.

"She did it. She caused the malfunction on Capital Station. I—I didn't know I was helping her until it was too late." My statement settled between us, plunging the conversation back into silence.

Lysander stared, but his expression betrayed none of his thoughts. After several seconds, he nodded. "To kill Felseven," he said, coming to the correct conclusion on his own. "And his supporters."

"I know what you're going to say—because I read your damn mind—but I can't report her. If I turn her in, I turn us all in, and then she'll never see justice for what she's done. Endellion could worm her way out of anything."

Lysander ran a hand down his face, his gaze distant, lost in thought. "She left us?"

"That's right. She wanted to leave the *Star Marque* attached to Capital Station."

"Why? She's done nothing but help me at every turn. And she's helped countless defects, and other crew members. My brother included."

"Endellion—" I debated whether or not to say anything, but I couldn't help it, "—doesn't give a fuck about defects. She doesn't give a fuck about you or anyone else. She turned you in to the HSN Navy Corps officers so she could have you as a pawn. She got a doctor who specialized in defect research so she could help herself. In the grand scheme of things, *Endellion couldn't care less about your life or mine.* If she thought throwing you out into the cold embrace of space would get her a little closer to power, she would fucking do it. Do you understand?"

Lysander glared at the floor. "She... revealed me to the Navy officers?"

"This is why I kept to myself," I said. "Nobody on this rig knows jack shit about Endellion, except for Sawyer. I haven't even begun to reveal the depths of her secrets."

I breathed deep, rage lurking in every pore of my body, ready to return to the surface the moment I remembered Endellion's many transgressions.

Lysander took the information better than I thought he would. "What're you going to do?" he asked, breaking the silence.

That was the big question.

"Leave," I commanded. "I don't have the patience to talk about this. If you think of a brilliant solution, you let me know."

Lysander hesitated for a moment. He gave me a hard stare before heading for my door. "Demarco," he said as the door slid open. "Thank you."

"Don't."

"You could've gone with her. What made you come back?"

I almost answered immediately, but I caught my breath before I uttered a word. Why *hadn't* I gone with her? The thought of betraying the *Star Marque* cut too deep. Maybe—because I was an asshole—I would have gone with her if she had *just* destroyed Capital Station, but I never would have trusted her again.

But not the *Star Marque*. She was the captain, and I was the vice-captain. We owed everyone aboard a duty. They looked to us for protection. I wouldn't fail them.

I could see why Endellion thought loyalty and duty were hindrances. They held back ambition. But they also stifled great evil. She made me think I was weak for valuing other things besides success, but how long could she have said that, when she'd left behind so many enemies and so much destruction on her path to glory?

"I couldn't leave the *Star Marque*," I said, strained. "Not when there was a chance that I could save it."

"That's why I need to thank you," Lysander said. "When I was in the HSN Corps, this is what they taught the officers to do. They taught us that selfishness is default and only a select few have the courage to sacrifice for the whole. The reciprocity of camaraderie, the notion of honor—that's what holds brothers together and makes civilization great. I... appreciate that someone without my background or training came to the same conclusion. I have a great deal of respect for you. Now more than ever."

Heh. Lysander. Maybe I should've listened to more of his bullshit in the past.

He glanced over and nodded. "If you need anything, Vice-Captain Demarco, let me know."

ONE WEEK FROM MIDWAY STATION.

Endellion had already been there for seven weeks. I'd thought we would never hear from her again, but I wasn't that lucky. She'd had the audacity to send a message to the *Star Marque* over the relay system. A vid message to the crew.

I almost didn't play it. I almost sent back a message of my own, calling her out. But I knew she would never be taunted into a fight.

The vid played for the crew over all the computer terminals and screens. I sat in the mess hall, watching the vid with the rest of them, my arms crossed, and my fingers digging into my enviro-suit.

Endellion stood in the middle of the screen, flanked on either side by soldiers. Her black-and-silver enviro-suit had all the markings and designations of a planet governor, and she kept her helmet over her head the entire time, even as she spoke, never revealing her face.

"Crew of the vanguard-class *Star Marque*," she said, in the same cold tone I had grown to hate. "This is your captain, Endellion Voight. You'll be pleased to know that I have earned the title of planet governor and for the next 20 years, I will preside over Vectin-10."

The statement chilled my core. A piece of me wanted her to fail —just to see her suffer—but I knew that would never be the case. Without Felseven and his associates to vote against her, there was nothing in her way. Not only that, but since several other governors had died when Capital Station crashed, I was sure the Vectin ministers wanted to fill the empty seats as fast as possible, especially with individuals who shared their goals and aspirations.

Their Stellar Engine would be top priority for all planets. More taxes, more materials, more labor. Endellion had won her seat by playing to those eager for change.

My thoughts returned to my surroundings when the cheers became overwhelming. The ground enforcers lifted their rum pouches and shouted.

"She's an inspiration," one woman said. "The first human governor since the Federation's formation!"

Another guy nodded. "That's right! Our captain's the best!"

"I have two messages," Endellion continued leisurely, but each word cut at my patience. "First, I would like to take this moment to name Clevon Demarco as the new captain of the *Star Marque*."

The cheering intensified. Enforcers all around the mess hall turned to face me. A few threw pouches. Everyone wanted to pat me on the arm.

I couldn't believe she had the balls to name me in the vid. Did she think I would still serve her while she was governor? All I could think about was stabbing her to death with her own cybernetic insides.

"Second," she continued, her voice almost drowned out by the commotion, but not quite. "I want to officially confirm the land I've promised each and every one of you. When you arrive at Vectin-10, you will be granted a six-hectare parcel of property. After that, you can terminate your employment with the *Star Marque* or continue under Captain Clevon Demarco's leadership."

I was deeply surprised. I'd thought she would renege on that offer, especially after she'd said it would make her look corrupt or tainted by favoritism. But I suspected *not* fulfilling her promise to an entire crew of enforcers would have looked even worse. That would have made her a liar, and she wanted to maintain some semblance of dignity.

"Six-hectare parcel of property?" someone next to me asked. "Outrageous."

"How large is that?" another asked.

"60,000 square meters. I once lived in an apartment on Midway Station that was 50 square meters. Unbelievable."

I tuned everything out and glared at the screen. I hated her. I hated that everyone there thought she was a role model of perfect stature. Her crimes sat forgotten, and I suspected that most wouldn't even want to hear them. Endellion had solidified herself as their messiah.

I stood from the table, white noise in my thoughts, blocking out everything else.

"Sawyer," I said, knowing she would hear me. "Call the officers for a meeting. I know what needs to be done."

QUINN, Lysander, Dr. Clay, and Sawyer sat around the massive table. I stared out at the transparent metal alloy wall that looked out into the darkness of space.

"—and then she altered the course of Capital Station's path to hit Galvis-4," Sawyer concluded.

Quinn and Dr. Clay widened their eyes.

I couldn't tell the entire crew, but if I was going to run the *Star Marque*, the officers needed to know. They needed to know why my objective would be to hunt Endellion down. They needed to know she was a tyrant, an autocrat of the highest order.

"I don't believe you," Dr. Clay said. "She had a harsh disposition. But destroying an entire space station? Never."

Sawyer tapped the PAD on her arm. A recording of Endellion's voice played back, and my blood ran cold as I remembered the moment with perfect recollection.

"There won't be any evidence after the dust settles. Capital Station was old, after all. A malfunction isn't outside the realm of possibility. Now let's go."

Keeping that recording would be hazardous. I would tell Sawyer to delete it later—and maybe even incinerate the PAD. While it would damn Endellion, it would cost us all. We didn't need it hanging around.

Quinn shook her head. "Endellion said that?"

Sawyer nodded. "She also said this."

A recording of my and Endellion's voices played back for the group.

"The Star Marque,*"* I said, strained over the speaker of the PAD. *"I won't leave without it."*

"Then you'll die with it," Endellion replied. *"Come, Clevon. You know this is for the best. Could you imagine me handing out hundreds of planetside estates once I became governor? I'd be accused of favoritism and corruption, and it would've been a dark mark on my political career. In a way, this is serendipity. The perfect end to a good run."*

Lysander glowered at Sawyer's PAD. "It's hard to hear."

"I never thought she would do something like this," Quinn said. "I knew she was ruthless—Yuan said some weird stuff when she was drunk—but *this?* I never would've guessed."

"And *you* saved the *Star Marque?*" Dr. Clay eyed me with a lifted eyebrow. "I suppose you truly *are* the hero here."

I was glad Sawyer hadn't played the rest of the encounter. I gave the doctor a nod. "Endellion's gone," I said. "But Sawyer was the backbone of her leadership. I'm the new captain, and I won't let Endellion's monstrous actions go unchecked. I plan to run the *Star Marque.* To make something great. And I want you all there with me."

"Us?" Quinn asked. "Really?"

"Yes. We could do things the right way, recruit people without harming them, and face Endellion when no one else can." I turned to Sawyer. "Are you with me?"

Sawyer pulled her knees up to her chest. I knew she still harbored some loyalty to Endellion, but she hardened her expression. "You have my full support."

Although Quinn and Lysander went to answer, I turned my gaze to Dr. Clay and matched his squinted glare. "Well?" I asked him.

He chuckled. "Well, what? You know the answer. I wasn't here for anything before. Endellion tried to kill me, but she didn't. I'm not invested in seeking revenge. As far as I'm concerned, I should stay away from all this and focus on my research."

"Stay," I said, "and I'll give you my piece of property on Vectin-10."

The others in the room caught their breath, half-gasping.

"Your entire parcel?" Dr. Clay asked.

"For ten years of service," I said, knowing I was paying him an insane yearly salary for an enforcer doctor. "I need someone who specializes in defects, and you're one of the best. Please."

Lysander stood. "He can have my piece of property."

"No," I said. "Keep it."

"I won't need it in a few years," Lysander said, staring at me with a hard-set gaze. "It's better this way."

"I want him to stay for you," I replied. "And for Noah, and Mara. And anyone else I might pick up. If Ontwenty and her research is anything like you all gush over, maybe you won't be dead in five years. Besides, I want you as my vice-captain—which means you'll have to stick around longer."

Lysander straightened his posture, more so than before. "You want me as your vice-captain?"

"You've got a moral compass. I don't. I want your guidance."

"I still need to agree," Dr. Clay said, interjecting himself into the scene.

"Well?" I asked.

"I'll do it. But only for ten years. Max."

"Good." I turned to Quinn. "Are you with me?"

She hesitated, and I knew I asked more of her than the others. She and Lee had plans. They wanted to start a family and leave the enforcer life behind. This was supposed to have been her last mission, the one to end them all.

"Demarco," she muttered. "I don't know. I'll have to speak with Lee about it."

Even if she said no, it wouldn't matter. We would get new pilots, and I would make it work, one way or another. Although I didn't share Endellion's "ends justify the means" mentality, I had become a fan of her determination. She never gave up, and neither would I.

"You have until we reach Midway Station," I said. "I want to keep you, but I understand if you go."

She nodded.

Sawyer swiveled her chair to face me. "Captain Demarco."

The title sounded weird, but I liked it. "Yeah?"

"We'll lose most of the ground enforcers when they take their land."

"I know. We'll get more, and then we'll take on more jobs. I swear, we'll be everything we were and more. And the moment Endellion makes the wrong move, I'll be there to see she pays for everything she's done."

The others at the conference table stood, and each regarded me with a resolute expression.

Thank you for reading!

Please consider leaving a review—any and all feedback is much appreciated!

ABOUT SHAMI STOVALL

Shami Stovall grew up in California's central valley with a single mother and little brother. Despite no one in her family having a degree higher than a GED, she put herself through college (earning a BA in History), and then continued on to law school where she obtained her Juris Doctorate.

As a child, Stovall enjoyed every portal fantasy, space opera, and magic series she could get her hands on, but the first novel to spark her imagination was Island of the Blue Dolphins by Scott O'Dell. The adventure on a deserted island opened her mind to ideas and realities she had never given thought before—and it was the moment Stovall realized that story telling (specifically fiction) became her passion. Anything that told a story, especially fantasy series and military science fiction, be it a movie, book, video game or comic, she had to experience.

Now, as a professor and author, Stovall wants to add her voice to the myriad of stories in the world. Everything from sorcerers, to robots, to fantasy wars—she just hopes you enjoy.

See all future releases with:
https://sastovallauthor.com/newsletter/
Or contact her directly at:
s.adelle.s@gmail.com

Other Titles by Shami Stovall:

The Ethereal Squadron

Star Marque Rising

FRITH CHRONICLES:

1: Knightmare Arcanist

CPSIA information can be obtained
at www.ICGtesting.com
Printed in the USA
BVHW031255280721
613096BV00004B/75

9 780998 045207